Also by Terri Prone

Racing the Moon
Swinging on a Star
Blood Brothers, Soul Sisters

About the author

Terri Prone is the head of the successful PR firm Carr Communications. The author of two previous novels, she has also written seven non-fiction books and a short story collection. She has a husband and son.

Running Before Daybreak

TERRI PRONE

CORONET BOOKS
Hodder & Stoughton

First published in Great Britain in 2001 by Hodder and Stoughton
First published in paperback in 2001 by Hodder and Stoughton
A division of Hodder Headline

A Coronet Paperback

2 4 6 8 10 9 7 5 3 1

A CIP catalogue record for this title is available from the British
Library.

ISBN 0 34073325 X

Printed and bound in Great Britain by
Clays Ltd, St Ives plc

Hodder and Stoughton
A division of Hodder Headline
338 Euston Road
London NW1 3BH

For Letty Cottin Pogrebin

איזהו חכם הלומד מכל אדם

PERMISSIONS

ACKNOWLEDGEMENTS

I'm grateful to Brian Looney, former editor of the *Irish Examiner*, for permission to give him a cameo role. I stole the one-legged Charleston from Gavin Duffy, the funniest man alive. Joan Dennehy provided the model of superb, understated nursing. Jean Boyce kept me moving – literally. The Ellickson clan lent me aspects of their life, a name and Dominique's sensitive efficiency. Hilary Kenny, Donal Cronin and Stephen Cullen read the first draft. My beloved mother, Moira Prone, read the proofs. Each gave advice and vital encouragement.

I had not realized, until Anton Savage pointed it out, that the GP is a short loving portrait of the late Dr David Chapman, the definitive family doctor and a dear friend. For that, and so much else connected with this novel, I thank Anton.

Tim 'Boomer' Carroll gave me time, research and advice about fire-fighting and fire-fighters.

I'm grateful to some friends who must be nameless who gave me permission to include personal references.

Tom Savage's love, faith and insight make it possible for me to write.

ACKNOWLEDGEMENTS

CONTENTS

CHAPTER ONE

The Spider and the Minister

When Little Miss Muffet laughed out loud during his speech, the government minister lost his place and his composure. 'I'm really sorry,' she said.

She stood up to apologise properly, collided with the spider and dropped her curds-and-whey bowl, which rolled towards the minister on its rim in a wobbling arc. When the minister picked it up, the spider used its front two hairy legs to applaud. Little Miss Muffet caught a foot in her petticoats and staggered towards the minister clutching an oversized spoon. He steadied her, one-handed. The spider covered its eyes in admiration. The audience laughed.

'My speech wasn't that funny,' the minister said, trying to make the best of the interruption.

'Oh, no, your speech wasn't funny at all,' Miss Muffet assured him, with disproportionate conviction. 'It was just he –' she gestured at the spider '– he asked me to marry him.'

The minister, despite evident anxiety to get rid of the curds bowl and finish his speech, knew better than to abandon this issue. 'You going to?' he asked.

'Jesus, would you?' she responded. 'Marry a spider?'

'I'm already married,' the minister said, realising too late that this sounded as if he'd be dying to marry the spider otherwise. 'Happily,' he amended. 'Happily married.'

The spider made a gesture suggesting that the minister would put a hand up any one of the spider's legs, given half a chance. The audience roared. The minister, young enough to blush, laugh and surrender, stepped back to the microphone. 'Ladies and gentlemen, it has been a great pleasure to announce vastly increased funding for the Irish Pre-school Playgroups Association. Although if I'd known they were going to make me look as if I fancied Little Miss Muffet's future husband, I'd have cut the money in half.'

Even as he said it, the spider danced hairily closer to him. Half to fend it off, and half to end any pretence at formality, the minister upended the empty bowl on its head. It looked like a biker's safety helmet.

'Put your arm around Little Miss Muffet, Minister,' one of the photographers called out.

For a moment, he hesitated, remembering his PR guru's instructions: 'Never let them put anything on your head. That's fatal in pictures. Remember Dukakis in the helmet.' The warning did not include bans on hugging ringleted figures from fairy tales, so he hugged her.

'Were you serious?' one of the crowd asked the spider. 'About wanting to marry her?'

'Course I was serious,' the spider said, taking the bowl off his head, clutching it to his chest as if swearing an oath.

'How well do ye know each other?' a journalist in black sweater and trousers asked.

'We don't know each other,' Little Miss Muffet said.

'You don't?'

'I've never met him in real life,' she said, and pulled off her wig. 'Nor do I want to.' She apologised to the minister again.

'Don't worry about it.' The minister smiled. 'But I do expect an invitation to the wedding.'

'You'll be waiting a long time,' she called after him. At which point the spider entwined several of its arms around her. From behind. Pointing her elbows, she started to fight him off. 'I'm not joking you,' she said to the spider behind her. 'I'm going to kick you in the crigs.'

'From *there*?' one of the journalists asked. 'That'll be a neat trick.'

'Spiders don't have crigs,' the spider said, letting her go and pulling off the balaclava part of his costume. A mass of tight light brown curls sprang loose around his head, causing some flashbulbs to go off as the two former characters finally got a look at each other. The spider removed the black glove from his right hand. 'Polo Cadogan,' he introduced himself.

'Polo?' one of the journalists queried. 'As in Marco?'

'Yeah.'

'Cassie Browne,' Miss Muffet said, forced to reciprocate.

'What does Cassie stand for?'

'Cassandra.'

'Posh.'

'How does Cassandra Cadogan sound to you, as a name?' the man in the spider uniform asked.

She belted him with the spoon. '*Don't* start that crap again. This is the first job I've got with this company and you've probably ensured I never get another one.'

'You've a job for life. I own the company. I'm much more than your average spider.'

'Get off.'

'He does, you know,' the journalist in black told her. 'Polo Cadogan, Street Theatre. That's him.'

Cadogan began to pull spider legs out of their suction cups on the sides of his costume. Shorn of the appendages, he was revealed as a solid six-footer in a slightly hairy wetsuit.

'D'you always propose to the other actors you work

with?' the journalist in the black jumper asked him.

'This is the first time.'

'Is it a stunt? For publicity? A joke?'

He tucked the spider legs under his arm, freeing a hand, which he held out to her, palm upward. 'You got a Bible?'

'You must be kidding. A journalist with a Bible?'

'Well, if you had one, I would happily swear on it that I'm deadly serious, not to mention persistent. No matter how long it takes, I'm going to marry that girl.'

'In a pig's fucking *ear*,' his intended said, trying to reach the zip at the back of her costume and failing.

'Unzip her, there,' Polo Cadogan directed the journalist. 'I can't undress her at first meeting. *Second* meeting, no problem.'

The journalist did as she was bidden, then picked up a pad of doodles from the tuffet earlier occupied by Cassie Browne. 'This yours?'

Blinking myopically, Cassie nodded.

'C'n I borrow it briefly?'

Distracted between the journalist and Polo Cadogan, who was whimsically inserting the spider's legs into Little Miss Muffet's frilly pantaloons, Cassie Browne shrugged and acquiesced. Which was why her cartoon of the minister appeared on the front page of the following day's *Irish Independent*, alongside a report from their colour writer.

Next morning, before she knew about the newspaper, Cassie stumbled through what she imagined to have been her father's morning tasks as if the guessworked mimicry would somehow reconnect her with him. Instead, it emphasised how different her recent mornings had been in New York, where the priorities were showering, dressing, getting out of the door and grabbing coffee somewhere, hand protected from burning by a brown cardboard sleeve around the white-lidded cup. Her father's generation made and ate three meals at home every day. His morning had been about the tiny explosion as the gas jet lit under a solid black-bottomed kettle, about crusts cut off before toasting under the grill, about taking the cutting-board to the back door to scatter crusts and crumbs for the birds.

Standing, now, at the door, emptied cutting-board held as if in readiness for a bread-landing, she laughed softly at birds fussing on the edge of safe distance from her. 'I know, I know,' she told them. 'You're thinking, Why doesn't that dope get the hell back in the kitchen and let us get on with eating, the way the old guy always does? Here's the bad news, lads. There's no old guy any more. There's no always.'

A bright-beaked blackbird hopped heavily closer to the food. In the distance, she could hear the sound of a motorbike, growing louder until it seemed to be outside. She ran around the house just as a helmeted man in black and red leather dismounted from the bike. Turn it off, she mouthed, flapping her hands down-palmed at him. He did. The silence seemed total. Cosmic. 'Jesus *Christ*,' she hissed at him. 'You've even shut the buggering birds up.'

'What did you say?' he roared.

'Ssssh, for Chrissake,' she told him, her face a rictus of fear of the neighbours.

He indicated that, through the full-head helmet, hearing was difficult. Its padding had a push-up bra effect on his face, fattening his cheeks into too small an exposed space. When he smiled – as now – his mouth opened up and down, rather than sideways. From behind him, he produced a folded newspaper and handed it to her.

'Are you sure this is for m—'

Her voice died. A full-colour picture took up five columns of the front page. Herself as Little Miss Muffet, spoon aloft. The minister. And the spider to one side. 'Fairytale Proposal at Government Launch,' said the headline. The motorcyclist's black gauntleted hand put another folded paper over the first. 'Watch this Space, says Spider' was the headline over this one, which revealed that Cassie Browne, a.k.a. Miss Muffet, had passed the time during the boring bits of the minister's speech by drawing cartoons of him with a tiny head and a big body. The paper ran her cartoon alongside the report. It looked, she thought, offensively professional.

The motorcyclist removed his helmet and put it, with the big-cuffed gloves, on the saddle of the machine. She glanced up in time to see him go down on one leather-clad knee to present her with a single red rose. This, for some reason she could never afterwards identify, made her conscious that she was standing in the middle of the cul-de-sac wearing nothing but a T-shirt and French-cut cotton pants. She tried to cover herself, using the newspapers.

'You'll get newsprint on your chest,' he advised her.

The retired architect from across the road drove up and considered the kneeling, leather-clad biker. 'Lord, Cassie, you're in demand,' he said, in his quiet way. 'Spiders yesterday, couriers today. All inflamed by your charms.'

'It's the same wanker,' she told him.

'I beg your pardon?'

She poked the biker so vehemently with the paper that it bent in the middle. 'Get up, you,' she said venomously.

He staggered to his feet. 'I also played the spider yesterday.' He extended a hand. 'Polo Cadogan, sir. How do you do?'

'Kieran Grant,' came the response. 'Polo as in Marco?'

'Oh, *Jesus*,' Cassie said, trying to make a skirt out of the *Irish Times*. Mrs Grant was watching now from the picture window of their house.

'You're my witness, Mr Grant,' Cadogan said. 'I went down on my knees to ask her to marry me.'

'Well, *a* knee,' Grant acknowledged. 'I couldn't actually swear you asked her to marry you, though, I didn't hear that.'

'Stay put, I'll do it properly with you here,' Cadogan said, folding the other knee and extending the rose, the bloom of which suddenly went sideways like a sleeper's head. 'Stand up,' Cadogan said to the rose, 'don't get brewer's droop before the job's done or I'll compost you.'

'Stop wagging it around,' Cassie said, exasperated. 'You're weakening it.'

'Don't you find that happens a lot?' Cadogan said to her elderly neighbour. 'If you wag it around, it weakens?'

To Cassie's astonishment Mr Grant roared with laughter. This was the man who had once reported her to her mother for saying, 'Shit on a swing-swong', when she'd fallen off a skateboard in front of him.

'Why don't you take the rose?' Cadogan asked.

'I'm not taking anything from you.'

'You took the newspapers.'

'That was before I knew who you were. And I'm not giving them back, because I want to read the stuff again.'

'But you won't take a poor droopy-headed rose?'

'Oh, *Jesus*,' she said, reaching for the flower.

He grasped her by the wrist. 'Cassie Browne, will you be my wife?' he asked, with pseudo-Shakespearian gravitas. Kieran Grant nodded approvingly as Cadogan got to his feet.

'Let me *go*!' yelled Cassie, clouting him over the ear with the two newspapers in a frenzy of repeated blows, one of which beheaded the rose. Cadogan let go of the stalk and her wrist and stepped back, knocking over the bike and falling on top of it. Kieran Grant made a courtly gesture and removed himself. Cassie, trying desperately to use the newspapers as a back-skirt, ran inside her own house. After a minute, she heard the motorbike roaring away.

Two national newspapers on her mother's breakfast tray would be a good thing, she thought, heading for the kitchen. They were somewhat frayed, though. This would undoubtedly counterbalance any points won. Her mother would compute the sums of mutual cancellation within seconds.

Beside her the telephone rang, startling her. She snatched up the receiver. 'Yes?'

'Were you never taught to answer the phone properly? You say hello, then you give the number.'

'I would have, but the only number that came into my mind was my own in New York,' Cassie said, laughing. 'So how's my favourite aunt?'

'Vastly improved by having a famous niece.'

'A famous – oh, you've seen the papers.'

'No, I heard Richard Crowley. *Morning Ireland*? He interviewed a reporter who was at the press conference you screwed up yesterday. You're in the papers, too?'

'I've a cartoon in the *Indo* – some reporter gave it to the paper and they used it.'

'Make sure they pay you for it.'

'Yes, Auntie Marsh.'

'I'm serious.'

'Yes, Auntie Marsh.'

'What does my big sister make of all this?'

'I haven't brought up the papers with her breakfast yet.'

'Oh, to have a dutiful daughter,' her aunt murmured. 'And a long-stemmed rose on the tray?'

'Long-stemmed rose my *arse*,' Cassie said.

'Such an appealing image,' her aunt said, and rang off.

The voice on the radio was talking about the government minister's press conference of the previous day as Cassie arrived with the tray. 'That's the one you were at,' her mother said. 'We must listen in case they mention you.'

'. . . all of the front pages this morning carry colour photographs of Little Miss Muffet and the spider who sat down beside her,' the radio voice said. Mrs Browne nodded and smiled. 'They also report that Miss Muffet disrupted the entire event when she interrupted the minister's speech.'

Cassie's mother froze. The man doing the newspaper summary told the story of the proposal and of its rejection before moving on to other stories.

'That minister is going to be our next Taoiseach, you know,' Mrs Browne said, scandalised. Oh, Cassie thought. It would have been fine to interrupt him if his glowing future was all behind him, would it?

Mrs Browne compressed her lips and shook her head. All my life you've been doing that, Cassie thought. All my life. Hinting that you could say the most devastating things, but you have too much self-respect to let yourself go. Screwing me by facial expression while getting jewels in your heavenly crown for not putting it into words.

'He's not going to like this cartoon, either,' her mother said. 'The minister. Is. Not. Going. To. Like. it.'

'Why not?' demanded Cassie, cursing herself for asking. Go on, the little manic voice in her head encouraged. Put your wrists into the handcuffs. Bring your own ball-and-chain, too, did you?

19

'You've given him a little head,' her mother said.

'I give everyone a little head.'

That's right, the tiny voice sniggered. Talk dirty to your mother. Fill her in on your filthy practices.

'The minister doesn't know that,' her mother pointed out.

'Thanks be to God for small mercies,' Cassie said piously.

The phone rang and her mother's hand fluttered towards it. The movement suggested infinite willingness to serve family needs, qualified only by bereaved exhaustion. Cassie lifted it.

'Is that Cassandra Browne? Will you hold for a call, please?'

'Cassandra?'

She hesitated.

'Minister?'

Mrs Browne pulled the front edges of her bed-jacket closer. Ma, Cassie thought, we're not on reality TV.

'Cassandra, I'm ringing you on the instructions of my wife. She says we must have the original of the cartoon in today's paper.'

'Even though I only gave you a little head?'

'My wife says you've caught the essential me,' the minister said. 'So obviously, *she'd* only give me a little head, too, if she had her way.'

Please, dear God, Cassie prayed, if this man's wife is listening to this conversation, let her have a mind so clean it squeaks.

'What do you charge for originals of your work?'

For a split second, Cassie was enthralled by the sentence. 'Minister, as soon as I get the cartoon back from the *Indo*, it'll be on its way to you. As a small apology for being so disruptive in your press conference.'

The minister allowed that this was unnecessary,

but very generous, and he looked forward to receiving it. Cassie put down the phone and leaned against the wall.

'Of course, you didn't get his address,' her mother said, going back to her breakfast.

The phone rang again. 'Is Cassandra Browne at home?'

'That's me.'

'Hold for a call, please, Miss Browne.'

Another one for you to talk dirty to, the little voice muttered in her head.

'Cassandra?' The voice was male, but high. Cockney.

'Yes.'

'I run the High Five talent agency here in Bond Street. We'd like to sign you up. We specialise in gorgeous girls portraying fairytale figures for fantasy purposes.'

'I beg your pardon?'

'Yeah, I know you mayn't have thought of this loine of work before, but lemme tellya, it has—'

'A lot going for it, I'm sure, and you could live off my immoral earnings.'

Toast and tea went the wrong way and Mrs Browne began to choke. Cassie freed a hand to thump her on the back, but she refused to sit up to facilitate this, apparently convinced there was more dignity in suffocation if she was leaning back against her pillows when it happened.

'Well, we wouldn't be living off your moral earnings alone,' the cheery light voice responded. 'We've go' a lo' of uvver girls, too, you know. All short.'

'All what?'

'Short. If you want a little goin' over by Little Red Roidin' 'Ood, you don't want Big Red Roidin' 'Ood, do ya?'

Cassie's mother closed her eyes in a suffering Victorian way, wearied by her fight with the toast.

'Listen, you,' Cassie said, with sudden decision, into

21

the phone, 'you should be in jail and I'm cutting you off.'

'Well, could I interest you in living off *my* immoral earnings?' he said, in a quite different voice.

'Wh—'

'I'd rename the company, once we were married. Polo and Cassie Cadogan Street Theatre. How does that sound?'

'Shite,' Cassie said. Her mother clasped a hand over her eyes.

'OK. What about—'

'What about leaving me alone, you lunatic?'

'Why would I do that?'

'Because if you don't, I'll slice off bits of you.'

'Which bits?'

'The essential bits.'

'*Oooh, lovely!*'

'I meant your head.'

'Freudian slips show you're really in lust with me.'

'I wouldn't lust if you were—'

'The last spider on God's earth,' he finished.

'I'm cutting you off.'

'What a waste,' she could hear him saying, as she put the phone down.

Her mother indicated wordlessly that her appetite had vanished as a result of Cassie's profane phone calls. Cassie bent to take the tray just as the phone rang again. 'Is this Cassandra Browne's home?'

'Yes, and—'

'Hold for a call, please.'

'Hello, Cassandra? This is Brian Looney, editor of the *Examiner*. I want to meet you to discuss running a series of your cartoons in the paper.'

'You're a bloody sight better at doing a Cockney accent than you are at doing a Cork accent,' Cassie said. 'Plus you could've thought up a better name.'

'Sorry?'

'Not at all. Any time. Loony? Great name that would be for an editor. Anyway, it's the *Cork Examiner*.'

'We changed the title and the masthead in 1997.'

'You think by persisting you'll convince me this time you're real, don't you?'

'Miss Browne, I have no idea why you think I should be imitating myself, but when you have a chance to think it over, maybe you'd ring me.' He gave her a number.

'Goodbye, Polo.'

'Who?'

Cassie put down the phone. The same man, Cassie told her mother, except this time pretending he was the editor of the *Cork Examiner*.

'The *Examiner*,' her mother corrected. 'They're always giving out to people on radio programmes who call it the old name.'

'Loony, he said he was,' Cassie said, doubt beginning to chill her skin.

'Brian Looney.' Her mother nodded. 'He's the youngest editor of a—'

'Sssh,' Cassie said. 'I'm trying to dial the number he gave me.'

'Brian Looney here,' the voice said.

'Mr Looney—'

'Cassandra?'

'I'm really sorry for being rude earlier, I thought you were someone else.'

'You thought I was the fucking spider,' the editor of the *Examiner* said comfortably.

'I'm sorry. I did. You said you wanted cartoons.'

'That's right.'

'Why?'

'Because we haven't carried regular political cartoons, and our readers would probably like them. D'you always concentrate on people's shape, not their faces?'

'Yes.'

'Why?'

Was it, Cassie wondered, because she was so small and everybody looked tall to her with their heads a long way away? Was it because she was short-sighted and people appeared to her in shapes and movement, rather than in faces and features?

'Not that it matters,' the editor's voice said, filling the silence. 'If that's the way you draw people, then we could call the cartoons *Pinheads*.'

'I don't know anything about politics.'

'Good. Prejudices won't get in the way of what you observe. If you can get to Leinster House today, I'll have one of our people meet you and sign you in. You might have to sit in the public gallery because of not having a press card, but you can watch and do up some drawings and then we can sit down and come to an agreement. Right?'

'Right, Mr—'

'Looney,' he said helpfully.

'Looney,' she agreed.

Her mother waited for an explanation. Cassie gave it – waiting for the negative. I spend my life with this woman, she thought, my knees slightly bent, waiting for the distinctive tug of rugs being pulled out from under me.

'Cartoons,' her mother said thoughtfully. 'Like Martyn Turner.'

'No, mine wouldn't be big on faces. Martyn Turner's great on faces. You know the lovely sad doggy baggy eyes he gives Bertie Ahern.'

'Your father would like that. He loved good cartoons in the old *Dublin Opinion*. He would be very proud to see his daughter's drawings in a national paper,' her mother said.

The two of them stared at each other, knowing that to

tolerate each other they needed Ben Browne, if only as a quoted myth.

'You'd better dress properly,' her mother added more briskly. 'You can be sure they don't allow jeans in the Houses of Parliament.'

CHAPTER TWO

The Knitted Girl and
Ronald McDonald

'You're not supposed to make notes in here,' a uniformed man told Cassie in the public gallery of the Dáil.

'Am I allowed to draw?'

'To draw what?'

Water, she thought wildly. Conclusions. 'Cartoons.'

'I wouldn't think so,' he said, perturbed by the possibility.

Cassie put down her pencil and notebook. The uniformed man stood behind her for five minutes, then left. An opposition backbencher was reading a bad speech badly when a group of school-uniformed girls thundered softly into the gallery, hushing each other in theatrical hisses and falling over their thick-soled shoes. Their teacher pointed out which side was government and which was opposition. The horseshoe-shaped chamber below them had perhaps seven public representatives, scattered throughout the benches like survivors of a flash-flood. None, the schoolgirls quickly announced to each other, was familiar from TV.

'Not even *him*,' the girl nearest Cassie said, nodding at the speaker.

'D'you think he ever will be?' Cassie whispered.

'No.'

'Why not?'

'Like, *bor*ing,' the girl said. 'Look at him trying to lick up to us now he sees us up here. Oh, vomit.'

A hand descended on Cassie's shoulder. She jumped. It was the political correspondent from the *Examiner*. 'There's a bit of activity on the plinth, so I thought I'd bring you out there.'

The plinth turned out to be the raised section in the front car park part-owned by a television reporter whose delivery had the assaultive quality of the unarmed deranged. When he finished, his place was taken by a red-haired young woman who seemed ready to announce the impending end of the world and who, after her introduction, began to interview a woman who unravelled under the vehemence of the questioning.

The knitted girl, Cassie thought, beginning to draw. That's who the interviewee was like. The day her mother taught her to knit, Cassie knitted a girl. A very bockety girl with a triangular skirt and arms as long as her legs, described by Cassie's mother as a ridiculous waste of time. If Cassie wanted to draw things, God knows, there were enough pencils in the house, so why didn't she knit something to wear? That was what knitting was for. Expert at finding alternative vents for his wife's constantly molten, barely subterranean rage, Ben Browne distracted her on to another topic while he took the blue bockety girl and flattened her out on the pages of one of his favourite books. When he closed the book on her, he put it up on the shelf so that pressure from other books would hold her flat. Cassie watched this, sliding her gaze sideways to the kitchen, where her mother was banging saucepans to underscore whatever Point she was Making. (When Cassie discovered capital letters, she assumed they were meant for her mother's exclusive use.)

'You're very lucky,' Ben Browne murmured to his daughter, patting the spine of the book as if it was Cassie.

'You have a great imagination. A happy imagination. You can make yourself happy with very little. A great capacity to have.'

Cassie stored away the good things her father found in her, and told them to herself again later. Someone might say, 'Cassie's always in good humour,' and she would think, I can make myself happy with very little. A great capacity to have. It was as comforting as a warm pad on a muscle strain.

Without warning, someone sat down beside her and laughed out loud. The red-haired reporter, pale with interrogative concentration, glared across. The big, blazered woman beside Cassie laughed the more. 'That's a *great* drawing,' she told Cassie. 'Doing her as a knitting pattern is so funny. Do Amanda. Go on.'

'Who's Amanda?'

The big woman nodded at the red-haired reporter, and Cassie cast an assortment of anxious lines down on the paper. The reporter emerged as a collection of rigid tall pencils, each perfectly sharpened but somehow fearful. 'You're very good,' the woman beside her said quietly to Cassie, and stood up to be interviewed. 'If you draw me, I'll kill you.'

She had hair like a raven's plumage. An uncompromising glistening black blunt cut where layering might have better served the square face. Brandy-brown eyes under optimistic-arched eyebrows. Painted nails and good jewellery. How much more time and thought, Cassie wondered, went into the hands as opposed to the feet, shod in inexpensive flat shoes? And why were the hands held high, gesturing, protecting – protecting what?

It was only then that Cassie understood what she was observing. This woman hated being big-busted. There was no pleasure for her in the great fullness of breast under the tailored blouse, the jacket without lapels. The last glance down before the camera rolled was not the stroking self-glance of a woman satisfied with the shape and heft of herself, but rather a fearful foreboding of bust-gap and bra-gape. I know how to caricature you, Cassie thought, as the interview ended, and the woman flicked red-nailed fingers at her farewell. I also know why you didn't want me to draw you.

The woman was replaced in front of the cameras by a minister, two toddlers and a tree. The tree was fake with a man inside. The children watched this awkwardly moving confection of *papier-mâché* and real tree branches with wide-eyed terror. The photographers chivvied them all into varying configurations and the mothers of the two toddlers peeped around the cameras to wave reassuringly at them. The red-haired reporter sat on the bench to be out of shot. 'These photo-opportunities,' she said, gesturing at the minister, the tree and the toddlers, 'they should be banned. Exploiting children . . .'

The tree began to lumber towards them, wagging heavily from side to side, its upper branches wobbling excitedly. The two children, less frightened now that there was less attention on them, tagged along, and the line of photographers opened up, so Cassie was suddenly in the centre of a circle, facing a fake tree.

'I knew you wouldn't be able to stay away from me,' the tree said.

'Oh, for fu—' Cassie said.

'Watch your language in front of the children,' the tree said, then pulled the two toddlers close and whispered to them. They giggled. 'Are ye ready?' the tree asked. The two toddlers nodded. 'OK, then, one, two, three—'

'Will you marry him?' the children yelled.

Around her, she could hear reporters making the connection with Little Red Riding Hood and the Spider.

The man in the tree pulled his arms inside the trunk. 'Well, *will* you marry me?' he asked again.

'No, I bloody well won't,' Cassie said.

All the tree's branches fell off at once, leaving him standing in his own discarded foliage like the arboreal victim of an environmental disaster. Onlookers said, 'Aw,' in saddened sympathy, laughed at their own reaction, then applauded the tree for its cleverness. Cassie slid off the bench and pushed her way blindly through the laughing people behind her, across the yellow-and-black striped metal car barrier and out on to Kildare Street at a run.

She felt badly about not thanking the political correspondent, and said so when she talked, later, to the editor. No problem, he said, and talked terms. Within days she had a contract.

The day she arrived home, having posted the contract back to the editor, signed, Cassie could see her mother on the telephone through the frosted glass of the front door. The fragmented shape turned as soon as Cassie put her key in the lock, her mother gesturing to her to drop her belongings because the call was for her.

'Well, Father Quigley, by coincidence, she's just walked in the front door, so you can talk to her directly. Hold on and I'll put her on to you.'

Cassie took the phone, cupping her hand over the mouthpiece. '*Who?*'

'Father Quigley,' her mother said. 'He wants to talk to you.'

I know it's Father Quigley, Cassie's thought-voice said. It's bloody obvious it's Father Quigley because you called him that. I'm asking you who the hell effing Father Quigley is? '*Why?*' she hissed frantically, over the sealed mouthpiece. Her mother did a flapping gesture, which meant 'Ask him yourself' and 'Have you no manners, keeping him hanging on there?' Cassie sighed. 'Hello, Father Quigley.'

'Ah, yes, yes, yes, young Cassandra, isn't it?'

'That's right.'

'Ah, very good, very good, very good. Now, wasn't it very fortunate that . . .'

Cassie slid down into a sitting position at the end of the stairs, trying to concentrate, to find out what this old man wanted, to distinguish content from the plethora of warmly meaningless repetitions. He must, she assumed, be a friend of her father, although he sounded older than her father had ever sounded. But then, she thought, with a sudden stab of tears, her father had never spoken without knowing what he was going to say. He would have felt it was a form of theft, to demand your attention before he was sure he could justify taking up your time.

'. . . and from a good Catholic home, too.'

'Mmmm,' said Cassie, desperate to get the old cleric to keep going, because she had now lost the thread of what he was saying.

'So you will, my child?'

'I'm sorry, Father?'

'You will marry young Polo Cadogan?'

'I – what?'

'Got a good thing going, financially, in that street theatre business,' he went on. 'Making a mint, he is. In addition, is he ever hung.'

'*What?*'

'Well, I shouldn't boast,' Cadogan went on in his ordinary voice, 'but girls have fainted with fear at the sight of it.'

Before she could stop herself, Cassie laughed.

'Plus, I make women laugh,' Cadogan confided.

Cassie's mother, coming out of the kitchen, nodded, unseen, at the sound of her daughter's laughter.

'I suppose you're big as a tree,' Cassie said.

Her mother, unnoticed, looked puzzled at this.

'Oh, a Californian redwood.'

'So you last for ever, too?'

'You could search the world and fail to find a woman I have left clawing the walls with frustration.'

'But that's probably because you did it all wearing disguise.'

'Now, that's an interesting point,' Polo Cadogan agreed. 'You might think that, given a choice, women would prefer Prince Charming to a toad, but I'm here to tell you, there's no turn-on for a woman to compare with being treed by a toad. I'm better at animals than arachnids, by the way.'

'What sort of animals do you do best?'

Cassie's mother retreated into the kitchen and closed the door very softly.

'The easiest are horses and cows, except you're always depending on the other half behaving itself. I have one cow's arse that when he's sober is just *so* authentic, but when he gets pissed, he gets so loose I have to hold on to his hair or he'd fall off in front of the kids, and the whole illusion would be wrecked. I also do a good coyote sound-effect.'

'Do it for me now,' Cassie said, and he did.

'My best sound-effect is a sick beagle,' he added. 'I rang an all-night vet a few weeks ago. I was going to put the sick beagle on to him. I told the vet my dog had been stung by a wasp and I wanted to bring the poor pooch around to his clinic and you know what he said to me?'

'No.'

'He said, "Is the dog still breathing?" I said, "No, I wanted to arrange an effing dog séance, you thick plank.

32

What the frig do you think I'm ringing you in the middle of the night for if my dog's stopped breathing?" I banged down the phone on him then. No way would I take my great sound-effect to a vet that stupid.'

'I shouldn't be talking to you,' Cassie said.

'Why not?'

'Because you're driving me bananas.'

'That's only because you don't really know me. Once you know me, you'll love me.'

Cassie's mother ventured out of the kitchen again.

'I'll love you because of your natural endowment?' Cassie said.

'Wha'?' he asked.

'Because – as you claim – you're hung like a horse.'

Mrs Browne came level with Cassie just as her daughter said this, and stumbled, whey-faced, past her up the stairs.

'Oh, Jesus,' Cassie said.

'You've come over all wobbly, just imagining it?' he suggested.

'No,' Cassie whispered, cupping her hand around the phone. 'My mother has just heard me – as she thinks – telling an old parish priest he's hung like a horse.'

'I'll come around and help you explain it to her.'

'No, you won't.'

'Why not? I can't keep following you around dressed as spiders and trees. Sooner or later you have to see me in civvies.'

'Other than spiders and trees, what should I be watching out for? Oh, yes, you do Prince Charming and a toad, too. And the arse of a cow.'

'I do the front end of the cow,' he said sulkily. 'It requires much more talent to do the front end. I do a unicorn, too. That's *really* classy. This pale blue unicorn that leaps in the air in the most romantic way. Rears up

33

and prances. Very New Age. There's *satisfaction* in doing
the unicorn. Every adolescent female within ten miles
goes all misty-eyed and buys unicorn posters from my
support crew. Much nicer than pillar-boxes.'

'Why would you do a pillar-box?'

'An Post get me to do a pillar-box whenever they're
launching a new stamp. Pillar-box puts its arm around
model posting letter. You know.'

Cassie began to laugh again. 'Don't you feel an awful
fool, being spiders and post-boxes and trees?'

'You didn't feel a fool being Little Miss Muffet until I
proposed to you.'

'That's true.'

'See?'

No, she told him, she *didn't* see, and this conversation
was going to end, right now. Oh, come on, he begged, let
me buy you dinner. No, she said. Lunch? No. A cup of
coffee? Oh, please, down on my knees begging you, just
a cup of coffee in McDonald's, I mean what kind of
commitment is a lousy cup of coffee on a Saturday
morning in a McDonald's?

Eventually, she caved in and agreed to meet him in the
Grafton Street McDonald's at ten thirty the following
morning.

Which had been a mistake, she decided, when on
arrival she found the street awash in pre-teen children, all
of them singing. At the centre of the horde was the Ronald
McDonald figure with the red hair and gloves seen in
pictures around McDonald's franchises. The song came to
an end. The clown figure asked questions of the children
near to him, getting chorused yes and no answers.

Suddenly, he pointed directly to Cassie, standing on
the path at Weir's jeweller's. A wave of head-turning
followed his big orange-gloved gestures to the children
and parents between where he was and where Cassie was

standing, and in response, the sea of children opened, so there was a tunnel between them. The clown figure beckoned her towards him. You stupid bloody eejit, she thought, whyn't you pick on one of the young mothers who'd be delighted to be a star in front of their kid? Briefly she considered ignoring him or running away, but the thought of the disappointment among the younger children if a grown-up rejected their hero impelled her towards him. The only consolation, she thought, was that his helpers looked just as pissed off as she felt.

When she reached him, he took her hands in his big padded gloves. 'I'm shy,' he told the surrounding children. 'Do you ever get shy?'

Several nodded at him.

'I'm too shy to say what I want to say,' he told them. 'Isn't that awful?'

More nods. The helper nearest him hissed at him out of the side of her mouth: 'You're not supposed to be *doing* this.'

He ignored her, collecting Cassie's hands into one of his and using the other to do an eeny-meeny-miny-mo count of some of the children nearest him to select one for a special task. The children began to scream, 'Me! Pick me!' Ronald McDonald picked a freckle-faced girl, and stage-whispered instructions to her. Suddenly realising who he was, Cassie tried to haul her hand out of his. He pulled her into a tight one-armed embrace.

'You're going to get fired,' the helper hissed. 'I hope you realise that.'

He ignored her and finished his instructions to the freckle-faced girl. 'Out loud, now,' he said to the child. 'Out loud so everybody can hear you.'

'Princess Cassandra,' the child shrieked. 'Ronald McDonald wants you to marry him and – and – live happily ever after. What is your answer?'

'You're definitely going to be fired,' the helper said, not even bothering to hiss. 'This breaks every rule. Like, *every* rule.'

The children were yelling at Cassie to say yes. To cut the thing short, she gave Ronald McDonald a theatrical hug and kissed his white face. She could feel greasepaint on her lips and covertly wiped it off so that the children would not see the physical transference of bits of their hero. The children cheered, Ronald McDonald announced something that made them cheer even more, and steered Cassie across the street and into the franchise restaurant. He nodded and waved at family groups as he passed, finding a roped-off table obviously set aside for his use, and sat down there, making sure Cassie was on the inside, so it was less easy for her to escape.

The hissing helper, eighteen going on fifty, put her hands on the round-cornered table and her face so close to the clown's that Cassie wanted to warn her about greasepaint transfer. 'What the fuck got into you, you cretinous git?' the helper asked. 'You *know* what you're allowed to do and you *know* what you're not allowed to do. No offence, miss,' she said dismissively to Cassie, 'but this Princess Whoever-you-are crap could get us all fired.'

'I take the blame,' Ronald said, in Polo Cadogan's amused voice.

'Fucking *right* you take the blame,' the helper said, maddened further by this.

'I hereby fire myself,' the clown went on, with un-expectedly cold brusqueness. 'I will never, ever, as long as I live, play Ronald McDonald again, thanks be to Jasus, and if you don't go and get Cassie and me cups of coffee right now, I will take off my wig, take off my shoes and start taking off my makeup using my trousers as a towel. Your choice.'

Whatever message the fierce little helper got from the

cool eyes within the painted face put a stop to her rage. Without a word, she walked away, and within a minute, a wine-uniformed server put two cups of coffee on the table.

'See?' Cadogan said, producing a drinking straw and sucking his coffee through it. 'Made me lose a good job, you have.'

'D'you always drink coffee through a straw?'

'Ronald McDonald always drinks coffee through a straw, because otherwise he leaves half his face on the cup,' he replied.

'Yeah, I know. Some of it came off on my mouth.'

'First time you kissed me,' he pointed out.

'And last.'

'Without makeup, I'm much more pleasant to kiss. Have to do my own breath-freshener, though, from now on. "Ronald McDonald,"' he went on, his big gloves pawing the air as if turning over the pages of a reference book. "Ronald McDonald will be pulled away from the children every twenty minutes so a team member can spray his mouth with breath-freshener." No Ronald McDonald anywhere in the world, from Moscow to Moate, is ever going to be caught with bad breath.'

'It sounds like training for the SAS.'

'Cassie, my love, the SAS is a picnic compared to Ronald McDonald. I've done him for a year and a half. Now the business is going well, I no longer need him. They can get some other poor anonymous hoor to be jolly –'

'– within tightly prescribed standards –'

'– And breath-sprayed –'

'– at tightly prescribed intervals –'

'– and made up.'

'Meanwhile, there's three hundred kids out there who think Ronald McDonald is going to get married.

That's probably the most damaging thing he could do. McDonald's franchises all over the world will have to issue press releases saying he's gone off Princess Cassandra.'

His fatly gloved hand gathered hers on the table.

'The majority of those kids are here with their separated fathers,' he told her. 'They think marriage is a temporary thing. If Ronald got married and divorced, it wouldn't cost them a thought. Isn't that sad?'

Cassie looked around her. Almost every table was occupied by a family group led by a man.

'The Saturday Sacrament,' Polo Cadogan said, rising. 'It'll take me ten minutes to get out of this gear. Please stay here for those ten minutes. Please.'

In less than ten minutes he reappeared, to take her across Grafton Street to Bewley's. 'I preferred this place before it was self-service,' he told her, as they picked up coffee and found a table. 'I always have great ska embarrassing waitresses. Waiters, too. But waitresses are more fun. If you tell a waitress that her looks have you in a state of rampant arousal, she'll belt you with a tray and expect a great tip. Tell a waiter that his looks have you in the same state and he'll go outraged-maiden on you. Have you noticed that?'

'It wouldn't occur to me to try to embarrass a waiter.'

'Why not? They spend their whole lives embarrassing us. They hide behind things so when your mouth is absolutely –' pursing his lips, he inflated his face so his eyes popped '– they can arrive to ask you is everything all right, how's your meal, anything else you'd fancy, have you left room for dessert? It's a duty to get back at waiters and waitresses.'

She concentrated on her coffee. It would, she estimated, take five minutes to drink it, which was all the time she should give this guy. Not that he was entitled to any time at all. On the other hand, she partly owed her new cartoonist's contract to him. She told him about Looney's phone call and her subsequent visit to Leinster House to do sample drawings. He asked her if she had an agent. She laughed. 'I've only had a contract for two days,' she pointed out. 'What would I need an agent for?'

'Because you're very talented. The cartoons you draw don't need captions, even. So they would make sense outside Ireland.'

'Me and whatshisname with the sticky-up tie?'

'Dilbert. Right. Make sure you own the name.'

'What name?'

'*Pinheads.*'

'But the editor of the paper thought that one up.'

'Doesn't matter. Get him to call it *Cassandra's Pinheads* and you have a brand.'

'Like Polo,' she said. 'As in Marco Polo. Doesn't it make you want to drop a ceiling on someone when they say that, in response to your name?'

He shook his head, very seriously. 'If it makes them remember me, it's good for business, so I give them an extra-warm smile. Anyway, *they* don't know every other tosser in the world has come up with the same comment. It's like the spiral-staircase thing. You know the spiral-staircase thing? Well, then, what's a spiral staircase?'

Cassie's index finger automatically sketched a rising circle in the air. '*Don't* tell me everybody does that,' she said, laughing.

'Try it on people in the next few days. Be amazed.'

She went back to her cooling coffee.

'So, Little Miss Muffet is the end of your career with us?' he asked.

'Only reason I did it was that a pal of mine rang me. Orna Dennehy?'

'Oh, Orna knows you, does she?'

39

'She knew I was home because – because of my father's death, and she was stuck for someone to be in the background for the minister's presentation. She knew I wouldn't have a job to go to – so.'

'Home from where?'

'New York.'

'"If I can make make it there I'll make it anywhere,"' he sang. Tunelessly.

'A lot of people do that, too, when they hear New York,' she said impatiently.

'Why were you in New York?'

'My boyfriend is doing postgraduate work and I decided to go with him.'

'You a student, too?'

'I'm a drop-out.'

'Don't go down that road, don't ask any more questions, landmines ahead, poison gas and combat-ready cockroaches.'

Was her defensiveness that obvious, she wondered. It must be the result of spending a few weeks with a mother, unmediated. When Ben Browne had been alive, Cassie's disasters were all part of the learning experience. He was always sure that she would learn much more from any failure than from easy success, and somehow convinced her mother of it, too. It was one of her phrases, she remembered. 'Easy success.' The problem, she thought, is that failure is pretty easy, too. Effortless, even. She shrugged at him. Wordlessly. Caught somewhere between *none of your business* and *you wouldn't be interested*.

'I was one of the people you like to torture,' she said. 'I waited tables.' And, the little voice in her head announced, that's as far as we go. A couple of questions about you for politeness and then I'm out of here.

'My father died last year,' he said, unasked.

'Were you close to him?' He gave this more consideration than she felt it was worth. I don't care that much about you or your father, she thought. Get on with it, would you?

'I was so far from him, I have to remind myself I was his son,' he said quietly. 'He was fifty-three when I was born. He was an alcoholic and a drug addict.' She could think of no appropriate response to this, gazing at him, silently. 'Tell me what you think when I say alcoholic and drug addict.'

Ghostly stereotypes lined up shakily, scabbed, scarred and skinny, shaking, dead-eyed beneath cinder-dull uncombed hair. She shook her head.

'You don't have to tell me, I know. Except my dad wasn't like that. My dad was Dr Cadogan, GP. Everybody's favourite family doctor. He built up such a practice, he could have retired, but they wouldn't let him. Go out in the middle of the night, he would, always. Course, he might have to give himself a syringe of a waker-upper, but he'd be there.'

The coffee forgotten, puddling in the bottom of the mug, she puzzled at the mixture of sadness and pride in the way he talked. Puzzled particularly at her own conviction that the sadness was there because he perceived she needed it to be there.

'Sometime when we're heading for County Louth, I'll stop the car in our townland and let you just wander for a few minutes. If you mention him, you won't believe the stories they'll tell you about how wonderful he was. I never saw a man as good at working the system. Never let a pattern of narcotic prescription develop so he'd be caught that way. Never injected in the same places lest he run out of veins. Never dealt with a problem when he was under the weather. Balanced his internal chemistry like a scientific experiment. You look shocked.'

'Well, he was a doctor.'

'More drug addicts and alcoholics among doctors than most other professions.'

'Yes, but . . .'

'Yes, but they all hit bottom sooner or later?'

She nodded.

'Not if they're clever enough. My father never hit bottom. But he could see it ahead of him. Just after he turned seventy, he said to me that, sooner or later, all of his patients got some disease or had some accident that put them in the hands of other people. He dreaded that.'

'So what happened?'

'He drove into a bridge.'

'Deliberately?'

'Oh, yes. Didn't leave a note or anything that would screw up his accident policy, but I have no doubt. He was doing over a hundred. Bang. Gone. A very clever man.'

'Would you do that?'

'Oh, Cassie – and not hear the final round of applause?'

As their laughter died, Cassie could hear one of the three women at the next table saying she was going for refills of coffee. Polo leaned over to her with a five-pound note. Would she do him a favour and bring back two extra coffees? Milky? And a couple of sticky buns? Because if he got up to get two cups, the girl he was with would leave, and he really needed the extra ten minutes to get off his mark with her. The woman looked at Cassie and laughed when she didn't deny his claim.

'The sticky buns are another aspect of my father's legacy to me,' he said. 'Didjever notice kids of very much older parents are always fat? When your father's a grandfather's age, he hasn't the energy to play football with you, so he gives you money for sweets instead.'

He was not actually fat, she thought, but would always hover on the edges, like John Travolta or Russell Crowe. The woman from the next table came back with the tray and shared out the coffee and buns. Theatrically, he took her hand and kissed it. She called him an eejit. It was the amused endearment of the middle-aged, Cassie thought. A younger woman would have called him a spa.

'What happened to your dad?' he asked, sitting back down in the brown bentwood chair.

For a second she thought of refusing to answer, but it seemed too heavy a response to his talking so unguardedly about his own father. 'He went off to the local garage shop to fill my mother's car with petrol, because he always tried to make sure she never had to bother. Came back with an evening paper. Sat down in the armchair and died as if he was falling asleep.'

The image of her father, head confided against the side cushion of his favourite chair, swelled her throat with the need to cry out. It took her by surprise, this emotional ambush. At the funeral, she had stood, stunned with jet-lag, silent and dry-eyed among her older, weeping relatives, neighbours visibly tempering their disapproval of her frozen demeanour by murmured acknowledgements of how much of a shock it must have been and how difficult to get a flight. Now, six weeks later, in a warmly crowded café, the backwash of unexperienced grief stupefied her. People had said at the funeral that his death was so like him, so typical of him, so quiet and considerate.

'I must stop this,' she said. 'This is ridiculous.'

He said nothing, gesturing at her to butter her sticky bun, as if the trivial physical activity would pull her out of the emotional trough she was in. Except that overlaid like a ghost image on the hand that held the knife was her father's hand, holding his favourite knife and spreading the marmalade he liked best on brown bread. Marmalade with a three-masted ship on the label. Spanish Gold. Steepling her arms from elbows planted on

43

the table, she buried her face in paper napkins and wept, wondering as she did why such an inconsequential link would unhinge the stability she had maintained for a month and a half, why a recollection of a silhouetted argosy on a jam label would affirm a death, up to then, not quite real.

She blew her nose in one paper napkin, stuffing it into her pocket, mopping her face with the other. Taking a deep breath, she looked around and found herself being watched with evident dismay by the woman who had brought the coffee, who seemed to be having second thoughts about the wisdom of having done so. A gust of broken laughter went through Cassie, who did an it's-nothing-it's-a-good-thing flip of her hands at the woman, who looked mortified at having been caught.

'You finished?'

Steering out into Saturday sunshine so bright, it was momentarily like coming out of a matinée in a cinema. As they walked up Grafton Street, he stopped to give stick to the buskers, all of whom greeted him with affection. When he reached the old man who played the banjo, the musician abruptly changed the tune he was playing. Polo Cadogan laughed. 'D'ja hear that?' he asked the semi-circle of listeners. 'This mean bollix wants to show off my inadequacies. He knows I'm the only man in the world who can do the Charleston with only one foot.'

Cadogan was big, but not handsome. He was a complete stranger to all of the people who had been listening to the banjo player. He was not famous. Yet the group accepted him as if he wore a scarlet letter, E for Entertainer. Somehow he had the right to halt them, talk to them and create the expectation that he would also amuse them. 'This one,' he said, patting his right thigh, 'this one can do a great Charleston. But *this* one,' he advanced his left leg and looked at it in wonder, 'useless.

44

God knows, I've tried. Won't learn. Can't learn.' He opened his hands helplessly at them. Waited.

Someone at the back yelled, 'Show us, then!'

Whence, Cassie wondered, came Cadogan's certainty that someone would ask him to perform? You'd expect it of someone born in a theatrical trunk, stage-bred of stage-bred parents, but this man – this Meathman, son of a doctor?

Cadogan gestured the circle of watchers to move back a little, to give him more space in which to be seen. Then watched his own right foot as it trembled in time to the banjo, beginning to dance with the fast fluency of an old hoofer.

'Wha' abou' the other one?' someone yelled.

Still dancing, one-footed, Cadogan wiped his face with his hand. 'You don't want to know.'

'Yeah, we do. Show us the left.'

'The left hand?' Cadogan called out, so even the back row of the circle could hear him, offering his left hand floppily to them, continuing to dance, one-footed. Half the crowd were laughing, disbelieving how well he was able to do it.

'No, the left foot,' the crowd yelled back, configured into a pantomine audience by his cues.

'My Left Foot?' Cadogan asked, and – still dancing – for a few seconds transformed himself into a mimed reference to Daniel Day Lewis's cinematic version of Christy Brown, saying, 'Fuck off, would ye?' Those who up to now had been straight-faced began to laugh, too. Only when he had the whole semi-circle cheering for his left foot to get its chance did Cadogan make a huge gesture of surrender, stop his right foot, and try to get the Charleston going with his left foot. Cassie couldn't decide whether to watch the performer – his left leg apparently fattened with wet cement, trying, but

45

missing, crucially missing, the banjo-beat every time – or watch the watchers, straining with their faces to make that errant leg work. She had not often seen so many in an audience with tears squeezing out the sides of their eyes. The most affected seemed to be the ones who had halted, at first, with an air of duty, of giving a fair trial to an amateur.

Without warning, the banjo player segued into a dirge-like slow melody, and Cadogan, boneless, sank to his knees on the reddish pavement of the pedestrianised street. Money clinked into the banjo player's upended leather hat. Cadogan bounced to his feet, the two men bowed and hugged each other. Then Cassie was walking again towards Stephen's Green, Cadogan beside her, slapping at his red-dusted knees.

'More than half that money should go to you,' she told him.

'I'll never be without money.' He mopped his face with a striped hanky. 'That's one of the reasons I'm a good catch for you.'

'Midas,' she said.

Oddly, this seemed to disturb him. 'He was the lad that everything he touched turned to gold, right? Nah. I just attract money. It's not the same thing. Peter, I'm really sorry for being this late.' This last was addressed to a man sitting on one of the park benches overlooking the pond. Cadogan's hand dropped on to the man's shoulder as he led Cassie around the bench.

'Cadogan, you never change. It's always "See you at half nine or a quarter to three."' Seeing Cassie, the man stood up and extended a hand. As tall as Cadogan, he gave the impression of being smaller. If she was drawing him, Cassie thought, she would draw him melted. Melted by life. Not totally runny, but softened at the edges. The image tweaked a half-smile across her face, that half-smile noted, she realised, by the melted man, who looked a question. She ignored it.

'I'm sorry, I wasn't listening to Polo – your name again?'

'Peter Thornton.' The man sat down again, making a half-move of the hand towards the remainder of the bench. Sit down. If you want to. Don't if you don't. No skin off my nose. Almost to prove her independence of him, she sat.

'I'll get us drinks,' Cadogan said, and was gone.

Thornton turned down the corner of the page he had been reading, closed the book. His hair, she thought, was about three weeks past when it should have been cut. It was top-heavy, black floppy fringe falling into his eyes and loose bits at the back curling upwards in contradiction to its general straightness.

'So you're the girl Polo's going to marry.'

'I'm the one Polo *says* he's going to marry.'

He shrugged, as if what she had said meant the same as his own statement, and silently watched the families at the water's edge, feeding the ducks. Feeling under no pressure to keep up even a semblance of conversation with this surly individual, Cassie looked around her. Teenagers under trees, fondling each other or lying flat, black knit Spandex pulled up to expose white midriffs to the sun. Business-suited men short-cutting along the paths, heads tilted to mobile phones. Girls in citrus-glowing dresses raising their faces, closed-eyed, to the sun in pleased conjecture; would it last the weekend?

There had been a pen-and-ink sketch, Cassie thought, in one of her father's much-loved *Dublin Opinion* annuals, of much the same scene, perhaps fifty years previously. In the drawing, the skirts of the dresses were full, the bodices pencil-slim. But the pleasured reality was the same. So much the same, it brought a lurch of unexplained sadness to her and she thought she might ask her mother if she could take those annuals. Her mother never looked at them. She imagined going through the cartoons again, meeting the drawings that had made her laugh when she was small. One showing the soles of a man's shoes as he disappeared into a morass of papers on a desk, with the caption 'The Minister has gone into the matter.' Another with a weedy little man pouring a bottle of ink over his boss's bald head, with the caption, 'Guess who won the Sweep, Mr Muldoon.' The Sweep, she thought – the equivalent of the lottery today. And nobody but a poseur with a fountain pen had bottles of ink in the office now. Difficult to do that cartoon, these days, she thought. Couldn't very well have the little man beating his boss with an ink-jet cartridge.

'He'd be able to keep you in the style to which you're accustomed.'

She dragged her attention back to the man at the other end of the bench. 'Neat trick,' she told him. 'Sexist, stupid and offensive all in one go.'

'Sexist and offensive maybe. Stupid?'

'You know nothing about my style.'

He half smiled at her, somehow taking in a slow glance at her baguette bag and shoes. Then the smile faded completely. I can read you like a book and cost you like a spreadsheet, she understood his look to say. Then the heavy fine hair flopped over the eyes. Disengagement. At ease.

Her relief at Polo's return surprised her. Yet she was disturbed by her irritation at his naked need to have this older man approve of her. Disturbed even more by the realisation that this older man's disapproval of her moved her slightly closer to Polo Cadogan. She found herself planning the moves before she made them. Hook the bag-strap over shoulder, stand up, drink from the can, put it on the arm of the bench and go. No goodbyes, no conversation, no nothing.

'Girls in their summer dresses,' Thornton said, as she drank from the can.

'Don't go,' Polo Cadogan said, his unvarnished dismay appealing. She smiled at him and shook her head. He raised both hands in surrender. She moved. 'But I'll ring you,' he called after her.

Maybe not after your friend tells you I'm a type without depth, she thought. He'll tell you my bag and shoes cost a fortune. That I could shop for Ireland.

As she walked down an overcrowded Grafton Street, a woman, slightly surprised-looking, smiled at her. A responsive smile. Cassie had smiled first – at the realisation that no matter what the waspish derelict with the too-long hair said against her, it would not only fail to deflect Polo Cadogan, but would be transmuted into something exciting, something wonderful, something essential to her uniqueness by Cadogan's infatuation.

The good advice friendship gives is data-based, justified by evidence, she thought, and so is without currency against the ecstatic irrationality of affection. Even if you don't want the affection, the power it gives is pleasing. To be secretly touched, if not used. Her smile faded, but slowly, as a counter-thought came heavy as a pendulum-swing: perhaps even unwanted, unused power corrupts?

CHAPTER THREE

The Lover and the Sub-Let

'That's the one thing I'm sure of,' Cassie told her aunt on the telephone. 'For him, it's real. In the beginning, I thought it might be a publicity stunt.'

'Might have been that, too. Good career move.'

'Mostly for me, though. It's me who's getting cartoons on the front page of a national paper every day.'

'Thank God I work in a library where I get to read the papers for free. I'd be broke, otherwise. You'll be glad to know I always leave it folded so your cartoon is the first thing people see.'

'What people? The homeless guys who spend the day in the library for warmth?'

'Oh, so you're choosy about what fans you'll accept?'

'Far from choosy. Every time I see someone look a second time at one of my cartoons, I want to go home with them and wash their dishes.'

'What does my bereaved older sister think of all this?'

'It has her so confused she fell over in the supermarket.'

'Run that past me again?'

'Ma skidded on a spilled yogurt and landed on her arse in the supermarket. Well, *I* think she landed on her arse, but she says she landed on her wrist. But that's because, as you know, Ma is so well-bred she doesn't have an arse. She wouldn't *know* an arse if it got up and bit her.'

'Which, in the nature of things, is not likely.'

'She went over to Beaumont Hospital and spent a hundred years in A and E until they X-rayed her and found nothing.'

'Always knew she had no guts.'

'You *know* what I mean. They found no breaks, although that's not the way she tells it. According to her, the X-ray revealed acute trauma of the bones in her wrist. The kind of acute trauma that's just a fraction away from complete crushing to powder.'

'Yeah. If she sticks a pin in herself, that pin is always just one centimetre away from her jaguar.'

'Jugular.'

'Jugular, right. I was close, though.'

'Beaumont put a weeshy bandage on her tiny paw, but she bought more on the way home. Bandages. The little one wasn't giving her enough support, she said. So I ended up winding three and a half miles of bandage around her hand and she now looks like she's ready to take on Mike Tyson. She has one highly visible injury. Total strangers ask her what happened to her.'

'Sure, God love her,' Marsha said, in the tone Mrs Browne always used for sympathy. Warm and runny.

'And her recently bereaved, too,' Cassie supplied.

'God never shut one door but He shut two,' Marsha offered.

'God never oiled one floor but He oiled two.'

'But doesn't He pick broad shoulders for big burdens?'

'Don't let Ma hear you saying she has broad shoulders. She's made of paper-thin porcelain, remember?'

'Lucky she met your father and convinced him of that. Your father believed it was his job to protect her from everything because she was so effing fragile. He was a sweet man, your father, but not realistic. I think maybe it was because he was an only child.'

'Be careful, Marsha. Be very careful.'

'Shit, you have a point. Well, there's only children and only children.'

'You've a pretty good test case at home.'

'Colm will expect a much better present than usual next month from his aunt and godmother, now she's a wealthy cartoonist.'

'Marsha, what I love best about you is the subtlety of your reminders.'

'Cassie, without my reminders, my thirteen-year-old would not get the computer game he wants on the fifteenth. Look under Tomb Raider.'

'You proud to be the mother of a necrophile?'

'Any kind of qualification is good.'

'True. Listen, I have to go. Ma needs to be taken to a solicitor.'

'The will, is it?'

'No, different solicitor. This one's the ambulance-chaser with the ads telling you if you feel even a bit hung-over this morning, there's probably someone you can blame and definitely someone you can sue. She wants to sue the supermarket.'

'For landing on an arse she doesn't have?'

'Marsha, if it keeps her mind off how much of a failure I am in life and how my failure is probably due to living-in-sin Niall, who'll never make an honest housewife of me because he's lost respect for me because why would any man marry a woman when she's giving it away for free to him—'

'My big sister never said that.'

'No, but it's the sub-theme.'

'It's the sub-theme'll get you every time.'

'Especially from the recently bereaved.'

Cassie put the phone down, smiling to herself. Marsha had been an afterthought in her mother's family, arriving twenty-seven years after Cassie's mother. Becoming an aunt to Cassie before her teens had been an unexpected benefit of this position. A benefit for both.

A late-born only child, Cassie found in Marsha all the advantages of an older sister without the territorial battles of a sibling relationship, all the excitements of close friendship without the risks. When Marsha married Liam, she had one underage bridesmaid, Cassie, who had grave reservations about the nuptials, mainly because Cassie thought Marsha should hold out for someone who looked like George Clooney and did something interesting like be a film star or a doctor in an emergency room. But, above all, who had looks you'd be likely to remember. Marsha admitted at the time that her husband-to-be had the sort of forgettable face every serial killer needs. 'Liam Dungan has all the right features, but they add up to nothing in particular.'

I wonder if Marsha's happy, Cassie thought, clearing space on the surface allocated to the computer, scanner and printer the newspaper had given her. It's easy to mistake being funny for being happy, and Marsha's always funny. Particularly about Liam. Like when she gave out about golf and I asked her what the problem was in him disappearing for four hours now and again.

'Four hours?' was the response. 'Four hours? Yesterday he disappears at eight thirty a.m. At eleven last night I have to get out of bed because can he find the goddamn keyhole in the front door? When I open it, he falls full-length into the hall, holds up a Parker ballpoint and says, "See what I won you!"'!'

Marsha's reported anecdotes about Liam make him a more memorable and interesting person than he is, Cassie thought. Or maybe the Liam she experiences is more memorable and interesting than the Mr Plain Vanilla I know. Who the hell knows other people's relationships? Half of me worships at the shrine of my parents' happy marriage and the other half of me shrivels at the hard work my father put in to sustain the myth of my mother. But maybe she wasn't a myth to him. Maybe it's me who turns her into a malign myth because she has always seen through me. Even when there was nothing to see, through me.

'I know why you were down at the swimming baths,' Mrs Browne would say, glancing away from the teenage Cassie as if she wasn't worth looking at, even if she had to be talked to. 'Don't tell *me*,' she would add.

Should Cassie say she was at the local pool to swim, her mother would nod, not in agreement, but in acknowledgement of an expected lie. The nod accepted that nobody other than a fool would try a line as lame as that one, an explanation so patently spurious. Sometimes the smirking mother-nod would make Cassie desperate. 'But I *was*, I really *was*,' she would shriek.

Her mother would turn, eyebrows up, ridging her forehead, and invite Cassie to turn on the waterworks now, go ahead. This would make the girl cry, even though fulfilling the invitation would leave Mrs Browne's eyebrows up half-way to her hair while she smiled in confirmation of her own prescience. As Cassie got older, her mother saw through her all the time, spotting bad secrets in most of what she did. There might be a malign, covert significance to an action as simple as Cassie squeezing a pimple and leaving a red swelling on her chin. 'Well, we all know what's behind *that*,' Mrs Browne would say, lining up the red bump beside sleazy sex-seeking signals like fishnet tights worn with scarlet patent high heels.

Ben Browne called what his wife did 'teasing', as if she didn't mean her comments. 'Why do you rise to it?' he would ask Cassie. 'Your mother's only teasing.' The way he put it, this was yet one more endearing aspect of a lovely person. If her mother was present, she would giggle in response to the comment, the giggle defusing the tension between her and her daughter and somehow confirming Ben Browne's view: sure I was only egging you on to see how you'd react. Only in fun. Just a joke. No harm in it. No offence meant, no offence taken, I hope.

Perhaps it was a function of their time, this benign interpretation of his wife for public consumption by the husband. Perhaps it was unique to them. Cassie could find no present-day equivalent, although many of her girlfriends used reported speech to push their partners into the all-seeing, all-protective role. 'Joe says it's typical of me; I'm far too soft,' they would claim.

Half the time, Cassie thought, the Joes had not said anything, it was the girlfriends making it up. She had once asked her own long-term boyfriend, Niall, what he was thinking, when a long silence had fallen. He wasn't thinking or feeling anything, he said. And she needn't do that girl thing of him hiding from his own feelings, for fuck's sake: he'd never *met* a woman who didn't want to attribute thoughts and feelings to men who were just minding their own business.

Later, watching him, she realised Niall's moments of greatest pleasure were when his eyes went out of focus, when he thought and felt nothing, when he was adrift although not asleep, subject to yet uninvolved in the stream of half-consciousness smoothly swelling his brainwaves past coma but not peaking them into active thought. He was like a cat purring and preoccupied pleasurably by the involuntary pastime of purring.

A wave of affection washed over her. She lifted the phone and dialled. After three rings, he responded. She could hear him shifting in the big waterbed.

'Cassie. I tried you – was it last night?'

'Doesn't matter. How you doing?'

'Working. Signed off on the study, beginning to write it now. There's a visiting guy giving a couple of extra sessions and they've been really good. You'd have enjoyed them.'

This ISDN line is good, she thought, closing her eyes to listen to the sounds from the tiny sub-let in Manhattan. Murmuring to keep him talking. Bringing him up to date about the success of the cartoons, the TV producer who was interested in doing a series about cartoons and cartoonists. 'Weird,' she said, laughing. 'Five weeks ago, I knew nothing about cartoons, now I'm earning a living from them and perceived as an expert. Even my mother is impressed.'

He gave her messages for her mother and they talked about cheaper transatlantic flights coming up because of an airline price war. He could come to Dublin for a week or ten days, or she could go to New York. The sub-let was paid for a couple of months in advance, so he hadn't really given much thought to what would happen now that she wasn't going to be coming back in the immediate future. Well, she couldn't, really, not with her mother on her own. Not to mention the cartoons. That was too good an opportunity to turn down. They could talk again about all the implications – and e-mail, once she had her address. The conversation petered to a comfortable conclusion.

Cassie played it back in her head as she worked out which lead went into what slot on the back of the computer. More and more, since she started drawing the cartoons, she was thinking in pictures even when listening to people. Now, she sat back on the bed, eyes narrowing, registering a mismatch between the sounds so recently heard. There had been those continuing rustlings of him moving in the bed, kicking away the comforter, wriggling loose from a tangled sheet, yet the loud whisperings of the fabric hadn't been reflected in his voice. There had been none of the gusting volume or expelled air of someone moving into a more comfortable position or pulling themselves upright.

The wonderfully clear new telephone line provided by the newspaper for electronic transmission of her cartoons had transmitted movement in their New York rented bed in their New York rented apartment. Movement, but not *his* movement. Plus, Cassie thought, there had been that moment when she was talking and *all* sound had stopped. He had put his hand over the receiver while Cassie was speaking. She could see him doing it. He did it often when they were together. To make a comment on the conversation he was having. Identify for her who he was talking to. Give her an estimate of how long the conversation would last. Check out a dinner invitation with her. Putting your hand over the receiver was the habit of someone sharing living space with another. The only people living alone who ever did it were smokers who didn't want to subject the caller to great ugly hawking phlegm-raking morning coughs. Niall was not a smoker. Nor did he have a head-cold.

The reason now clinically clear to her, she lifted the phone and pressed redial. This time, he was even quicker on the pick-up.

'Niall?'

'Cassie?'

'Yeah. This'll be brief.'

'No hurry – this is a bonus, pet.'

'I took most of my stuff when I was coming home. What's still there you can regard as your own. Except, of course, the girly clothes. I suggest you bundle them up and drop them at Goodwill. But you might tell her to have a look at two pairs of shoes I left. One's by Manolo Blahnik and the other's Walter Steiger. Waste to send them to Goodwill.'

She could hear him in the background to her driven monologue, making bluffed-out blusterings about not knowing who she was referring to or what had got into her or really what she was even *talking* about.

'Tell her she's really welcome to them. Unless, of course, she's got big feet. But then, compared to me, most girls have got feet like barges, don't they?' Cassie amazed herself with the bubbling, all-pals-together laugh she produced to accompany this. 'She might want to give them to someone else. They're hardly worn. Tell her that, Niall. Tell her she's absolutely welcome to them. You might tell her she's welcome to you, too. I hope you have a great time together and the earth moves and all that. I really do. I wish her well. I owe her. She's simplified so much for me. Even if she has big feet, tell her she has great timing. She's saved me an awful lot of hassle, hasn't she? Have a nice day, Niall.'

Have a nice life, Niall, she added silently after she had put the phone down, ludicrously elated. This is like running away, she thought. Like clearing out cans of water chestnuts you always meant to eat but are now three years past their sell-by date. Like throwing away an expensive dress you know damn well you'll never get thin enough to wear.

She plugged the server in. Electronic wheezes began. She fumbled her way into the word-processing programme, typing two-fingered:

> Why am I not more upset? I have been with him nearly three years.
>
> He ws my first real love.

The misprint made her giggle.

Ws he really?

Ys, he ws.

Why ws he?

Because.

Serio?

He ws there. He ws nice.

Sr Annunciata always said "nice" was a legal term meaning neat and should never be used in other circs.

Pleased with her ease at finding the inverted-comma button, Cassie surveyed this last statement for a moment, wondering if a full stop should go in after the abbreviated word for Sister.

Well, OK, he cleaned up good. He ws polite to my parents. He ws clever and worked hard.

Reading her own typed words forced her to realise that the precipitate parting just accomplished was the end of nothing very significant.

But – three years.

So?

You're right.

How're you going to tell your Poor Widowed Mother, though?

How about I tell her the truth?

Oh, shit.

Why not?

It's all about bed.

So?

She'll extrapolate.

And?

Realise I used to be in that bed. At the same time he ws in

it. Ergo we ws probably up to every four-letter awfulness in the book.

Ws yiz?

No more than any other two people working three jobs.

Here's the tough one. Here's the question where you can telephone a friend for help. The earth move?

How the hell would a friend be able to help on that?

If it moved, you'da told pople.

Well, if I knew a pople I might have told him, but it's not something you'd tell a friend.

You'da boasted.

Would I?

Women tell each other about being multi-orgasmic.

No. Kids still at school write notes to each other full of crap to impress. No real woman has ever (hold on till I find the italics) *ever* told me about the quality of her orgasms. Anyway, if the earth moved, it didn't do it often enough to endanger the planned progress of tectonic plates.

You're just bitching.

Yeah. If I were doing it with the right fingers, I could even get Brownie points for it.

Would you be this *insouciant* if Polo Spider hadn't appeared, slavering?

What's *insouciant*?

Look it up in the thesaurus under Tools.

Doesn't recognise it.

Crap computer. Give it back.

Not only doesn't it recognise it, but suggests what you really mean is "in somebody's clutches".

Well, if you weren't in Polo Spider's clutches, would you be this laid-back about that unfaithful shitty slobber moving Big Foot's tectonic plates all over your bed in Manhattan?

Smelly Big Foot.

You don't know that. You have no evidence for that.

ESP.

Oh, OK.

Polo Spider's made me laugh more in three weeks than Niall McGrady did in three years, let's be honest. But that's not the point. The point is I'm out of there, I'm gone, goodnight, not sorry for the three years. Not the worst in the world, that unfaithful Arseface. Left no scarring. No replacement needs. Its over.

It's.

This is now, that was then.

Ws.

Effing right. Ws.

CHAPTER FOUR

The Condom and the Pajero

In the following weeks, Cassie was constantly fighting a structure cast around her life by the half-recollections of strangers. Introduced to her at parties or in pubs, someone would say, 'Oh, you were Little Miss Muffet,' their faces brightening at the remembered laughter.

Then there were the reminders, like the mention in a Sunday gossip column, of Polo Cadogan joining her gym as part of his continuing pursuit of her. What kept her from viewing this as stalking was that it solved other problems: few people asked about and even fewer remembered her former boyfriend. Niall was an assumption built into the story, but expendable, like the curds-and-whey in the Little Miss Muffet fairytale: a prop, a scene-setter, an establisher for the opening shot. You had to have a man in order not to seem naked, desperate and over-available in the first place, but only to the point where along came the spider. Then you soft-focused the first guy, doused the lights, killed the sound and tipped his picture into a black plastic sack.

It did, however, bug Cassie greatly that her mother was pleased to read about her in gossip columns. It was as if her cartoons were playtime, but to be up there in little emboldened mentions along with the ageing rock star and his beautiful mistress, to be mentioned beside the politician bonking his secretary, to be pictured adjacent to the silk and his PR guru wife was real achievement.

Mrs Browne was also convinced that being publicly juxtaposed with the transiently topical was the same as meeting them in reality, so she kept asking Cassie if the rock star's mistress was as innocent as she seemed, and how was the politician's wife bearing up?

'Ma, I don't *know* these people,' Cassie said, 'People in gossip columns are not important. They're not even real. They just dress up to go to parties and get mentions.'

'They're famous, though,' her mother said. 'They wouldn't be famous if they weren't important. Loads of people go to parties, but you don't read about *them*.'

I wonder, Cassie thought, if I should buy one of those clear plastic things people wear at night to stop their teeth grinding, and use it whenever I'm near my mother? I'm not home a full six months and my teeth are noticeably shorter already. They'll be stubs by Christmas.

'D'you think she's had a facelift?'

Cassie glanced at the two pictures of a TV presenter lined up side by side. 'Before and After?' queried the headline. 'Ma, I don't care.'

'But do you think she's had one?'

'Well, if the picture on the right is supposed to be her, post facelift, I'd sue the shit out of the surgeon, if I was her.'

'There's no need to be crude.'

For fuck's sake, you ask me crap questions about crap issues involving crap people in whom I have shag all interest and when I say 'shit' you berate me. Ma? I'm twenty-three.

'It's important for someone my age to keep up to date.'

Nobody but you, Ma, could interpret ferreting around in the facelifts of the nearly famous as keeping up to date. Nobody but you could get a truism, a lie, a crazy and a bulging bagful of widda-woman pathos into one short sentence. 'You're a remarkable woman, Ma,' Cassie said. Her mother simpered. Please, Cassie thought, let's have what the night-time radio phone-in programmes call 'closure' on this, OK? Heart sinking, she allowed her gaze to be directed to another picture on the gossip page.

'I was thinking of having him handle my serious-injury case,' her mother said.

Be bloody difficult, Cassie thought, since he only does major criminal stuff, preferably with ambassadorial Ansbacher outlaws or terrorists mixing extreme nationalism with equally extreme capitalism.

'But they settled out of court.'

Please don't ask for how much, came the unspoken addendum, delivered in a resigned sigh. It's all over now, said the sigh. Could have done better. But I would have had to be Hard. And – you know yourself – I could never be Hard. Many could. Not me, though.

The doorbell buzzed and the telephone rang at the same time.

'That's SDS for me,' Cassie said.

'I'll give it to him,' Mrs Browne said.

Her mother regarded couriers and SDS vans drawing up at her home in recent months as a demonstration of superiority over the neighbours, since they only got deliveries from an ordinary navy-trousered An Post cyclist. 'It's a torment to poor Cassie when she's trying to concentrate, all these couriers and vans arriving,' she would tell the other people living in the *cul-de-sac*.

The phone call was from Polo Cadogan, wanting to know why there was a message on his phone telling him she couldn't meet him the next day after his photo-opportunity.

'I'm flying to Paris just after noon.'

'For how long?'

'Three days. Not that it's any of your business.'

'Course it's my business. Aren't I your future husband? Why Paris?'

'The editor thinks my version of the Paris collections might be fun.'

'He's barking mad.'

'He has a vintage Merc,' she said, knowing that Cadogan lusted after classy old cars.

He decided to gloss over this evidence of successful sanity. 'What time's your flight?'

'Why?'

'Jesus, you're the most suspicious wagon I ever met. Ever strike you I might want to be helpful to you?'

'No.'

'You're right. I just want to cop a quick feel.'

'My mother is listening.'

'I'll cop a quick feel of your mother, too, if she wants. Meet me at the twiggy fellas in College Green at eleven and I'll take you to the airport in my new Pajero.'

'What's a Pajero?'

'A triumph of engineering from Mitsubishi. A seven-foot-long comfortable Jeep high off the ground that weighs a ton. Piss off a Pajero, the Pajero wins. Except in Spain. They're not allowed to sell it in Spain.'

'Why not?' Cassie asked, surprised. She didn't think of Spain as being in the vanguard of car-safety standards.

'*Pajero* means "wanker" in Spanish.'

The 'twiggy fellas in College Green' were the John Behan angel-sculpture on the island in the middle of the road. When she arrived, pulling her new wheeled garment bag behind her, the island was already over-crowded with photographers inadvertently elbowing bystanders and gawkers off the kerb.

'Cassie! Howya, love!'

The joyous cry came from the middle of the mêlée, from the middle of the fountain, as a huge purple plastic shape bounced up from among the angels and waved.

'Only a few minutes more!'

The shape bounced up again to promise her this. Polo was inside a rounded, tube-shaped shiny plastic form with a wobbly smaller bit above the head part. A condom. *A condom?* Could it be? He bounced up again. It was. Definitely.

'OK? You won't go away?'

The wobbly rubber bit vibrated anxiously on the top of him.

'No, I'll stay.'

'What the point?' a young black man near her asked.

'Sorry?'

'What the point of the purple thing?'

'Don't ask me.'

'You *know* the purple thing,' he said, offended by Cassie's refusal to inform.

'The purple thing know *her*, too,' his girlfriend said, by way of a clincher.

Cassie let go of the handle of her luggage to make helpless gestures. Someone grabbed it and ran.

'You know *him*, too?' the black man asked, impressed.

'No – no – he's stealing it.'

'Stop thief,' yelled the black man. 'Him with the red bag – thief. Robber!'

This put the thief off rhythm, and the hesitation was fatal. The crowd took up the cry of 'Stop, thief!' and several ran after him. Cassie, half laughing at the sound of a phrase she had never expected to hear in real life, half panicked because her passport, wallet and tickets were in the bag, dithered.

'Is that your bag, Cassie?' the purple condom asked, on another upward jump.

'Yes,' she said.

'That *fucker*!'

Polo took off like a bullet up Nassau Street, gathering the rubbery purple skirts of the condom, eagerly photographed by the press. When the crowd disappeared around the corner, the cameras, for want of anything better to do, lined up on Cassie. She turned her back to them and looked at the cannons in the car park of the Bank of Ireland.

In response to a growing noise like a football team procession after victory, she turned, to see the purple condom, now clutching her scarlet clothes-carrier, borne shoulder-high by the crowd. When they deposited him in front of her, the rolled-up skirts of the condom unfolded to his ankles in a curiously graceful movement. 'What am I?' he demanded breathlessly.

'A purple condom,' she replied.

'Come on, don't give me any of that small-talk,' he gasped. 'What am I?'

'The fastest condom in the West?'

He turned to the observers, the little trembly empty bit of plastic over his head flopping first to one side, then to the other in a way that made him look infinitely pathetic. 'This woman's mink coat, her Versace gowns, her diamonds, her gold credit cards, her tickets to Paris are in this bag,' he gasped for breath, 'this bag I have just recovered for her from a . . .' as he drew another breath, several people suggested derogatory terms applicable to the bag-snatcher. Even inside the condom shape, Polo Cadogan managed to look reproving, so that they laughed. '. . . from a *villain*,' he said firmly. The PR man from the condom company, in a wild bid for extra coverage, clutched the purple condom at mid-level and announced that this proved the incredible versatility and flexibility of the brand. Media and bystanders jeered him, starting a slow handclap.

'Don't I deserve a kiss, at the very least?' Polo Cadogan demanded.

The PR man looked mortified and withdrew his arm.

'Cassie,' Cadogan clarified. 'Do I not deserve a kiss?'

The crowd roared agreement. A big grey vehicle – the Pajero – pulled in on the double yellow lines behind her. Cadogan passed the retrieved bag to the driver, who stowed it and got out, holding the driver door open for Polo.

'Not going without a kiss,' he insisted, and Cassie, making the best of it, threw her arms around his rubbery costume, kissed him through the mouth-hole cut in the front of it and pulled herself away, the skin of her arms peeling off the rubber with the slurping sound of suction letting go reluctantly. He insisted on bringing her round to the passenger door of the Pajero and handing her up the steps, in spite of the uniformed Garda moving purposefully towards this pedestrian-created traffic jam. Running around the front of the high vehicle, clutching the skirts of the condom one-handed, he made pacifying gestures at the policewoman, gave a final bow to the crowd (the loose rubbery bit on the top now flapping happily at them), dragged himself up the steps into the driver's seat, gave a thumbs-up sign to the man who had delivered the car and got it moving.

As Cassie sat back in relief, she saw pedestrians crossing in front of the Pajero and drivers of surrounding cars pointing to it and laughing. 'I wonder if Mitsubishi could sue you for bringing their vehicle into disrepute?'

'They should pay me,' he said, accelerating. 'This is the stuff of an urban legend. The day the condom drove the Pajero.'

'The condom people should pay you double, anyway. They're going to get twice the publicity they planned on. Although I could've done without that runty little crawler from the PR company trying to make sales points about his products.'

'Get off – what you didn't like was him having his arm around me,' Cadogan said, passing the Rotunda on his right and rolling down the window to look at his reflection in the darkened glass doors of the wax-museum building.

A child, sitting beside its mother on the steps of the museum, stared, terrified, at the purple thing driving the big van. Strangling on his excitement, the little boy gestured one-handed to get his mother to look, tipping his ice-cream cone so that the softening central scoop fell off into the crotch of his shorts. 'Would you *watch* what you're at?' the mother said, swiping at his skinny upper arm, back-handed. The jerky movement made the central scoop of her own cone fall into one of the shoes she had kicked off her tired feet. '*Now* look what you made me do.' As the Pajero rounded the corner into Dorset Street, Polo and Cassie saw the little boy's arm flailing after them, his mouth a huge circle, simultaneously spilling liquid ice cream and bubbling protest.

'This rate, we'll be lucky to get to the airport without causing a riot,' Cassie said.

'This rate, we'll be lucky to get to the airport at all,' he responded.

The roof of the car was bending the condom over and his eyes were no longer in line with the eye-holes in the purple plastic.

'Pull in, for Chrissake,' she said.

'I can't pull in in the middle of bloody Drumcondra.'

'We're not in Drumcondra yet.'

'Whatever. Look at the traffic. Pull in? Like, where? Like, how?'

'Better than being killed.'

'We're not going fast enough to be killed.'

69

'Famous last words.'

'Can you find the air-conditioning? I'm a bag of sweat inside this bloody thing.'

Cassie located the cool-air button and turned all the air outlets towards him. He lifted the lower edge of the condom to let in the cold air under the costume. This had the effect of inflating the purple shape below the seatbelt like a frou-frou skit. He unclicked the seatbelt. The incoming air inflated his purple shape right up to the narrow bit at the top, which stood up and looked positively cheery for the first time. 'Swollen, you're even more interesting to people out there,' Cassie told him.

Rolling down his window, he yelled at the passers-by that they all only wanted the one thing.

'If you don't take your head in and shut up, I swear to God, I'm getting out right here and now,' Cassie told him.

He pulled his head in, but only to open the sunroof and stick the top of the purple condom costume out through it while trying to get the eyeholes lined up with his eyes.

'You'll just drop me at the airport, right?'

'You afraid I'll walk you into Departures as a condom?'

'Not that it matters. No doubt there'll be a picture of me embracing you in tomorrow's papers. My mother will be scarlet.'

'She had no problem with Little Red Riding Hood.'

'Miss Muffet. In my mother's scheme of things, a spider beats the shit out of a condom any time. One of them eats flies, the other – I don't think I should have started this sentence.'

'When we get near the roundabout at the airport, there'll be delays. I'll get out of the costume then.' This settled, he blew kisses to other drivers. Cassie edged towards the steering-wheel.

'It's OK,' he said huffily. 'I'm totally in control.'

Something about a man dressed as a condom with half

his purple head sticking up through his own sunroof claiming to be totally in control of his vehicle made Cassie laugh so much that she could not even be helpful when he was trying to pull the costume off himself and stow it behind them. The space behind their seats was already occupied by her wheeled garment bag and she made a half-hearted effort to shift it, because he seemed to be having so much trouble.

'You just tell me when the lights change, OK?' Polo Cadogan instructed, kneeling on the driver's seat and fumbling in the area behind it.

'Green,' she said, after about twenty seconds.

He made a couple of fast final pokes into the rubbery material before righting himself, grimacing at protesting horns, and getting the big car moving again. At Departures, he dropped her, promising to park and join her in minutes. She wheeled the red case across the tiles to the check-in and joined a small queue.

'Nice bag,' the woman in front of her complimented.

'Thank you,' Cassie said, and opened the top pocketed section to get her ticket. The pocket, over-stuffed to bursting, vomited its contents on to the floor. For a moment, Cassie thought she might have the wrong bag, but no: there among the things on the floor were her tickets and passport. People dropped to their hunkers to help her gather what had fallen. One by one, they glanced at her in disbelief. The skin of her forearms prickling with shock, Cassie realised that the tiny individual packets in their hands, on the floor, even on the shoes of the woman next to her all contained condoms. Small condoms. Large condoms. Plain condoms. Glitter condoms. Condoms shaped like bunches of grapes. Condoms with little blisters 'For Extra Pleasure' on them.

She stood for a moment, her eyes closed, until the man behind her in the queue pointed out, mildly, that it was her turn at the desk. He and his middle-aged wife gathered up the last of the condoms and ladled them into the pocket on her case while she agreed with the uniformed woman behind the desk that, no, she wasn't a vegetarian and, yes, a window seat would be great. Her hands trembled as she retrieved her boarding pass and passport.

The young woman behind the desk told her that she finally needed to ask her some questions. Had she packed the bag herself? Cassie essayed a nod but the girl looked unsatisfied. Perhaps it was like being in court, Cassie thought. You had to be heard by the stenographer. Yes, she had packed the bag herself. Had the bag been in her possession since she packed it? Yes, it had. (Cassie could feel, rather than see, the helpful respectable couple behind her exchanging glances.) Anybody ask her to carry anything on board for them? Nobody, she truth-fully confessed.

Even the roots of her hair were perspiring, Cassie noted. This was a first. She had never been embarrassed enough on any previous occasion to get dewy around the follicles.

'Darling, do you know what they have over there in Hughes & Hughes?'

Polo Cadogan slid an arm around her waist, beaming at the couple behind her, nodding at the ground staffer behind the counter. The desire to slap away his arm was tempered by the fear that, without it, she might fall over.

'The Pope's book. You know the one with his poetry and everything, that's become a bestseller? I told the girl over there it was exactly what you'd want. Oh, I'm so sorry. We're delaying these people, darling. Beg your pardon.'

Apparently abashed at having blocked the people behind her in the queue by his preoccupation with sliding the book out of the small paper bag for her to see, he did a shrugging, blithering self-abnegation, which drew vastly more attention to himself and Cassie than a shouted 'Look at us!' before walking her away from the check-in desk, arm around her waist, taking her tickets and passport from her as if they had been married twenty years and she was no longer the full shilling.

'I. Will. Kill. You.' she told him, as he ostentatiously checked the time on one of the big clocks before seating her at the coffee bar.

'My little presents announced themselves, did they?'

'Dozens of them.'

'Closer to a hundred, actually.'

'All over me, all over the feet of the woman in front of me, all over the floor.'

He glowed with delight, ordered two coffees and handed over a fiver.

''Scuse me, Miss?'

Cassie started as if stung. Turning, she realised that the peculiarity of the voice was due to age: the boy was halfway between soprano and man.

'My da said he thought you dropped these.' He held out two packeted condoms, his palm hilled in the middle by his eagerness for her to see every detail. She snatched them, dropping them deep into a pocket.

'Tell your dad we really appreciate it,' Polo told the boy warmly. 'Tell him she'd have been lost in Paris without them.'

The boy nodded and disappeared.

'They're the best condoms of all,' Polo said, drinking his coffee without waiting for her to start on her cup. 'They're the ones tested to withstand two quarts.'

'For fuck's sake,' the baseball-capped teenager on the next stool said. Cassie, about to drink her coffee, gusted half the foam off it with a laugh.

'Show the man,' Polo told her, holding out his hand so

73

that she had to dig into her pocket and deposit the two packets in it. He used a plastic coffee-stirrer to point the young man's attention to the tiny print. 'See?' he said. 'Two quarts.'

The young man clearly wanted to ask something, but was inhibited in some way by Cassie's presence. Me either, Cassie thought. I mean, yes, of course you want your condoms reliable. Strong, even. But—

'Practically bullet-proof, they are,' Polo assured him. 'Here, have these on us.'

The man looked at Cassie worriedly from under the peak of his cap.

'Oh, no, she's fine, she's fine,' Polo said, patting the stranger on the shoulder. 'She's got hundreds in the case. And it's only a short trip.'

The recipient eased back down on to the stool and waved the two condom packets at them as an appreciative goodbye.

At the ticketed Passengers Only sign, Polo Cadogan made sure she had passport, tickets and boarding pass. Told her she was to take care of herself.

'I suppose,' she said, through gritted teeth, 'you want me to bring the condoms home safely, too?'

'Oh, no,' he told her in surprise. 'I won't need them. What I'd be hoping for is we'd have lots of babies, very soon. Maybe four. Maybe five. Go on now, you don't want to have any hassle before boarding.'

She allowed him to hug and kiss her, mainly because she had no energy left to hit him.

CHAPTER FIVE

The Dried Frog and Slane Castle

Cassie's cartoons of the Paris collections were picked up by several overseas publications. The size of the extra cheques thrilled and frightened her. The temptation was to cash them and live, but the thought of paying huge income tax in a lump scared her into getting an accountant.

When I told him a gallery in Temple Bar wanted to stage an exhibition of my originals [Cassie e-mailed her Aunt Marsha] his eyes lit up, insofar as an accountant's eyes can light up. He's gone off to see if he can get me classified as an artist (as opposed, I presume, to a newspaper hack) because if he can, I pay no tax at all. Now, you and I would see this as a hell of a *coup*, maybe even a *stroke*, but my mother would see it as me cheating my way to success to which I am not entitled, so don't tell her, if you're talking to her. Of course, if you *are* talking to her, it'll be her that's doing the talking, because of the frog in her tea.

You know part of my mother's constant self-affirmation of her upper-middle-class status is rejection of tea-bags? She keeps loose tea in a tin caddy. The day I came back from Paris, she hardly said hello to me before bringing Exhibit A to my attention. Exhibit A being an inch long, absolutely flat, dried dead frog. She'd been doling miniature shovelfuls of tea into the pot and found

75

herself unintentionally shovelling a desiccated frog.

You know what she did? Photocopied him. Sent the photocopy off to the tea company. Invited them to consider her pain and trauma. When she showed me the frog, I thought it was the coolest thing – like freebies in cereals, you know? I thought she should put him in a glass and pour hot water on him because maybe he'd expand like those flattened dry sponges in the shape of sea-horses and octopuses. She was raging I didn't immediately see the horror of having dry frogs inflicted on you without notice. I think she was *really* raging because she had me mentally lined up as a witness, testifying in court that she is half the woman she used to be and I wouldn't be worth a toss in court if I thought dry frogs a bonus.

Marsha, she got two and a half thousand quid out of them. Had to hand him over, though. Well, slide him over. She made a big thing of never touching him, on the basis that he probably had exotic Sri Lankan viruses in him which would unleash horrors if he was touched. I miss him. He was so perfect in all his details.

The reply came a few hours later.

I didn't get to read your message immediately, because one of my colleagues here was telling me she saw you on *Questions and Answers* and thought you were great. (No, no, don't apologise for not telling me you were going on. It's perfectly all right to show me up to my colleagues as not being close to the Famous Cartoonist.) I asked her did you have your glasses on and she said no. Which probably explains the fearlessness she ascribes to you: you couldn't see there was anybody else on the programme with you. Why don't you get contact lenses, now you're filthy rich? I wear the disposable ones. Another thing, now you can afford it, get a house. A property boom is starting, which means house prices will soon go through the roof. Unless, of course, you move into Polo Cadogan's mansion?

In fact, Cassie's first visit to Polo Cadogan's mansion happened that week. He was going to take her to see Carlingford Lough, he told her, one of the most beautiful parts of Ireland. It was a disgrace she knew nothing of the beauties of Meath (where he came from) and Louth (one county up). On the way back, he would show her his home. That would, of course, soon be *their* home.

Her agreement came without struggle, partly because she was curious to see where he came from, but more because she was now used to Cadogan's constant courtship, his capacity to appear anywhere, at any time, in any guise. It was like a radio alarm clock: there every day, annoying in intent and implied control, pleasing in reliability. Sometimes, just as the alarm-clock radio, even in waking its owner, plays a favourite piece of music, so Cadogan's antics, even as they embarrassed her, amused and warmed her. She began to enjoy the unremitting outrageousness, the predictable unpredictability of him taking over and melding together total strangers in public places, the reluctant but half-admiring laughter he evoked in victims of his practical jokes.

In the beginning, she would blush and pretend she was not with him, even seeking to initiate a conspiracy of put-down glances with other people in the area – who *is* this countrified OTT creep? This gave way to a shrugging, distanced, tolerant helplessness: 'What can you do but laugh?' More recently, she had simply enjoyed the carnival he created.

He would arrange to pick her up and drive her home from wherever she was sent by the newspaper, despite her protests that the paper gave her taxi vouchers. On days when he was doing a photo shoot, he would arrive in the Pajero, its back section filled with strange props. Other days, he would drive his Porsche. The first time he arrived in the Porsche, Cassie slid silently into what she saw as a small, misshapen vehicle. He asked her opinion of it.

'Well, I suppose it's a start,' she said, trying to let him down gently.

'A start on what?' he demanded.

'A start towards a sports car.'

'This is a fucking *Porsche*!'

'OK.'

'Do you know about Porsche?'

She shook her head, tempted to tell him she didn't know about Mitsubishi, either, but that the Pajero was a hell of a lot more comfortable to travel in. It was the Pajero he took on their trip, so she would get 'a good, elevated view' of all the beauty spots in which he took particular, almost proprietorial, pride. North of Julianstown he gave her the impression of owning everything, including football and hurling teams.

He drove her through the mountains, slowing to show where it was possible to see right into Northern Ireland, slowing again when they had a view of Dundalk Bay. Some of the sunshine slanted from behind puffed clouds, theatrically picking out townlands as if they were spotlit. His accent thickened, she noticed, as he talked about his home place. She poked him along with little cue-questions, not quite listening to what he said, but enjoying the enjoyment he took in saying it. The Cadogans, he told her, had lived for more than a hundred years just outside Stackallen. The place-name was new to her. 'You've heard of Slane Castle, though.'

'Place where they have rock concerts? Lord someone.

Henry Mount Charles. Some teenager always drowns in the local river.'

'The Boyne,' he said, somewhat let down that she didn't know the name of the river. 'Our home looks across the river at Slane Castle.'

'So you get the music for free?'

'Well, a couple of times I've been working there on the night anyway. Warming up the crowd.'

'You'd be good at that, I imagine.'

'I'm probably the best alive at it.' It was said with such understated casualness that it took a moment for the scale of the boast to strike her and make her laugh. 'I'm deadly serious,' he said, looking surprised. 'You ask me am I good at sport, I tell you no. You ask me can I Charleston, I say yes, one-legged. You ask me am I good at warming up an audience, the answer is that I've travelled all over the world to watch guys doing it. Comedians on the way up. Old comedians on the way down. I'm better than any of them by a mile.'

The Pajero pulled between two fat rounded stone pillars and crunched along a gravelled curving driveway, serpentined in that late Victorian way designed to surprise the arriving guest with a sudden, total view of the big house. A red car was parked to one side of the front door, books thrown along its back window. The car itself, although big, was dented, rust crusting the edges of the dents.

'That another of the fleet?'

'No, that's Peter's.'

'Peter?'

'You know Peter. You met him that day in Stephen's Green. Peter Thornton. He stays here a fair bit.'

He halted her on the gravel to make sure she got the full sweep of the view, the angled beauty of the castle, the rich grazing lands sloping to the river.

Inside the house, he showed her first the rooms where

his father had worked. The patients' waiting room. The examination room. The storeroom for supplies and medical reference books. They were less luxuriously furnished than the rooms where the family lived, which were filled with solid, old-fashioned furniture and indications of inattention: an empty bird case and a picture on the floor against a wall, its glass cracked, waiting for someone to have the time to get new glass put in the frame. There were no family photographs on display, and she wondered aloud at their absence.

'My father was a fine photographer in his young days,' he said. 'Somewhere, in an attic, is his old box Brownie camera. There are albums of photographs of my mother early on. Very few after I was born. Maybe his hands shook too much. Maybe he lost interest. I don't know. Never cared enough to ask. I never wanted to take pictures. *Be* in pictures, yeah, but not take them . . .'

They ended up in a big old stone kitchen with an Aga, an electric cooker, plus a machine to make every kind of coffee and a microwave.

'If Peter's living here and his car is outside, where is he?' she asked.

'Walking somewhere with a book in his arse pocket,' Polo Cadogan said. 'When I walk, I walk. When he walks, he reads. I kid him he never kicked the breviary habit.'

'What's that?'

'Priests have to read their breviary every day for an hour or something.'

'Oh, he was a priest.'

'Still is, I suspect. I have no idea if he ever officially left. But he hasn't done priest stuff in the last couple of years.'

'Why not?'

'Well, calling your bishop the king of cowardly avoidance behaviour and an irresponsible little shit tends to lead to a parting of the ways. There he is now.'

They watched the distant figure walking up one of the tracks foot-beaten out of the lush grasslands near the river. Although he was not carrying a book, he walked slowly, shoulders down, as if walking was a demanding physical activity.

'Walks like he's walking on cinders,' Polo Cadogan said softly.

The man's hair was even longer and limper than the last time she had seen him, so when he noticed them at the kitchen window, he had to tilt his head to get the heavy fringe to one side. He raised a hand in greeting, his face serious, and they could hear him coming in at the back door and going upstairs.

'He's not joining us,' she said, relieved.

'No. Unless I make a big thing of it, he stays in his room when he's in the house.'

'Why does he live here?'

'Because I told him my house was his until he found somewhere else, or found something he wanted to do.'

'Why would you give a man unlimited squatter's rights in your home?'

'He was close to my father.'

'That's not a good reason.'

He searched in an overhead cupboard, found a packet of peanuts and decanted them noisily into a saucer. Put it in front of her. Coffee and peanuts? She took a handful out of politeness, realising too late that they were honey-roasted, orange-stained with awful sweetness. Ate one. Washed away the taste with the coffee, which tasted bitter. He had all the machinery for hospitality, she thought, but only a schoolboy's skills. A schoolboy's hands, too, pale and plump and bulging at the fingertips from bitten nails. Upstairs, she could hear faint movement. Funny, how some quite big people moved softly, almost scuffing along, not lifting their feet high off the floor, while smaller people like her mother came down heavily, heavily, on every step of the stairs, every movement of her upstairs as easy to map mentally when Cassie was downstairs as if black footprints appeared on the ceiling.

'I know it's not a good reason.'

She had to backtrack to remember what they had been talking about. Nodded slowly to indicate a persistence of interest she didn't have.

'I didn't get a great Leaving Cert,' he said, shrugging.

It must help, she thought, to have a dead mother and a busy drug-addict GP father if you don't get a great Leaving Cert. Better a non-judgemental father whose lack of reproach peels away your protections so that your mother's gusty sighs and high-pitched listing of points achieved by this neighbour's daughter and that first cousin get scored in your memory. All these years later, at her father's funeral, when Cassie was sympathised with by the neighbour's daughter and the first cousin, she saw the points they got in the Leaving Cert like a TV scoreline across their foreheads.

'I was going with a girl from Galway,' Polo said slowly. 'She was doing communications studies.'

You got her pregnant, she filled in silently, and he nodded at the unspoken truth of it.

'She was nineteen,' he said, then half moved his hands as if he had been trying out an excuse that was irrelevant.

Cassie scrubbed off her fingers the burnt-orange salty oil from the nuts. Wrapped the nuts in one tissue, then another. Created an unimportantly busy silence.

'I had money. My da would always give me money,' he said. It was a reproach, a condemnation. But of himself, rather than his father. It said, 'I was bought. He dealt me the wrong currency, for a father, but in accepting it, I became the son he required. Who could be paid off in bundles of the notes patients gave the doctor. I could be paid to be absent. Inattentive.'

'We went over together. I didn't want her to be on her own, it was my – it wasn't her problem to go through on her own, you know?'

Cassie nodded, considered ameliorating his evident misery by mentioning money she had lent to girlfriends, of providing a place to spend a couple of nights to bleed, to talk, to cry, before a friend went back home, afterwards.

'It wasn't late. Maybe six, seven weeks. We knew what we were doing. She has – she had three sisters younger than her and her family would have been devastated. They were really professional, too, in the place. They said only two guys out of ten go with the girlfriend. It was like they were praising me for bolstering up her courage. Jesus.' His face was blotched from pushing his knuckles against his cheeks.

You don't have to tell me this, Cassie thought, knowing the thought to be untrue.

'That's what I was doing. Bolstering up her courage. They told me some of the girls from Ireland lose heart, even when they've had counselling beforehand, they just cry, they come apart. The clinic people said they never try to persuade someone, that wouldn't be right. Some of the girls go home pregnant. Although some of them go back, did you know that? They still can't get the courage to tell their parents or their friends or the place where they work or their husband. So they go back, weeks later, when it's *really* a – when it's more difficult and everything. But I was there, big hero, wasn't I? To give her courage and be supportive and all that shit, and I minded her afterwards, did all the right things, minded her, let her cry, let her talk, promised her she'd get over it, that it was just a bundle of cells, just a blob. That she had a life. A great life ahead of her. The Easter break was a few days after we came back, so she went down to Galway. The night she went, I went to the parochial house in Drogheda to see Father Thornton. Nobody could have been as good. He didn't ask me anything. I just told him. Jesus, I must have told him six or eight different times. He just kept making cups of tea for me. He smoked all the time. He used to smoke. Untipped Players. Lit one from the end of another the whole evening. Except – except at one stage, I asked him and he got his stole and he kind of sat sideways and heard my confession. I told him at the end of it that I would never get over it, that it was the worst thing I had ever done, that she'd have gone ahead with the baby if I hadn't had the money, if I hadn't been there with her. That I would always try to stop other people doing it.'

It was so long since Cassie had been to confession, she could not remember if absolution could be made conditional. 'Did he ask you to be against abortion?'

'He didn't ask me anything. He didn't comment on anything. Except at the very end, he said nobody should ever make big decisions when they were in a state of emotional turmoil. I said I was so sure that I could guarantee I would come back to him three months later or six months later or a year later with the same decision, but he just went . . .' Polo Cadogan put his index finger to his mouth in a hushing gesture. 'Any time after that I tried to talk to him about it, he put me off.'

'Did this have anything to do with him fighting with the bishop?'

'No. It wasn't long after that he fought with the bishop but he fought with the bishop because of telling his lordship about a local priest interfering with little boys. The bishop was horrified, told him he would take immediate action. Which he did. He sent the priest to Devon. To another boys' school. Peter found out maybe three months later. Went straight to his lordship, wouldn't even wait for an appointment, reamed him up down and sideways and said the worst thing about the bishop was – quote – "that he was such an appallingly plausible apologist for a system that was corrupt to its core". He also told the bishop he was going to tell the British police. *That* changed things.'

'So the bishop fired him?'

'No bishop could fire a priest for that. No. Peter just walked away. Stopped saying Mass. Hearing confessions. He was never much for wearing Roman collars and stuff, so he doesn't dress that differently. It's a tragedy, though. He was such a good priest.'

'Maybe he'll go back?'

'Never. That's – what? Four, five years ago? There was other stuff, anyway, before that. Something involving my father. But I've never got into it with him. He does work for some hospitals plus he's a third-level examiner in Latin and Ancient Greek. He gets by.'

They could hear soft footfalls on the stairs. Polo Cadogan sat where he was, calling out to the man to join them. He came to the doorway, car keys a-jingle, dangling from one hand, the key-ring around a finger. 'The prophet of Troy,' he said, his other hand dipped at his forehead in a satirical salute to her.

Spare me, Cassie thought. Polo looked confused. 'Cassandra,' Cassie told him dismissively, getting up to rinse her cup, 'told the Trojans that accepting the gift of a big wooden horse from the Greeks would bring them a shitload of grief. But would they listen?'

'I'm going out to get something to eat. Anything I can bring you back?'

'You must be hungry by now,' Polo told Cassie.

'She's hungry,' the dark man said. 'I'll deliver. Just place your orders.'

Good, Cassie thought. He doesn't want to get into a threesome with Polo's adoration being ladled all over him, either. Polo went to the side of the big fridge, where menus from a couple of hotels and takeaway food joints were held up by magnets in the shape of pick-up trucks, and surveyed them. Peter Thornton began to toss his car keys in the air and catch them behind his back. Which made Cassie aware of how high the ceilings were in this old house, compared to more modern homes. He never missed catching the keys, though he never turned to see them, introvertedly absorbed in the pleasure of his sure-handedness as a child playing ball alone in a backyard.

Polo, now at the phone, pointed to Thornton. 'I know what you'll have,' he told him. 'D'you trust me to order for you?' he asked Cassie. 'Course you do,' he added, not waiting for her answer, and began to flirt with whoever was at the end of the line, persuading her to take an elaborate order he would pick up.

Cassie got the impression that the hotel did not do takeout food, but was used to breaking its rules for him. His whole life seemed to be about persuading people into a laughing conspiracy. Thornton was looking at his car keys. Furiously, she thought. *Furiously?* As she watched him, his face, gaunted by rage, unclenched as if he were doing relaxation exercises, and he shrugged his eyebrows at her. She stared at him. I'm way behind you on this, she thought. You assume I share your understanding of some mutually annoying manipulation, but I have no clue what it is.

'Oh, and Claire?' Polo said, walking the telephone to the full length of its ringleted flex's extension in order to pick up his own car keys. 'You heard about the suicidal tug-boat, didn't you? You didn't? Wanted to scuttle itself.

Why? Discovered its mother was a tramp and its father was a ferry. See you in fifteen.'

Cassie smiled. Thornton scowled. Polo Cadogan headed past him. 'Now, boys and girls, I'll be back with the best food ye've ever tasted in no time. Make yourselves useful. Set the table. Put out the wine – Peter, you know where it is.'

'Better than you, I know where it is.'

He was gone, footsteps running through the hall, crunching on gravel, beaming at them like a child, spinning the steering-wheel with the heel of his hand, the heavy car spitting grey stones at the turn. Now I know why Best Friend Peter is pissed off, Cassie thought. He doesn't like Polo setting us up to be stuck together any more than I do, but spotted it sooner. 'We don't have to *talk*, you know,' she told him, turning back from the window. 'He wants you to approve of me so you'll persuade me to marry him and he wants me to approve of you so I'll listen. We both know it, so what's the problem?'

He smiled and stretched and put down his keys. 'You're doing lovely work,' he said. 'Your cartoons.'

She made a move that simultaneously acknowledged the ritual compliment and dismissed its importance.

'You make readers see politicians in a new way. See past the spin to elements of their reality they sometimes don't want seen.'

'It's an accident, if so,' she said. 'Others read into the cartoons a significance they don't have. I just draw them the way they look to me.'

'Fact you don't consciously know the traits are there is beside the point. While you're working at a conscious, apparently simple level, unconsciously – subconsciously, even – you're moving deeper.'

'You flatter me.'

87

He looked surprised. 'No, I don't think you quite understand. I'm not saying you're clever or insightful.'

There's a relief, Cassie thought. Shit, wouldn't want you to think stuff like that.

'I'm saying cartoonists do their best work when they haven't a clue what they're at. Even when they can't fecking *see* what they're at, like Thurber.'

Her father had liked Thurber, particularly a drawing of a man and a woman in bed, with a seal peeping over the headboard. The caption had the man snarling, 'OK, OK, have it your own way. You heard a seal bark.' The memory of it made her laugh aloud. 'D'you know the seal one?'

He nodded, half smiling.

'There's no reason that should be funny,' she said. 'It's not even well drawn. Why does it work?'

'Thurber used to start out drawing one thing and end up with something else. That's why it's so funny. Most political cartoons are so effing *purposeful*, so anxious to make their point, they don't make us laugh, they just make us accept the point and recognise the people being portrayed. Your editor is a very smart operator, to see how different your stuff is. How . . .' He paused for quite a long time to select the right word. 'How guilelessly cruel it is.'

One recent *Pinhead* cartoon showed a high-level government figure, female, sideways-on, her great solid corporation extending out further than her bust. When it appeared, people laughed and winced, recognising the awful accuracy but vicariously experiencing the hurt of the subject. Cassie was floored that the unintended acuity of her observation of the fat politician would be experienced by that politician as deadly, acid-burning, public-shaming, long-time-scarring cruelty. 'I don't like being cruel. I shouldn't have to be cruel.'

A shadow of contempt crossed his face. I was *not*, Cassie thought, reactive rage boiling her cheeks to a scarlet shine, I was *not* seeking to be approved of by you, you son of a bitch, for avoiding cruelty, I was not doing what your expression says I was doing, being a two-faced woman, stabbing with a shiv and then looking wide-eyed at it: 'This is a *shiv*? Never knew . . .'

'All good cartoons are cruel,' Peter Thornton said. 'Otherwise they belong in kids' comics. Great cartoons are unintentionally cruel. That's the distinction.'

He sat back, hands clasped behind his head, elbows pale through the worn knit of a navy sweater. Content that Cassie would consider this definition. Confident that she would need to consider it. You arrogant bastard, she thought. Polo has enormous confidence, enough confidence to decide to take over a whole streetful of people, enough confidence to be sure that he can entertain them, squeeze gobbets of laughter out of the grimmest of them, warm them so much by the shared experience that they will take on some of each other's essence and be briefly melded into a unity. Polo has enough confidence to embark on an outrage the end of which he cannot possibly envisage, knowing that, no matter what offence it causes along the way, he will still, at the end of it, be friends with its victims, perhaps even better friends than before. Polo has a unique, delighted but never surprised confidence in himself and his capacity to enthral and entrance others.

You? You have arrogance. The arrogance that I would wait for you to find the right word. The arrogance that it was *you* who needed to be satisfied with the rightness of the word, not me, your listener, your audience. The arrogance of talking about my profession as if you knew more about it than I would ever know. The arrogance of knowing that, on this, you are right, and I can't disagree without trivialising myself. 'Shit,' she said aloud.

'Yeah,' he said.

'We should set the effing table,' Cassie said.

'We should.'

He pulled open doors and drawers. Plates, glasses, cutlery. Cassie selected three sets of everything. He located a bottle of wine and a plastic insulator into which he put the bottle, surrounding it with water and ice.

'Polo implied something about the wine. What was that?' she asked.

'I drink too much.'

When she turned up a half-empty packet of red paper serviettes, he shook his head, went into the room next door, came back with three linen napkins, hand-embroidered. 'If he brings good food, he'll take a dim view of raggy serviettes,' he said.

'You an alcoholic?'

'No.'

'How do you know?'

'I can drink one and stop. I can drink none and be happy. If I drink to extinction, I do so with complete awareness. It is not a process that takes me over. It is a decision I make. Sometimes. Too often, probably. But the . . .' Again, he paused, looking at dust-motes in mid-air while he selected from an apparent competition of possible word choices. '. . . responsibility is mine.'

'Or guilt.'

'Guilt comes into it only if the drinker harms someone else.'

'You said you could drink none and be happy.' He grunted acknowledgement of having said it. 'That's not true. You're not happy.'

Now sitting again at the end of the oblong table, he considered this, as emotionally detached from the issue as if they were discussing trigonometry. 'Probably should have said I could drink none and be content. Or serene.'

Oh, stuff serene, thought Cassie. Like you'd choose

serene if you could get happiness. I probably couldn't draw you, she thought. Because you're between things. You're between young and middle-aged. Between great physical power and lassitude. Between cynical and sour. Out of nowhere, a cartoon from her father's old collection of *Dublin Opinion* annuals came to her, whole and intact. It showed a politician making a speech. 'If we do not pull up our socks,' the politician was saying, 'we will slide rapidly downhill.' If Polo's friend Peter didn't pull up his socks, she thought, he would slide rapidly – and terminally – downhill. Maybe Polo hoped to help the sock-pulling.

'Talking about drawing cartoons makes me uneasy,' she confessed, after a moment, changing the subject somewhat to her own surprise. Letting him off the hook. Or perhaps letting herself off the illusion she had him on a hook. 'Doing them without thinking is probably my greatest strength. If I had to analyse the process – if I had a degree in psychology that made me wise and analytical, I maybe wouldn't be as good. I have to do it without thinking.' Go on, do your contempt expression again, she thought, wishing she could unsay it. Except that he looked at her, not with contempt but with something closer to recognition in his face.

'To be able to do a job without thinking,' he said, so softly she had to strain to hear him, 'that's the ultimate. That's what I've always wanted. I remember, when I was twelve, thirteen, on the top deck of the bus going back to boarding-school in the autumn, looking out of the window, knowing I was privileged, knowing I was accounted lucky, a kid from a working-class home, bright enough to study, a mother with enough faith and sureness to find the money, find the ways to educate me. Going back to school to thicker books, more complex ideas, longer references to learn, and looking out of the window at lads stripped to the waist and brown at the end of August, burnt brown, maybe their shirts tied around their middle, maybe a T-shirt thrown over a hedge nearby, and they shifting soil out of a trench, the rhythm of it unthought as a heartbeat, laughing and joking among themselves and one of them leaning on a shovel, smoking, giving stick to the rest of them. I would envy those lads so much. That was the life, I thought. Doing something you didn't have to think about. No fear. No complexity. No moral choices. No comparatives. Just being able to do something physically satisfying. Something with an end result every day. Every *day*. Something you could do without thinking . . .'

In the distance, they could hear the Pajero turning off the main road.

'We should have the oven on and plates warming,' she said.

'Why do you always need to be guilty about something?' he asked.

'Why do you always need to be a superior pain in the tits?' she asked.

Silently he turned on the oven. Then he ran the water until it steamed, plugged the sink and submerged three dinner plates in the hot water.

Arriving in the kitchen, Polo unloaded everything on to a surface, embraced her as if he hadn't seen her for a week, then examined the table, schoolmarm style, clucking his tongue reprovingly. 'No butter.'

'There *was* no butter,' Thornton said testily.

'Is now,' Polo said, slapping a gold brick into his hand. 'No salt and pepper. Always plenty of salt and pepper in this house,' he added, with theatrical reproach. 'C'mon, now, Peter, move your arse, gotta get this show on the road, Cassie doesn't know where we keep the pepper and salt. Cassie, sit down and be impressed. Open the wine, if you like.'

'I don't like. I get cork everywhere.'

'Well, dry off the warm plates, then.'

'I never before came across that thing of warming plates by drowning them,' she said, fishing them out one by one.

'Easy knowing you never went camping.'

Thornton put a butter dish on the table and went searching for salt. Polo put mint leaves decoratively on top of the starter and positioned the three small plates on the table before filling the warmed dinner plates and putting them in the oven. Out of bunched paper towels came hot crusty rolls. Cassie found and held a basket for them, took the basket to the table. Thornton was opening the wine with the efficiency, she thought sourly, of someone well used to the task.

'Right. We're done. This is it. Cassie.' Polo Cadogan, very much *mein host*, indicated by a sweeping hand where she was to sit. 'Peter.' Thornton waited until she was seated, then sat. Finally Polo took the head of the table, flapping his napkin out of its folds.

'These are beautiful,' Cassie said, running her fingers over the silk-threaded bumps of the embroidered flowers on the napkins.

'My mother did them. You would think, would you not, that my father, since he saved her work carefully,' Polo said, cutting up his bread like a farmer in a hurry to go and make silage, 'would be proud of her? But was he? Never. "Your mother's minuscule minutiae." That was how he always referred to her embroidery. Told me once she had gone all the way to Dundrum to learn a particular stitch. Made it sound like evidence of a per-version. I mean an *embroidery stitch* . . .' His face, as he sucked the life out of the words and rolled them in his mouth, took on the prissy contemptuousness of a bitter old man.

'Was his father like that?' Cassie asked Thornton, determined to be polite.

'Dr Cadogan was a clever man who knew the full extent of his cleverness.'

For a moment, Cassie thought Thornton was showing off.

'And that's always a tragedy,' he added, half to himself, standing up and taking away the starter plates.

Polo got tea-towels to handle the hot plates from the oven. 'Oven gloves are a girl thing,' he told her, and she giggled at being caught thinking precisely that.

'Saucepans with plasticated handles are a girl thing,' Thornton said.

'Electric can-openers are a *really* girl thing,' Polo added.

'Meat tenderiser you sprinkle is a girl thing.'

'That's right.' Polo picked up. 'Real men beat their meat with perforated hammers.'

'No,' Thornton corrected, deadpan. 'Only masochists do that.'

She tried not to laugh, but failed. 'I'll never be able to buy sprinkly meat-tenderiser again,' she said, eventually.

'It's very good for bee-stings,' Thornton said.

'Now *that*'s a girl thing,' Polo said, waving a full fork at him. 'Knowing stuff like that. Reckitt's Blue.'

'What the frig is Reckitt's Blue?' asked Cassie.

'You don't want to know,' Thornton told her. 'You're a career woman. When have you ever felt a gap in your life that cried out for Reckitt's Blue?'

'Maybe all the time,' she told him. 'I constantly have gaps in my life – if I knew what this crap is, maybe it would fill all the gaps.'

'No, the gaps are for marriage and motherhood,' Polo told her.

'Oh, Jesus, we're not back there again.'

'Peter, I hope you convinced this woman she has to marry me.'

'Never got a chance. She saw through the subtle way you left me here with her. Never let me talk about you at all.'

'What did ye talk about if ye didn't talk about me?' Polo asked, baffled.

'She interrogated me about my drinking,' Thornton said, refilling Cassie's glass and then his own.

Polo Cadogan did a disgusted snort. 'If she found out that I let a lush stay in my house, it'll take me months to get her to the altar.'

'He says he's not a lush,' Cassie said.

'No, I said I wasn't an alcoholic.'

'That's precisely the kind of pedantry that makes you a pain in the tits,' Cassie said.

'My da used to define people on what he called the gin scale,' Polo intervened. 'He said most people are born one gin under. One decent gin, and they become human. Some people are born two gins under – Peter, now, he'd have to be a two-gin-under man. Depressives are three gins under.'

'Except that three gins won't bring them up to normal,' Thornton said, 'since alcohol's a depressant, anyway.'

'People like you, Cassie, are born one gin over. Think life is basically OK and that something good's likely to happen during the day. Da said I was born two gins over, and he's right. When I'm at parties, people always assume I'm pissed as a porcupine, but that's just the high of the party.'

'It's also because you sweat like a pig in heat and start stripping off before half the guests have arrived,' she suggested.

Thornton snorted and his drink went the wrong way. Polo thumped him on the back with enormous force and not much attention.

'How early does this gin scale manifest itself?'

'Good question. Probably at birth. Da's theory from the days when he used to deliver babies – before they all got delivered in hospitals by sucking machines – was you could tell what sort of personality any baby was going to have if you paid attention to it in the few hours after birth.'

'Everybody pays attention to their baby directly after birth.'

'No. They make the baby do exams. The mothers are zonked on drugs—'

'The fathers are zonked on drink?' Thornton suggested.

'They're all claiming it looks like them in the nose or the eyes or the mouth—'

'Some gobshite is going, "Would you *look* at the perfect fingers?"'

'The weights-and-measures statistics are being collected,' Thornton added.

'Mobile phones are going like crazy—'

'The new parents ringing everybody they ever met to tell them.'

'The people who get rung up have to say things like "Oh, she must be *so* tiny and beautiful" if it's under six pounds, or "Oh, he must be such a sturdy strong little chap" if it's over seven pounds,' Cassie said.

'And the fathers are saying things they can't know, like that their wives are great. Tired, but in great form,' Thornton said.

'Which is the point where I ring my wonderful aunt and say, "Marsha, would you buy me fifty quid's worth of baby crap, because I have to go into the Rotunda tomorrow to goo over so-and-so's newborn and pretend it's not a squinched-up version of every other repellent newborn ever born."'

'You don't believe that,' Polo told her, with warm conviction, as he got up to organise the next course.

'She does, you know,' Thornton said, over his shoulder, while he scraped the scraps from their plates into the rubbish container.

Polo began to whip cream in too small a bowl. When the third white blob hit her, Cassie held out her hands for the metal container. 'Whipping cream is *definitely* a girl thing,' she said, demonstrating her skill at whipping fast but in a contained motion, giving it back when it peaked gently.

Polo sugared the cream lightly, and dolloped in on to raspberries in three bowls. Thornton put one bowl in front of her and one in Polo's place before taking the third, quietly scraping most of the whipped cream into the sink and sluicing it away before standing where he was to eat the cream-stained berries.

'I'm not into babies,' Cassie said flatly.

Polo's amused glance indicated he took this as her being *agent provocateur* for further discussion. Thornton looked questioning.

'I think babies are all the same, I hate the smell of what goes into them and comes out of them, I hate the way parents kid themselves their babies are unique, special, wonderful. I hate the way they inflict them on other people. I hate the way other people – especially, over-whelmingly, women – are forced by . . . oh, I don't know, culture, expectation, race memory, all the sugary shite that flows around the whole procreation myth into saying, "Can I hold him?" when they never really want to hold him because babies *always* cry when they're given to someone else, or their mother thinks you're going to let their head fall back and snap their neck and half the time you'd love to do that just for spite and the mothers always want the babies to cry so you can give them back feeling like a complete and utter gobshite and the mother can then prove to everybody what a natural mother effing earth she is because looka, didn't he belt up the minute she got him back in her arms?'

Thornton shovelled extra sugar on to his raspberries directly from the bag left on the draining board. They must crunch between his teeth when he ate them, she thought, because it wasn't caster sugar. 'How are you on toddlers?' he asked, in the tone of a market-researcher.

'Toddlers are worse than babies, because toddlers interrupt everything and parents always think everybody else's toddlers are badly behaved but theirs are wonderful. Toddlers you have to talk to. So you start asking questions about Barney the Bloody Bastard Behemoth and both kid and parent think you're crap because he grew out of bloody Barney *years* ago, and if you mention *South Park* you've impugned the parent's control although you know by the way the kids' eyes light up that they get to watch *South Park* on the sly because they're faster than gunslingers with the remote control and by the time Mammy moves a step from the front door, long before the briefcase is out of her hand, the station's changed and they're watching bloody *Big Bird* or something similarly acceptable. So you end up asking them their names and their age and they hate you because every fool adult asks them that.'

Thornton threw the rest of his raspberries into the rubbish and said nothing. Polo talked with affection and pride of his nephews and of the ten-year-old twins his company sometimes employed.

'We all know ten-year-olds who are OK, but what do ten-year-olds turn into?'

Polo looked puzzled.

'Teenagers,' Cassie told him. 'Jesus, I'd rather be dead than have to spend time with teenagers. They know everything and they're so cool icicles form on them and anything you're foolish enough to reveal about yourself allows them to categorise you and cut you down.'

She was half aware of Thornton boiling a kettle and making instant coffee. Just as well, she thought. It would be better than the real coffee the high-tech machine had produced for Polo earlier. 'You'll be delighted to know the medieval church fathers believed parents would do away with their kids quick as look at them,' Thornton said, putting a mug in front of her. 'They banned parents from taking their babies into bed with them, since so many accidental baby deaths were happening that way. Because the deaths weren't accidental.'

The two younger people looked at him, silenced. He raised opened hands to them – a gesture oddly clerical in its grace.

'So maybe she has a point,' he told Polo, trying to lighten his tone. 'Maybe all babies aren't that lovable.'

'I can't imagine any sane human being killing a baby they knew and loved. I know you'll say they didn't love them, but,' Polo drank his coffee scaldingly black, apparently not noticing that it was instant, 'it's a belief I have – people wouldn't have abortions if they could see the shape, the individuality, the *humanness* of the baby.'

'Foetus,' Cassie said.

'It's only because they think it's a foetus, not a baby, that they can do it.'

'It's because it's a foetus, not a baby, that they need to do it.'

Thornton put four spoons of sugar into his coffee and stirred it as fast as Cassie had whipped the cream. 'I wouldn't go the anti-abortion route, if I were you, Polo,' he said, half to himself. 'Not if I wanted to get this girl to marry me. I'm not sure a lot of happy marriages start on a shared passion for the prevention of terminations.'

Polo got up and opened the last bag he had brought from the hotel. 'Here, Thornton, you do the *petit fours*,' he said. 'I'm doing the cheese.'

'*Petit fours*,' Thornton said, with concentrated venom. 'Pointless little friggers. Painty little tarts got up to look like something they're not.'

Polo put a huge glass of brandy in front of each of them and sat down with a can of Coke. He seemed still pre-occupied with the earlier conversation, taking *petit fours* one after another and eating them without noticing what he was doing, Cassie thought. That was probably why he was a little overweight. He ate, half the time, without noticing he was eating. Largely because he was per-forming – entertaining some audience, no matter how small – at the same time.

'What about your biological clock?' he asked suddenly.

'Oh, fuck my biological clock.'

'You don't often get an invitation like that,' Polo said to Thornton.

The older man took his brandy and said he thought he would leave them to it.

'Before we've established when we're getting married?' Polo asked, laughing.

'It's not when, it's if,' Cassie said.

Thornton, headed to the door in that slightly crouched hushed gait of his, shook his head. The move maddened Cassie with its know-all quality. I will not feed into this man's leftover ex-priest omnipotent act. Omniscient act, she corrected herself.

'When you were a priest, did you ever advise someone not to marry someone else?'

He stopped and half turned at the door, nodding. 'Once. Only once. My best friend, after he left the seminary.'

'Why?'

'Because he asked me to do the ceremony. I told him she was a living bitch. He told me at least it wouldn't be dull. At least it wouldn't be dull.' He stood there, as if completing an oral exam, waiting in dutiful sadness. When they didn't ask him another question, he raised the brandy glass to them, half salute, half parting, and climbed the stairs. Softly. Effortfully.

Cassie became conscious of a disappointment in Polo. She had not thought him capable of being deflated, but now he seemed bereft, a plump child eating sweets for comfort. 'We don't have to like each other's friends,' she said, after a long silence. 'There's no law that says we must.'

He began to move around the kitchen, putting first butter into the fridge, then milk and cream. Putting a lid on sugar, tying off the rubbish bag. When he picked up his car keys, she rose. 'He's your friend,' she said, feeling some need to reassure him. 'I'm not going to say bad things about him.'

That was stupid, she thought, climbing up into the Pajero. It implied a continuum. It was like a condition for a shared future. Some sort of concession, hardly noticed in the relentless warming persistence of this man's pursuit.

He got the car into first gear, settled his back more comfortably into the big seat, put on music, took her hand. And she let him.

CHAPTER SIX

Syndication and Surrender

'Right throughout today, people have been asking me how I persuaded Cassandra Browne to marry me. And I've told them the truth. I didn't persuade her. I wore her down. Anyway, with the property boom the way it is, it was the cheapest way she could get away from her mother.'

Cassie's mother roared with laughter and clapped, along with the rest of the guests. Polo Cadogan, good in front of any audience, was inspired on the day of his wedding. People talked about the speech for years afterwards. Talked about how the morning suit somehow pulled him together more than usual, so he looked almost handsome. Mainly, though, they talked about how funny he was.

You had to hand it to that Cadogan fella, he had a hell of a knack for just telling the truth and making you fall over yourself laughing at it. Sometimes even when it wasn't that funny a truth. Sometimes when it had a sting in its tail. Yet even as the sting found its way deep into your sensibilities, you laughed and you surrendered to this big outrageous man who used laughter the way warriors use weapons. He surrounded you with it, impaled you on it, stabbed you with it, then won you, so that you shrank down to become a tiny part of the helpless weakness of surrendered laughter.

He told the guests at the wedding that Cassie didn't like

children. That she didn't want babies. That she thought all teenagers should be put down. They laughed more and more with every statement. As did she. She knew it was true. They believed it was *maybe* true. By the time he was finished with it, though, it was a truth hammered flat, thin and shimmering, the nuggety fight in it gone, ready to frame, filigree and link something different, the memory left only in the essence of it.

He said that, too: announced he would tell his grand-children that only for him they wouldn't even exist on this earth, because their grandmother, when he met her – whoo! He sucked air through his teeth, shaking his head at the formidable fight he was taking on in this woman. The wedding guests stole glances at her to see if the fight showed, and were reassured it didn't, because of course the fight never shows in a bride puffed, taffettaed and soft-laced on her wedding day into a parody of the past, a contradiction of the quotidian, a pale prayer for the future, shrouded in a sparkling cloud of dreams.

All counthry bhoy on the make, he told them he might not look much, although this morning suit had cost a week's wages, so he'd *better* look worth it, they could have got cheaper if they'd settled for polyester in the shirt, but the new wife had insisted on silk – *silk*, it was far from silk that he was raised, he could tell them, and he had doubts about that stuff, too, coming from worms, at least cotton only came from the bog, he didn't mean that kind of bog, would they remember where they were and not be lowering the tone of his wedding, please.

He might not look much, he repeated – and coped with the confirmatory heckles – but once he set his eye on something, it never got away from him. He'd told yer wan (giving a country gleck of his head towards the bride, as if secretly to let them know whom he meant), he'd told her she was going to marry him the first time he ever laid eyes on her, and her with thick glasses on her and all, not the expensive contact lenses she was dolled up in today.

Now, his own eyesight was good, thanks be to God, because he wouldn't fancy trying to put those yokes into his eyes first thing in the morning. Especially not after some of the parties you'd be at in Dunlops' or McEniffs' or Donegans'. (Separated rounds of applause from the partying families referred to.) And taking those lens things out was even worse. There was a lot he was looking forward to on his wedding night (he stood, deadpan as Jack Benny, blankly astonished at what he was hearing from the more ribald fellas from up the hills above Stackallen). There was a *lot* he was looking forward to on his wedding night, but there was one thing that was not included. He was not looking forward to the noise when she took them off her. The contact lenses. Had they heard them coming off? Like two bathing caps. Scwuuulch.

Some of the lads did warn him, he told them, that the day after the wedding or maybe the day after that again, she'd stop all this jig-acting with fine clothes and contact lenses and go back to the milk-bottle glasses, but Jasus, he didn't think he'd mind. She didn't see as much through the glasses and you could do a lot at the side, where her blind spot was. And there wouldn't be that scwuuulch.

He thought the lads were trying to put him off her, but they didn't understand that from the first day he'd met her he'd known that she was his and he was hers for life. That he'd follow her to the ends of the earth. (Jesus, if she'd said she wanted to live in *Limerick*, he'd have gone with her.) That nothing would ever separate them. Not time, not illness, not diminishing looks (his, he rushed to add). Cassie had seen a sample of how committed to her he was during the time she kept trying to lose him. It was only the smallest sample of the reality. He would trail her no matter where she led, tread in her footprints, follow whatever line she drew (even if it was only the size of a *Pinhead*). He had kept a cassette in his car since the week he met her, and every time she gave him temporary walking papers and told him she wouldn't see him for a week or a month, he would play it to keep himself going.

The band played the introductory notes, Polo held out his hand to Cassie and the guests stood to celebrate the new couple as they moved on to the hardwood dance-floor, their applause masking the music completely at first, then dying so that their feet found the beat before the melody resolved itself, Cassie moving swiftly at his lead, but careful with the dipped hem at the back of her full-skirted dress, unable to identify the tune. Over his shoulder, she could see the lead singer moving in to the microphone so it could better pick up the intense, almost whispery tone of his mimicry. Sting, he was imitating, she thought. Yes. Sting. Polo's arms tightened around her, and he whispered the words with the singer.

> *Every step you take*
> *I'll be watching you.*

He held her at arm's length, told her he loved her and went out of step. It was not an easy tune to dance to. Unless you were close enough to shut your eyes and go with his lead, not seeing the smiles, the little waves, the nodding, nodding guests, the shiny sweated faces tired from laughter yet locked in laughter shape.

> *Every step you take,*
> *Every move you make,*
> *Every breath you take,*
> *I'll be watching you.*

This was the first song of many, all ordered and introduced by the groom. He *plámásed* and begged oul' aunts to do their party pieces, immediately following their quavering renditions with highly professional performances by members of the street-theatre group. He told funny stories to calm down nervous singers, and a couple of times told anecdotes of personal kindness related to some cousin or schoolfriend or co-worker or competitor, inviting them to sing, for the wedding guests, a song with particular relevance to the day. When he insisted on Peter Thornton singing, he did not mention that he had failed to persuade him to be best man. Thornton talked briefly with the band, caught the note they gave him, and, without introduction, sang a country song new to Cassie.

'Odd song, for a wedding,' Marsha commented later, when the two of them were in the bedroom reserved for the bride to get into her going-away clothes. 'All wistful and heartbroken. But he knows how to sing, all right.'

'He better not lose his hair,' Cassie said, turning her back to Marsha for unzipping.

'Polo?'

'No. Peter Thornton. He's always doing this head-tossing thing to get the fringe out of his eyes. If he goes bald, that habit's going to make him look weird.'

They stood for a moment, looking at their reflections in the mirror, bride and matron-of-honour. Then Cassie stepped out of the gown, looking younger and at the same time less innocent in lacy underwear.

'"*You Had To Be There*",' she said. 'Is that what his song was called?'

'Something like that. Maybe "*I Guess You Had To Be There*". Liam says it was a big hit for some blonde American country singer.'

'Tanya Tucker.'

'No.'

'I don't know any other blonde American country singers.'

'Yeah, you do. Everybody knows the one with the boobs.'

'Oh, Dolly Parton. She's not a singer. She's a phenom-enon like global warming.'

'I was watching him to see how drunk he got.'

'Who?'

'Thornton – Polo's pal the ex-priest. You said he drinks. He didn't drink much today. Kept pretty far away from your Polo's set of right-wing Catholic brainboxes, too.'

'That's one of the reasons I like Polo so much,' Cassie said, scrubbing off her makeup. The makeup artist from the street-theatre company had come to her house that morning to give her a particularly elaborate makeup for the wedding pictures.

'That he has bright right-wingers as friends?'

'That he's good at pointing out how often liberals are completely *il*liberal. It doesn't affect me, because I really don't believe in anything much, but I see his point, you have to be kind of *brave* these days to be unfashionable and say you believe in God.'

'Or sin. D'you remember sin? I think it's time we revived sin. "Inappropriate behaviour" doesn't have anything like the kick of a good, preplanned mortal sin.'

'Let's revive blame, while we're at it.'

'Guilt, as well. God, if we could dust off guilt, wouldn't it be—'

Without warning, Marsha put her forehead down on her knees and began to cry. Cassie, seated beside her, gently kneaded the back of her neck. Muffled apologies came from under Marsha's dark hair. Cassie patted her into silence. Two floors below, they could hear the dance music, with short gaps between tunes, no doubt, Cassie thought, filled by her new husband, whose starched pleated shirt must now be awash in sweat.

'Be a great photograph,' Cassie said, when the sobbing had become sporadic.

'Mmmf?'

'Two girls in sexy underwear on the edge of a double bed.'

Marsha straightened up, looking sideways at the reflection in the mirror. 'Thanks for the "girl",' she muttered.

'Oh, we strive to be inclusive,' Cassie said. 'We even let old aunts in. If they look OK. Now, you look less than OK in the face because of bawling, but running repairs'll take care of that. Due south of the face, though, you're fine. The coppery bra and pants are really cool.'

'If it was a picture, people wouldn't know for sure it was a wedding day,' Marsha said, staying very still, her eyes seeking out the details in the room. 'There's the wedding dress and the veil thrown over the lamp. But my dress isn't salmon pink or peacock blue. Thanks be to Christ.'

'If it was a picture, what would viewers make of you crying?'

The two figures on the bed looked into the eyes of their reflections as the tune from below changed to something faster, happier. It seemed louder, too, as if more people were joining in the singing.

'Would they say you had found out something upsetting?' Cassie asked gently.

Marsha shook her head slowly, smiling grimly. 'No. Nothing like that. I haven't found out anything. I simply stopped trying to avoid the truth.'

'About?'

'About my husband. My son. Myself. Oh, Cassie, this isn't the time or the place.'

'I would have thought it was a great time and place. What truth about your son?'

108

'That he's not a terribly nice person.'

'Give him time.'

'How much time? At adolescence, they take away your kids and put imposters in their place. Awful imposters who know you enough to humiliate you, who know almost to the penny what they can take you for, who have no memory for the hurts they do you, no sense that you are real, that you are as young as they are. That's the weird thing. I think I'm twenty-eight. I don't mean I try to look twenty-eight or act twenty-eight. I am twenty-eight. I've no sense of being older, or having any great accumulations of wisdom or confidence.' She pulled the hair away from her face, hard, and stared at herself. 'When I was twenty-two, I knew stuff. I knew Liam's limitations – hell, I could have listed them off to you. I knew my own strengths. Now I don't know anything. I can see things coming: what Liam will say every day and what Colm will say and what I will say. Every single day it boils over like a mad chemistry experiment leaving me making the noises of a controlling old parental fool, Liam paying Colm off because that's the easy way, and all of us looking at each other as representing everything each of us despises most.'

She let the hair back down on her shoulders, and Cassie brushed it into shape. 'C'n I ask you something, Marsh?'

'What?'

'Why'd you get undressed?'

'What?'

'I had to get undressed, because I'm going away. You're the matron-of-honour. You get to stay. You go home in the clothes you came in.'

The two of them gazed at themselves in the mirror, Cassie now fully dressed in casuals, Marsha still in the bronzy bra and pants. Marsha laughed, embarrassed. 'At least I cooled down,' she said, getting back into the dark top and skirt.

'Marsh?'

'What?'

'Nothing I can do, right?'

'Nothing anybody can do. Nothing to be done. There's miseries a thousand times worse than my piddling problems in every marriage, I should be ashamed even to—'

'Oh, shut up.'

'What actually matters in life is work. Not home. Work. Not spectacular, hit-the-jackpot, make-the-million, sell-the-dot-com-company-on-the-stock-exchange work, just work. Small to medium achievements. Little private triumphs. The only place where there are certainties.'

'You shouldn't be reduced to lowest-common-denominator business certainties,' Cassie said. 'Jesus, that's an awful bleak prospect.'

'The whole thing's a bleak prospect,' Marsha said. 'They trick you into not noticing.'

'Who's "they"?'

'Circumstances. Events.'

'Births, marriages and deaths?'

'Sort of.'

'And court cases, like Ma gets into all the time?'

Marsha giggled. 'My beloved sister probably won't talk to me for a month, because without thinking this morning I told her I hardly recognised her without a neck-brace on.'

'The neck brace got its P45 when she got the five thou for whiplash. Next injury will be at ankle level, you mark my words.'

Marsha pinned the wedding dress into its plastic protector and patted it. 'I'll get this later,' she said, blundering into Cassie's embrace, the two of them standing, heads bowed in half-understood shared sadness, a silence filled with chosen, then rejected offerings growing between them, separating and conjoining them.

'I shouldn't have said any of this,' Marsha said. 'Polo is a different kind of man from Liam. He truly worships you. It must be wonderful to know that he'd upstakes and follow you, never let you go. And always make you laugh.' Her voice died on the unspoken agreed truth that Liam never made anybody laugh.

'Not to mention the syndication deal,' Cassie said, shifting the scene.

'Right across America – it is brilliant. You should get your hands insured.'

'Not my brain?'

'I don't think you can insure your brain.'

'Do me a favour while I'm gone?'

'Anything.'

'Find out about very heavy insurance for my hands.'

'Lloyds of London do legs, I know that.'

'My legs are not worth a shite. Locate someone who does hands.'

The door to the bedroom was knocked on and simultaneously opened. 'Who says your legs are not worth a shite?' Polo Cadogan asked his wife.

'I do, and I'm the one with the trained eye.'

'Mrs Cadogan, you wear specs thick as glass bricks and you're telling me you have trained eyes? Give us a hoult, Marsha. At least *you* can see a foot in front of you. Not to mention being a bit of all right. Bit more height to you than this one here. The genes fell off in her generation.'

'But not the judgement.' Marsha smiled.

'Oh, Jesus, not the judgement. She knew when she saw a good thing.'

CHAPTER SEVEN

Oscars and Sick Bags

What followed their honeymoon was six months of what Cassie described as pointless travel. The American syndicate wanted her to attend political conferences and ceremonies like the Oscars.

'I can see Gwyneth Thingummy on TV same as anybody else, same *time* as everybody else, in a huge bloody close-up, why the hell are they dragging me five thousand miles to see her in the distance?' she asked Polo.

'Authenticity. Our cartoonist on the spot. Everybody does it. Soon as somebody runs a disaster or a famine or an air crash, they put their guy on a plane. Of course, by the time he gets there the story's a day old and, anyway, who from a tiny little station in a tiny little country hanging on to the tits of Europe is going to get close to any of the real drama? The reporters from little local stations are gonna watch it on CNN in their hotel room, they're gonna sit in the back row of the general briefing, and then they're gonna stand in front of a camera and let on to be the brave boy at the front. The whole thing's fulla shit. But that's OK, because we all *know* it's fulla shit.'

'Do we?'

'Sweetness, if people were looking for reality from their news media, my company would be on its knees. Big reason I'm in business is that no newspaper wants straight pictures any more.'

Cassie looked at the big framed pictures around the

white walls of the office he had built into the room where his father's patients had once waited in a U-shaped tier of chairs. Captains of industry, government ministers, leading academics, a few bishops and a lord mayor or two were in supporting roles in each picture, deferring to, laughing with, and occasionally looking resentful of Polo or one of his team dressed up to simulate fire extinguishers, syringes, light-bulbs, fireworks, hot-water bottles or whatever object best exemplified the theme of the promotion.

'If it's not entertaining, it's not news,' Polo said. 'Don't get an overactive conscience about it. You're sitting in your first-class seat on the plane –'

'Business class, but go on.'

'– thinking, I really don't need to take this flight, I could get an idea of Gwyneth Paltrow's shape from CNN, this is false pretences. It's not. It's part of your brand image. Play it down and they'll pay you buttons. Play it up and you'll be able to retire before you're thirty.'

Polo wouldn't retire before he was thirty, Cassie thought, because of his ferocious need to have an audience. An appearance on any TV programme led to hours of him walking around downstairs after he arrived home. She would sit half-way down the big, graceful staircase in the old house, wait until he came into the stone-flagged hallway, then say, 'Boo,' very softly. He would bound up the stairs to kiss her, to apologise for waking her, even when he hadn't. Then an anecdote from the night's recording or transmission would force itself out of him, and he would swing over the banister or jump the last three steps into the hall to play out all the parts, spotlit by his own charisma.

Or he would take her hand and pull her upright, dancing her down the stairs and into one of the warm rooms, tucking her into the corner of a couch, all the while talking, acting, mimicking so that her laughter moved from half-hearted to overwhelming to painful. He had a genius for noticing the tiny, pivotally characteristic details in the way people moved. She sometimes learned how to cartoon a public figure by watching Polo's mimicry of that figure, and out of those midnight-feast festivals of comedy in the quietness of a stone-spackled Meath big house came skits for reviews and satirical programmes on TV.

He was better on TV than on radio. The very shapelessness of him, the lack of defined handsomeness, allowed him to assume an external persona at will. One minute he was talking to you. Next minute he was subsumed into a mad parody of someone you would never see again without association with the wild, warped funniness of his impersonation.

Early on, when she half suggested that her work become part of the assets of his company, he said no, she was her own woman and should have her own company. He would not be either a shareholder or a director of that company nor was she in his. That was the only way they could stand back from each other and be of most use to each other. So she asked Marsha to find an accountant, and Marsha said she would do better than that. She would take over the business side of *Cassandra's Pinheads* so that all Cassie would have to do was observe and draw.

'Why?' Cassie asked. 'Or, rather, how? You going to give up the day job?'

'Going to job-share,' Marsha said. 'You can afford to pay me ten K a year.'

'According to Polo, I could afford to pay you three or four times that.'

'I don't want three or four times that. I want variety, but I also want security. Keeping up half of the day job will give me security, and there's a woman wants back half-time now that her kids are at school age. Running your company will give the variety I need. Not to mention *powerrr*.'

Marsha's use of power freed Cassie to try new possibilities and fail, but to try and sometimes succeed. There was the possibility of a *Simpsons*-type TV cartoon series based on *Pinheads*, which never got past (literally) the drawing-board although, much to Cassie's delight, the failure netted her company twenty-five thousand pounds in option fees. On the success side, the syndicated cartoons of international figures and types appeared every week in hundreds of newspapers throughout the world, resulting not only in a continuous set of income streams but in a matching set of cuttings from overseas newspapers.

An extra disadvantage to all this travel was pointed out in a magazine profile of the *Pinheads* cartoonist. 'Internationally syndicated cartoonists may travel first class,' the journalist wrote. ('Bloody business class, I *told* her,' Cassie said) 'But the same recycled air you get in tourist circulates in first class, and so Cassandra Browne is on antibiotics for the third time this year to combat a respiratory infection she's convinced originated in flight.'

For that reason, Cassie was extremely glad that no further trips were planned for at least three months. The thought of a long flight – or even a short one – seemed suddenly onerous beyond bearing. At the very end of the last trip, when the 767 taxied up to the airbridge, the seat-belt sign was switched off and passengers retrieving their carry-ons from overhead bins, she had thrown up at length into an air-sick bag. Bad enough, she thought, to get sick when the plane is flying, when there's turbulence to justify it, when other people are turning green and there's a feeling of all together now, lads, one, two, three, puke. You don't wait until people are hanging around with nothing to do but watch you upchucking noisily into a tiny bag. Not to mention the unspeakable awfulness of handing the same bag to a steward. Thank for you taking such *good* care of me. Not at all. It's a pleasure. Yeah, right . . .

She should, she thought languidly, tell her doctor about antibiotics making you air-sick. He knew about them making you depressed, but that variation might be new. Air-sick and car-sick. It wasn't bad if she did the driving, but the thought of being driven in the big oversprung Pajero by Polo made her queasy. When she got to the end of the capsules, she told herself, she'd feel fine.

It did not help that her mother was not speaking to her. Cassie's mother was the ultimate expert in 'cooling' people, and if Cassie hadn't been travelling so much, she would have picked up the unmistakable signals before Marsha told her she was being cooled.

Cassie, in bed trying to persuade herself that bronchitis was not helped by lying flat but unable to muster enthusiasm for the alternatives, let the phone sit against her head on the pillow while Marsha brought her up to date on how Pinheads Ltd was doing. 'Really well, is the bottom line,' Marsha said. 'Do not tell anybody I told you, but you are probably going to get one of those awards for the *Queen of Compo* series. Of course, my sister, your mother, is likely never to speak to you again as a result of that same series, but, shit, you win some, you lose some, right?'

'I've lost you,' Cassie said dully. 'Why would Ma not be speaking to me?'

'You have made her the laughing stock of the nation,' Marsha said, imitating the way Cassie's mother spoke. 'You have held her up to the ridicule of her friends. You have destroyed her reputation with all right-thinking people and if you were not her daughter,' Marsha finished, abandoning imitation, 'she would sue the shit out of you.'

'Why would she shoo the sit out of me? Why would see sue the—' Cassie began to laugh, weakly.

'Oh, Jesus, Cassie, get Polo to inject you with caffeine or something, would you? I've already told you, she says you've made her the laughing stock of the nation, the ridicule of her friends—'

'Yeah, right-thinking and so on, but how?'

'The Compo Queen? Nuthin' personal, Ma, but I've just invented this bad oul' bint that busts her butt for the insurance? I've come up with this mad old cow who'll amputate her ears, her tits, her tail, her anything if it'll let her sue the corporation, the supermarket, the bank or the man next door who sprayed his cauliflowers with something that makes her come all over weak.'

Cassie lay back on the pillow. Unintentional cruelty, she thought. That's what Peter Thornton said is what makes me so effective. 'Did you ever insure my hands?' she asked, idly.

'Yup. You put your hands under a guillotine, hold them out and get them struck by lightning, or Polo gets notions that he's an Arab prince and you've been unfaithful and he chops them off, you get two million. Adjusted for inflation,' Marsha added tidily. There was a moment's silence. Then: 'Of course, you could let your mother cut the hands off you, which I'm sure she'd be delira to do, get the two million and give it to her to pay her off. That might work.'

'I'll get Polo to talk to her,' Cassie said.

'That *would* work,' Marsha agreed. 'Does he have time to placate his wife's parent?'

'Oh, yes,' Cassie said, comforted by her own certainty. 'Oh, yes.'

Taking over her father's role as moderator and interpreter of her mother, Polo loved to spend time with Mrs Browne. He loved her melodramatic self-presentation, the stories of insuperable obstacles overcome in each encounter with the telephone people or the men who came to paint, the accounts of egregious slights at the hands of acquaintances getting above themselves or friends showing their true colours.

'Outsiders might think Cassandra Browne lives in an interesting world,' he said, coming into the drawing room after one of his Compo-Queen-mollification trips, 'but she actually lives in a grey world compared to the one her mother lives in. Your mother meets someone, gets friendly with them – and from then on, they're an unknown quantity. It's like she's a member of the Resistance, knowing any of her pals could be turned by the Nazis, so she has to keep an eye on them, be super-sensitive to signs of slipping on their part. Sort of a moral military policewoman. Though she's not upset when she finds someone out. Jesus, it sets her up. Confirms everything she ever felt about human nature. If your mother is ever in *really* good form, it's because she's found out something appalling about some erstwhile friend of hers. Or yours.'

'If she knew your friends, she'd be running surveillance on them, too,' Cassie said, trying to match his exuberance.

'Oh, she warns me regularly that financial controllers should be checked on without notice, because the minute you get comfortable, that's the minute they start stealing. She tries to get me worried about Orna, too. Reminds me it was Orna wished you on me as Little Miss Muffet and Orna probably knew you'd cock it up.'

'My mother never used that expression.'

'She didn't use any expression. She used dot dot dot:

"Cassandra would never mean to bring any trouble on you . . ." Or she does it with non-verbals.'

Polo grabbed Cassie's empty coffee mug and, sitting down opposite her, began a series of Mrs Browne's gestures, the ones that had always provoked Cassie, as a teenager, into mad profane pointless shrieks. She watched her husband's unpleasing malleable hands now take on her mother's cast, the index finger of the left hand circling the rim of the mug slowly, delicately, the move of a quiet condemnation. Then Polo put both hands around the mug, holding it tightly, tightly, refugee-style, evoking Mrs Browne as Cassie remembered her, so often, in conversation with Ben Browne, sending the message *Look at how chilled I am by my daughter's uncaring nature*. From the mug, one hand went to his chin, a finger tracing the outline of his lips as he watched Cassie, eagle-eyes, predator in waiting for the glint, the gap, the gaffe that would invite diving, beak brutal, blunt, aimed at the back of a neck, talons arched and hooked ready.

'But you *like* my ma,' Cassie said, wonderingly.

'Course I like your ma,' Polo said, taken aback by the comment. 'Your ma's a great bit of stuff. Gave me a bag of scones to take home to you and all.'

He went off to make tea, to butter scones, while Cassie wondered how he could evoke precisely what clenched Cassie's hands into fists within minutes of contact with her mother, yet be so totally affectionate, so unjudging, towards her. Perhaps if you needed someone's traits as source material for your own, you loved them for the donations. Polo imbibed, ingested, *inhaled* the clues and characteristics of everybody around him later replaying them with an emphasis and selection bordering on genius, so audiences understood for the first time what they had previously only observed. He did it without

119

noticing whether the unconsciously nuanced subtext delivered by the moves, the expressions, the mannerisms was negative or positive. His curiosity about the physical, and appetite to imitate it, was absolutely devoid of the moral, clean approval or disapproval. It was just *there*, to be Hoovered up and transmitted to his every synapse and sinew, so the unfinished look of him took on brief perfection as someone else.

'You'd probably be a good detective,' she told him, when he came back with the tea and scones. 'You'd spot someone in a crowd by the way they walk.'

'Nobody would effar escape me!' he said, twirling an imaginary moustache, then stealing one of the scones. He ate sloppily. Without a mother to say, 'Close your mouth when you're eating', 'Swallow that before you talk', 'Don't put in another mouthful before you've finished with that one', he had grown up with the eating habits of a happy, hungry animal. On his feet again, he spewed crumbs and didn't notice the butter melting into a shiny yellow runnel on his thumb as he explained how good he would be at following a target who might be trying to escape him.

'I'm just short of tall, just shy of memorable, a notch south of good-looking but not ugly enough to attract your attention. Put a baseball cap on me – better still, put it on backways, slouch me a bit –' he went rubbery in demonstration '– and have me do my vacant preoccupied look,' this drew a laugh from her, 'and I could be close behind anybody and they'd miss me on a backward glance. Including you. I did it in the beginning. Half the time you'd look around, you'd see me, but you wouldn't register me. It's a thing I have to teach the kids who join us for the summer-festival work every year. Imagine this.' Out went the pale hands. (Even during the sunniest summer, he never got tanned, unwilling to lie still long

120

enough.) They sketched a central oval, lower than waist level. 'There's your playing area. Town square. Centre of a town hall if it's raining. Middle of a ballroom in the local hotel, even. Now, up here.' He gestured past himself on both sides at ear level. 'Up here and over there, you've maybe five kids, mingling with the crowd, ready to run down the path into the central bit to say a line or whatever. Problem is, while they're up here,' another gesture past his ears, 'they're being AcTORS ActING. They're displacing air. They're not talking, they're not gesturing, but something about them is saying to the passers-by, "Look at me, I'm different." I have to teach them to do "Don't bother looking at me, I'm the same, only more so." Takes them ages. I call it yellow-packing. Reducing yourself to a generic. Brillo-ing off all the characteristics that make you into a noticeable individual.'

It would be against nature, she thought, running away from your own identity, your own life, pretending not to be alive, yet not pretending to be noticeably dead, as she had done in childhood, lying flat on her back with a rosary in her hands, eyes closed, imagining how much her mother would regret when she saw how beautiful Cassie looked in death. Polo trained people to cease – briefly – to exist. 'You could be dangerous,' she said.

'If you ran away and didn't want to be tracked, yeah,' he said in a distracted way. 'So just stay where you are and that's not going to be a problem. No, where it's dangerous isn't to other people. This thing of being able to fit in . . . The first year I was in Dublin, I was wandering around like the redneck I was, and went into this pub for a Coke. Looking around me, going, "Hi," with nods to anyone looking civil, drinking my Coke, minding my own business. Adjusting. That was the problem. I was adjusting to the atmosphere, the way the others were sitting, talking. Everything. Next thing I get propositioned in letters a foot high by a fella about fifteen years older than me. I left scorch marks on the carpet. Had this crazy urge to go back afterwards and say to him, look, no offence, it's not that you're older and it's not that I'm anti it, I'm sorry, I'm sure I was giving off all the signs and it must have been like a belt in the gob with a stale kipper when I left so fast, it's just I pick up signals and send them back out faithfully, like a mirror, but that's all I am. A mirror.'

She asked him to bring her the last of her antibiotic capsules, to save her having to climb the stairs. He looked worried. Rarely if ever sick himself, he was frightened by hard, hacking coughs, frightened even more by un-characteristic lassitude. I must take brewer's yeast or something, Cassie thought, and get back to my usual bouncy self, because he can't cope with me in wilting-violet mode.

Not even an iron tonic swallowed in rust-tasting table-spoonfuls brought her back up to par in the next few weeks. Polo was doing research for a new play about eco-warriors in Manchester. The trip meant that for one week he was not at home to be worried by her watered-down personality and pallor, although he phoned her constantly to tell her about the environmentalists he was interviewing.

'These are the guys – lots of them women – who dug tunnels and padlocked themselves inside them so the cops would have to manhandle them out of it, the pictures would scream police brutality, the establishment knocking hell out of poor idealists. Course, the pictures couldn't show the police in the tunnel, trying to cut free people who were crapping in their own jeans because what else could they do, locked in position for days, the pictures couldn't show that the cops had to wash them and give them water and medicines, feed them oxygen.

Nobody wants to know that stuff. They won't believe it, either, about a bunch of tree-hugging vegetarians.'

Cassie was silent, swallowing rapidly to control the instinct to vomit. Polo had a genius, when she was sickish, for coming up with disgusting descriptions calculated to bring the sickishness to full flower.

'It's all a beauty contest,' he told her, the zest in his voice overcoming the periodic fading of the mobile-phone signal. 'Tree-huggers win over cops. Looks are everything. Rats are intelligent, resourceful, great students and brave as hell, but when you ask people what animal they'd like to be, do they ever pick a rat?'

'Rats are incontinent,' Cassie said, wondering why she currently seemed drawn, magnet-fashion, to nauseating aspects of every topic.

'So are dolphins, but everybody wants to be a dolphin.'

She suspected he didn't know anything about dolphin toilet-training or lack of it, but had to admire his comeback speed. It made him good on chat shows: the killer line always came to him quickly. Sometimes, after a programme, an opponent protested that the information Polo used to win his point was inaccurate, but even when he cheerfully and publicly acknowledged it might have been a bit skewed, he never lost as a result.

'Think about it,' he instructed her. 'When the zoo invites photographers in to take pictures of newborns, what are the newborns?'

'Pandas and koalas. Baby tigers because they look like kittens. Baby seals with those huge big eyes.'

'Right. Beauty-contest winners. You never see pictures of newborn skinks or aardvarks or hyenas.'

At this point, the connection failed. Just as well, Cassie thought. She was already somewhat behind time to get a good viewing seat at the press conference her editor wanted her to attend that morning.

Right now, she thought, sliding open the wardrobe door, she had no problems picking clothes. Three pounds below what she regarded as her impossible target weight, she could probably fit into the wild silk suit Polo had brought back from Hong Kong, which had always flattered her (Well, if he thinks I'm *that* thin . . .) but been wearable only on rare occasions following liquid or fasting diets. She tried it on. The waistband was still a little tight, but wearable.

She might, she thought, as she got into the car, do a series of cartoons about dieting women and their shapes. Dieting women and the tricks they use to conceal weight gained. Or rather, she thought grimly, pushing the speed a little now that she was on the main dual carriageway heading towards the city, the tricks they *believe* conceal weight gained. Like those 'tummy control' trousers that give you an absolutely flat panel below the waist. They just shove everything upwards, so you get a spare tyre that would suit an artic.

The images crowded, thick and fast, into her head, so she could not wait to put down on paper the reminders, opening a pad on the passenger seat for quick sketches at every red light. Most of the images came from her own largely unsuccessful yo-yo dieting and the tips picked up over the years from women's magazines. Up-and-down stripes, never side-to-side stripes. (The sketch showed vertical stripes relentlessly outlining every bulge on a massy woman.) Bright scarves at the neck to attract attention. (The drawing showed a tiny flirty scarf waving but drowning as a huge tsunami of flesh rose from below neck level.) Tights and shoes the same dark shade as your dress. (Here, the lines indicated a silhouette – huge, monotone, threatening.) High-heeled shoes so that onlookers, when you said how overweight you were, would dutifully respond, 'But with your height, you can carry it.'

Quietly certain that the new series would be a winner, Cassie sat, half her mind on the conference, the other half examining the cruelties and vulnerabilities that would dance together, like Hieronymus Bosch-coupled contradictions, creating unwilling welcome laughter. It didn't matter so much that there was cruelty involved if the cartoonist was clearly one of the people being mocked. Cartooning was handy that way. You could make laughter, money and a little more than fifteen minutes of fame out of the worst things in your life.

CHAPTER EIGHT

Pills and Problems

One week later, having waved Polo off with his Humpty-Dumpty suit neatly stowed in the back of the Pajero (he was the visual in a public-health seminar that touched, among other things, on the dangers of cracked eggs), Cassie opened her laptop, bumped the viewing size of the print to 150 per cent, the better to see it as she typed, and began.

I am pregnant.

You haven't been tested?

No.

You haven't bought one of those kits in the pharmacy?

No.

Well, then.

I am pregnant, though.

How the hell could you be pregnant?

Same way every other plank in the world gets pregnant.

You just know.

I just know. Oh, God, I just know.

How do you just know?

I know because I have morning sickness.

You have all-day, every-day sickness.

I've been sick before. With nausea. This is different.

How?

It's a complete and total nausea like a black wall.

You couldn't be pregnant. You're on the Pill. As in, today is Tuesday, take the one that says Tuesday. You missed any?

No.

Never?

Never.

Not once?

What part of never don't you understand?

So how could you be pregnant?

There are things that affect the way the Pill works.

Like?

Travel. A lot of air travel, moving between time zones, cocks up (you should pardon the expression) your body clock. I did a lot of air travel earlier this year. I didn't know whether I was coming or going. (Again, you should pardon the expression.)

Where's all this dirty talk coming from?

I'm pretty good at dirty talk at the best of times.

This isn't the best of times.

You might sing that if you had an air to it. At the moment, everything leads miserably, unraunchily back to sex and its consequences. Show me an iguana, I'll give you a sexual connotation.

So air travel made you pregnant.

No, air travel is one of the factors which can diminish the efficacy of the Pill.

You've been reading the warning labels. Post-factum.

Yeah. Post-factum is your only man.

Apart from labels, what are your sources?

Life, the universe and the Internet.

And?

Antibiotics can—

Don't tell me. Diminish the efficacy of the Pill.

You got it.

That's an Americanism.

Remember the air travel? Mainly to the States. Look at all I got out of it. Pregnancy and phraseology.

Other evidence?

I've gone up a bra size, and if I breathe normally, I'm four inches bigger around the waist.

Calories will do that.

I've eaten shag all in recent weeks, and what I did eat, I threw up. I've actually lost some weight.

You haven't been taking exercise. Haven't been to the gym in three months.

There are no muscles in boobs, which is why they move due south with gravity and time. Not all the pec exercises in the world will move them due north. Female body-builders get massive shoulders and humungous chests, but teeny little poached-egg tits in the middle of the muscle.

Egging to move south?

Right. The fact that I'm not exercising would not result in my boobs swelling.

Might help you get a porter-belly, though.

Grain of truth in that. Except that what I have is *hard*. We're not talking about the soft mushy gloopy stomach you get when you get fat. This is firm to the touch, like a table.

A round table.

Oh, ho ho fucking ho. And furthermore, you know all those

tests where you see how much you can pinch of yourself, and if you can pinch an inch, that means how fat you are? I can't pinch *nuthin'*. It's like trying to pinch a perfectly inflated football. Can't get a purchase. It's like trying to pinch an egg in its shell.

But what about changes in pigmentation? Aren't your nipples supposed to change colour permanently or something?

Something.

And?

Here I confess complete failure to observe.

You mean you haven't looked?

Sure, I've looked.

Well?

I've nothing to compare with.

Meaning?

I never looked *before*. I have no idea what the hell colour unpregnant nipples are.

You make your living through observation and you never observed the colour of two things on your own torso, located but a glance away?

I work in black and white.

Just as well.

Not only am I pregnant, I am pregnant with a male.

Polo.

No, I mean the collection of molecules is male.

The what?

You want me to call it a foetus?

Better than 'the collection of molecules'. Polo would call it a baby.

He would, wouldn't he?

Is it going to be?

A baby?

Yes.

What else would it be?

You know what I mean.

I know what I mean. The answer is, no. No, I'm not getting rid of it. Not because I suspect it might be late in the day anyway, at this point, not because I have any great feelings about abortion one way or the other, not because I would have to do it without telling Polo. The decision made itself. No ifs, buts, internal arguments, nothing.

Oh, so you welcome the pregnancy?

I *hate* it. I couldn't welcome it less. I wish it had never happened. I am appalled it did happen. I worry about the consequences of the way it happened. But I won't have an abortion, and don't ask me any more stupid questions about why, I don't know why. It's possible to be certain about something, convinced about it, without having an intelligent rationale for the certainty or even wanting one. Today is Monday, OK? I just know it's Monday. I might prefer it was Sunday, but it's Monday. All day. I'm pregnant and I'm not going to terminate the pregnancy. Full stop.

Kind of a contradiction, that.

Life's full of them. Shit happens. So do pregnancies.

You 'worry about the consequences of the way it happened'?

From the moment these molecules clumped, I've been bombarding them with antibiotics, every one of them carrying warnings: Don't use if pregnant.

So you're frightened that the baby will be disfigured?

I'm terrified that the baby is damaged, deadly hurt, destroyed, set up for leukaemia, cleft palate, handicap of all kinds. And don't start the termination crap again. I know, I know, I know. If I was going to have a baby, wouldn't it be better to get rid of all those possibilities and start with a clean sheet?

That's another of those sex-related phrases.

I'm too tired to care. Plus I want to cry again.

Been doing that a lot?

All the time.

Why?

I don't know a feck.

What are you going to do?

I'm going to an obstetrician (see, even know how to spell it).

You lie. The spellchecker fixed it for you.

And after that, I'll have more data.

About whether it's a boy or a girl?

No, I have that data.

Not scientifically confirmed.

It's not scientifically confirmed that today is Monday, either. It just is.

How far d'you think you're gone?

Three months? Maybe more.

And then you'll tell Polo.

And then I'll decide when I cannot *not* tell Polo.

He does have rights, you know.

Ah, shut up. I'm closing you down.

131

After her visit to the obstetrician, Cassie was sorely tempted to tell Marsha, rather than Polo. Partly because, with Marsha, she could talk freely about how spurious the man was when he did his sums, telling her with a smile, 'Your baby should arrive in the second week in April.'

Your baby. They probably got trained to put in the possessive, she thought. Not *the* baby. *Your* baby. Probably sent a warm tremor through most mothers-to-be. Sent a cold tremor through Cassie. Who had already indicated she wanted to see no scans. The obstetrician, probably used to warmly mushy mothers-to-be, she thought, deflated more and more at the failure of his efforts to create anticipatory chumminess about the future birth. He mustn't often meet pregnant women who behaved like old-time detectives: just gimme the facts. How long? When? How healthy? Anything else I need to know?

The obstetrician, baulked of chumminess, opted instead to berate her. This complete lack of antenatal care was understandable in her case, but not good. Not good at all. He would recommend these clinics and that course and the other appointments. Cassie took the individual sheets of paper from him without comment as he made himself busy filling them in and tearing them off. Makes you happy, that's fine, she said, evading the open ends of his recommendations, flagged by an awkward inflection, like a question: *This class puts mothers very much in control?* Any decent woman, Cassie thought, would feed back to this man the consent, the agreement, the surrender his goodwill sought. Frig him, Cassie thought. They're recommendations. I'm a free agent. Not only will I not act on them, I will not be emotionally blackmailed by an overpaid baby-catcher into agreeing with him. Neutral responses are much more fun. Let the wanker swing.

When she told him she never noticed any movement from the baby, he told her movement was patently *there*. He did another shrug. You're gonna end up like a pagoda, you keep doing that, she thought. There was a body of research, he murmured, which suggested that women actively planning a termination did not feel movement at stages in pregnancy where women not planning termination did.

She looked at him levelly. Wouldn' you *love* for me to break down right here in front of you and confess all? Wouldn' you? Wouldn' you just come into your own, sitting down and intertwining your fingers until I stopped crying? You don't like when a patient sends the wrong signals. We can go one way (blushes and glowing smiles so wide you could tie them at the back) or we can go the other (tears, panic and confessions of guilt, regret or doubt) but it galls the shit out of you if we sit here expressionless, saying, no, you can't play, no, we won't *let* you swim in our emotional pool. Because you know what? You do motor mechanics, not emotions. You get high pay for not getting in the way of a process women have been doing all on their oniers for millennia and just occasionally going in with soup spoons to give the kid a yank.

Four and a half months gone, she thought, glancing at the shops as she drove home. A line of headless mannequins bulged repellently at her from Mothercare. No maternity clothes, she thought. Not a smock. Not a pair of trousers with those disgusting extra panels in the front. Not a Princess Di dress with a Peter Pan collar and a central bow. That decision made, she considered the issue of baby movement. Her insides churned with hunger because she had been instructed to 'attend fasting'. The wavery churning continued. OK, you've made your point, she informed her hunger, palm on her stomach to emphasise the point. The palm registered a wavery, corrugated-iron movement that had nothing to do with hunger noises. She sat, locked in position, until beeps from other cars unlocked her.

That was what he had been talking about. That was baby movement. It had been there for weeks, unrecognised, unlabelled. Hell, it – it – had presented itself and got no round of applause. If it was a chip off its father's block, it would be in there not knowing what to do with itself, cheated of the audience response its DNA yearned for. It better be a chip off its father's block, she thought, because its mother clearly wasn't up to the job. Didn't recognise morning sickness. Didn't recognise a baby doing knock, knock, I'm here. Didn't recognise a bump even when the bump had no self-doubts at all.

Anyway, wasn't it obvious this kid was a chip off the paternal block? Look at its sense of timing. Wants to be announced to coincide with Christmas, so grandmother-to-be and father-to-be can come over all dewy with empathy at every reference to the Christ-child during the festive season. Joy to the world. All the boys and girls. (Boy, in this case.) Joy to the fishes in the deep blue sea—

'Well, fuck that,' Cassie decided, glaring at the Christmas decorations in the department-store windows. There were little sparky lights all over the Mansion House, too, she noted furiously. 'I can get through Christmas without telling,' she said aloud, to hear the proposition. It sounded difficult, but doable. 'I can get through Christmas without telling,' she said again. And did.

She didn't admit to the pregnancy until the Christmas lights had been put away and Polo was beginning to get bored checking, every second night, to make sure the members of his company subcontracted to various pantomimes were still up to scratch.

One morning, the electric clock took the pneumatic

deep breath it always took ten minutes before it went off. The morning sickness might be dying away, she thought, beginning to sit up. A slimy wall of contradiction made her lie back down, eyes open. A growing crack in the ceiling plaster looked like a mad toothless oul' fella cackling at a dirty joke. She tried to make some of the other cracks into an image, but they stayed as ordinary cracks. Maybe the message is get the ceiling plastered, she thought. Unbidden, the sickly sweet smell of ceiling plaster coiled around her nostrils and she closed her eyes fiercely against the association.

The alarm clock lifted the two of them about six inches off the bed, Polo because he was dead asleep, Cassie because she was grimly awake. His soft fingers groped for the snooze button. She poked him with an elbow. 'Get up.'

'Awright.'

Polo was the definitive heavy sleeper. Once he went to sleep, his faculties deserted him, including free will. If you could get him one notch out of coma and lock him there, he was completely obedient, if poorly co-ordinated.

'Have a shower,' she told him, when he stood by the side of the bed, baffled to find himself up earlier than normal.

'Awright.'

After the shower, the glimmerings of Polo's natural good humour began to show. 'You going to stay there like a sackrofigus while I'm up and doing?'

'Up and doing what?'

'Jesus, I don't know,' he said, towelling his thighs as if he should.

'It's not a sackrofigus, anyway.'

'What is it, then, smartarse?'

'It's that thing like a coffin, only not a coffin.'

'A sackrofigus.'

135

'It isn't. But you've mucked up my memory of what it is by saying the wrong name all the time.'

'Saying sackrofigus?'

'Stop it!'

'I'm impressing the knickers off myself being able to say a word like that when I should still be in bed, unconscious.'

'You're not able to say it right.'

He flapped a hand dismissively in the air. 'That's minutiae. Jesus,' he said, delighted. 'Minutiae and sack-rofigus before breakfast. Not many men can do that. You stay there and I'll bring you up a tray. What would you like?'

'Just tea.'

'Just *tea*?' he checked, reversing back through the bedroom door. 'Not coffee?'

Don't even say the word, she thought. Day or night, that drink, that drink I totally love when I'm normal, now makes me ill even to think about. The smell of it is worse than the smell of wet ceiling plaster. The spectral smell of wet ceiling plaster and coffee, mixed, squeezed her capacity to speak. 'Tea. Black,' she half snarled.

He would never have made it below stairs, she thought, brushing her teeth in the bathroom. He was far too noisy and freehanded in the way he clashed crockery and cutlery around. Every week she threw out plates and saucers because of rough-edged bites taken out of them by too vigorous contact with each other. Nor did he ever check if he had a cup unbalanced by partly standing on a spoon rather than sitting squarely on a saucer. Even now, she thought, she could bet one of the cups was wobbling as he came up the stairs. There was too much noise for everything to be in its proper place. She ran a brush through her hair and was back in bed, pillows tiered, when he arrived with the big tray.

136

'Sarcophagus,' she announced, triumphantly.

'*Gezundheit*,' he responded, settling the tray securely. 'Bet you can't pronounce it the way I did, now, though.'

He poured milk on a bowl of Rice Krispies and made a performance out of being annoyed by how chatty they were.

'Shurrup, would ye? She wouldn't have got me out of bed early, cheated me out of my just snores, if she didn't want me to do something. Put out the garbage. Sell off my Porsche. Buy her a mink.'

'Buy her a cot.'

'Buy her a Merc, b——?'

The Rice Krispies disputed among themselves without competition for a moment.

'Buy her a cot for the baby,' Cassie elaborated.

OK. That's it. Out. Done. Said. Not too vomitously cute, either, the way I got it out. All right, where does it go from here? C'mon, Polo. Your turn. You wanted this to happen. You were resigned to it not happening, although if we'd been relying on condoms, I swear to God I'd believe you stuck a pin in one. React, please. I've allocated ten minutes to reaction time. She looked up from the cup of weak tea at him, shamed to find him, bowl of cereal just below chin level ready for another shovelled mouthful to be taken out of it, looking at her with his eyes filled with tears.

'Cassie, you're not joking?'

One stray Rice Krispie flew from the side of his mouth and fell into his teacup. There you go, Cassie thought. No loss of protein there. Bit more bite to your cuppa. She shook her head. No, this is no jest. You're the guy does the practical jokes, not me.

He put bowl and spoon down with the exaggerated trembling care of a drunk, and came to the side of the bed. She patted the place beside her. Permission. He sat down, very gently, and then suddenly was in her arms, the fresh sweet-smelling damp hair of him where she could kiss it while he told her what it meant to him, how wonderful she was, how grateful he was.

'Not grateful,' she whispered. 'Grateful' would be appropriate if I had conceded, surrendered, given in. Given you the generous gift of a son. There is no generosity in this unwilled invasion, this carrying without intent, this hard, rounded change you seek with your hand. A pilgrim at a shrine, he asked her questions, asked them again, repeated the answers, hands gentle on the bump, tears and laughter colliding as he gave out to her for keeping it a secret for so long. Even then she lied, telling him she was four months gone, wasn't sure when exactly the birth would be.

At one point, he held her, almost held her *down*, one-handed, while he rang the office and told Orna he would be late. Not in until after lunch. Just take care of it, OK? OK. Turning to Cassie with a face of such naked joy that a bile of resentment rose in her, knowing she would have to pretend, to talk about this thing for hours, the smile sagging on her face, suspended between her ears, the desire to snap sitting like heartburn below her voicebox.

Every now and again he would walk the room, talking about what she had gone through, awed by her control in the face of something so unexpected, so unprecedented. Never did he use the word 'unwanted'. Never, in all the rapturous eulogies, was there praise for her continuing the pregnancy. Somewhere stony in each of them was the knowledge that another possibility must never be articulated, lest it reveal too much that neither wanted to know.

For Cassie, that morning most resembled the weeks after their honeymoon, when he edited and re-edited the video footage of their wedding, remembering, every time he had a final version, some other incident, some other shot that could not be left out, because it would diminish the entirety of the taped memories. That morning, even when Cassie came out of the shower, he wanted to sit her down again, have her tell him about the antibiotics and the sickness and when the realisation had come to her. He sat, stroking her hair, touching the back of his fingers softly to her cheek, doing tiny head-shakings of admiration at her self-control, her discipline. Trying out the phrases praising her that he would spend the next few weeks saying to their friends and acquaintances. She knew this, and was wearied by her knowledge of it.

Trying to shift him into the routine of fatherhood, away from the transfiguring-revelation stage, she mentioned appointments, classes. His excitement shifted, dates and times now caught in its crosshairs. She gestured at her shoulder bag so that he brought it to the bed. Handed him the bits of paper the obstetrician provided. He sat down (one hand reaching out to pat her leg in reassurance – reassurance of what?) to read them, nodding at the wise saws they contained about antenatal care, checking against the calendar on his watch when the next class was.

'I'm not going to classes.'

'Of course you are,' he said, continuing to read. 'I'll come with you.'

'Polo.'

'We'll have to do extra to catch up.'

'Polo, I'm not going to classes.'

'You have to.'

'They change the law when I wasn't looking?'

'But, Cassie, it's all part of the system.'

'Precisely the reason I don't want any part of it.'

'They teach you how to breathe.'

'Hey, Polo, you know something? I've learned to do that all on my tod. Here's how it goes: free demo. From

139

what I hear, the only variation for birthing babies is,' she giggled at the association, 'you just put your lips together and blow. If you want to get lessons in putting your lips together and blowing, Polo, off you go.'

'I will,' he said.

'Even if I don't?'

'Even if you don't,' he said, 'I will.'

So I will, she finished for him in her mind's voice, him standing, lower lip pushed: sturdy sulky toddler. I will, so I will.

'And I'll be there on the day,' he said, squaring up for a fight on this one too.

'Good,' she said. 'I'll need you.'

Which made him cry again, she could not see why, but held him awkwardly, sideways. Then he wanted to know who else she'd told, and was chuffed to hear he was before Marsha. 'You're my husband,' Cassie said. 'The baby's *father*.' And realised as she said it that only those formal claims had prevented her from talking to Marsha first. Schoolboy planning to steal a teacher-pleasing task, he asked if, since she would obviously tell Marsha, maybe he could tell her mother? Of course, she said, so eager to fend off his returning gratitude that she almost went too far, almost said she had no desire to tell her mother at all, ever. Every time she thought of her mother as a grandmother, it brought the ache of knowing this baby would never know his grandfather.

Eventually, he pulled himself together. He was off, he told her. Had to go. Although it would be much better if they could be together all day. Not, she thought, smiling at him with renewed enthusiasm now this pre-primal scene was nearly over. Even then, he ran back up the stairs twice after reaching the front door.

'I won't get unpregnant if you go to the day job,' she told him, the second time. 'That's not the way it works.

140

Works the other way. I'll be even more pregnant when you get back tonight.'

He laughed. She could hear his delighted snorts as he ran down the stairs for his third attempt at leaving. To you, it is an announcement of glad tidings: your pregnant wife will be more pregnant this evening. To me, it is a life sentence without parole.

CHAPTER NINE

Watching and Waiting

She was braced for impassioned hugs, for 'I'm thrilled for you, Cassie,' said quietly but with great warmth. Disbelief or astonishment would not have been a surprise, either. Unanticipated was Marsha continuing to eat her warm goat's cheese salad as if Cassie had said nothing. Cassie, offput but not sickened by the pink of her salmon mousse, continued to eat. Very slowly. Small mouthfuls, put down your fork. Take a drink. See how your system copes with that. Doing OK? Right, once more into the mousse, dear friends.

'I'm just wondering if there's a safe response,' Marsha said eventually. 'And if there isn't a safe response, which is the safest of the unsafe responses I could opt for?'

'Why would there not be a safe response?' Cassie asked, knowing the answer.

'Because (a) you said you were never going to have children, (b) you said you couldn't stick children, (c) you said Polo was not going to persuade you to have children and that if he wanted to use your pre-wedding announcements on all of these topics as justification for later annulment and divorce, way-hey.'

'Best-laid plans,' Cassie said.

'Best-*laid*? Jesus!'

The laughter made Marsha less cautious. 'Accident?'

'Yeah.'

'But we are talking baby, future tense, here?'

'As opposed to?'

'Being part of the statistic – what is it? Five thousand?'

'Baby,' Cassie said.

'Would there be a significance, do you think,' Marsha asked, a raised forkful of salad, 'to the fact that my niece does not say, "I am going to have a baby in six months time," she makes with the monosyllables and just says, "Baby"?'

'It must be your brains qualify you to be an aunt.'

'What'll be my relationship to this infant? If you make me a grand-aunt, so help me, I'll split you.'

'Marsha, you may not believe this, but your title in the new situation hadn't occupied my thoughts that much.'

'You just don't care, do you?'

'Not a bit.'

'Even if the sense of advancing age makes me suicidal?'

'Doesn't matter. You don't have the courage for suicide.'

'Suicides are not courageous. They're cowardly.'

'Tell me about it. Tell me arranging to suffocate at the end of a rope is cowardly.'

'There's easier options. Stick your head in an oven.'

'Doesn't work with natural gas. You'd just get a crick in your neck and leftovers from the Sunday roast in your hair.'

'Who does a Sunday roast, these days?'

'Nobody, but I wanted you to get the reference to my happy childhood. To my endlessly skilled mother. Never mind meat and two veg, if you pushed her she could do gravy, too. Followed by apple pie filled with little perfumy nails.'

'Cloves.'

'Hate them.'

'You hate anything your mother cooked.'

'And you love anything *your* mother cooked?'

'Oh, yes,' Marsha said. 'Oh, yes. I begged for my

143

mother's cookbooks when she died, all filled with drawings of terribly slim women with bunchy fringes,' her hand sketched a 1940s hair-do with bouffant front, 'and aprons, wearing high heels in the kitchen and producing fairy cakes with little spirals of steam coming off the top for two children with freckles across their noses, their little paws on the edge of the table, their eyes sparkling with greed.'

The waiter removed their plates and ostentatiously swept the crumbs from the white tablecloth. Offered the menu, had it waved away, offered coffee, had it accepted. By Marsha.

'My mother was a *wonderful* cook,' Marsha went on. 'The smell of the fresh raspberry tarts she used to make. Wonderful nutty brown bread. A fruitcake she called a "farmhouse". Upside-down cakes. Pancakes. Anything pastry. Anything baked. Fecking *jam* to die for.'

'D'you do any of that stuff?'

'And have it go mouldy while the pizza place delivers?' Marsha fished sweeteners out of a bag big enough to hold a single-decker bus. Cassie shook her head, indicated the lack of a coffee cup. 'You being careful?'

'Can't face the C-drink. Makes me gag to think about it.'

'Barrels of laughs, pregnancy.'

'Barrel being the operative term.'

'You're not showing much. How far have you to go?'

'Three months.'

'You *cow*!'

'Do cows produce calves in three months?'

'I know shag all about the gestation time of effing cows. I meant you're a cow for being six months gone and not telling me.'

'I'm six months gone and I *am* telling you. Sooner than anyone other than Polo.'

'What about your mother?'

'Polo's telling her.'

'Coward.'

'Whatever you're having yourself.'

'Why didn't you tell me sooner?'

'Marsha, I didn't *know* sooner. I only got a glimmering maybe five weeks ago.'

'It's a neat trick, all the same. A three-month pregnancy. Seeing as how you never wanted one in the first place, it's the best way to do it, probably.'

Cassie drank iced water and signalled the waiter for the bill.

'I hate to sound like a TV reporter,' Marsha said, 'but I have to ask you how do you feel about this event in your life?'

'Shitty.'

'What about that sense of fulfilment?'

'I have fuck all sense of fulfilment,' Cassie said quietly.

'What about your consciousness of burgeoning womanhood?'

'Burgeoning arseholehood,' Cassie grumbled, signing the credit-card slip.

'Well, in that case, how're you coping with Polo, who – it's fair to assume? – is on cloud nine and a half since you told him?'

'I'm coping badly,' Cassie said. 'I'm trying, but within minutes of Polo arriving, I want to hit him with a chimney. He's so goddamn solicitous, I feel I'm playing Elizabeth Barrett Browning in *The Barretts of Wimpole Street*. He keeps saying "our son".'

'Not a crime.'

'No, but Jesus, I'm back to grinding my teeth the way I used to when I was living at home with Ma. I had to tell him I was deeply superstitious about buying anything for the baby before the baby was born – is born – *gets* born, because otherwise, oh, Christ, we'd have him stencilling buggering bluebirds on the wall of what he is already calling the nursery – the *nursery*, when did you ever hear a fella from Meath talking about effing nurseries? It's like I'm his audience, and if he works really hard on his performance, he'll bring me along with him like a good audience, make me warm to the whole baby idea. I don't tell him how much I hate it, how much it disgusts me, because what's the point?'

'What's the bit you find disgusting?' Marsha asked carefully.

'Marsha. Have you ever looked at an eight-month pregnant woman sideways? It is horrific. It is impossible. Every time I think about it, it gives me this cold feeling.'

'Women have been having babies for a long time and a lot of them say it's worth it. Some of them say it's the best thing that can happen to you.'

'They're just stupid. There's all this research that says women at work are happier than women at home, healthier, too, higher self-esteem, everything. In spite of all that, you have silly cows *choosing* to get pregnant, losing their shape, their future, their autonomy, their promotions, getting morning sickness and then the final thing hurting like hell. What the hell else can anyone dumb enough to make those choices do except go all bleary-eyed and say, "The pain was worse than anything I've ever experienced, but you forget the pain when you hold your own baby in your arms for the first time."'

Her high-voice mimicry featured wide eyes and fluttering fingers. Marsha laughed and said nothing.

'How bad is the final thing?' Cassie asked in her normal voice.

Marsha looked at her, one eyebrow raised. 'The final thing? As in the giving-birth thing? Cassie, you're going to have to at least pretend to be a normal person, because

– unless you're on to something I've missed – this hands-off, nothing-to-do-with-me approach to motherhood doesn't work. If you're asking me about giving birth, the answer is I did it without epidural, I wanted to do it naturally, Liam was useful for rubbing my back and I would sum it up as one great orgasm.'

Cassie and the waiter were equally surprised by this, the waiter more curious because he came in at the end of it and wasn't sure what Marsha was talking about. 'Childbirth,' she tersed at him.

'Oh, my dear,' he said, blinking. 'One great orgasm?'

'Trust me,' Marsha told him.

They walked to where Cassie's car was parked, Marsha unfurling a full-sized umbrella from what looked like a fat spectacles-case.

'Don't tell me,' she said, her voice slightly hollowed by the arch of the umbrella. 'You don't own an umbrella. You can tell how rich people are by their complete deficit in the umbrella department.'

'I'm not going to buy anything for the next three months. Not an umbrella, not anything.'

Marsha looked sideways at her, impressed. Cassie's expenditure on clothes, particularly shoes, had been likened by Polo to the spend of a lapsed member of Gamblers Anonymous.

'I wouldn't waste it,' Cassie said, opening the car.

They exited on to the wet road, Cassie flicking on her windscreen wipers as if they should have known it was wet outside. 'Go on, say it,' she said, as the car picked up speed.

'Say what?'

'Whatever you're afraid to say. I'll stay speaking to you. I don't have that many aunts who are my best friend.'

With enormous attention to detail, Marsha returned the miniaturised umbrella into its container and slipped it into her vast bag. 'I'm glad I'm your aunt, I suppose, is what I want to say,' she said, gathering her property together as they came near to where Cassie was to drop her off. The car slowed to a thrumming stop. 'I wouldn't want to be Polo,' Marsha said. 'And I wouldn't want to be your little passenger. Right now, I wouldn't.'

She leaned over to kiss Cassie, halted when her niece turned to her, eyes full of tears. 'I know you think I'm just being selfish, being a bitch,' Cassie said. 'It's just I feel taken over. Getting married didn't change things. It was still *my* life. I could do anything I wanted to whenever I wanted to. But once a baby is born, you never have a day afterwards you don't have to think about it and plan around it. That's probably all right if you like the baby. If you love the baby.' She flicked off the ignition key, so the wipers halted mid-windscreen and the window developed puddled waves of water flowing down from the car roof.

'You don't love Polo, and you've done pretty well on that front.'

Cassie stared at Marsha, who drew a sour little face in the misted window beside her.

'On a scale of one to ten, I'd rate the two of you an eight and a half,' Marsha said. 'The paradox is that I *do* love Liam, and on the same scale we'd get a six. On a good day. What's love got to do with it?'

The two women sat in a silent cell, surrounded by the eternally uninvolved sounds of weather, questions coming, then turning away, unasked, pretences suggesting themselves, then wilting in the face of the simple truth of their friendship. Cassie leaned over so Marsha could get her arms around her, the two locked in temporary warmth inside a chilling car. Then Marsha opened the door, hefted the oversized bag, and ran up the steps to the library, letting the car-door swing closed behind her. It failed to latch, the inadequate click alerting her as she reached the shelter of the porch.

Cassie leaned over to push it open again. 'No consideration,' she yelled through the rain. 'Forcing me to do your work for you, and me pregnant.'

The two people sheltering under the library porch looked at Marsha, as if her expression would explain this shout.

'Worse than pregnant,' she yelled back.

Half lying across the front seats, Cassie laughed and waved, then pulled the door closed decisively.

CHAPTER TEN

Fainting and Fighting

The fact that Polo Cadogan fainted at quite an early stage in the proceedings was the best part of the birth, in Cassie's opinion. Cassie was making no fuss about early contractions and Polo, having done double-time, as he put it, on the antenatal courses, was ready to assist at every stage in the procedure.

'You're only two fingers dilated,' the hospital midwife told Cassie, dismissively. At this point, Polo passed out. The midwife, who looked as if she had been delivering babies for three or four centuries, wiped her face with her freshly ungloved hand. 'A doctor is going to have to examine *him*,' she said.

'Why? He just fainted,' Cassie said.

'Whacked his head on the floor,' the midwife said, irritated by this aggravation of a normal faint.

'Always OTT,' Cassie said, craning around her own bump to look down at him.

The midwife went to the nurses' station to telephone for help. At no stage did she so much as touch Polo, who, after a few minutes' lying face down, began to stir. 'Stay where you are, you,' she ordered him.

For just a moment, Cassie considered offering her his first name, but decided against it. 'You' allowed the midwife to be much more forceful, and there wasn't much possibility of confusion, anyway, since Polo was on his own on the floor.

Two orderlies came in with a wheelchair and horsed Polo into it. He made weak protests. The orderlies, obviously more scared of the midwife than of this swooning spouse, ignored him, wheeling him out of the door, which shushed pneumatically closed behind them.

'Where are they taking him?' Cassie managed to say, simultaneously crushed by something a quantum leap away from a period pain.

'What do you care?'

How true, Cassie thought, as the wave of pain retreated. I need all my attention on this. Did I imagine the scale of the last pain or was it as bad as I thought it was?

'You could still have the epidural, you know,' the midwife said.

It was like she was a third-party commentator, Cassie thought, giggling. This birth thing had nothing to do with either of them, and the epidural was a floating issue similar to a proposition in an examination. Epidural. (Discuss.) Cassie drew a deep breath and everything below her lungs got caught in a crusher. Nothing happened for thirty seconds. The indrawn air puffed her at the top, the crusher held her in the middle. Then she let out the air and the crusher gnarled, rolled and ground her into oblivion. For ever. Waves of black with red edges rolled down behind her eyes and eternity happened.

Then the pain retreated, leaving everything nearly normal, except for a horrified muscle-memory and a sense of guilt – if I hadn't let that breath out, everything would have been under control.

'I'm going to break your waters,' the midwife said.

As in, I'm going to replace this battery, turn this page, do something else of minor importance. Which made perfect sense to Cassie. Waters? Piffling inconsequential matter affecting someone vaguely attached but not

151

actually involved. The only consideration worth even a moment's thought would be if –

The crusher grabbed Cassie again, this time with no breath in her lungs, so after half a minute, she had to breathe in, which cued the crusher to start its roiling, burning, pulverising action unhappily ever after for ever and ever for all eternity infinitely.

'– if breaking the waters started a contraction,' Cassie finished, aloud.

The midwife stood over her, questioning. 'What did you ask me?'

'Who knows?'

'How are you doing?'

'You tell me. I'm absent without leave. I wish.'

'Your husband wants to come in and help you.'

The crusher got going again. I must cope with this, Cassie thought, before it dragged her under mud, under water, under roaring hell without any hope of –

'– egress,' she said.

'What?' the midwife asked.

'Never mind,' Cassie said.

'What about your husband?'

'What about him?'

'He's back. He wants to help.'

'Tell him to fuck off.'

'You're sure of that?'

'Tell him nicely.'

As the crusher started again, in the long distance, Cassie could hear the midwife's unemotional voice, as clear and detached as if she was making a public announcement. 'Your wife told me to tell you nicely to fuck off.'

The literalness of it made Cassie laugh, and it was the laughter, this time, that made the pain so bad. The lifeline throughout the labour was the completely unsupportive surliness of the midwife. If she's that bored, it must be routine, Cassie would think, grasping for the hope in it. If she's that unimpressed, this must be the way it always is.

'I know you won't believe this,' the midwife said, at some point, 'but this is going very fast.'

'Why don't you fuck off, too?' Cassie asked.

'No, you need me,' the midwife said, unmoved. 'I'll fuck off later.'

Then the obstetrician arrived, all business, now the *real* symphony can begin, everything up to this was just tuning up, no insult, ladies, we're a professional team here, of course, you get to put my gloves on me and I get to say reassuring things to the patient, but very quickly because I have timed it so perfectly, here's the infant's head crowning, so I can be just interventive enough, instruct the mother firmly, here we go, you have a beautiful son, Cassandra, now I'm pressing down on your tummy and I want you to push again, everything's gone so well, just a little needle sensation here, keep you warm and comfortable for a little while before we bring you into recovery, here he is.

They handed a small, heavy, blanketed bundle with a hat on it to her. She searched the room, batted the obstetrician out of her line of vision, fastened on the midwife, who, unnervingly, was smiling. Don't smile, Cassie thought. Stay in role. The midwife came closer, bent over.

'It is OK? Tell me the truth.'

'Your boy is a beaut. Perfection itself.'

Survives early assault by antibiotics, Cassie thought confusedly, comes out a beaut. The midwife started to straighten up but waited when she saw Cassie wanted to say more.

'I'll remember you all my life.'

'No, you won't. C'n I fuck off now?'

'Do me a favour? Give me a bit of paper and something to write with. Thanks. This is my best friend's name. And number. Ring her. Tell her what you said to me about him being a beaut. But tell her – these words, please – tell her it was nothing remotely like a goddamn giant orgasm and I'll never speak to her again as long as I live.'

'You don't mean that, though.'

'I don't mean anything,' Cassie said. 'You can let Polo in now.'

'Your husband?'

'Yeah.'

'Don't forget to give him a hard time over fainting.'

It wouldn't have mattered what kind of time Cassie decided to give Polo when he arrived in the room. She had the impression that he would never experience un-happiness again, even if a band of masked terrorists were to drag him out of the place with the intention of shooting him. He held her and the baby in one vast embrace, then lifted the baby, cradled its capped head against his chest, wanted her to admire the fact that the baby was feeling the fabric of its father's jacket.

Polo walked around the room, awash in gratitude and delight. Cassie watched him sleepily. He did fatherhood very well, she had to hand it to him. He even asked her, now and again, if she wanted the baby back, but what would she want it back for when he was so good at holding it? It wasn't crying or anything. Most of what Polo said, she placidly observed, did not demand much of an answer. It was like a litany in the old days in church. Blah blah blah prafrus. Blah blah blah prafrus. All she had to do was the prafrus bit. Wasn't the baby so sturdy, so you could tell he'd be a little footballer, couldn't you? Oh, yeah. (Prafrus.) The lovely shape of his head, would you look at it, so perfect in the cute little cap, isn't it? Yeah, absolutely. (Prafrus.) Hands like yours, Cassie, small but broad across the knuckles, better than him having hands like mine, right? Oh, I don't know. (Prafrus.)

Nurses appeared every now and again to ask how she was. They would look approvingly at Polo, wandering round and round the room, but check with him if he wouldn't like them to take the baby away for a while? No? Oh, fine, fine. Indulgent smiles all around, they were off to the next room, the next family.

At some point, her mother was there, preceded by a wave of Opium, kissing Cassie on the forehead like a perfumed bishop and telling her she was so proud of her. Polo absorbed Mrs Browne in the baby while Cassie damped down the irritation resulting from other people's pride in her. Proud of her for what, for Chrissake? Wasn't as though she had suffered in silence. She'd have suffered a whole lot noisier if she'd had the breath. Proud of her for having a baby? Jesus, there must be an awful lot of free-floating pride if having a baby is a cause of it. Proud of her for having a beaut? Got lucky. Must have had an umbilical impervious to drugs and travel.

Somewhere during this internal colloquy, Cassie's mother disappeared. Marsha may have happened around the same time, but Cassie was never very sure. But the sleep that descended was total, dreamless. Heavy to sodden darkness.

When she woke, it was because hospitals corporately and collectively wake at half five or six in the morning, nurses finishing their tours of duty with a flourish, handing over to the incoming rota who embark on their tasks with a self-righteous air, a half-sent message of reassurance: yes, the standard of care up to now has been a bit iffy, but we're here to show you how it should really be done. Do not fear, the day team's here. We will open curtains, rattle charts against the end of your bed, be cheery, cheery, because this is a maternity hospital where good things happen and mothers are happy unless they're the small proportion who get the baby blues. Negligible proportion, really, but you have to watch out for them.

The thought police are here, Cassie thought, retreating to the bathroom. Have I the energy to do the whistle-while-I-work performance? Short answer, no, but I'd better do it anyway, because if I don't do it they'll have counsellors in here on top of me asking me the ten questions any five of which answered wrong mean I've got post-natal depression. Folks, this ain't post-natal depression. This ain't depression, post- or ante-. This is a state of mind to which, if I wasn't in a hospital, I might give you an argument about being entitled to, but in a hospital, the authorities own your states of mind and all your emotional reactions and if they don't stack up, those states of mind, they zap you for your own good until they do. So don't give the thought police any argument, just smile and smile and be a mother.

'Are you all right in there, Cassandra?' a voice asked, after a tentative tap on the bathroom door. Never heard that voice before, Cassie thought, therefore it's a strange nurse, don't gimme that first-name crap, you don't know me at all, I could be Nelson Mandela in here, you just read it off a notice outside the door.

'Fine, couldn't be better,' she said, coming out into the bedroom, where a strange nurse was holding a bundled baby. Hers, she supposed. Nurses wouldn't carry rival babies into new mothers. One of the mothers might decide her own wasn't up to scratch, gimme that *café au lait* one third from the left.

The two women stood for a moment as if they were starting an argument.

'D'you want to get back into bed, Cassandra?'

It was a sweetly voiced order, rather than a question,

and although she was dying to get back into bed, brought out the fight in Cassie. 'No, I'll stay out for a while,' she said, holding her hands out for the bundle.

'No problem, if you want to walk around for a while,' the nurse said, calmly rejecting the open hands, instead putting the baby into a crib at the end of the bed. 'You wouldn't want to walk around carrying the baby. Too much danger of fainting.'

It's Polo who faints at babies or impending babies, Cassie thought, but decided not to fight about it. For just a moment, she considered a walk down the corridor. Oops, no, thought police on patrol. She walked over to the crib and traced the baby's forehead with her index finger. It wrinkled its nose. She did it again. It did it again. She laughed. The nurse, filling in details on the chart, looked up and smiled. One Brownie point earned already, Cassie thought, as the nurse finished her paperwork and left.

Cassie immediately lifted the baby out of the crib and walked around with the bundle, notching up conscious positives about it. Neat shape. No bad smell. Has hair. Sleeps. Does not snore. No, you couldn't put that in the list. Babies probably didn't snore, so it wasn't a virtue. The shape of the baby's head went wavy, sending the unmistakable message that its mother was about to prove the nurse right by fainting. Cassie got to the bed, put the bundle in the middle of it, then lay down flat beside it. Symptoms of faintness retreated. She turned on her hip and propped her head on her hand. Wobbly? No. Grand.

The baby opened its eyes. Not fair, Cassie thought, to have it looking at a ceiling when it had never seen a ceiling before and when this particular ceiling – she glanced up at it – was so smoothly plastered there was nothing much to see in it. She turned the bundle on to its side and propped it with the towel she had carried from the bathroom. 'Hello,' she said, helplessly, after a while.

The baby did nothing much in response to this gambit, although she could see it was fingering the open-weave of the blanket bundled around it.

'Tell you what,' she said. 'I am never going to bring myself to do this coochie-coo lark. So let's pretend you're a human. Humour me, OK?'

The infant seemed to be confused as to where she was, so she moved closer, with some difficulty.

'The world is full of people who'll do the coochie-coo stuff,' Cassie explained. 'They'll see all sorts of resemblances but there aren't any, actually. You're just a baby. You could be any baby.'

The baby watched her gravely.

'Now, if I was normal, I would think you were hearing every word I said, and thinking deep thoughts about it,' Cassie said. 'But I'm not normal, so I know you have no thoughts of any kind.' The baby sighed deeply and Cassie laughed. 'You make a good straight man, though, kid, I have to hand it to you. How about we do the finger-in-palm bit? That always works.'

She put her little finger into the baby's palm and its tiny hand closed around it.

'See? Told you. Never fails. Course, you're going to be driven bananas, over the next few days. Every halfwit who comes into this room is going to put their finger in your palm and be convinced they're having a bonding moment with you. It's clever hard wiring, though, you have to admit that.'

Not letting go of her finger, the baby began to change expression, its concentrated stare giving way to a frown and a thwarted lip.

'Working up to a whinge, are you? Feck. Figured you

158

would do if I didn't coochie at you. You babies are all the same.'

The baby made a noise, which seemed to surprise it more than it surprised Cassie. Both of them considered it for a moment, then the baby did it again. Cassie hauled herself up against the pillows into a sitting position. 'Shit, I should have brought you with me,' she told the baby from a distance. 'Pivoting on my arse after what I went through yesterday is not an easy proposition. How the hell am I going to get you up here? Any suggestions? I mean, there's two of us have the problem, not just me.'

The baby gave up on her and began to complain in earnest. By stretching out with her left hand, Cassie could reach the end of its blanket. She hooked a finger and pulled. It unravelled as it came, presenting the baby feet first, but the end result was that the baby was within reach without painful pivoting. She took hold of it by the ankles and pulled it further. The movement seemed to distract the baby from its complaint for a moment or two. When she had it at hip level, it was possible to pick it up and lay it on her chest. 'Now you're supposed to listen to my heartbeat,' she told the top of its head. 'This is when you cop on, "Hey, that's the noise I've been listening to for the past nine months, all is well."'

The baby shifted around as if to avoid any contact with her, heartbeat or no heartbeat.

'You're right,' Cassie muttered. 'Bore the shit out of me, too, a heartbeat for nine months. For Chrissake, nothing but boom boom bloody boom. No melody, not even a bit of a lyric. You'd need the attention span of a foetus to stick with it.'

The baby protested and squirmed. Any minute now, Cassie worried, a nurse was going to walk into the room to find Cassie failing to bond. She shifted the baby, wondering why it was without its little hat today. It squirmed and protested some more. Suddenly, light dawned. 'I know what you're at,' Cassie told it. 'You're looking for a boob. That's what you're at, right? Right. You don't have much of a sense of direction, yet. Nor do you know about this button thing.' She opened the top of her nightdress and half pointed her breast at the baby. It snuffled and searched. 'Jesus, you're like one of those blind mammals that roots for truffles,' she told it impatiently. 'Would you *look*? Here. This bit.'

The baby got the hang of her anatomy and swallowed half a breast, to Cassie's astonishment. Maybe she never looked much at Madonna-and-child paintings, she thought, but the image she had was of babies decently addressing nipples, not suctioning half a mother into them.

A nurse knocked and entered the room in one busy movement, started to smile, then came to the bedside double quick. 'You're not down for breast-feeding,' she stated.

Cassie laughed. The baby opened its eyes at the disruptive movement, then went back to work.

'You're not, really,' the nurse said, in a panicky voice.

'What's the punishment?' Cassie asked.

'No, you don't understand,' the nurse said. 'You're not down for breast-feeding. You'd have had instructions in advance.'

'There you go,' Cassie said, placidly.

'I'll have to get someone to show you how,' the nurse said, desperately.

'I know how.'

'No, I mean how to do it properly.'

'I know how to do it properly.'

'Ten minutes on each side and everything?'

'Precisely,' Cassie said, with great casualness. Shit, she

160

thought, I have no idea how long he's been going on that one, but what the hey?

'You're sure?' the nurse said, anxiously.

'I'm very sure,' Cassie said, becoming very sure by saying it. 'But I'll do better if you darken the room a little and just leave us to it.'

Relieved to have something to do, the nurse lowered the blind half-way, dithered a little, then left.

'I lied,' Cassie said to the baby. 'I haven't a clue about this method, but I couldn't tell her I was following your lead, could I? I'll make it up to you later. Problem now is you have to go the other way.'

The baby ignored this. Cassie gently pulled it, discovering that its cheek muscles were considerably stronger than she would have ever imagined. She had another go, riveted to see her own breast, somewhat depleted now, stretching as the baby sucked on for dear life. 'What the hell am I going to do now?' she asked it.

It struck her that she should break the suction. She inserted a finger at the edge of the baby's mouth. For a moment, it looked as if she might lose the finger, but by curling it up under the baby's lip and pulling the child away with the other arm, she managed to separate herself from it. It bellowed. 'Wait, wait, *wait*,' she begged it. 'Hang on, for Chrissake, nobody's trying to starve you, there's another one here just as good. Better, in fact. Much better. Listen, you dope, if you shut up roaring, you'd be able to see it. *Look!* Oh, feck this for a game of soldiers, I'm just going to gag you with it.'

With inexpert desperation, she plugged the baby's open mouth with her boob. The silence and instant adherence was marvellous. The baby sucked with hunger enough to suggest it had never had a go at anything in the way of food before. Cassie looked at her wrist-watch. 'Ten minutes from now,' she told it, 'you have to come

161

off that one, and you know what? There isn't a third. Jasus, you'll take the shagging hospital apart and disgrace me. However, you know something? I'll cross that boob when I come to it. You just get on with the work, I'll do the timing.'

She lay back a little. The baby adjusted to the shift, putting one hand on her breast as if to assert ownership. She grinned at it. After about seven minutes, she noticed that the sucks were becoming intermittent. 'Hey, matey, you're not making good use of the time you're booked for,' she said, making a move at detaching it. It went back immediately to full-time work. After another minute, however, its rhythm began to drift.

'You're like a windscreen wiper at "intermittent",' she explained. 'No action, then a quick sweep, then no action. You know what I'm going to do? I'm going to wait until there's no action for two minutes because I figure that means you're asleep and then I'll slide you . . .'

The baby's head slid away and she had herself covered up in a minute. This could work. A nurse in a different uniform arrived, officer-class written all over her. A staff nurse, Cassie thought. The staff nurse lifted the baby and put it in the crib. 'I believe you've opted to try breast-feeding?'

'I forgot to burp the baby,' Cassie said.

'Don't worry about it,' the staff nurse said, tucking in the baby's blankets with such vigour it looked like imprisonment. A tiny bundle held down by tightly tented blankets. Immobile. Pinned. Cribbed, cabined and confined, Cassie thought.

'Burping babies is largely a myth,' the staff nurse added. 'Makes parents feel good, does no harm, but does he look as if he's missing it?'

Cassie craned with some difficulty to see. 'Is he not very tightly . . . ?' she asked.

162

'The tighter you blanket babies, the less they cry. Leave a baby's legs and arms free, they frighten him because he doesn't know what they are. That's why papooses and swaddling worked. Except in hygiene terms.'

Hygiene terms? Cassie was about to pursue this out of curiosity, but the staff nurse had a tube of ointment and a few brisk instructions, which she asked Cassie to repeat. Cassie decided that since this woman had accepted Cassie's amateur breast-feeding, she'd play along and repeat her instructions. Nurses left quicker if you didn't fight them, and this one was no exception. She should, Cassie thought after she'd left the room, have asked her to pull up the blind again. On the other hand, sleep wasn't a bad option, either.

While she was thinking about sleep, it happened to her.

CHAPTER ELEVEN

Roses and Convertibles

They hawked the baby around, the women crooning rapturously, the men either refusing to take the child, ogling it half-heartedly over a partner's shoulder or taking it with such lack of comfort that it protested. Mostly, when it cried, it cried in a temporary, huffy way. To Cassie's concealed delight, the only time it did flat-out in-out, strangling-for-breath, inconsolable, desperate crying was when her mother picked it up.

Everybody else brought gifts. Cassie put Post-it notes on them after the visitors left, so she would know to mention the dotty little Babygro in one thank-you note, the darling Oshkosh denim pull-ups in another. As the day went on, the room filled with all of the flowers Cassie hated: lilies, chrysanthemums, miniature roses tight-wound in pursing prettiness, feathery fern fizzing around the outside of every display. Polo promised to bring in a container to allow for them all to be taken home. She blinded him with a look. It was easier than trying to talk over the baby's roaring.

Anyway, she didn't want to give her mother a reason for lecturing her: all these *beaut*iful flowers, you couldn't just throw them there, this isn't even a religious hospital where they could go on the altar, these roses would be so perfect on that antique table in your drawing room. Prevention, Cassie thought, was truly better than cure where her mother's advice was concerned. Go on, Da, she mentally invited him. Tell me how marvellous she is to be able to visualise the perfect place in my home for those tight-arsed midget roses. Tell me how thoughtful she is *not* to bring gifts, because wouldn't I have the hassle of transporting them home? Not to mention the wisdom of waiting to see what everybody else gives so she can then fill the gap. I can hear you, even over that baby's bawling. Your mother doesn't have a mean bone in her. True. But any generosity she has is awful strategic, Da. You used to buy gifts for people on impulse, for the pleasure of their amazed delight at receiving something out of season; unpinned to the justification of birthdays or anniversaries.

At eleven or twelve, I learned to defend you against your own munificence, trained myself not to say 'Oh, isn't that lovely' about items in shop windows, knowing the item – or a better version of it, a super-charged, deluxe, guaranteed version – would surface in my life within weeks. Always with an explanation designed to obviate guilt on my part. I needed top-of-the-range roller-blades because they were great for a cardiovascular workout. That was the funniest of the explanations. Me, thirteen, ready to stick it to every other kid in the neighbourhood that I had skates with a population explosion of ball-bearings, skates so fast not even the boys, the ice-hockey tough wannabes, could catch me, being provided with a justification I could hardly pronounce.

Mrs Browne knew when she was beaten, although she still managed to hand the baby to Polo with an air of relinquishing a treasure, allowing the truncation of a perfect relationship between her and the child. That the child, once in its father's arms, brought its yowling into a shuddering holding pattern did not escape Cassie's attention. Any malicious satisfaction derived therefrom, however, was speedily erased as Mrs Browne, gathering her gloves and handbag, delivered herself of the view that it wasn't good for a baby to be called It. The comment was made on a sigh, the inference to be drawn inescapable: is it any wonder a baby would cry so hysterically, even in the embrace of an expert like herself, when it knew it was being wilfully deprived of its proper identification? All of *her* children had names long before they were born, she sniffed.

'He has a name,' Cassie said. 'His name's Ben.'

Her mother turned at the door, all the censorious tightness washed out of her face in a melting misery of memories, of gratitude, of affirmation, so unguarded in its testimony to her love of the dead man that Polo instinctively put his arm around her and hauled her into an awkward embrace with the baby squashed between them. 'Sure what else could we call him?' he asked her gently, repeating the question contentedly as he laid the baby down in the crib. 'I'll take your mam to the car,' he told Cassie. 'Be back tonight.'

The two of them went off, leaving Cassie to wonder at the ease of him. He had suggested all sorts of names in the run-up to the birth when Cassie had been of no mind to consider them. He must have had some investment in one or two of those names, yet he now accepted her unilateral decision without petulance. She must suggest the baby's middle name be that of his father. What *was* his father's name? Funny, she always thought of him as Dr Cadogan.

'You can't be called Ben Doctor Cadogan,' she said, in the direction of the crib. One of the baby's shuddering sobs followed this, in apparent relief, making her smile.

'Well, that's a surprise,' Marsha said, entering the room quietly.

'What is?'

'Finding you with a smile on your face. Jasus, I was

expecting thundering glares. Specially when I met your mother, being escorted, weeping, from the premises by your husband.' Marsha hugged her. The baby gave another shuddering sigh. 'You've been beating this kid already, I can tell,' Marsha said.

'Ben.'

Marsha raised her eyebrows and regarded the bundle with her head on one side. 'Ben. Not the worst,' she said. 'Could've been Tyler.'

'Or Jason.'

'Or Justin.'

'More fun if you'd named him Jesus. Whenever I read books with Hispanics in them called Jesus, I regret not naming Colm that way. That'd teach him.'

Marsha dragged a chair into position and turfed a number of wrapped packages on to the wheeled tea-tray at the end of the bed. 'Don't waste your time opening them. None of them will fit him until he's one and a half. Every new baby gets half a million things that fit up to six months. Then the poor sprog goes into a famine. Six months passes very quickly.'

Cassie shifted in the bed. They had given her an in-flated circular cushion not unlike a child's inner-tube for floating in the sea. It was supposed to be more comfort-able than sitting on the flat surface of the bed.

'I hear it wasn't an orgasm?'

'Oh, the midwife rang you?'

'She passed on your message faithfully. Did add, though, for a first labour it was fast and easy. Ten hours. What're you complaining about? Could have gone to thirty.'

'The fastest, easiest ten hours of baby-delivery does not an orgasm make.'

'We'll agree to differ.'

'Bloody right, we'll agree to differ.'

'So have you been hit by the wonder of motherhood?'

Cassie gave her a killer look.

'Oh, well,' Marsha said. 'Realism has its merits, too. How well are you coping with Polo's sustained ecstasy?'

It made up, Cassie told her, for her own objectivity.

'Objectivity?' Marsha tried out and rejected the word. 'Objectivity? About your own baby? Better not use that word to anyone other than me. They'll think you're unnatural. I *know* you're unnatural, I just keep quiet about it. Don't mention the war. Don't mention natural motherhood. Don't mention big orgasms – at least, not in the context of labour.' She stood up, pushing the chair back to where it had been before she shifted it. 'I'm out of here.'

'Why you going so fast? My unnaturalness getting to you?'

Her aunt laughed. 'Your unnaturalness is no problem to me. You can be as unnatural as you like, on my time. No. Reason I'm going is that you've had dozens of well-wishers in here all day. Every one of them has stayed too long, you've smiled so much your face is sagging and this place smells like a hoor's parlour. All the flowers. Hey, Ben, bet all the visitors picked you up every time you got settled and pissed you off, too? Well, lad, you can stay where you are, as far as I'm concerned. I'll get to hold you plenty when Ms Unnatural up there needs a babysitter so she can go off to be a career pinhead. Hang in there. Don't let her erode your self-esteem. Show me any bruises, I'll inform on her to the Welfare. Get you taken into care. Maybe even get to foster you. Wouldn't that be a plan?'

She was gone less than ten minutes after she arrived, and sleep descended, unannounced, on Cassie. Sleep so heavy that when she surfaced again, it was dark, they had taken Ben to the nursery and pulled the coverlet over her. She turned on the light. A note in childish handwriting was held down by a glass of water. Didn't want to disturb her. Good to see her sleeping so peacefully. Ben likewise. All his love, Polo.

Spotting the glow of Cassie's bedside light through the over-door slice of thick glass, a nurse came into the room. 'There's something wrong with me,' Cassie realised and said.

Her breasts were swollen, hard and hot to the touch, terrifyingly painful. The nurse said her milk was 'coming in'. Once she fed the baby, it would be all right, it really would. She foosthered around the hospital room, tidying in a desultory way, as if predicting the end of discomfort ensured that discomfort went away instantly. Cassie's did not, and she asked if she could feed the baby now. Right now. Please. The nurse said it was usually done on demand. 'On demand' seemed to apply only to the infant.

'Please bring him to me,' Cassie said, as if she knew this was the right thing.

The nurse came back with Ben, the baby blinking in a baffled way at the lights, and handed him over with an air of 'on your own head be it'.

'Thank you,' Cassie told her in dismissal.

The baby fisted a hand into its mouth, settling itself for more sleep.

'Hey,' Cassie said softly. 'Need you to do me a favour.' She pulled the tiny hand away and presented her breast instead. The baby began to nurse, tiny eyebrows raised with effort and surprise. 'Five minutes, each side. That'll do it,' Cassie explained, shifting him midway.

After ten minutes, the soreness was gone and Ben was contentedly asleep. She felt absurdly grateful to him. In the morning, when they began to educate her for her departure, she sat through the instructions paying no attention whatever. Took the plastic bag of freebies.

Nodded agreement where there was no absorption, never mind agreement. Polo had brought in a couple of outfits, erring on the side of looser fit, but because she had gained so little extra weight; once in clothes she looked as if she had never had a baby. Polo walked her to the car park, half swinging Ben in the most elaborate baby-carrier-cum-car-seat she had ever seen. She halted after the third row of cars, trying to spot the Pajero, or her own Camry.

'Here we are,' Polo said, setting the carrier down beside a convertible Mercedes.

'Don't tell me,' she said, shaking her head at him.

'OK, I'll say nuthin,' he said, latching the baby seat into the back of the car. 'D'you want to drive your new car?'

'Why not?'

She slid into the driver's seat, where he gave her a tutorial. This opened the roof, you just had to remember to depress that first. This raised the seat, this lowered the back. She registered all the little icons on the controls and told it back to him. The baby half woke, making some general criticisms. For a moment, she worried. Did he need to be fed? No, fed less than an hour ago. Changed? He was changed directly after the feeding. Polo leaned over the back of the passenger seat to check that the belts securing Ben were all firmly latched, then did an elaborate in-your-own-time gesture to her. She started the car and drove out of the car park, Ben making his point more loudly. A few traffic lights later, she tried to change gear. The car bucked and caused Ben to cry louder.

'It's an automatic,' Polo pointed out, mildly. 'You don't have to change gear. It does it for you.'

Soon, they were on the northern road, the car seamlessly, soundlessly, imperceptibly gaining speed. The diminution of Ben's complaints matched the smoothing out of their journey precisely. Now, *there*'s a handy thing to know, Cassie thought. If he's crying, go somewhere.

The engine noise or the rhythm of the car puts him to sleep.

Polo fiddled with the controls of the radio/CD-player. He would put LMFM first, she knew without asking him, then RTE 1, then 2FM, then 100FM because he loved Eamon Dunphy. It was a little like the car, she thought. When Polo did you a favour, he did you the favour he decided you needed, rather than establishing the favour you wanted. Under the dream-car-I'll-never-get category, Cassie's number-one choice was always a red convertible BMW, not a silver Merc. The Merc was probably more expensive and reliable, so Polo would have decided it was a better gift. His generosity was enormous – and oddly controlling.

'Your mobile phone gets powered up while you drive,' Polo said, now that he had the radio sorted. 'But you never have to lift it up. I've programmed in your ten most frequent numbers, so all you have to do is two button pushes to get any one of them.'

Ben gave a deep sigh.

'God, you'd think sleeping was awful hard work, wouldn't you?' Polo said, looking back at him.

'Lovely to be in a car so quiet you can hear him sigh,' she said. 'Thank you. By the way, would you shift the cot into our room when we get home?'

He nodded, surprised. A fortnight earlier, when he refused to postpone any longer the decoration of what he now always called the nursery, although up to four months previously it was always referred to by him as 'Peter's room' (though his friend had moved to Dublin before their wedding), she made no objection, once the paint dried, to Polo's installation of a brand-new luxury cot near one wall. I just don't want to be blamed, she told herself now, concentrating on the road extra hard because, without gears to change, it was too easy to slip

171

into a fugue, mesmerised by the trees whipping past, the geometric sameness of the interrupted white lines on the road. I just don't want to be blamed for not having him close. If anything happened to him. A wash of skin-chilling fear came up over her and she slowed the car in reflex response.

'What's wrong?'

Nothing, the headshake told him. Nothing. Just the sudden realisation that this baby might die, might go blue-limbed silent in the sussurating night, might stilly look at the distant ceiling, wide-eyed, untroubled because of oncoming death, might be to the touch cold-heavied in rigor, in *rigor*. Her throat closed at the thought of it. It happening two doors and a landing away. Too far to hear, to sense, to see, to wake.

They were less than three miles away from Stackallen. The car gained speed again, Polo talking about not opening the boot unless something else was done first. She nodded, staring at the road, fierce-faced in apparent attention, but counting off the miles and then the mile-tenths on the speedometer until the Mercedes was smoothing its way around the curves of the driveway, the car was parked softly on the stirring gravel, and she could reach into the back for the baby, to be reassured by the warm weight of him, the flustered breathing of him as she lifted him out of the car cot, the sweet smell of him.

She flat-handed him to her in the front seat of the new car, eyes burning with the choking relief, speechless. Polo ruffled her hair the way he would ruffle the hair of a little boy who had won a race or given a great smart answer. Told her to take her time, as if he had the permission to give. Took bags from the boot and began the series of trips that would bring their son into their home.

Drying her eyes on the edge of the cotton blanket, Cassie organised the baby-weight so the carrying was comfortable, hip-closing the door, turning at the top of the three stone steps up to the house door to aim the electronic lozenge at the Merc and make all four doors obediently lock themselves at once. No, she didn't need Polo to carry Ben, she'd manage fine. Maybe he'd make a cup of tea, though? That'd be great.

She walked slowly up the shallow sweeping stone steps of the big old staircase, touching her lips through the soft baby hair to Ben's skin, his scalp, the infinite softness of his round forehead, side to side caresses. Brought him into the bedroom. Changed him without waking him. Lay down on the bed beside him, unable to keep her hands away from his skin. There was a yearning desperation in her like nothing she had ever previously experienced, a terror-filled sweetness, a passion that took her over, shook her in its maw. This is what falling in love means, she thought, searching her son's face for its every wonder, comfort and joy. And then she whispered it to him. Once. Again. So softly and so often that it became a whispering song, matching the march of his decided breaths, the pulsing promptness of his heartbeat.

CHAPTER TWELVE

Washing Machines and Parties

'She's stopped paying any attention to me,' Polo told Orna in the office. Delightedly.

'Haven't you enough people here, paid to pay attention to you?'

'It's not the same.'

'About bloody time she stopped paying so much attention to you,' Orna said, meaning to insult him, knowing she was wasting her time. Nobody could reach Polo now. Fatherhood had inflated him so that he no longer walked but bounced, shined him so his skin glowed like an apple in a supermarket display.

'I'm turbo-charged,' he told Cassie, arriving home early day after day. 'Our son has even made me into a better manager. I'm getting through things twice as fast. Problems? I ace them.'

He mimicked a killer tennis serve so well, she wondered why it was he fell short of realising his sporting ambitions. If he could imitate the constituent portions of a great player's game, it seemed contradictory that he could never pull all those portions together into a winning sequence.

Increasingly in demand as an after-dinner speaker, he was constantly requested for annual dinners at golf clubs, having developed a part-speech, part-skit based on the styles of famous golfers. This unathletic softish shamble of a man would arrive, mid-dinner (because that allowed him to leave the office at four, rush home, riot with Ben, and get to the venue by about half nine), eat pudding if the main course was finished, fiddle, white-handed, with his dinner-jacket sleeves during the introduction, wander to the microphone and become John Daly. Not a word. Not a greeting. Daly was just *there*, draggled, hung-over, hair sticking up at the back, hitting the ball with great violence for want of anybody closer to serve as a target. The round of applause was eager and reluctant, grudging and abandoned, all at once.

From that point on, at each dinner, Polo was a man possessed. Possessed by a demon called comedy, a capacity to evoke stars the audiences knew in ways they could never pin down. Possessed, too, by a demon called pathos, as he reminded them of the sunny greatness of a man like Ballesteros, made them witness and watch the greatness shift into something else, something immeasurably less, stealing the sun from the open Spanish face.

The clubs that hired him always thought of him, in advance of the performance, as a category of celebrity guest: a merely funny man, a well-paid retainer. They never noticed when the relationship between employer and servant changed so that it was *he* who now owned them, conducted them, controlled their glee, surfing their laughter so the impetus was highest at the end, allowing him to leave them sated, simultaneously wanting more, coming up to him afterwards like subservients eager to be recognised by him, get the scrofula of lonely seriousness king-touched off them for ever, have audience with him.

He did not often talk about that shift in power he could achieve, but she knew it fascinated him. Some part of him always scrutinised what he could make happen, interrogated the dynamic, wondered about its application elsewhere, speculated about the malleability of the minds before him. He had a theory that if you could make people laugh, you could make them do anything, forgive anything, be open to anything. Humour, he said, was the ultimate key to power. Nobody copped on to this, because, he said, most of those who yearned for power were humourless, missing out on the skill, the trait that could win them ultimate power, whereas those who were funny rarely wanted anything other than fame or the self-sustaining power of audience amusement and applause.

In day-time casuals, scruffy from shifting costumes and props in the tiny city-centre office, he would walk the house carrying Ben while she drew her cartoons, or if her work was done, would talk to her over his son's head, understanding his own theories as he heard himself telling them to her, simultaneously nagging himself about the time, the need to break off, the need to get dressed up for the evening gig, eventually and reluctantly relinquishing the baby to her. 'The show-off must go on, right?' he would say, depositing random kisses on the two of them before rushing out of the front door, jumping the three steps, fastening his watch as he went. The Pajero was cluttered with plastic oblongs containing the instant shoe-shine sponges he used at traffic lights to get his shoes polished before performances.

It was after one of his noisy departures that the baby smiled for the first time. Wind, thought Cassie. Even though she refused to read baby books and tried to avoid listening to the baby talk of other parents, somewhere along the line the message had got through to her that the first smiles are not smiles at all, just facial reaction to internal digestive activity. Ben looked at her, pink-faced from all the excitement Polo had induced, and smiled again. She smiled back. Then laughed, because the wide-mouthed grin she was getting looked like a comment on the child's father: *Yer man's a hoot, isn't he?*

'I mustn't attribute thoughts to you that you can't have,' she told Ben firmly. The smile went away, the baby's eyes searching her face. 'But if you *were* thinking he's a hoot, you're not wrong, you're right,' she told him, rubbing his tummy gently.

He gave her another grin.

'D'you know something?' she said, lifting him over her head, not minding when he dribbled joyfully on her. 'It's all lies they told me about babies. That's no more wind than I'm Janet Jackson. That's a smile, no argument about it. You're just in great humour, that's all there's to it. Betcha I can make you smile any time I want to. You on for a game?'

She propped him on their bed, half sitting, held in place by pillows, and knelt in front of him, where he could see her. 'Now, here's a thing,' she told him, in a deep voice filled with gravitas. 'There are serious problems in the world, and when we think about them, we get very serious faces. Like mine, right now? See this for a serious face? You've got a serious face on, too. But then, someone like your mad father appears and you know what? We lose the seriousness. We smile – whee – like this.'

She demonstrated a big smile, instantly getting one in return.

'Oh, do you know something? You are so clever,' she said. 'You've got your priorities right. Get to the smiling first, we can worry about the great thoughts later. On the other hand, I think we might discuss a nappy change at this moment in time, because I don't know about your olfactories, but mine are getting signals that you have taken action. Maybe involuntary action, but highly effective action nonetheless, requiring reciprocal action from

177

me. You know something? You're training me. Teacher and pupil, that's us.'

She collected nappy-change supplies and went about the task. Ben followed her with his eyes, smiling at her when she came back into his line of sight.

'That's another thing I got wrong,' she told him. 'I thought parents were the teachers and babies the pupils. It's the other way around, isn't it? I'm the pupil, you're the teacher. How'm I doing so far? Oh, kid, I'll go for the honours course if you keep giving me smiles like that.'

Fresh and clean, Ben was carried with her as she disposed of the dirty nappy, his eyes a-droop with oncoming sleep. Cassie was surprised by how much the baby slept, but adapted, so that instead of one seven- or eight-hour block of sleep, she took four or five shorter sleeps, lying down with Ben beside her on the king-size bed and shoving the telephone on to the answering-machine, muting its ringing noise. Increasingly, he woke her, a flailing little hand reaching out for her face, a wordless noise alerting her, so she opened her eyes to see him, grinning at the ceiling, arms and legs winding up for whatever activity was on offer. She might lie on her back beside him, talking to him. About how fortuitous it was that, although she was doing fewer cartoons, she was earning more, and how neatly this fitted with his arrival. About how embarrassing it was to be so totally in love with him, and how she couldn't tell anybody but him about this overwhelming experience.

Although the local woman who came in three times a week in the mornings was willing, indeed eager, to mind Ben while Cassie 'went into town', in the first three months, Cassie never took advantage of that willingness. Indeed, she preferred the days when the woman didn't come in. During those days she would tuck Ben into a light fabric sling, wandering the house, doing tasks in a random, almost casual way, discussing them with him as she went. One morning, when he cried unceasingly, she found herself with him in the utility room, trying to sort coloured from white clothes one-handed. 'This is just not going to work,' she said to him, straightening up. 'Have to put you down for a minute, OK?'

Ben roared on, uninterested in negotiation. She slid him out of the sling, then wondered where best to put him. The softest option was the clothes at her feet, but they were dirty. The washing-machine was in the middle of its most aggressive cycle, great heavy-toned swooshings of hot water making it advance in a slow drunken march, three inches at a time. She threw a bath-towel on the hard top of it before setting Ben down on the towel.

'Won't be a second,' she told him.

Not that he could hear her, she thought. The slurring, sodden percussion of the washing-machine in the enclosed utility room made sure of that. It was not, accordingly, her comforting reassurances that silenced him – so completely and instantaneously that she was hauled up out of mid-crouch to investigate. The washing-machine was moving from aggression to absolute frenzy. Ben was vibrating counter-clockwise on top, taking the towel with him, an expression of equal parts delight and amazement on his face. Lest the commotion frighten him, Cassie moved forward so he could see her, but he very decidedly ignored her, concentrating fiercely on this spinning, thundering agglomeration of sensations.

The machine spun itself to a clunking halt, and in the sudden silence, Ben looked bereft. She held on to him, one-handed. Then, from way below him, came a loud rapid metallic trickling as the drum refilled for its rinse. He listened with wonder to the changing tone as the trickle first entered a relatively hollow space, then gradually became a flow into deeper water. Fill complete, the machine began its much more stately rinse revolutions, a portly matron circling with heavy grace. Ben's expression went from gleeful to contented to dreamy. By the end of the rinse cycle, he was fast asleep. Carrying him up to the bedroom, the bath-towel still around him, Cassie giggled at the realisation that all the washing of curtains, towels, tablecloths, rugs and other household items she'd been intending to do for some time could now substitute for taking Ben out in the car whenever he was having a truly bad teething day.

'And that was before I found out about the tumble-dryer,' she told Marsha on the phone.

'What's wrong with the tumble-dryer?'

'Nothing. But if I set Ben down in that springy chair thing you gave me, about six feet away from it, he gets totally mesmerised by it. If I need him to go to sleep quickly, I dry a completely white load. If I want to stimulate him, I dry a mainly white load with maybe one red sock and one blue sock. He keeps trying to work out when each of them is going to come into the central window next. His hair sticks out because of the steam, so he looks like a mad little Einstein. If I simply want to give him a great time, I dry a mixed load. Applause, applause. Laughter.'

'You're probably spoiling him as a TV viewer,' Marsha said. 'He'll expect all the programmes to go round in circles on the screen. And the presenters to come out clean and dry and hot at the end of it. Covered in little worn-out sheets of Bounce.'

The worst day, in those early months, was the day Ben rolled over. Unexpectedly and successfully, he rolled from his back to his front. So successfully, in fact, that the impetus caused him to do it again, in the process coming off the edge of the bed where Cassie had put him while she went to get rid of a dirty nappy. Ben hit the uncarpeted floor of the bedroom with a whack calculated to stop Cassie's heart, and screamed in reaction to the fall in a way she had never heard before. Almost afraid to lift him, for fear his spine might be severed, she eventually gathered him into a blanket, got him out and into the car, and drove to the local doctor, who was just finishing his surgery.

'Come on in, come on in,' the doctor said, waving away her apologies, tilting his head to hear what she was saying over Ben's continued screams. 'Put him down there and we'll have a look at him,' the doctor said, pointing at his examination couch. 'Oh, my, aren't you a sturdy boy?' he continued, prodding Ben approvingly in the tummy. 'Such a sturdy boy, and you only what? How many months?'

Cassie told him. Ben told him, too, although precisely what information was being conveyed was not clear.

'You're right, you're right. You're right,' the doctor agreed, as Ben screamed up into his face. 'You're absolutely right. Now, let's see about this head of yours,' and he probed firmly, confidently, around the back of Ben's head. This greatly distracted Ben, who seemed unsure as to whether the head-probing was being done by the same person asking him the questions. He paused in mid-scream and gulped. 'Nothing that painful back there, then?' the doctor asked, and Ben made a lengthy, tearful statement. 'Ah, yes,' the doctor said. 'One of those. Happens all the time. Very painful at the time, was it?' Ben sobbed some more. 'D'you know what I think?' the doctor asked, in quite a loud voice, but still in confidential tone, as if discussing something slightly iffy with Ben. 'I think you came down on your forehead because you do have a bit of a haematoma there. It must have been quite a surprise to you, as well, I imagine?'

He bundled Ben up and handed him to Cassie. Ben

snuggled his head into the warmth of her neck and snuffled the remainder of his disappointment with the way the world was treating him into the depression above her collarbone.

'The great thing about babies,' the doctor said, 'is that they fall like drunks, all relaxed, because they don't know what's coming up to hit them.'

Cassie burst into tears at the thought of the bedroom floor coming up to hit Ben.

'They're like rubber balls, too,' the doctor said, seeming not to notice this. 'They bounce. Rarely do themselves any harm. It's marvellous, really. Marvellous.'

Without ever telling her to move, he had her half-way to the front door of the surgery, the unstated diagnosis clear. Flustered, she apologised for making a fuss.

'Oh, no, no, no,' he said. 'Mothers don't make fusses. Mothers are the great experts about their babies. The rest of us are only amateurs. Mothers know the whole story. Isn't that right, young fella?' He patted Ben on the back, stood at the door until the baby was sleepily secured in the car seat, then retreated. Which allowed Cassie to begin the apologies she would make to Ben, out loud, all the way home. He slept through most of it and when he woke up, seemed to remember nothing bad .

The following day, Cassie did a *Pinhead* drawing of the doctor, with a caption saying, 'You do have a haematoma, there, at the back.' The drawing showed the GP as Ben would have seen him. She scanned it and sent it to Marsha, who knew about Ben's accident. Minutes later, Marsha rang her. 'Why'd you do this?'

'Thought I might have it framed and give it to the doctor.'

'Oh, fine, but keep thinking Ben's POV.'

'I beg your pardon?'

'Ben's point of view. Watch people and see them the

way he sees them. Make notes of the idiot things people say to babies. I think there's a series in it. Not for a paper here, maybe for one of the parenting magazines.'

This instruction led to one of the few drawings with a big face Cassie ever produced. It showed a huge, bulbous, jowly, big-pored, eye-bulging countenance, drawstring mouth opening to reveal fender teeth, over the caption 'You wouldn't make strange with me.' Something in the cartoon spoke to mothers driven mad by strangers who first invaded their baby's space, terrified the baby into a screaming fit, then blamed the baby for 'making strange'. Marsha contacted an international company specialising in goods for babies, doing a deal which had the cartoon, signed by the cartoonist, framed and selling for fifty pounds a time. (Unsigned copies went for twenty pounds.)

Marsha was in her element managing Cassie's business. She was without hesitation, without shame when a marketing idea took hold of her. Cassie would sometimes hear her talking to Polo, teasing out a possibility with him, but then putting him firmly back in his box when she had the information she needed. She negotiated contracts, got accounts done on time and allocated Cassie a strict budget so that what she called Cassie's Multiplier Effect could be controlled. (Cassie's Multiplier Effect was a tendency, when she found a pair of shoes she liked, to buy them in all colours. Or when she came across an outfit she wanted for Ben, to buy three of them, for fear the washing-machine began to eat, rather than clean.) She even presented Cassie with a contract covering their professional relationship, which ran to several dozen pages and seemed to cover every possible eventuality short of Cassie being hit by a low-flying 747.

'Why do I need all this?' Cassie said, skipping paragraphs on the mental plea of urgency, even though

Marsha was playing with Ben in a way that seemed to satisfy the two of them completely.

'If you read it properly, it will become clear to you why you need it,' Marsha said relentlessly.

Cassie sighed melodramatically but read then signed the contract. What the legalese added up to, she decided, was empowering Marsha into a metaphorical crouch in front of Cassie, flick-knife shining as she whipped it from side to side threatening anybody who wanted to exploit Cassie, now or in the future, alive or dead, married or widowed, able or disabled. That was OK with Cassie. Marsha had become such a high-flying, tough-talking, deal-doing agent *extraordinaire*, the transformation allowed Cassie to live in a bubble where nobody fought with her, underpaid her, overworked her or forced her to do sums.

Only at parties did Marsha, accompanied by her husband, seem to retreat to something like an 80 per cent version of herself, deferring to Liam and retreating to the kitchen seeking to be domestically helpful. At the Christmas party when Ben was eighteen months old, Cassie, coming down the wide staircase after checking on him, couldn't see her among the guests. She halted, level with the star on their sixteen-foot tree, looking for her.

'Careful,' a voice said directly below. 'I could put a hell of a caption on *that* pose.'

Cassie laughed. In the very early days of her cartooning, the *Examiner* had worked out that although Cassie could come up with funny images, she could not come up with the captions that would propel them into provokers of open-mouthed gusts of laughter. A staff sub-editor would do that, they told her. After a fortnight of the staff sub-editor producing such inspired captions that Cassie would end up hugging herself and liking the cartoons twice as much, she asked his name. Erik the

Red. Erik the *what*? Erik the Red, the editor told her. He did have a surname, but nobody could remember it. He had the reddest hair in captivity, hence Erik the Red. Early on, Cassie thanked him by phone and sent him fan mail. Then insisted his name go on the cartoons, and that he be part of the international syndication deals.

At no stage did she learn his surname – when his name joined her own on the cartoons, it appeared as Erik the Red, which he always claimed as a potent factor in the Norwegians buying her work. He was rarely in Dublin, so they were a couple of years in remote-control partnership before she learned that the man with the heroic Viking name was a great-headed crumpled-paper figure in a wheelchair, tiny hand constantly fidgeting with the electric control unit so that the machine was never at rest.

The first time he came to their home, the wheelchair had to be humped, backwards, up the stone steps by Polo, who at the same time did a guilty apology for not having a ramp.

'Your father was a doctor?' Erik asked, mildly, as Polo, getting the chair into the hall, relinquished it.

The red-faced embarrassment seemed set for further complication when Ben, newly walking, tottered into the hall and spotted the new arrival. 'Car!' Ben yelled, delightedly. (His first word had been car, which Polo found both funny and hurtful.) 'Car!' The child threw himself across the intervening space and climbed Erik like a ladder, settling on his withered lap and bunting him with a nappy-padded bottom.

'That movement means "go", I take it?' Erik said over Ben's head.

Cassie nodded. Erik treated Ben to a whirling, fast-forward, sudden-retreat experience culminating in a spirited wheelie, which addicted Ben to him for life. Erik claimed he needed to keep a spare battery in Stackallen because of the power Ben forced him to expend on every visit. The fact that Ben was now so heavily asleep was due to earlier races around the big Christmas tree as Erik's passenger. Cassie came down the stairs to where she could sit level with Erik, leaning against a rail of the banister.

'Who were you looking for?' Erik asked.

'Marsha.'

'She was here earlier. Wants you to do children's books. An extension of the drawings you did from Ben's point of view. Except with stories.'

'I can't do stories.'

'I can.'

'Children's stories?'

'Children's stories.'

The two of them sat in a pine-scented oasis, the warmth, music and laughter surging around them.

'The drawings usually come first . . .' Cassie said slowly.

'But how could you draw anything until you knew the story?' he finished.

She smiled at him, knowing he either had stories already written, or that they would arrive as soon as the festive season was over.

'Tell me something.' He was fiddling, fast-fingered as always, with the control of the wheelchair, but because the power was so depleted, it could respond only sluggishly, drunkenly. 'How did someone as bright as Marsha end up with a plank like Liam?' he asked.

Someone at the other end of the great hall was embarking on a solo, hindered by helpful shushings louder than the conversations they attempted to subdue.

'She loved him.'

'Oh, please. This is the sort of guy whose hangers all point the same way.'

'Sorry?'

'Rigid little bollix would always have the hooks of his hangers lined up in the wardrobe like so.' Erik hooked one of his tiny fingers in the air to illustrate. 'Doesn't do relaxation even on alcohol. Goes from prize-winning altar-boy to footless sot with no pause in the middle for hilarity. Or even fun. Or even human being. He could die over there and you'd only notice it when he began to smell.'

Polo hove to with a drink for Erik, trailed by one of the girls from the street-theatre group who wanted to be introduced. Cassie shook hands with her through the banister and left Erik with her. In the kitchen, Marsha was loading dishes into the dishwasher. Cassie came up beside her and closed the dishwasher door. 'That's for tomorrow.'

'You've got a lot of people staying over tonight,' Marsha pointed out. 'Helps to get ahead of the grot.'

'You really don't like socialising, do you?'

'It's not that, it's just that I'm the designated driver.'

'Marsha, you know bloody well we have room for the two of you to stay.'

'And have my splendid sixteen-year-old son decide that my house is "free gaff" for the night, so I'm picking up used condoms from behind couches for weeks?'

'He wouldn't.'

'He would.'

Marsha poured herself a bitter lemon and drank it thirstily, leaning up against the now busy dishwasher.

'Erik was telling me your Cunning Plan.'

Marsha's face lit up. 'Think it'll work?'

'Of course it'll work. Think you can sell it?'

'Wouldn't have suggested it if I didn't know I could sell it.'

'Well, that finishes wheat around here,' Cassie said, and laughed. 'One of Gobnait's great phrases: "That finishes wheat around here." I have no idea what it means.'

Gobnait was the local woman who came in to clean the big house. Cassie put a hand to the small of her back, easing the stiffness there while considering when she should present more food to the eighty or ninety people in the house. The tacitly agreed deal she had with Polo saw him in charge of drinks and maintaining the party dynamic, her in charge of food.

'I suppose I should go exchange witty repartee with my spouse,' Marsha said, and the two of them laughed at the idea.

'As in badinage?' Cassie suggested.

'Deffo. Nick and Nora one-liners,' Marsha said.

'One-liner, singular, I suspect, if Liam is as tranquil as he seemed to be when I noticed him last,' Cassie said.

Marsha giggled appreciatively at the 'tranquil'. 'Liam brings tranquillity to a new level,' she said.

'Beyond comatose,' Cassie offered.

'But short of fossilised.'

'No harm to anybody.'

'No good to anybody, either.'

'Which has the spin-off that he is not feeling up any of the street-theatre girls. He is faithful, even.'

Marsha raised her empty glass in an ironic toast. 'Faithful he certainly is. Of course, he's not feeling up anybody nearer home, either, but heck, you can't have it every way.'

'You could if you wanted, Marsha.'

'Please, Cass, not in the middle of Christmas. Not the leave-him-you're-your-own-woman-he's-not-good-enough-for-you-the-kid-is-old-enough speech.'

'OK.'

They smiled at each other in a conscious conspiracy of silence, the unsaid secrets hanging between them like looped decorations.

'Allowances must be made,' Cassie said.

'And after Christmas, after the leftovers, we have to go back to work, boo-hoo,' Marsha said. 'Work, which knits up the ravelled sleeve of care.'

'That's sleep.'

'Sleep does it too. But work does it better. God invented work to distract us from real life. Getting paid is just the icing on the cake.'

'The cherry in the martini.'

'Olive.'

'Olive who?'

'You don't put cherries in martinis.'

'Onions?'

'I don't know what the frig you put in a martini. But it has to be shaken, not stirred.'

'The other way around.'

'Is it?'

'Listen, who cares? How many people out there would notice, at this stage, if you put an effing *turnip* in their martini?'

'Cooked. You're right. Frig 'em. Let them eat cake. If I could *find* the effing cake.'

Marsha half opened the kitchen door. One of Polo's troop was singing, an unsure but pleasing harmony line provided by a grey-haired man whose waistcoat was decorated with a fob watch. He looked, Cassie thought, like a cartoon of an eighteenth-century Whig. Marsha let the door slide closed.

'Senior counsel and director of elections,' she announced sardonically.

'Say what?'

'The eminent Garett Connell, SC. Brilliant barrister. Card-carrying right-winger. *Éminence grise* behind the electoral prospects of Wee Winnie.'

'Who the hell is Wee Winnie?'

Marsha straightened, brought her hands up in front of

her, palms out, and began to sing in a high soprano, composed roughly 50 per cent of breath. Cassie laughed, instantly recognising the former child star from a series of TV ads a decade or two earlier. 'I'd forgotten *her*,' she said. 'What did you say about electoral prospects?'

'Ask your husband,' Marsha said. 'Word on the street is he's her handler.'

CHAPTER THIRTEEN

Coffee and Car Keys

Just as Ben neared his third birthday, Orna and Justin tried to steal Polo's business out from under him. But for Polo's indiscriminate urge to perform, he might not have caught them in time, either.

Years before, when he first set up the street-theatre company, his father had suggested it might be kind to give some business to a retired friend of Dr Cadogan, a book-keeper squeezed into early retirement by a multi-national determined to speed up its processes. Polo handed over his books to Máirtín Doran, a man whose attention to detail was matched by a complete incapacity to prioritise within those details. Máirtín was paid for one and a half days' work a week, but spent all day, every day, in the overcrowded, undersized offices, dutifully worrying as much about company expenditure on toilet rolls as he did about bad debts running to tens of thousands of pounds.

Physically unprepossessing (Polo described him as parting his hair at the hip to try to hide his baldness), he mistrusted everybody except Polo, frantically seeking urgent meetings to report the use of a courier to deliver a parcel where the postal service might have done the same job for two pounds less. Orna, who cordially loathed the book-keeper, not least because she saw him as an in-house informer, maintained the only reason Polo tolerated his visits was that Máirtín amounted to an audience of one, and once Polo had listened to the latest dire warning, the payoff was the opportunity to try out a new skit on the book-keeper, who often laughed so much at his young boss's anecdotes that his carefully trained hair fell down at the back, trailing, unknown to its owner, in a weird parody of a bridal veil for the rest of the day.

Máirtín believed Polo hardly slept at night, worrying about the problematic deviations from best practice the book-keeper brought to his attention. This, allied to Máirtín's sense of being greatly favoured over others by being Polo's chosen test-audience, developed in the book-keeper a fierce loyalty, a commitment to protect Polo even where Polo saw no need for protection.

Scrutinising routine invoices might not be part of Máirtín's job specification but it was part of his personal makeup, so one evening when Orna and Justin were already gone, but Polo was still in the office because of an early gig in the city, Máirtín quietly brought his boss over to his work station and scrolled a series of figures up in front of him. Polo's understanding of billing systems was rudimentary but functional. After a moment, he asked for some of the figures to be run again. Smirking to himself, Máirtín brought them up on the screen for a second time. Then a third time. 'Justin's discounting a series of cabaret invoices for the Higgins Hotel Group,' Polo murmured. 'Now, why would he do that?'

'There's no correspondence on file from them asking for any reduction,' Máirtín said. 'Nothing to indicate they thought they were being overcharged.'

'They weren't being overcharged,' Polo said. 'They're getting great bloody value. So, why a discount?'

'Justin didn't ask your permission to discount the bills?'

'No. He'd know I couldn't agree. Oh, yes, yes, Máirtín,

I know I signed off on these, but I didn't realise they were discounted, and I certainly never gave formal – or, indeed, informal – permission for it to happen.'

'There are two possibilities, and only two possibilities,' the book-keeper said quietly. 'One is he's getting a kick-back. The other is he's planning to set up on his own with Orna and take them as first client.'

'With Orna?'

'There is, in my opinion, an unsavoury intimacy between that pair,' Máirtín said.

Polo considered this, Justin was married, but rarely spoke of his wife with anything but thinly veiled dislike. If Orna and Justin were planning to set up a business of their own, imitating Polo's highly successful household-name theatrical mélange, then a big, recurring, profitable contract like the one with Higgins Hotels would be the perfect insurance against losing money in their set-up year.

'Can we get into their computer files?' Polo asked. 'Justin's or Orna's?'

'They would have a lot of files they'd share on the network with the rest of us,' Máirtín answered slowly. 'But they would have others more personal to them. In theory, we can't get into those files.'

'How do you mean, in theory?'

'Passwords.'

'Oh, shit, yes.'

'On the other hand, people are very predictable when it comes to passwords,' Máirtín said, punching keys on the computer as he spoke. Where Polo was sitting, a few feet away, turned out to be the best possible vantage-point. He could see a list of documents suggesting themselves, all belonging to Orna, all password pro-tected, all carrying ambiguous titles.

'People use the names of their pets, or their home phone number, or their mother's maiden name,' Máirtín said, typing in what Polo knew to be the name of Orna's cat. The protected documents immediately opened. Without comment, the book-keeper revealed them, one after another. Correspondence between Orna and a junior manager in Higgins. A recent arrival, Polo thought, who wasn't around when Polo first established a great working relationship with the Higgins managing director. The letters from Orna were subtle, but nonetheless delivered the good tidings that the new manager must be delighted to show his bosses the great deal he managed to do with Polo Cadogan's company. It must be great for his image, and he only new in the Higgins Group, to be able to demonstrate so forcefully that he could save them money.

The book-keeper silently opened the next documents, saved off e-mail transmissions. A series of love-letters between Justin and Orna. Polo figured in some of them, as Orna proffered mild guilt feelings for Justin easily to eradicate, which – as the documents scrolled up the screen – he duly did, pointing out to her that Polo had more work than he could cope with, and that the profits for the past year alone must be close to a million smackers, so Polo would hardly notice, let alone be beggared by, the removal of the Higgins Group from his client list. In fact, Justin went on, Polo was doing so well that when he lost his two best people, himself (Justin) and Orna, he would probably be *grateful* not to have to handle the Higgins cabaret contract without their expertise. If she could imagine a slightly different scenario, it was quite possible that Polo might even have set them up in a subsidiary company and handed Higgins over to them, but one way or the other, she was not to worry her little head about Polo, although the fact of her caring so much about her boss was one of the aspects of her character Justin found so admirable. Indeed, that fragile vulnerability inspired him to write a poem about her. The verses were attached.

'Can you imagine Sinead's face when I send her all this?' Polo asked, shrugging himself into his overcoat.

The book-keeper looked horrified at the prospect of Justin's extremely verbal wife ever seeing his love-letters to another woman. 'You're not going to do that?' he asked tremulously, his back hair coming down in one damp depressed scarf at the possibility.

'No, I'm not,' Polo said, checking to see he had his wallet and car keys to hand. 'But there's a lot of pleasure in imagining the possibility, isn't there?'

Looking even more scared, the book-keeper nodded.

'Máirtín, do me a favour?'

Eyes still on the screen, like a pornography addict ogling photographs of bound women, the other man nodded again, his back hair keeping in time, half a beat later than his nose.

'Print out all the passworded files on his machine and on hers. Drop them over to me on your way home – you know where I'm headed? But before you go, put a new password on *everything* on both machines. So no matter how early anybody is in tomorrow morning, they can't get into anything without the new password.'

Máirtín began to scribble on the back of a business card.

'I'm not likely to be first in,' Polo said, 'but just in case, what password are you going to put on?'

The book-keeper silently handed him the card.

Coup! it read.

The two men grinned at each other, the book-keeper promising that before Polo left the venue in which he was performing that night, the printouts would be waiting for him in an envelope at Reception.

What amazed Cassie, reading the printouts that night while Polo tried to get Ben to go to sleep, was how elated her husband was. Half laughingly aware that his own excitement about the aborted treachery within his business was exacerbating Ben's desire to stay awake, he told his son, with no conviction whatever, that Ben should really surrender to this sleep thing because nothing entertaining was going to happen when Ben was unconscious. This never worked with Ben, who lived by an unspoken creed: the minute you woke up, excitement started and lasted the whole day, whereas the minute you went to sleep, nothing ever happened. When the child resentfully succumbed, Polo put him down with such clumsy expedition that Ben woke up all over again.

Which meant that by the time Polo joined Cassie in the stone kitchen for big mugs of weak tea, she knew the documents almost off by heart.

'Is there anything as revolting as someone else's love-letters?' she pondered aloud. 'It's like that telephone conversation where Prince Charles told Camilla Thingummy he'd like to be her Tampax. I'm sure it was fantastically arousing for the two of them, it's just to outsiders it sounds so tacky. Same with these.' She waved them in the air.

Polo had no interest in the differing interpretations of other people's love-letters. His focus was on the following day, which he planned as if it was a new pageant or pantomime. He would go in very early, he told her, which would surprise the hell out of everybody, but he would say Ben woke him at dawn and he couldn't go back to sleep.

'No, you won't,' Cassie said. 'Leave Ben out of it.'

She was right, he agreed. Wouldn't sully their son's

name by *mentioning* him to the wankers. He would just be in early to ring someone in – in Brussels.

He snapped his fingers at the idea of Brussels. They were negotiating to do a series of health-education playlets for DG10, so he could legitimately be ringing Norman Morley. In fact, now he came to think of it, he probably *should* give Morley a buzz. Cassie smiled. Polo rarely let his eye come off the business ball.

He walked around the kitchen, predicting the sequential arrival of his staff. Máirtín would probably arrive early, not having slept a wink because of knowing Orna was going to get her comeuppance. The book-keeper was neutral to negative about Justin, but Orna held long-term hate status with him.

'I feel guilt by association,' Cassie said, tucking her feet under her because they were getting cold on the stone floor. 'Remember it was Orna who had the idea of me playing Little Miss Muffet?'

This he dismissed. Long before Little Miss Muffet, he, Polo, had seen Cassie with Orna, even been in a group in a pub with them, and decided she was going to be his wife. It was he who'd come up with the spurious reason for Orna to ring Cassie at short notice and beg her to get them out of a hole by playing Miss Muffet. Orna wasn't an initiative-taker.

He put the kettle on again, not noticing Cassie's reaction to this information. Instead of being relieved, she felt worse, without fully understanding why, but was distracted by his enthusiasm in laying out the drama of the following day. Máirtín would be able to get into his computer without hassle, knowing the new password, so the first person to be locked out would be Justin, who usually arrived precisely ten minutes before Orna, mainly, Polo surmised, because the two of them could not travel together from wherever they were shacked up, so one had to leave first, the other following an artificial gap in time later. ('Shacked up', Cassie thought. What a curiously old-fashioned expression. It was the sort of thing her mother would say, animadverting to the sexual amorality of her daughter's generation.)

'What will Orna do?'

'She thinks there's nothing she doesn't know about computers,' Polo said, walking around the kitchen, too preoccupied to notice the kettle reaching a full boil and safely switching itself off. 'So she'll spend at least twenty minutes trying everything.'

Giggling to himself, Polo explained to her that Justin always parked his company car directly outside the office for the first two hours of the working day, right beside Orna's. At coffee break, mid-morning, the two of them would run downstairs and swap car-park positions, to avoid clamping. Tomorrow Polo would ask Justin for a quick loan of his car to nip over to the coffee shop to get coffee and Danish for everybody – big treat, arising from the early arrival of Polo, hence his personal need for coffee and sweet stuff and his expansive wish for every-body to share in the goodies. Justin would laugh and hand over the keys, indicating that he'd be very pissed off if Polo didn't get back in time to get his favourite parking place before the rest of the nine-to-fivers arrived.

Because one of the girls in the coffee shop was a big pal of his, Polo said, he would persuade her to help him with the delivery of the coffees. She would travel the short distance back with him, the cardboard tray with its cut-out spaces all filled with tall Styrofoam cups on her lap, a bag of warm Danish between them on the front seat. She would bring a couple of black plastic rubbish bags and, while Polo made his way up the two flights of stairs to the office with the drinks and pastries, she would load all of Justin's personal belongings from the car into the black plastic bags, leave them in the lower hall of their building, and drive the car away, parking it behind the coffee shop, the last place on God's earth Justin would think to look for it, holding the keys under the counter in the shop until Polo came by later on to collect them. She would just adore the whole episode, Polo knew.

'So you arrive with the coffee and the Danish . . . ?'

'And Justin is listening to Orna on the phone to her pal Darren the computer whiz, who is taking her through a series of steps she's already gone through, but she does them just to make sure. I put coffee and sweeteners and Danish beside her, making a big thing of not interrupting whatever important task she's involved in, then suggest Justin joins me in the office to enjoy the coffees.'

'Asking Máirtín to make sure everybody else gets their fair share?'

'Oh, better than that. Better than that. Realising I've forgotten two of the coffees, he offers to collect them and picks up Orna's keys from her desk, because everybody knows he parks his car near a DART so needs to borrow someone else's wheels.'

'The heroine in the coffee shop repeats the performance, so both of their cars—'

'Both of our *company* cars,' Polo corrected severely.

'End up stashed behind the coffee shop.'

By which time, Polo established, he would have tricked Justin into admitting everything, and when Máirtín arrived back, because he *was* Máirtín, he would come to the boss's office to confirm that he had returned, was not skiving off. At that point, Justin would be released by Polo to share with Orna the little matter of the new password. Máirtín would provide both with letters of resignation, effective from the moment of signature, and stand over them until they signed. Polo would offer them black

199

plastic sacks into which to load their possessions and the book-keeper would stand over Justin and he, Polo, over Orna, just to ensure that the company's property didn't get mixed up with their personal property. That task complete, they would be told there were a few more bags containing a few more items belonging to the two of them downstairs. They would go down the stairs weighed down with fat rubbish bags, their briefcases, coats over their arms, and only then realise that they were without means of transport.

She watched him, alternately hugging himself with schoolboy aren't-I-so-evil glee and then standing, eyes narrowed, in consideration of a complication. You have been good to both of these people, she thought. They have done you a bad turn. You must remove them from your staff immediately, and of course it makes perfect sense to prevent them having access to anything which might facilitate their making off with any of your business. The steps you outline ensure an efficient, speedy removal. Because you are a showman in your every fibre, inevitably you seek to make the removal not only efficient and speedy but dramatically satisfying into the bargain. However, there is an aspect of your pleasure which is spitefully punitive. Malevolent, in its detail. And, she realised, unfolding her legs so her feet touched the cold stone again, impregnable in its decisiveness. Nothing I can say will change the plan you have laid out. If I raise questions about it, you will give me explanations that obviate, to your own satisfaction, any apparent malice on your part, while teaching them to be better people from this point on.

Polo hugged her, too high on his own intentions to attribute her silence to anything other than weariness at the end of a busy and exciting day. As she climbed the steps, she could hear him rinsing out the two mugs. Turning out lights. Whistling, tunelessly, through his teeth.

The following day played out for Polo almost exactly as planned. He telephoned her before lunch to tell her about it.

'Who's there in the office with you?' she asked.

The book-keeper, she thought, before he told her. He would want the book-keeper to get the vicarious kick of overhearing him telling the saga to his famous wife. The book-keeper would probably suggest she should do a cartoon of the whole thing.

'Hang on,' Polo told her. 'What?' A murmur in the background drew a delighted, snorting laugh from him. 'Máirtín says there's great material in this for a cartoon,' he told her. 'Have to go. Getting rid of people is very complicated, you know. There's all sorts of perks to be stopped, insurance and pensions and health insurance frozen.'

Putting down the phone, she opened her computer where the latest children's story from Erik the Red was waiting for her as an e-mail attachment. She printed it out and read it to Ben, who chortled at all the right points. Erik had a genius for portraying the normal day-to-day behaviour of parents so that a pre-schooler laughed uproariously at it and felt extremely superior. Ben made her start at the beginning and go through to the end a second time, drifting off into the early-afternoon nap that was becoming a rare event for him. She slid him gently on to the bed beside her, pulling the notebook computer on to her lap and beginning to type.

If I had the moral fibre of a slug, I'd tell Polo to stop taking such pleasure in screwing the two of them.

He'd still take pleasure in it, though.

I probably would, too. In the same situation.

No, you wouldn't.

Let's not get high-minded about me and him. He's endlessly patient and pleasant to my mother, and I'm *not* endlessly patient and pleasant to her. I'm in her company roughly three minutes before I'm ready to kill her.

It's all about compromises. Marriages that survive are filled with compromises made by people who swore before they got married they'd never compromise.

Shallow-profundities time, is it?

Who swore, particularly, they'd never repeat the compromises their parents made. Like refusing to see anything but the positive in their partner.

It's not the same.

But it's abundantly similar. Still, it's been tried and tested. Whatever works.

Whatever works to *what*?

Whatever works to keep you away from the black hole in the middle of everything.

Polo is a good father.

Liam is a good provider.

There is no similarity between the two.

Marsha says you don't love him.

Outsiders always have a skewed view of the relationships they observe.

You build them up, praise him, flatter. So it's easy to miss you never say you love him.

I sign messages to him 'Love, Cass'.

Not the same thing.

I just try to be honest.

The last refuse of the self-serving.

I think you mean 'the last refuge . . .'

True. But it's an interesting, even Freudian misprint, don't you think?

Look. This is a happy marriage. He's happy. Ben's happy. I'm happy.

You are?

I genuinely am. Mostly because of Ben. Ben's just the most surprisingly wonderful turn-up for the books.

Children are children for a very short time.

Oh, spare me the obvious.

Children aren't created to paper over the cracks in parental relationships.

You know something, you're an awful pompous computer.

Question is, am I an awful secure computer?

Jesus.

Precisely.

Jesusjesusjesusjesus.

Think.

He wouldn't.

Think it out.

Polo would never read something on my computer.

Never?

Why should he?

If you're saying, 'Polo would never read something on my

computer', that's one thing. If you're saying, 'Why would he?' that's quite a different thing. Like you think he would read documents on your computer if he had a good enough reason to.

But –

– a good enough reason as he saw it. Not as you saw it.

I – – – – – –

You can fill a whole line or a whole page with dashes. But what are you thinking?

I'm thinking I shouldn't have started this.

This what?

This goddamn dialogue with a fecking hard disk.

And you do know nothing ever really gets wiped off a hard disk. Remember the Menendez brothers – the ones who did in their parents?

An expert was able to retrieve documents they deleted, thought were gone for ever.

Indeed.

Polo's not a computer expert.

Polo is constantly underestimated by you. From the moment he saw you, Polo has been out ahead of you, gathering and using information in a way that – that—

Terrifies the living bejasus out of me, if you must know.

Except he has never ever used being out ahead of you, out-thinking you, except to be good to you.

He used it to pursue me.

You were flattered.

Up to a point.

Up to a point called marriage.

But that's sort of 'the end justifies the means'.

Meaning?

I have to assume Polo – although he has the – the cast of mind, the methodology, to manipulate and control my life . . .

. . . ?

I have to assume he'll never use it badly. To my detriment.

You have to assume – no, you have to *guarantee* that you will not give him cause to use it to your detriment.

That's not difficult. I signed on for marriage. I'm not going to start flashing at the postman or bonking somebody at our next party.

Postperson.

I'm not going to do any gender non-specific flashing.

You miss the point.

I do?

If you assume Polo has the methodology and the mindset to manipulate and control you, but won't use it in a malign way unless you give him cause, it doesn't matter that *you* are satisfied you haven't given him cause or won't give him cause. If *he* decides he has cause, that's the trip switch. Not in your jurisdiction, kiddo.

I could do something without knowing—

You mightn't even have to do something. If he perceived you to be endangered in some way. Morally . . .

Oh, this is too ridiculous for words.

Amazing how edgy the word 'moral' makes you.

Inquisition. Ducking-chairs. Not really what I anticipate from a generous, successful, funny man who worships the ground I walk on.

As the witches said about the men standing around the bonfires.

Ah, crap.

Maybe. Interesting, though, that you're still knotted up about the possibility of him reading this document.

Well, of course I am. It would be very hurtful to him.

Now you're being completely dishonest. Now you're inputting smarm on the off-chance he actually *does* read it.

Oh, Jesus.

Because you know he would. Even if there were no bad outcome, the need for a special password to guard against the possibility rattles your fillings. Just a bit.

Ben's beginning to stir.

He's not alone.

Give over the predictable comebacks.

You know why I won't give over the predictable comeback lines?

No, but I'm sure you're gonna tell me.

I won't stop them, because you're typing them in. And you're typing them in because you think if you keep tip-tip-tippying there, something you tip-tip-tippy in will make you laugh or make it all right, or take the shadow away or disguise the black blackblackhole in the middle. It won't.

I know. And yet, I am happy. That beautiful boy is going to turn over towards me in a minute, his eyes are going to open, he's going to smile at me as if I was the best thing in the world. I am very happy. I'm not under constant threat. Correction, I'm not under immediate or proximate threat. I need to focus on the best sides of the man I married, I need to get on with a very satisfying career—

And you need to think up an awful good password.

That's true.

Lemme tell you what wouldn't be good. Anything to do with Ben. ANYTHING. Not your maiden name. Not the name of Orna's cat. Not the name of your best friend in school. Not the name of your former boyfriend. Not your old address. Nor your address in Manhattan. Nothing to do with Miss Muffet.

OK, OK. I really have to finish this – because Ben is really waking up.

Don't postpone it.

The password?

As in: think up a killer phrase that Polo would never as long as he lives work out.

OK, OK. Look.

Yeah?

I think I know how to do it.

So I'll hear from you later? When you password all this stuff? When you definitely *don't* password the stuff you'd never mind him reading?

Right.

Right.

What struck Cassie as the perfect method was based on something she knew Polo occasionally did, and was rather ashamed of doing. It was heretical, he once told her, laughing in a shamefaced way. But when he was having a major doubt about some planned course of action, then, in spite of his religious orthodoxy, he would take the big old gold-leaf family Bible in his father's library, would stand, eyes closed, and break open the great tome at random, taking whatever advice was thus presented to him, whether it was a psalm, a parable or a single sentence.

After Ben was in bed for the night, before Polo came

home, she took the Cadogan family Bible, broke it open, smiled at the sentence at the top of the left-hand page, and was careful, when she closed it again, not to put any of the satiny, snake-tongued place markers at the point selected. She would have no problem remembering the password she painstakingly applied to a number of documents on her computer.

CHAPTER FOURTEEN

Geese and Aeroplanes

Gobnait came in three times a week. Always had, even before Cassie's arrival. In fact, she once confided to Cassie, the easiest year for her was the year Father Thornton was in what was now the baby's room.

'I not a baby,' Ben said, stumping up to Gobnait, tummy and lower lip advanced.

'Sure, you're a prize-fighter,' Gobnait said, as if it was obvious.

Ben thought about whether or not this was a better option than babyhood and went to get advice from his mother. 'Are I a prize-fighter?'

'More a champion swimmer.'

He nodded. He knew he was cool in the pool, the only one of his playgroup who didn't need armbands. 'I'n a champing swimmer,' he corrected Gobnait, who snapped her fingers at her own mistake. 'You thought I was a baby,' he told her, scandalised.

She smacked the palm of her hand off her forehead. 'I need my head examined, so I do.'

'She needs her head esamined,' Ben told his father later.

Polo looked surprised. Cassie explained. 'Gobnait says Peter Thornton was the dream lodger,' she went on. 'From her point of view. Never threw anything on the floor, never left food around, washed his own clothes.'

Ben began to run one of his little cars up and down his father's thigh. Polo took it from him to admire it.

Realising there was something stuck in it, he attempted to poke the obstruction free with his finger. 'Lump of Plasticine got in here,' he said.

Ben roared at him, incoherent with rage at the damage his father's probing finger was doing. He snatched the little vehicle back and began to prod and pat the dirty blue lump of modelling clay occupying most of the front seat, burbling protest and rage. Polo did a hands out by the shoulders what-did-I-do-wrong gesture at Cassie. She put her index finger first over her mouth, then pointed it at Ben. Ssh. Watch him. Listen to him. Although Ben and his father adored each other, their time together a constant maelstrom of messing, rolling around, trick-playing and laughter, Cassie felt Polo missed the marvel of Ben's own observations, activities and constantly building skills.

Satisfied, now, that the Plasticine was back the way it should be, the way it was before his father interfered with it, Ben brought the car back, turning it sideways to give his father a better view. 'D'you *see*?' the little boy asked, sternly.

'I do,' Polo said obediently.

'Wrong answer,' Cassie hissed.

'*What* do you see?' Ben asked his father.

Polo closed his eyes, trying not to laugh at being caught out. 'You tell me,' he said cautiously to Ben. 'It's your car.'

'Gubney's mamma!' Ben said triumphantly.

Polo started to nod, then backed off pretending to see, in the lump of Plasticine, a passenger he very definitely didn't see. Being caught out twice in a row would not be a good thing. Cassie murmured helpfully that Gubney was Ben's version of Gobnait.

'And this is Gobnait's mamma?' Polo asked, slowly, looking at the shapeless blob filling the passenger side of the little car right up to the roof. Ben nodded.

'*Bad* mamma,' he said.

'Yeah, she's not the most shapely,' Polo agreed.

'Sexist,' Cassie muttered.

'*Bad* mamma sending babies,' Ben said, throwing car and Plasticine passenger on the floor.

'Apparently she was overheard to say it was about time I got pregnant again,' Cassie hissed. 'Ben took this amiss. Wouldn't want showers of siblings.'

Gobnait put her head in the door. 'Nessan's picking me up in a few minutes,' she said. 'Anything you want to add to the rugs that I'm taking to the dry-cleaner's?'

'No,' Cassie said. 'I was just telling Polo here that you think we're extremely mucky compared to his old friend Peter Thornton.'

'On the other hand,' Polo said, 'you didn't get much skit out of Peter. More laughs out of us.'

Gobnait agreed that Father Thornton – not that he was still Father Thornton when he was staying in the Stackallen house, but old habits die hard – was very quiet and serious. Although sometimes, around this house, you'd be glad of a bit of quiet and serious. 'Just before he went off to live in Dublin, though, I thought he was showing a bit of life,' Gobnait said, going over to the window to watch out for her husband's car. 'I remember telling him I was praying for a girl this time around and asking him did he think God answered prayers like that. "Don't ask me, Gobnait," he said. "I no longer believe in God." And I said, "Course you don't. How could you stand the competition?" The minute I had it said I was afraid he'd go thundery on me, but he roared laughing – there's Nessan. 'Bye. Gimme a kiss, Ben. 'Bye.'

Nessan's truck pulled up on the gravel outside.

'Gubney's mamma,' Ben said.

'Don't point, Ben, it's rude,' Cassie said.

Polo went over to the window, dropping on his

211

hunkers behind his son, his knees forking out on either side of the little boy, who automatically leaned back into him, the child's blond hair and his father's browner curls gilded by an evening sun now throwing a long oblong across the parquet floor behind them, echoing, in light and shadow, the tall window with their intermingled shapes at the bottom of it.

Cassie moved quietly to the bureau to slide out the Olympus. She was good at capturing the little tableaux of informal family life. Polo, who associated photograph-taking with receptions, announcements, weddings and graduations, never thought of the camera except on official occasions. He did have, however, a genius for holding the naturalness of the moments Cassie picked to photograph. As she clicked the battery switch to On and sorted the depth of field on the camera, he talked softly, half to his son, half to her.

'Ben, that's Gobnait's mother, is it?'

'In a *car*,' Ben emphasised. 'The *whole* car.'

'She looks *exactly* like the way you had her in your car,' Polo said.

'I told you,' Ben said, a little fight left in his voice, although his father's admission mollified him.

Once she had her pictures taken, Cassie came up behind them to wave to Gobnait. The delay was caused by Gobnait loading bags for the dry-cleaner's into the back of the truck. As the gears ground into place for departure, Gobnait's mother raised a hand in a wave so royal she could have gone into competition with the Queen Mother. Trying not to laugh at this, her first sighting of Gobnait's mother, Cassie put away the camera.

'Belongs in *The Guinness Book of Records*, for starters,' Polo said, out of the side of his mouth. They were good at Parent Code, that oblique patois mothers and fathers use to share information but prevent kids from announcing the information to third parties who would experience the announcement as a personal insult.

'The maternal figure recently seen?' Cassie asked.

'The maternal figure contained, with some difficulty, in a vehicular device,' Polo confirmed. 'We're either talking obesity at a level making Pavarotti look like an anorectic wimp. Or we're talking that African disease . . .'

'Elephantiasis?'

'The very thing.'

'Gubney's mamma is a heffalump,' Ben said, with an air of summing it all up.

Polo opened his mouth to contradict, to warn, then noticed his wife, laughing but shaking her head at him. 'What gets forbidden becomes twice as interesting,' she said, trying to sound casual so Ben wouldn't want elucidation. 'If you show outrage, you can bet your ass the phrase will be repeated in precisely the context and to precisely the person most calculated to make you wish you could emigrate instantaneously.'

'You have to admit, though, the sculptural rendition of the subject does have artistic merit,' Polo said, picking up the car to show Cassie the Plasticine bulging out of the door and up to the ceiling. It was almost obscenely funny in its freehanded accuracy.

'He's his mother's son,' Cassie said. 'Thinks visual. I've been trying out the proofs of the children's book on him. He knew instantly what the drawings meant, even though they're not like anything you'd expect in a – in a—'

'In a normal children's book?'

'Well, you know what I mean.'

'Yeah, you mean a children's book written by a normal author, not a supercrip, and illustrated by someone who could draw Thomas the Tank Engine, not a bunch of adults with tiny heads up at the top of bodies like cliffs.'

'I really *hate* Thomas the Tank Engine,' Cassie said.

'Not as bad as I hate buggering Barney,' Polo said.

He said it with such passion that it was fairly predictable that this would become Ben's pet phrase for the following ten days. Asked what he'd like to eat, during that time, Ben said, 'Buggewing Barney.' Asked who his best friend was, Ben would give the same answer. He even used the answer when a lady in the garage shop asked him what he wanted to be when he grew up.

'She had a hearing aid, though,' Cassie told her mother. 'So when she looked puzzled, I made up an answer that satisfied her. Of course, Ben was all for contradicting me, but I carried him out of that shop so fast . . .'

'Did he get upset?'

'He screamed the bloody car down,' Cassie said. 'Which isn't like him.'

'He's got something wrong with him,' her mother said, looking at the little boy wandering without apparent purpose around her back garden. Cassie's mother had an ordered, even military approach to gardening. Every plant grew in its own row, its own circle or its own square, with roundy pebbles rather than grassy patches in between. Mrs Browne further favoured stand-up stalky flowers like tulips and lilies. Her garden stood to attention. Ready to take a salute. She was the general, pulling on gauntleted gloves before moving through the ranks, a weeding tool under her arm like a marshal's baton.

As a child, Cassie imagined the tulips sagging slightly in relief when her mother stowed away gloves and tools at the end of her tour of duty. 'Did you see what she found around my ankles?' one would say to another. 'A dandelion. Scarlet, I was.' The tulips always seemed to have their big green leaves at the ready to conceal some mortification, until at a certain point – the point, Cassie believed, when her mother had inspected them to such an extent that they'd lost all hope of ever being promoted to corporal – they would let go, their leaves hanging down in 'Shit, what do I care?' mode. It was only at that point that Cassie identified with any tulip.

'I can tell he's off-colour,' her mother said.

Cassie glanced up at the broad-based wooden clock on the mantelpiece, to check how long she'd been with her mother. Polo's theory was that their relationship could withstand six minutes forty-five seconds of each other's company. He maintained he did studies of the two of them, using a stop-watch.

'Probably whooping-cough,' her mother said. 'I told you he should be vaccinated.'

'Polo didn't want him vaccinated. He says there's conditions running in his family that amount to contra-indications.'

Polo has theories, her mother's expression said. He's a lovely boy, so you have to let him off with a lot, but when it comes to medical matters, a mother should take responsibility, not be listening to theories from a nice, badly informed husband. Ben came in from the garden with a caterpillar on his hand. The caterpillar seemed a bit off-colour, too, Cassie thought. If Ben gave him a poke with his finger, he would undulate a bit, but most of the time he lay dormant, occasionally lifting his head to survey Mrs Browne's dining room without enthusiasm.

'I think he'd prefer to be out in the sunshine,' Cassie said.

'He's a girl,' Ben said.

'Oh?'

Ben gave the caterpillar such a determined poke that the little creature telescoped and unwound extra fast to get away from his finger.

'He grows into a butterfly,' Ben said, going out to

deposit the caterpillar on a broad leaf. Being a butterfly was a girl thing, therefore any caterpillar with that career plan had to be female.

'Look at him coughing,' Mrs Browne said.

Sure enough, Ben's shoulders were being shaken by coughs. As they watched, he threw up. The two women made a run for the garden, Cassie to tend to Ben, Mrs Browne to get a hose to sluice away the evidence of his visit.

'I *told* you it was whooping-cough,' Mrs Browne said, winding the green hose back on to its hook, much to Ben's dismay. Never having seen the hose in action before, he wanted a go, but in Mrs Browne's scheme of things, a hose was a gardening tool, Not A Toy. There go the capital letters again, Cassie thought, strapping her crying son into the child's seat, where he turned his face to the window on his own side to avoid eye-contact with his grandmother.

'Don't worry about it, Ma,' Cassie said over her shoulder. (*As if you would.*) 'He shakes off infections very quickly.' (*Not to mention grandmothers. Jesus, Ben, don't sulk at her quite so obviously.*) 'And the sunshine in Portugal next week will do him the world of good.' (*Ma, so help me, if you say, 'Sunshine is no substitute for Proper Vaccination', I'll drive over you, so I will.*)

'Sunshine is not a substitute for proper vaccination,' Mrs Browne observed, on her way back up the path to her front door. (*Good move, Ma. I'd have to take out one of your pillars to drive over you.*)

'Didunt give me a goodbye kiss,' Ben said.

'Get off,' Cassie said. 'You didn't want a goodbye kiss.'

'Didunt even *try*,' he said.

'That's true,' said Cassie, letting down the roof.

Usually this manoeuvre enthralled Ben, who followed its every stage, almost applauding when the boot of the

Merc swallowed up the folded roof and clicked itself closed over it. Today, he ignored it. 'Grannies are s'pose to give goodbye kisses,' Ben went on.

Cassie got the car moving, wondering if a declarative style of conversation based largely on There-Should-Be-a-Law statements was a genetic inheritance. Ben didn't see enough of his grandmother to imitate her so maybe it was passed along in the genes.

'They're *S'POSE TO*,' Ben yelled, over the wind noise as the car moved on to the northern road.

'You want to sue her?' Cassie yelled back.

'What's sue?'

'Take her to court and get a judge to put her in prison.'

Cassie tweaked the position of the rear-view mirror so that it allowed her to see her son, rather than the road behind her. Ben was nodding in beatific delight. Cassie did a thumbs-up to him and pushed the rear-view mirror back into its proper position, knowing the slow pace of the answering smile meant he would be asleep within minutes, the feverishness cooled by the breezes whipping within the car with its roof down. Wanting to sue his granny this early might be an indicator that he had inherited her litigious ways, Cassie thought. On the other hand, Ben only wanted Mrs Browne put in prison. He hadn't been looking for compensation.

Three days later, when the three of them set off for a villa in Portugal lent to Polo by one of his barrister friends, Ben had got over the bad-tempered feverish stage of whooping-cough and was back in his customary high good humour. At the check-in desk, he engaged in a spirited negotiation with several uniformed staff, to persuade them that his comfort and safety on the flight would be best assured if he was allowed to sit in one of the great plastic bath-shaped containers used to hold oddly shaped pieces of luggage such as baby-seats and pushchairs. In the duty-free, while Polo and Cassie tried to remember Mrs Browne's favourite perfume, he filled their temporarily abandoned wire basket with the most expensive champagne available, until a young male traveller nudged Polo and said he 'wouldn't mind attending any party catered by that kid'. In the departure lounge, he riveted a group of pensioners by telling them, in surprisingly accurate detail, what happens inside a jet engine when it ingests a goose or a swan. 'It's mostly gooses, though,' he concluded consolingly, to one worried-looking woman. 'Swans don't fly as high up as gooses.'

The woman's anxieties seemed relatively unassuaged by this offering, and Polo had to distract Ben to prevent him offering further unhelpful detail. This he achieved by telling Ben about the time Gobnait, as a little girl, met her father's goose when this goose had small goslings to which Gobnait, in the opinion of the goose, posed a threat. The goose advanced on Gobnait, hissing, its wings out at full sail, and Gobnait (who even then was decisive, Polo indicated in an aside to Cassie) grabbed the goose, one-handed, around the neck. Carrying Ben down the air-bridge, Polo grasped an imaginary gooseneck with his free hand, keeping his arm straight. Ben mirrored the action.

'Goose couldunt bite her,' he said, nodding at Gobnait's historic wisdom.

'Aren't you smart? No, the goose couldn't bite her. Then her daddy came home and scared the goose away so it was all grand. Now, here's our row. In you go,' Polo said, decanting his son on to a seat.

'That story ended kind of suddenly,' Cassie said, sideways, to Polo, shoving bags into the overhead locker.

'Yeah, well, I couldn't tell Ben her father didn't come home for three hours so the poor kid was left strangling a goose for all that time.'

'Wouldn't say it did the goose any favours, either.'

'Being shamed like that in front of all its kids.'

'Probably flew twice as high to get away from Gobnait and got ingested by a passing jet.'

'Oh, Jesus, give over with the jet ingestion, we don't want him going to find that poor terrified pensioner to frighten her with more details. How does he know that stuff, anyway?'

'Open-door information policy.'

Ben was riveted by the aeroplane's safety video, putting his hand on the thigh of a complete stranger to his right in order to lean over and verify the voiceover statement about floor-lighting showing the way to the exits. The passenger whose thigh was thus employed was slightly startled by the sudden pressure, having wrapped himself in blankets and tucked his neck into an inflated U-shaped pillow for immediate sleep.

'Did your car crash and go in bits?' Ben asked him.

The man blinked, mystified. Over Ben's head, Cassie gestured at the man's neck pillow. 'Ben thinks it's a neck brace for whiplash,' she explained. *Thanks, Ma.*

'Oh,' said the man. 'No,' he explained to Ben.

'Well what went in bits?' Ben asked.

'Nothing,' the man said, looking irritated at the inefficacy of his monosyllables.

'Well, why is your neck held up, then?'

Cassie embarked on an explanation of inflatable pillows, unintentionally making them so interesting that Ben began to campaign for one. Polo came to the rescue by announcing he was fed up with nobody to talk to and Ben was to go in the middle between his mother and father and keep the two of them entertained, not just be talking to his mother. The passenger to Ben's right opened one eye to watch his removal, greeting his replacement, Cassie, with a relieved look. He seemed to think it unlikely that she would put her hand on his thigh in order to see aisle floor-lighting.

When a bout of coughing struck Ben, he was standing on his father's thighs, holding on to the back of the seat in front of him, holding forth about Gobnait and the goose. The coughing was so sustained and spectacular that the man on Cassie's right woke up and fixed Ben's convulsed little back with a look of pure, unconcealed hatred. At the same moment, the man in the seat Ben was holding on to straightened up – also out of sleep – but wasted no time directing any looks, approving or dis-approving, at the cougher. Instead, the passenger vacated his seat with surprising grace for a big man in his late fifties. The seat was hardly empty when Ben threw up into it.

Stewards and stewardesses descended in force on the area with cleaners, sprayers and – unless Cassie imagined it – a bucket of sand. The passenger who had vacated his seat with such good timing was offered a seat across the aisle and accepted it.

'You do know, of course,' he said, leaning into their row and speaking quietly, 'it's illegal to take a child suffer-ing from a communicable disease on to an aeroplane?'

Dumbstruck, Cassie stared at him, conscious of the passenger beside her stirring with new interest. Maybe he could sue this kid. Polo thumped the speaker on the upper arm. 'Arthur Staunton,' he said, apparently delighted that Ben had chosen a friend to throw up on. 'Jasus, howya?'

The big grey-haired man in the expensive casuals greeted Polo with equal warmth. 'Of course, you're going to Quinta da Lago also,' he said, extending a beautifully manicured right hand to Cassie. 'Mrs Cadogan? How do you do?'

Cassie nodded. Ben had been transferred into her lap

by Polo as he stood up to talk to the Staunton man, and her son was now demanding an explanation of why most coughs didn't make you throw up but this current cough did.

'Ask this man,' Polo said to Ben. 'Ireland's most eminent surgeon.'

Staunton did a 'Please, no applause' grimace at Polo, then sat down in Polo's seat and explained whooping-cough thoroughly and civilly to Ben, who listened, wide-eyed. When the explanation was finished, Staunton, like a man concluding rounds with students, started to rise. Ben caught him by the front of his sweater. 'Whassa surgeon?' Cassie disengaged Ben's hands from the big man's glazed cotton sweater and tried to pat out the wrinkles he had made in it.

'A surgeon is a doctor who opens people up to fix what's inside them.'

'Opens them up how?'

'With a very sharp knife.'

'You're bad to be a surgeon,' Ben said, horrified.

'It doesn't hurt them,' Staunton said. 'I magic them asleep first.'

'How d'you magic them?'

'Anaesthesia.'

'He magics them asleep with Annie's—'

'Thesia,' Cassie and Polo finished. In chorus.

'And then I go in and find out what's wrong with them.'

'All the way in?'

'Yes, I – oh, hang on,' the surgeon said, carefully. 'I don't put my entire body in their insides. I just put my hands in.'

Ben looked greatly disappointed by this, and for some reason, his disappointment vexed the surgeon. Or so he let on. 'How could I go inside you if you were sick?'

Staunton asked, somewhat querulously. 'You're too small. If I put myself inside you, I'd burst you.'

'You'd burst me,' Ben agreed, giggling. 'You'd burst me up in bits.'

The man next to Cassie got up in a marked manner and disappeared down the aisle.

'So if you were really, *really* sick, not just with whooping-cough,' the surgeon said, lowering his voice ostentatiously at the diagnostic phrase, as if to protect Cassie from being exposed to the rigours of aviation law, 'I'd magic you asleep, then I'd open you up and find what was wrong with you.'

'Germs,' Ben said.

'Sometimes. Or one of your bones might be broken.'

'You'd take it out and throw it away,' Ben said, demonstrating with a sweep of his arm that connected, at its widest point, with the face of the passenger beside Cassie, who had just arrived back. The passenger clutched his nose, beginning to make a fuss, reducing the scale of the fuss as he remembered that the man talking to his assailant was a surgeon who might offer to do an examination, which might hurt more than the initial blow. Cassie apologised profusely and made Ben do likewise.

'No, if one of your bones was broken, I might pin it together and then close you up again.'

The surgeon made another attempt to stand up, but Ben, sure at this point that he was great value and loath to let him go, clutched at his jumper again. 'Why have you a caterpillar on your front?'

'It's not a caterpillar, it's a crocodile.'

'Why's it not a caterpillar? It's green,' Ben told him.

'It's a crocodile because it has a big mouth with big teeth, see? Caterpillars only eat lettuce and flowers. Crocodiles eat people.'

'Why have you one on your front, then?'

The surgeon straightened to laugh. Also to rub the small of his back. 'You want to explain to your son the phenomenon of fools like me paying a fortune to serve as walking advertisements for brands like LaCoste?' he said to Polo. Cassie began to draw a big crocodile for Ben, who quickly became absorbed in it, advising on the length of teeth required to chew up people so the crocodile wouldn't get hiccups when he swallowed them. The passenger in the outside seat disappeared again.

'He *always* getting up and down,' Ben said, with deep disapproval. 'No respeck for others.'

Recognising one of her mother's permanent plaints, Cassie lowered her forehead into the warm space between Ben's shoulder-blades, laughing into his back. Shaking her head, when she surfaced, at Polo: too complicated to explain, this minute. Later, maybe, when there isn't engine noise to contend with. Polo and the surgeon stood for quite a while in the aisle facing into the middle row of seats, the surgeon flexing his legs before cramping his circulation by sitting down again. By the time Polo slid into the outside seat again, their imminent arrival at the Portuguese airport was being announced, and Ben was sweetly asleep, in the seat between his parents. Tranced by engine noise, Cassie thought. It was ever thus. Washing-machines, flying-machines, driving-machines. No wonder his first word was 'car'. As the landing-wheels bit, both parents instinctively flat-handed Ben against the sudden jolt, smiling at each other over his head.

Within minutes of disembarkation, the child was not only awake but back to asking questions. Were they there yet? Nearly there; they just had to hire a car first. Hire it where? Over at that counter, see where Daddy is? But hire it where? Cassie looked down at him and realised he thought she meant 'higher'. No, she explained, hire can also mean to borrow for a while. Pay money and borrow for a while. Give back the car at the end of the holiday. Oh, Ben said, was her car hired at home? No, it was waiting in the garage for when the holiday was over. Ben wanted to know *why* her car wasn't hired to someone else. One of the men greeting Polo as an old friend laughed as he overheard this. 'Good businessman in the making, there, Polo. Never mind house swaps, he wants to do car swaps. Get Mammy's car to make money while she's in Portugal.'

Polo introduced the man and four or five others, all clothed in the casual arrogance of good education, career success and temporarily abandoned happy families. They wandered around the passport-checking area rehearsing golf swings and threatening to beggar each other at poker.

Ben wanted to know precisely where Portugal was, relative to Meath. Meath he knew. He didn't want to be bothered with Ireland, so when Polo started the geography lesson by putting Meath in its wider national context, Ben lost interest.

'Asks you for a drink of water, you give him Niagara Falls,' Cassie teased. 'Look at him. Filled with lassitude.'

'Not to mention longitude, courtesy of his father,' Polo agreed.

In the car, they watched the scenery in silence for a while, Cassie figuring that there was perhaps another ten minutes in the journey and trying to imagine herself back to Ben's age, when everything was shapeless in time terms, every question about duration answered unsatisfactorily by adults who said things like 'Soon, now,' or 'I'm not answering that question every five minutes, you know.'

'We should look around while we're here at property,' Polo said, pulling the hire car up in front of a three-storey villa.

'Why?'

'Long-term investment. Nice place for later.'

'Later than what?'

'Oh, you know,' Polo said, not letting go of his son's hand even though Ben wanted to be free to go faster than his father could, given that his father was also carrying a suitcase. (The suitcase had wheels, but any time Cassie pointed them out to Polo it seemed to affront his manhood: real men don't wheel suitcases.)

She thought about long-term investment. The future, for Polo, stretched ahead like a long, straight country road. He apprehended his life in phases. His company had a tryout phase, then – around the time she met him – it settled, consolidated, developed a set of specialist units. Now it was delivering profits and was managed to a great extent by the heads of those units, so he was in a personal tryout phase, free to experiment. He talked occasionally of being the first man ever to float a theatrical group of companies on the stock exchange. Or maybe sell it off to a private investor a few years down the line. Do something different. Or take early retirement, spending the winter months in a warm climate, in a villa bought earlier for investment.

She sat back on her heels, the case empty in front of her, the sound of Ben's conversation with his father coming in through the open window. Maybe, she thought, this sense of continuum was a function of him belonging to a family based in the one house for more than a century, whereas she had no idea where either set of her great-grandparents had lived. Somewhere in the West, she thought. Maybe.

It might be comfortable to have an understanding of the future as a series of links you could plan for and envisage, instead of having the future hijack and ambush you unforeseen, as it seemed to do to her all the time.

Curious, she thought, that someone so visual as herself could not imagine Ben at ten or fourteen or twenty. When she tried, it was like trying to imagine him a year before he was born: the future impenetrable as the past, as if neither existed or could exist.

'We have our own nobody else swimming-pool just to our own selves for a swim this minute,' Ben hollered, coming at her with such enthusiasm he upended the two of them into the open suitcase.

'I think I'll close this and travel home,' Polo said, making as if to shut the two of them into it.

'We wouldunt fit,' Ben said, with the airy confidence he had very recently developed about his father's more obvious joking threats. Six weeks earlier, he would have panicked at the notion of becoming human luggage.

Sitting in the suitcase, Cassie started to undress him, his little togs beside her at the ready. Polo always flung his clothes off himself with such vehemence they wore out twice as fast as was normal, leaving them in fabric worm-casts around their bedroom floor. In his Y-fronts, he now opened and closed drawers until he found his own swimsuit.

'You going to join us?'

Cassie shook her head, saying she wanted to explore the villa, come to terms with the kitchen. As she wandered the marble vastness of the place, she could hear the two of them cavorting in the pool. The luxury of it, she thought: not to share a pool with other families, where you constantly felt obligated to ask your own child to 'keep it down', 'stop splashing' and not 'run on the wet tiles'. Or where someone else's child became an obnoxious focus of attention because his parents or her parents did *not* insist that the child keep it down, stop splashing and not run on the wet tiles.

The day after they arrived, Polo brought most of the

brigade of 'golfing buddies' together for drinks around their pool. Ben pounced on Arthur Staunton, validated the details he recalled from Arthur's surgical briefing on the plane, then more or less demanded the next instalment. Using a beach ball, the surgeon explained collapsed lungs, Ben climbing off his lap with some difficulty at the end (the surgeon was in shorts, Ben in a swimsuit so their skin adhered in the warmth) to pass on the new information to Cassie.

'My grandchildren don't flatter me with their attention half as much as your beautiful son does,' Staunton commented.

The men arrived in groups of two and three from different villas within the campus, discussing whether or not they would themselves purchase property in a place like Quinta da Lago. The consensus seemed to be that being so close to other Irish people made little sense. It would, one of the barristers opined, be remarkably akin to the old British raj: expatriates *in* a country, but never of it, never learning it because they travelled in the cultural equivalent of a sterile bubble.

Listening to them from a slight distance (half reclining on a poolside couch with Ben asleep, his head on her hip) she noted their lack of irony. These men talked of their wives, their children, and in some cases their grandchildren, with uncomplicated affection and pride. Theirs was a lambent, not lacerating, wit.

'*La crème de la crème,*' a voice said behind her, summing up her own thoughts.

It took her a moment, as he sat down on the next couch, to recognise Peter Thornton, and before she thought about it, she indicated her surprise at his presence.

'Your husband is convinced that if he watches a good golf swing long enough, he'll get one himself, so he brought me out as a walking object lesson.'

227

'You're a good golfer?'

'Anything athletic, I'm good at.'

No woman would ever say that, she thought. There would be a modifier included. *I'm fairly good at.* Or the praise would be attributed to someone else. *Some people say . . .* On the cusp of speculating aloud why it is that a man boasts openly and comfortably, a woman covertly and guiltily, she remembered this man's argumentativeness and left it alone.

'You, on the other hand, refuse to consider learning golf,' he said, watching the light flickering eye-shocking reflections off the slightly choppy pool water. She smiled, nodding. 'Because to be a female golfer would typecast you. Make you just one among equals.'

Partly true, she admitted. But there was a missing component. Each of the men clustered around the pool had mastered a speciality combining the intellectual and the physical. Peripheral to the expression of their expertise were factors that might influence the outcome. A jury might respond irrationally. An ambient virus might infect a recovering patient. But those factors carried no negative implication for the bewigged man arguing or the green-masked man operating. Each would be paid enormous sums, each would be adjudged to have done a superb job. Until age or illness clawed holes in their competence, they would be in control. For them, she surmised, the appeal of golf lay in its unpredictability. The tighter you grasped it, the less you were in control, like Ben when he swore that this time the wet soap would not escape him. That was the occasion his squeezing hand would propel the slimy bar completely out of reach.

'Take your youngfla for a walk when he wakes up?' Thornton asked.

It took her a moment to work out that he meant 'young fellow'. She nodded, knowing Polo often brought Ben with him when he dropped in to Thornton's Dublin apartment. Ben seemed to like him. As they sat in silence, Polo detached himself from the group in response to noise from his mobile phone.

'Wee Winnie, no doubt,' Thornton murmured. ' "Oh, Polo, they've asked me such a difficult question, tell me what to say, they've asked me what day it is".'

'Who'd be asking her difficult questions?'

'Journalists. She's running in the general election.'

'Is there a general election?'

Thornton laughed and nodded. 'You'd better learn how to draw her now, because,' he nodded at the men around the pool, 'if they've got anything to say about it, she'll be a power in the land before long.'

'Why the hell would they want to push a half-wit who's already had her fifteen minutes as a child-star in a bloody yogurt ad?'

'Because they all want to call a halt to . . . directions Ireland has been taking, and she might be the catalyst that'll do it,' Thornton said. 'She's not a half-wit either. Anyone who can get *that* amount of intellectual fire-power behind her, free, gratis and for nothing, ain't a half-wit. Listen to the discussion.'

'Why?'

'Give you your daily dose of rage,' he said, wandering away.

She would not listen, she thought crossly, and would be far too busy with Ben for eavesdropping, anyway. He now knew how to dive to the bottom of the pool, and spent the next half-hour retrieving shiny pink copper pennies from its surface, bringing them back to her for her to toss high in the air, the coins spilling, splaying into sparkling separation, tiny smacks on the surface followed by slower, random sinking, avidly watched by the little boy planning the order of his attack. To get one coin on the smooth tiled bottom of the pool seemed to Cassie worth celebration. To get two in one dive was the bare minimum Ben was satisfied with. Thirty seconds of silence, as the tubby little shape of him barrelled beneath the water, his firm round back dappled with evening sunshine refracted through water, then minutes of gasping, spewing, chattering noise as he reported, delivered, celebrated, then more silence.

The ultimate triumph was retrieval of all three coins in one dive. Just as Cassie began to worry that he would get the bends, he decided he wanted to go back on dry land and have a cuddle. He picked out a poolside couch far from the group, and she slid him out of his togs, enveloping him in a great soft bath-towel that hid his arms and legs, briefly reminiscent of his baby months. Dragging another towel around herself, she climbed on to the bed and took him on top of her, fingering his damp dark golden hair, patting the thick towelling surrounding him. In the safe shelter of the bath-towel, she could see him sneak his thumb into his mouth. 'You're just the best boy,' she told him softly. 'The very best. Best boy in the world.'

It became a murmuring mantra encircling him with sound, wrapping him in repetitious warmth. Every now and again, he would croon in time with her, moving his cheek against the fabric between them, his eyelids drooping. It can get no better than this, Cassie thought. Letting her head fall back, she closed her eyes, momentarily considering a search for her sunglasses, dismissing it because the oblique rays were untroubling. Amplified by the shimmering surface of the unoccupied swimming-pool, the voices and cutlery-rattling were clear as a radio play. But not *like* a radio play, she thought. Whenever you tuned into a radio drama, you instantly recognised that these were not people having real conversations.

What was going on across the pool was real. One over-weight warty non-golfer with dull grey hair curling up at the nape of his neck was structuring the apparently casual comments of the others.

'Look, we could get dozens of guys trained in media skills,' one of the accountants was saying. 'But it'd be a waste of time. Media coverage is all second-hand, these days. Journalists talking to other journalists.'

'All illiberal liberals,' someone else said. 'Ready to defend to the death your right to have your say – unless your say is conservative.'

'But isn't that what we should be going for?' Polo suggested. 'Attacking the way liberals dehumanise conservative thinkers? Instead of waiting around to be attacked?'

'How?'

'With humour. Nothing opens up people to ideas like humour.'

'Humour,' conceded the surgeon, 'but humour that is bitingly clear about the fact that media liberals only theoretically accord freedom to conservatives to state and argue their case. Radio programmes, when they're forced to have conservatives on, actively seek stereotypically rejectable conservatives, so that the manner of the discourse obviates any possibility of their viewpoint being more widely adapted.'

'Positioning,' another man said. Cassie thought he had something to do with advertising. 'That's the key. Liberals always portray conservatives as big, rich, power-ful figures—'

The group began to laugh and point at each other. He fought the merriment. 'No, come on, listen, that's a real problem. Conservative values are wrongly positioned. We have to reposition so people understand that being pro-family, pro-life and pro-Church at the moment is to find yourself disenfranchised, disempowered, caricatured, silenced, ridiculed, slandered, libelled and robbed of the basic citizen's rights it would be illegal to deny anybody else.'

There was a long, acquiescent silence around the table, the only sound the clinking of ice-cubes as they melted and rearranged themselves inside the drinks.

'Are you asleep?' a voice said, right beside Cassie, who almost knocked Ben off the lounger with her startled leap. She patted him back to sleep, trying to make her own heart stop racing. The man was standing carefully so that his shadow was cast over the two of them and she didn't have to squint against sunshine. '*Piña colada* with alcohol,' Peter Thornton said, holding out the drink in his left hand. '*Piña colada* without alcohol,' he finished, holding out the drink in his right hand, which she took. 'You OK over here?'

She nodded, trying to get her mouth around a straw emerging from a traffic jam of pineapple chunks and miniature paper parasols.

'Nothing to contribute to the summit conference?'

Without waiting for her response, he was off, padding softly around the pool in battered boat shoes, sitting down at the crowded table, but slightly at an angle. You never quite belong, do you? Cassie thought. There but not present. She smiled to herself at the memory of a joke Polo had made on some TV show about chickens and pigs. To the effect that in a bacon and egg breakfast, the chicken was involved, but the pig was committed. As far as she could tell, when it came to the defence of the illiberal realm, Thornton was involved, but not committed.

By the time the *piña colada* was finished, the scraping of chairs indicated the break-up of the informal meeting. Some of them remembered Cassie and waved across at her, others simply ambled off in groups corresponding to the different villas. Polo came bounding around the end of the pool, arms out to lift Ben, delighted with himself and the day's work. In a moment, Ben was curled, still asleep, head on his father's shoulder, and Polo was offering a hand to pull Cassie out of the lounger. She gathered toys and insect repellents, sunscreens and towels, stuffing them willy-nilly into big tote-bags. In the room afterwards, he asked her what she thought of what she had heard.

'Interesting,' she said, noncommittally.

'"Interesting"? What do you mean, "interesting"?' he demanded, as if it was a four-letter word.

'Well, it could be described as a right-wing conspiracy, couldn't it?' she asked lightly.

'No, it couldn't,' he said, instantly and defensively furious.

'Well, for a bunch of people who use "liberal" the way anti-Semites use "kike", you could have fooled me,' she said, less than coherently.

'What's so different about the way you and Marsha talk about right-wingers?'

She was too tired to argue, since the only point offering itself was that she and Marsha were right to be fearful of right-wingers, but what had that group of well-heeled, well-placed religious control freaks got to fear from liberals?

'Right-wingers hold back progress,' she said.

'Oh, Cassie, please. Progress towards what?'

'A more tolerant, compassionate society.'

'Cassie, in the past ten years, more legislation has been passed in Ireland to achieve the liberal agenda than anybody in their wildest dreams could have imagined. You seriously trying to suggest that we're more tolerant and compassionate as a result?'

'Well, gay people are not – not in danger any more of being taken to court for expressing their sexuality.'

'How many gay people were taken to court for "expressing their sexuality" before Geoghegan-Quinn brought in the pro-gay law?'

Cassie had no idea. Polo made a speech about how the law, pre-liberalisation, had been potent more in the breach than the observance, that it had been little more than a hypothetical threat. Irksome to vocal gays but no more than that. 'Yeah, we now have divorce,' Polo plunged on. 'Big deal. Big fucking deal. My God, you'd think, with *that* enormous ground-breaking civil-rights achievement, people would be breaking the doors of the divorce courts down to get free of the wankers they were married to. What happened? Yawn, yawn. No big rush. No great liberation. Even with a backlog of years, when divorce came in, the numbers were less than anybody predicted. But by creating a law that wasn't needed, Ireland sent a message to people getting married: "Hey, have a go, if it doesn't work, you can get unhitched quick as you got hitched."'

'If that's the message couples are getting, they must be pig-ignorant and deaf as posts,' Cassie said. 'Only a brain-dead moron would be under the impression you can get unhitched as quick as you got hitched.'

Polo brushed this away as minutiae clogging up the more important point he was trying to make. 'There's all these extra liberties, all these encouragements, as you'd see it, for people to bloody well overflow with shagging compassion and what was the other thing?'

'Tolerance.'

'Frigging tolerance, right. Produce me one example of that compassion and tolerance. Just one. One example of tolerance that wouldn't have been there before these laws were brought in. One single, solitary bit of evidence of compassion in play that wouldn't have bloody well been in play anyway. We've got more people committing suicide than at any time in recorded history. Loads of them young people who should be in a state of continuous orgasm, because what's to prevent them screwing from dawn to dusk and after? We've got more depression than in the worst days of the TB and flu epidemics or the war or the recession. We've got a fucking epidemic of alcoholism. We've got more illegal drug-taking than any other country in Europe. We've got more single-parent families than anywhere else. All the fruits of the liberal agenda you and Marsha are so effing self-righteously committed to.'

'I don't believe all that's the case. I mean, where does it say – How do you know we've got more single-parent families? I'm sure there are more single-parent families in Britain, maybe in the Scandinavian countries – but anyway, that's like saying single-parent families are wrong. That's like attacking women who chose to keep their babies and you're against abortion, aren't you?'

Bizarrely, Polo began at this point to polish his shoes. It was something to do. Some physical thing to do. Cassie, sitting in bed watching him, wished she had a similar task to quiet and occupy her trembling hands.

'Single-parent families *are* wrong,' he said, after a long time. 'We're just not allowed to say that any more. Every indicator – by every indicator, every measurement of family success, of bringing up happy productive children, single-parent families are less successful than two-parent families.'

He looked up at her, shoes and polishers abandoned on the floor, big knees crooked up into the air, asked if she would like a cup of tea. She nodded. He went downstairs ahead of her, searching for the light switches he had used earlier to darken the ground floor, fiddling so that the kitchen was bright enough to see, but dim enough to be kind to sunburned eyes. He plugged in the kettle and got mugs, teabags. She found teaspoons and a carton of milk. Space-walking around each other in the kitchen cotillion of the quarrelling couple: you first, no you, why thank you, don't mention it.

When they were seated at either side of the oblong kitchen table, facing each other across its narrow side rather than in more overtly hostile positions at head and tail of it, he opened his hand from where it was clasped around the mug: off you go. The floor is all yours.

'Let's accept, for the moment, that all your claims are absolutely accurate,' she said, trying to shift the discussion to an uninvolved, depersonalised, detached, disinterested level and instead sounding pompous, even to herself. 'It isn't necessarily cause and effect. The Ireland of our parents' time was narrow, judgemental, puritanical, full of shame, full of guilt, full of repression. It didn't take a liberal movement of thought to end all that. Once you had mass media, once you had television allowing people to see other possibilities, things were going to change. Look at the Soviet Union. Look at China. Change happens.'

'Change isn't always progress. That's the myth we have at the moment. All any shit has to say is "It's time for change," and everybody nods like it's inevitable. Change and entitlement and effing rights, that's all anybody wants. The minute you talk about duty or responsibility you're portrayed as a goose-stepping gobshite.'

Cassie laughed. Uneasily.

'I find it sad that women's autonomy can be defined by the numbers of tanks outside abortion clinics sloshing with dismembered foetuses,' he said. 'There's something wrong if Ireland will be regarded as a fully equal society only when we, too, have those clinics and those tanks.'

'Oh, *Polo*, why does this argument always come down to dismembered foetuses?'

'Because, Cassie, in case you hadn't noticed it, dismembered foetuses are the end product of abortions. We're all so politically correct, these days, it's considered an outrage to put a picture of a foetus on a poster, but not an outrage to put a real one in a disposal tank.'

She started to answer, colliding with his suddenly raised voice.

'Cassie, if we're all so open and tolerant and compassionate and liberal, why do you have to be *brave* among your friends because I believe something unfashionable? I'll tell you why. Because of people with loads of opinions and shag all else. They don't actually *do* anything good for anybody. They don't even give to charity, because that's "perpetuating the system", that's "patronage", that's "sustaining the cycles of deprivation". My *arse*. They believe themselves virtuous because of the category to which they belong. They think they're courageous because they keep fighting a battle they won years ago. They won, Cassie. They beat the Church. They became the Establishment. They rule. But they don't let on they won, even to themselves. They still convince themselves that they're the brave revolutionaries, speaking out, saying the unsayable, when what they're saying is smack dab in the middle of the national consensus of the brain-dead.'

'Polo, I don't know whether to laugh or cry or call for police protection. This is so unlike you. You're not a bully for good causes.'

'I have beliefs.'

'But you don't ever browbeat me with them. I've never heard you talk like this.'

'Well, to be honest, some of it's from a script I'm writing for Winnie,' he said, so sheepishly that, despite her rage, she was forced to laugh. 'But I do believe it,' he added hastily.

Cassie tried to work out what angle to attack this from.

'And so does she,' he added, reassuringly.

'I don't give a flying fuck what the superannuated star of a ten-year-old yogurt commercial believes,' Cassie blurted.

'No, all I wanted – I wouldn't want you to think she was false.'

'Of course she's false, if she's going to use your words.'

'But that's just because she's not able to articulate it the right way.'

'She doesn't pretend, then? She believed what she used to say about the yogurt?'

'She did, actually. Still eats that brand.'

'A mouth puppet for copywriters.'

'All the great thinkers had speechwriters.'

'Abraham effing Lincoln didn't.'

'All the great modern thinkers.'

'Like who?'

'JFK.'

'Great modern *thinker*? A lace-curtain Irish hypocrite on steroids – literally – screwing different women every day of the week while pretending to be a good husband and father.'

'He *was* a good father.'

'Much you know about it.'

Elbows propped on the table, face in hands, Cassie found – right in the middle of this argument – she was beginning to doze off. She wondered whether it would be better to ask Polo a question that would allow him to vent any further dogma left in him once and for all, with her sleeping through it, or to confess to overwhelming drowsiness. Her hands were gently peeled away from her face, his fingers curling around the tips of her fingers, folding them down into, she thought, a little swiss roll of fingers. 'C'mon, you're tired out,' he said. 'I shouldn't be battering you with my promises, the things I try to be faithful to. Only one is relevant to you: till death do us part'.

For some reason, Cassie thought, awkwardly climbing the stairs with his arm around her shoulders, that was the most threatening thing of all.

CHAPTER FIFTEEN

Of Mice and Men

He leaped out of bed at the sound of the alarm the next day as if there had been no battle the previous evening, no argument into the small hours. Interesting, she thought, stirring to watch him as he opened the curtains, whistling and then suppressing the whistle in deference to her supposed slumber, you are not often so filled with gaiety in the early mornings. You are a heavy sleeper, a reluctant waker, lying splayed, sodden and heavy without bones like a man in the street after a thirty-storey fall from a skyscraper roof. Not much in your ordinary work jump-starts you into such joyful anticipation.

He went next door for Ben, who seemed to have been awake. At the door of their room, Ben broke loose at a run, bouncing on to their bed in one leap, cracking his forehead off his mother's, giving the bump on her head a cursory rub of sympathy (his own head seemed to be made of concrete).

'Sharks have no feelings when they get in a feeding frenzy,' he told her, tugging at her arm to pull her upright in bed. Struggling to accede to his evident wishes, she smiled grimly. Chip off the old block, you are. Need an audience, just like your da. Won't be satisfied with a recumbent audience: audiences must sit up and pay attention. Leave them lying down, they'll go to sleep on you quick as look at you.

'They just –' Ben turned himself into a shark, surging

over the bed to eat his mother, biting through the thin bedclothes with surprising force. '– they eat and bite and swallow and *savage* everything, so much they'd bite their own tails off if their tails went in front of them. And not *notice*, even.'

'By Jesus, they'd notice plenty when they went to swim home to their mothers,' Polo muttered, heading into the shower.

'Why would they?' Ben asked Cassie, balked of his father by the closing shower door.

'They couldn't swim without their tails.'

'They could, so.'

'You couldn't swim without your feet.'

'I can so. I pull myself with just arms. I pretend my feet are stopped, sometimes.'

Cassie looked at him, taken aback by this.

'Erik swims all the time,' he told her, letting her make the links. 'They made him when his feet stopped. His arms are stronger than anybody else's in the whole world.'

This claim might be a little on the large side, she thought, but nonetheless Erik the Red undoubtedly was overdeveloped in the pecs and abs department.

'Well, then,' Ben said. 'They could, so.'

Back at the sharks, she thought. Do I care about sharks? Do I give a shit if the entire ocean is filled with half-sharks unable to get home to their mothers? Anyway, why the hell would an adult shark *want* to get home to its mother?

'Someone like you or Erik could teach yourself to swim over time without using your legs, but if a shark lost his tail suddenly, he wouldn't have had practice.'

'But he could learn,' Ben said triumphantly.

'Not if he was bleeding to death at the same time and his insides falling out.'

Ben went wide-eyed and a little trembly as to the lower lip.

'He'd never get home to his mother,' he confirmed. 'He'd just die there all on his own.'

Cassie closed her eyes and took a deep breath through her nose. Choices, choices. Did she now tell him that the shark wasn't on its own in the first place, and that if it was bleeding like a stuck pig and losing its entrails, another shark was likely to put it speedily out of its marine misery by swallowing the rest of it? Or should she theorise that maybe mother sharks had so many offspring they'd never miss the odd one that got done in by one of its delinquent pals?

'Maybe he'd grow another tail like a lizard,' Ben said hopefully.

'I don't think so,' Cassie said, opting, as she tended to do, for the painful truth.

There was a long moment of silence and bleak thought. The shower was turned off and Polo thudded out – one heel, second heel – on to the bathmat, beginning to sing tunelessly, the song taking on a corrugated rhythm as he vigorously towelled himself.

'Sharks are not good,' Ben said suddenly. 'I don't care about sharks. They can just die, so they can.'

'The thing is that any shark who was in a feeding frenzy in the first place was eating some other poor fish or even a person,' Cassie said.

'So he *deserves* it,' Ben said, relieved. 'Like Judas.'

'Judas?'

Delighted by her apparent ignorance, Ben told her that Judas was Our Lord's best friend, one of his team. (Whoever had told him this seemed to have left him with the impression that the Apostles played soccer or GAA.) But then he betrayed Our Lord and – Ben demonstrated, promoting his mother, briefly, to the Jesus role – showed the Romans who to grab hold of by *kissing* him and they crucified Jesus and then they gave Judas thirty pieces of silver and he went and hung himself up. Ben made it sound like good housekeeping, Cassie thought, watching her son fling himself in embrace around his father's newly dried legs. Polo involved him in a plan to bring Cassie her breakfast in bed, the two of them heading downstairs discussing the menu.

Cassie slid back into a supine position, trying to work out what, if any, was her objection to Ben being told Bible stories. The child had made the appropriate reductive reasoning from the story: actions have consequences, bad actions cause regret, sometimes bad fortune is retributory. Whoever told him the story had left the Jews out of it. During her own childhood, they had been villainised in every telling. But in Ben's version, even the Romans were portrayed in a guardians-of-the-peace role. It was just their job to pick up miscreants identified by kisses. The kiss-off, she thought. Wonder if that comes from the Bible?

She was glad to get home, glad to be away from the pleasant, principled, clubbable men who went golfing every morning and developed methods to change the thinking of a nation in the afternoon. Marsha had left a package inside the front door. 'Author's copies', it said, somewhat inaccurately, since Cassie had only illustrated the children's book. The real author, Erik the Red, was gone on a media tour of America, very excited, although the absolute requirement of the publicists that he learn to mention the title of the book every forty-five seconds enraged him.

When she unpacked the book, Ben sat down and read it from cover to cover.

'Did you know it already? I mean, did you remember it from the proofs or were you really reading it?' Polo asked.

Ben looked puzzled. 'I can read,' he said.

'Of *course* you can,' Polo said. His kindly paternal tone was understood in all its implications by his son.

'I can read like a grown-up,' Ben said.

'All right,' Polo said, losing interest.

'Even newspapers,' Ben said.

'OK, OK,' Polo said.

'There was this girl and this man and they were in a pub and they had drinks and the man had a lot of drinks and he put his hand in the girl's dress and said gimme a kiss and she said no and he said I'll make you and she said you won't and that's when the murder began. He put his two hands really *really* tight around her neck and squeezed and blood popped in her eyes and no air could get inside her so she died and he said look what you made me do.'

Polo didn't seem to know whether to applaud, laugh or cry at this tightly edited version of a murder case just concluded in the Central Criminal Court.

'You read all that by yourself?'

'Course I did.'

'You didn't hear it on the radio?'

'I *read* it. It wasn't even on the front page.'

This was true, Cassie verified, finding it on page four.

'I must buy some books for you,' Polo said.

'The library is full of books,' Ben pointed out suspiciously: you want to distract me from the good ones?

'But they're all adult books,' Polo explained unwisely.

'I can read adult,' Ben said, beginning to climb an invisible emotional scale.

Cassie distracted him, murmuring to Polo that books too old for Ben were likely to bore him long before he reached any questionable bits. Dr Cadogan's books amounted to a literary snapshot of thirty or forty years earlier. There were dozens of authors of whom she had never heard – who, she wondered, hefting a series of small, beautifully bound hardbacks, had E. Phillips Oppenheim been? Famous in their day, the writers' names now evoked nothing but slight pity for the forgettable. Then there were authors who had featured on her father's bookshelves. Plus a thick sprinkling of what her mother always described as the Classics. The books you were always safe to be seen with, as a kid. Louisa M. Alcott, Thackeray, Dickens, Captain Marryat, any Russian.

Because the antique library steps were being mended – a task that took several months at the beginning of Ben's sixth year – his choice was not limited simply by weight (he could not physically lift some of the bigger morocco-bound tomes) and verbiage, but also by author's name. This was because, without a ladder, he could reach only the bottom two shelves and was consequently confined to the letters S, T, U, V, W, X, Y and Z. Sensibly, he picked the smallest of the first reachable row on the left. Coming upon him, lying on his stomach, chin propped on hands, she asked about the book. It was about mice, he said. He gave the name of the writer, too, but it meant nothing to her.

She let him take it to bed with him, it seemed to fascinate him so much. It took him over for three days, like a mad, bad, wonderful secret. He would not let his father read it, telling Polo he would tell him the whole story at the end. He even tucked himself up in bed first thing in the morning to read it. Which was why, the morning a migraine kept her in bed, she woke from a drugged slumber in response to a jolting sensation. Muzzy-eyed, she fumbled her way to wakefulness. The bed. Was. Shaking. Ben, sitting on the end of it, was roaring crying: rocked with a grief that consumed and vomited him, that choked and drowned him.

'Honey, what's wrong, what's wrong?' she asked, looking for blood, for white bone poking through delicate skin.

'Lennie's dead,' he roared. 'Poor Lennie's *dead*!'

She tried to hold him, but the grief was bigger than she was. It tore him out of her arms and beat him to and fro, rocked him in shuddering horror.

'George shot him and he'll never get to take care of the rabbits and live off the fatta the land and he didn't mean any harm, he never meant any harm. Lennie was my friend. George was his friend, but he shot him.'

He was holding an old book in his hands, his tears darkening widening circles on the faded umber cloth cover. *Of Mice and Men*, it said. *John Steinbeck*, it said.

'Ben, it's a book,' she said desperately.

'I know, it's all about Lennie and George and the rabbits—'

'But it's not true. Lennie didn't really die.'

He stopped babbling his grief, looking at her, his eyes welling and overflowing with tears, the sobs pulling in his lower lip spasmodically.

'It's a story. John Steinbeck – see, this man whose name is on the spine of the book,' she turned the back of the book to him, '– he made up the story and the people.'

'He made up Lennie? He made Lennie up?'

'Yes, he did.'

'He made George just shoot him?'

'Yes.'

'Lennie was just made up?'

Cassie began to lose confidence in her method of consolation, and started to blither about the reasons behind John Steinbeck inventing a marginally disabled character like Lennie. It didn't help that she couldn't remember anything about the story.

'He's a pig,' Ben said, with enormous dignity and venom.

'Who?'

'John Steinbeck. Isn't he, Dad?'

'Is he?'

As Polo led Ben across the landing to his own room to get dressed, Ben began to tell him the story of *Of Mice and Men*, becoming upset all over again because of what happened to poor simple Lennie. Cassie got herself dressed, listening to gusts of grief interspersed with questions from his father. It probably helped, she thought, that Polo wouldn't have read the book. For the most part, Polo saw books as pleasing furniture.

When he brought Ben back, all dolled up and ready for school, Ben was sad but recovered and Cassie was ready for the day. She had, in addition, taken a quick run through his book, wondering what a six-year-old had made of the institution Steinbeck's characters called the 'cat house'. With luck, she hoped, this would be covered in the father–son consultation while she showered and dressed. Saying goodbye, Ben told her he was going to watch out for that John Steinbeck and tell him he was cruel and rotten to have shot Lennie even if it *was* only a book. 'And give Auntie Marsh my love,' he added, running to join his father in the car.

Which Cassie duly did, when Marsha arrived later for their monthly meeting.

'You making that up?' Marsha asked, sharply.

'How do you mean?'

'Did Ben actually say that?'

'He asked me why I was all dressed up, I said I was going to a meeting with you, he said to give you his love. What's your problem?'

Marsha looked apologetic, but muttered that relatively few six-year-olds spontaneously sent love to relatives. Relatively few six-year-olds, Cassie thought, finishing her Danish, woke their mothers at dawn in tears over literature from their grandparents' time. She tidied crockery to one side, knowing Marsha would want to lay out paperwork for her to read or sign or both.

'We're going somewhere else for the meeting, today,' Marsha said, and for the first time Cassie noticed that her friend was carrying only a handbag – no bulky briefcase.

'We're going in my car. Can you stand the come-down?' Marsha said, unlocking her Camry. Cassie slid in. 'From now on,' Marsha said, 'I suggest we alternate venues for our meetings.'

'Marsha, you make us sound very important. Venues, yet.'

This provoked a lecture from Marsha that Cassie was among the top thirty cartoonists in the world. Her draw-ings of politicians appeared on the Op Ed pages of leading newspapers while at the same time her strip/story series appeared in the comic supplements, sometimes of the same papers, while the children's books were reaching a third, quite different market. In fact, that was one of the things Marsha needed to discuss with her this morning. Cassie was invited to do a keynote address at the Annual Symposium of Editorial Cartoonists in Iowa about the relationship between thematic and political or editorial cartooning.

'What's this thematic stuff?'

'Mostly strip cartoons like Cathy Guisman's one about the girl who's always gaining and losing weight, gaining and losing boyfriends. Your series about how kids see and hear grown-ups. Gary Trudeau's *Doonesbury*'s sort of a cross-over between political and thematic cartooning.'

Marsha, Cassie thought, in a little over six years, had made herself into an expert, not only on syndication, tax law, book-keeping and budgeting, but also on the history of cartooning. The non-fiction section of Dr Cadogan's old library was now brightened by the dust-jackets of new books about cartoons and the men and women who drew them, mostly ordered by Marsha through Amazon.com.

'There's maybe a hundred and fifty full time political/ editorial cartoonists in the States,' Marsha said, as the Toyota reached Sutton Cross. 'They all seem to hate each other, so when they get together there's a great fight,' she went on. 'I think you should do the speech. It would filter back to Ireland and make people realise cartooning is important. Did you know it was cartoonists who invented the expressions gerrymander and McCarthyism?'

'Expressions on my lips every day,' Cassie said. 'Particularly in the supermarket.'

'Shut up, you recalcitrant ignoramus,' Marsha said, swinging the car off the road to the left, into the grounds of the old Claremont Hotel, negotiating carefully between oversized garbage skips filled with builder's debris, and parking where they could overlook the sea. To the right was Howth, the left arm of the pier snaking out into the sea.

Getting out of the car, Cassie faced into the strong wind coming off the sea, letting it whip her loose long red hair, a watery spring sunshine promising warmth, later in the day. 'God, isn't this so beautiful?'

The two of them walked to the white fencing separating the grounds of the hotel from the flat golden beach. In the distance, an old man was heading for Howth along the sea's edge, throwing a ball for a spaniel, which was splashing into the water one minute, then sliding, skating to a halt the next minute in the dry loose surface sand on top of the harder-baked core.

Marsha turned, led the way across the car park to the main entrance of the building Cassie remembered as a hotel visited on summer Sundays in her childhood, for lunch, before an afternoon playing and walking on the beach. 'Is there anybody there, said the traveller . . .' The line came, unbidden, to her mind, staggering her up against the metal containers inside the entrance. Her father would do that, whenever they walked a beach at sunset. Throw out a line of poetry for her to pick up and build upon. She always pretended to find it tedious: school under a different guise. But whenever he would forget, she would initiate it herself. 'Theirs not to reason why?' or 'Nothing is as beautiful as spring,' or 'How do I love thee?'

They would walk together, quoting in unison, filling in for each other, sometimes halting to deliver a particularly dramatic couplet face to face. On soft-dying summer evenings edging into September, watching out for wasps, picking ripe blackberries from the brambles along the road-edge of the beach, they would talk out quiet poems of love and loss and longing. On high-winded chillier days, they would orate lines pulsing with hoofbeats, with battle, with betrayal. Whenever they were basking, having remembered every line of a long poem, her father would puncture nascent smugness by quoting something new to her from Ogden Nash or a limerick from Edward Lear. Or make up the first line of a limerick and compete with her to complete it.

'You going to stay there all day?' Marsha asked.

'Sorry,' Cassie said, straightening up to examine what she had leaned against. A double line of locked metal cabinets with spaces on the front of each for names. Apartment letterboxes. The hotel was being converted into luxury apartments. Marsha opened the inner door. The lift had not been installed yet, she said. Cassie followed her up the wooden stairs, as yet uncarpeted, the wood dusty and paint-spattered. At the top of the second flight, Marsha let them into a penthouse apartment, two-bedroomed, with its own roof garden overlooking Dublin Bay. The view sucked the breath out of Cassie, who stood, spellbound, identifying buildings, old castles, sand-spits, watching boats crossing the open water.

'This has been the demo apartment,' Marsha said briskly, laying out her paperwork, having shoved a microwave coffee perker into the machine, pushing the buttons as if she had been using such gadgetry for years. 'All the apartments are now sold, and I own this one. Since, as you know, I have the visual sense of a brain-dead bluebottle, moving into something completely decorated where I have no choices to make is a Godsend.'

'When do ye move in?'

'What's with the "ye"?'

'You and Liam and—'

'Just me.'

'For business?'

'For business and everything else. My home.' Marsha did a sweeping gesture, then thumped her chest, gorilla-fashion, two-handed. 'Mine, mine, all mine, only mine, mine alone, just for me, me, me,' she carolled.

'I get the impression this might belong to you,' Cassie deadpanned.

'Happiness is knowing that nobody but your niece-and-client has a key,' Marsha said, handing her a set of keys, coppery-golden, sharp-edged with newness.

'Thank you,' Cassie said, taking seriously the signal honour bestowed, putting the keys into her bag.

'Imagine,' Marsha said, planking a milk carton down between them. 'The main keys to this house are in a Dunnes Stores bag but the spares are in a Ferragamo with matching shoes.'

'Oh, cut me some slack,' Cassie said. 'These are not new.'

Marsha looked up in the direction of the ceiling as if she was doing mental arithmetic. 'You're right. God, they're what? At least six weeks old? Tell us, Cassie, how many pairs of shoes do you own? A thousand?'

Nothing like that, Cassie indicated. You couldn't even say a few hundred. Marsha laughed, suggesting that this meant Cassie owned at least a hundred and fifty pairs. All of them carrying expensive designer labels. Cassie shrugged. As long as Marsha was in charge of her income, she figured she would always stay one step ahead of serious debt. Anyway, her credit-card suppliers were always offering her *more* credit, she pointed out to Marsha, so she must not have a bad reputation with *them*. None of which was what they were there to discuss, anyway.

'Divorce?'

'Right first time.'

'Shock, horror.'

'Lack of commitment.'

'What about in sickness and in health?'

'What about it?'

'You're breaking a promise you made for life.'

'Couldn't have put it better myself.'

'Sending out bad signals.'

'Nobody's watching my signals.'

'You will be lonely.'

'No. I'll be alone. Quite different. I've been lonely for a long, long time.'

'Some of your friends will cut you off.'

'Hoo-bloody-ray.'

'My mother will go ape-shit.'

'No, your mother would go ape-shit if it was her daughter divorcing. Her sister doing it will make her feel young, cool and modern.'

'You will experience loss of status.'

'Your arse.'

'Why didn't you do this ten years ago?'

'Because ten years ago, I was still addicted to hope. Best

narcotic in the world, hope. Gives a better high than heroin, a brighter buzz than crack. Reduces nicotine to ashes. Once you're hooked, though, it's worse than any of them. It's your daily fix, this belief that tomorrow will be better. You whore for hope on a daily basis.'

Marsha's appearance was oddly contradictory, blazing happiness out of a face filled with infinite weariness and defeat, puckers appearing at the edge of lips pulled together a million times to stifle protest, wobbly wrinkle-parentheses from nose to mouth and further, testifying to a million forced smiles, deep lines between the brows the scars of accumulated wounds.

Marsha leaned across the table and patted Cassie's cheek as if she were the one needing sympathy. 'It's all right,' she said gently. 'It's over. History. Past hurts don't mean anything in the present, any more than past happiness. Yeah, you remember it happened, but no matter how much you try to drum it up into the present, it has no reality. You can't make yourself happy, today, remembering your great moments of happiness in the past.' She thought about this for a moment, unsatisfied. 'Sadness stays current. But happiness doesn't. So, kid, enjoy it while you have it, because the year Ben becomes an adolescent he'll disappear, leaving a sordid, sulky, hostile uncooperative thing called a teenager in his place, and when that happens, not only will today's happiness not warm you up, you'll begin to think you imagined it. Fooled yourself.'

Cassie sent this down the instant disposal chute she had developed in her mind for almost all comments about babies, children and teenagers made by other parents, none of which ever related to the continuous happiness Ben had brought her. 'You are divorced, then?' she asked.

'Nope. It's under way, as of last week.'

'But it'll be years before it's through.'

'Like I'm in a hurry? You think I have a toy-boy in the deep-freeze I want to marry tomorrow? Get a grip, Cassie.'

'Will my godson come and stay with you for some of the time?'

'You really don't get it, do you?' Marsha said, half laughing. 'Technically, I'm divorcing Liam. Actually, I'm divorcing my son. Remember stories last year about teenagers in America going to law to get legal separations from their parents because they weren't getting along with them? I was reading about that, and the whole plan came together – snap – in my head. You probably noticed I've been in fierce good humour in the last six months. Impending freedom from your offspring'll do that for you.'

Cassie had no idea how seriously to take this. Her godson was no longer the charming, ash-blond kid she remembered from his First Communion, no longer the merry-faced ten-year-old she would take to air shows and carnivals. Partly because of Ben's birth, partly because of living in Meath rather than closer to Marsha's home, there had been little contact between them in recent years. 'Maybe Colm's just going through a phase,' she said.

Marsha said nothing.

'OK, file that one under Shite,' Cassie said, and the two of them laughed. 'But how much can a kid change?'

'How much can an adult change?'

'If you listen to my friends about their mates, employer and friends, adults can change completely, totally, absolutely, three hundred and sixty-five degrees.'

'That's days in a year. Three hundred and sixty is all the degrees you need. In fact, a hundred and eighty should do you.'

'You going for an annulment, too?'

'No,' Marsha said expressionlessly. 'I don't need the Church to tell me my son is a bastard. I know that without their help.'

The sun was rounding the corner of the building, filling the apartment with light. The two women wordlessly acknowledged the marvellous difference it made to the sense of space within the room, Cassie doing a thumbs-up, 'good purchase' gesture.

'I've never seen any adult change as much as Colm in his second ten years.'

'What about diseases that strike in the teens, like schizophrenia?'

'Cassie, if he was nuts, I'd have no problem. Mental illness is mental illness, same as physical illness albeit a lot more difficult to cope with. One of *my* girlfriends has a daughter who went through three years of the most awful depression – never getting out of bed. My friend used to ask me to go over and sit with the daughter sometimes, for fear she'd commit suicide when my friend had to go out. My son is sane. He's just changed from being one seriously nice kid to being the sort of evil presence you'd never allow to cross your threshold, if it wasn't closely related to you by blood.'

One of the reasons I love this woman's company, Cassie thought, is because I can be silent with her and she makes no judgements about the silence.

'Look at it this way,' Marsha said. 'Here's this – this –'

'Man,' Cassie said.

'Man,' Marsha accepted. Both laughed at the self-evident concession. 'Here's this man with money to burn, thanks to his gobshite aunt sending him cheques the size of lottery winnings.'

Cassie reddened. Being well-off to a degree never anticipated allowed her to buy off people. Once her mother stopped being the Compo Queen, Cassie felt obligated to send her cheques to compensate for the damages she would otherwise have litigated out of shopkeepers, builders and any local authority unwise enough to leave a kerb where she could fall off it. When she was invited to give talks to motivate current pupils at her old school, she would ask Marsha to send a letter pleading unspecified pressures and soften the blow by enclosing a contribution to the building fund.

The first time she'd sent an oversized cheque to Colm, she'd enclosed an apologetic note to the effect that she didn't want to insult him by picking a toy that this birthday made him too old for, or a book already read, so would he pick something for himself? Popularity was easily bought, she learned, if at Christmas she bought a dozen or so of those pocketed Christmas cards into which could be stuffed brand new fifty-pound notes. Present popularity without trace. The gifts she remembered from Christmases and birthdays past were the ones like the antique inkwell Erik the Red had given her, or the eighteenth-century slotted spoon designed for skimming tea-leaves from the top of a cup another friend had sent. Gifts that kept her connected to the giver. She gave very few presents connecting her, long-term, to recipients. Absorption in Ben disimproved her in some ways, providing her with an excuse to ignore all but the most obvious needs of people she should be close to.

'It's not just you who gives money to Colm,' Marsha said tolerantly. 'I did it, too. I gave up choosing gifts for him when the pleasure went out of it. Just stopped. "Here's the cash." "Here's a cheque." Of course, his father did the most efficient version – got him a credit card on Liam's own account. Colm, Son of American Express. The ultimate financial rite of non-passage. Money to burn, OK? Gifts are not going to bankrupt him. But does he remember anybody else's birthday or Christmas? No.

Does he feel guilty about it the way we feel guilty about *only* giving him money? No. He says, "I'm not good at Christmas presents," as if choosing gifts for those you love was a genetic strand missing from his DNA. It applies to a lot of things. He's not good at saying thank you. He's not good at getting out of bed before late afternoon. He's not good at helping in the house. He's not good at expending thought and time on others. I gave him the benefit of the doubt for a long time. No more. I've run out of doubt-benefit. I've been giving him the benefit of the doubt since he turned bad, since he stopped having any desire to please anybody other than him, and you know what it's got me?'

Obligingly, Cassie tried to snap her fingers and failed. Marsha provided her own percussive finger-snap.

'It doesn't work the other way, you see. I don't get given the benefit of the doubt. I'm this dismissable, contemptible, *negligible* figure that says things mothers in movies say. That's his great area of expertise: movies. He watches them all day, every day, except when he goes out drinking. He is as *knowing* as if he was middle-aged, but it's all drawn from films. He knows more about sex than I will ever know – from films. He has all the killer put-downs he's ever going to need – from films. He knows how every situation plays out, he is withered and wise and experienced, all at second-hand. He doesn't need real life, or risk. Why would he? He doesn't need to be approved of by me or his father, because we're just stock characters, the drunk and the nag. He doesn't need the high of achievement, of building and proving his own skills – he can buy easier highs. He doesn't need to read – he can check out the video of the film they made of the book. He's not interesting to talk to, because he has no ideas – everything loops back to a reference to *Pulp Fiction* or *Taxi Driver* or . . . Real life for him is a dull unedited version of what he can turn on in his bedroom anytime he wants.'

There has to be a cartoon series in this, Cassie thought, mentally drawing a limp, grey-draped male figure with cargo-pockets pulling him downwards, a tiny baseball cap reducing even his pinhead to anonymity. Jesus, came the next thought, I am such a *user*.

'Now, add it all up, and what you get is the kind of boring toxic person you'd never in your right mind invite into your home, never mind allow to live permanently in it. Who needs that, eating your food, stinking up the place, stealing from your wallet, leaving his girlfriend's push-up bras in your drying-machine and being unremittingly rude to you? So I'm divorcing him. I'm not going to fight over who gets custody of Liam: Colm can have him. I won't even demand visiting rights.'

How quiet are the miseries of some of our friends, even at this time of raucous radio victimhood, Cassie thought, ashamed, looking back over six or seven years of choosing simply to enjoy Marsha's acerbic smartass humour, choosing to read it as happiness, never as the black humour of someone not joking but drowning.

'This divorcing relatives has a big future, then? I think I've already got a sort of legal separation from my mother,' Cassie said, giggling a little at the idea. 'How come you can get along so well with my mother? She's difficult, too.'

'But she was my big sister, I was the flower-girl at her wedding. Nice husband. Got to be godmother to her baby. I have no hopes and dreams tied up in her. I had hopes and dreams tied up in my son and maybe sour hopes and dreams develop a smell. Maybe when the first ten years are an enchanting time, maybe when you've seen a boy develop the capacity to light somebody else up like a Christmas tree because of his charm, his wit, his looks, his sheer bloody niceness, and then the second ten years see it all going rancid, you realise you can't live with that, whereas an irritating older sister's manageable. You can live with a lousy son, but why would you? If there was hope, maybe, but I don't have hope any more and I'm tired of being a forty-year-old innocent, having my dreams torn up and used as lavatory paper by a middle-aged twenty-year-old who thinks life equals consuming. I'll be my own forty-year-old innocent where nobody can put me down with second-hand TV snideries. In short: fuck him.'

She beamed as she said it, and there was no acid burning in it. Just the clap of one door closing. Then she was on to business. More and more, she told Cassie, starting the agenda, people wanted to put a particular *Pinhead* sketch on a T-shirt or an ad. 'We're going to have to retain an international copyright-law firm that does constant sweeps to catch people using them without authorisation.'

'Do we have to be that possessive?'

'Yes, we do. Che Guevara. I say the name, what do you see?'

'Black and white picture, gorgeous bloke, long curly hair, military beret.'

'Right. Image on a thousand posters, a million T-shirts. Based on one photograph taken by one photographer.'

'That's usually the way it goes,' Cassie observed mildly.

'Who lives in Castro's Cuba. Who isn't that bothered that his nice pic is being used to remind people of the great Che who otherwise mightn't ever hear of him. Until someone in the US of A decides to put that face on a whisky bottle. Photographer takes the dimmest of dim views. Sues. Likely to have a more difficult route to his objective because he *didn't* get possessive up to now, so there's a million precedents of people stealing the image and using it to promote whatever they wanted, without let or hindrance.'

'I can tell you've been talking to lawyers,' Cassie said, gathering her belongings. 'I'd better surrender before you hit me with a heretofore.'

'I can do a pretty good Ultimo of the Sixth, too,' Marsha added, instinctively turning at the door of the apartment to admire it all over again.

'It's beautiful,' Cassie said softly. 'I hope you are always as happy in it as you are today. That view. To be able to see the sea – every day. It eases your soul, just watching the sea, doesn't it?'

CHAPTER SIXTEEN

Of Mice and Drunks

When Cassie picked Ben up outside the school that afternoon, he gave her his usual huge hug, uncaring about other boys of his age who turned their embarrassed faces away when their mothers, collecting them, offered kisses. But when he buckled himself into the seat, he did not embark, as he usually did, on an impassioned account of the incident or lesson that most engaged his attention on that day.

'I'm in trouble,' he said solemnly.

'Oh, dear,' Cassie said. 'Been found guilty of something awful, have you?'

'I don't know.'

The answer was miserable in its brevity. She signalled and pulled in at the side of the road. Once the engine was switched off, she hugged him all over again.

'She told me to give this to you.'

He handed her an envelope, slightly crushed by the tightness of his hold on it. Cassie opened it. Victorian handwriting. Perhaps Mr or Mrs Cadogan could attend the school at such-and-such a time, on such-and-such a day, to discuss some issues Ben's teachers had with his veracity?

'What does it say?'

Ben's voice was filled with a dread she rarely heard in it. She read the letter aloud.

'What's foracity?'

'It means truthfulness.'

Ben's eyes searched her face for the elusive meaning.

'It means they think you've been telling lies.'

'Oh,' he said, deflated.

'More than one teacher,' Cassie hazarded, rereading the letter. 'More than one teacher thinks you've been telling lies.'

'I thought it was just Miss Morgan,' he said, dolefully.

'Did you tell lies to her?'

'I can't remember. I don't know.'

He began to cry, turning his face to her because children from his school had caught up to where the car was pulled in, and he didn't want them to see him in tears. She started the car and drove home in silence, trying to work out what was best to do. In the driveway, she turned to meet so frightened a face that she could not speak other than to protest that he had nothing to fear from her, from *her*, but could only pat her own trembling mouth to indicate that they would be silent now, silent until they were safe inside the house, away from the harsh, probing sunshine and the shouts of children.

Inside, he followed her across the big hall into the cosy little sitting room at the front of the house, dragging his bag so listlessly that it hardly cleared the floor, dragging rugs into defeated, unnoticed half-pursuit of him, leaving them drawn to accusatory arrows on the hard floor: this way to the guilty party. She took the bag from him and threw it back out into the hall, pulling him down beside her on the small couch, trying to hug the belief and the happiness back into him.

'D'you know what I think?' she asked eventually. Asked the room, because his head was sunk on her, rocked by leftover sobs. 'I think I don't need to know about school. I think I'll send your dad in to talk to them. But I don't care what they tell him. Because I know you. I'm not going to be reached by any bad thing anybody in school says about you.'

He pulled himself into a crouching position beside her, watching her. She held his face, trying to efface the slug-trails of tears from the rounded cheeks with her thumbs.

'Ben, you don't understand. I love you no matter what. If there's a bad thing in school, your dad will go and whatever he finds, he'll help you close it into a box and bury the box and you'll go back to being our beautiful boy. OK?'

'OK,' he said dutifully, sure of nothing. Looking over his head, she could see the rugs, pointing into the room where they sat.

'Would you look?'

He followed her nod and something about the urgently defeated shape of the rugs made him smile, shakily. He got up to put them back in place, and had recovered considerably by the time Polo arrived.

'Show him the letter,' Ben whispered to his mother.

A whisper from Ben was so untypical, it stopped his father dead. Cassie silently handed over the letter. Polo read it. Looked at Ben, who began to weep. Looked at Cassie, who put her hands out, at knee level – what do you think? Polo stood, read the letter again and took up his mobile phone. Punched buttons. He would like to talk to the headmistress. Polo Cadogan. Ben Cadogan's father. When the headmistress came on the line, Polo outlined the letter. He was raising it with her because more than one teacher seemed to be involved, although only one had signed it or given their name. Ben and Cassie looked at each other, a mad flurry of surprised self-righteousness in their glance. No, no, Polo went on, it wasn't a problem, here's what he would suggest. He would suggest that tomorrow morning before school opened, he would be there, with Ben, although Ben could stay outside while he, Polo, met the teachers in the presence of the headmistress. He was sure it would be no problem for her to arrange it, teachers were always on the premises well before classes actually began, he knew. Yes, indeed, there was a time and a date proffered in the letter, but he was sure she would agree with him that six-year-olds didn't have the same sense of time adults had, and his little boy should not be kept on tenterhooks about – Polo groped momentarily for words – about an unresolved issue which would undoubtedly affect the behaviour of both child and teacher in the classroom tomorrow anyway. He was delighted to have talked to her and to have experienced such courtesy. He looked forward to seeing her in the morning.

In the morning, Polo dressed with particular care, choosing what was for him a grossly understated silk tie and one of his best shirts. She could hear him asking Ben to insert the cufflinks for him. He drank his cup of tea standing up, not to put a horizontal crease in either shirt or trousers.

'Booted and spurred?' she asked, smiling.

'Loins girded in fucking concrete,' he confirmed, steering Ben out of the door in front of him at the point of his rigid fingers, his hand held like a gun.

Just short of an hour later, the phone rang.

'Our son's veracity has been vindicated,' he said.

'Meaning?'

'Meaning two stupid fuckers who were quick to share their separate half-arsed bits of information in the staffroom but slow to check their facts are licking their wounds right now and it'll be a long, long time before either of them raises another cheep about Ben. I told them the law of slander could be used to defend six-year-olds just as it could be used to defend sixty-year-olds.'

A gurgling digressive thought struck Cassie that before

he got interested in politics Polo wouldn't have known the difference between libel and slander. He had been spending a lot of time, recently, with high-powered lawyers.

'One of the teachers has nothing to do with Ben. Doesn't teach him anything. Has no responsibilities whatever that involve him, right? Hold on a second.' Engine noise roared into the space left by his voice while he gave his full attention to some road manoeuvre. 'She just happened to overhear him telling a pal of his that his father played golf with a President of America. Which, of course, could not be true.'

Cassie began to laugh, looking at the silver-framed picture on the curio table showing Polo and a completely convulsed Bill Clinton on a golf course in Kerry. She could not remember the details of the elaborate joke the President's Irish hosts had sprung on him during a day off in his official visit in 1995. It had involved Polo playing one shot against Clinton and having his picture taken, though, that was for sure.

'So we knock that one down. Embarrassment all round. But then the other cow, who Ben is unfortunate enough to have all the time teaching him, this other cow has it written all over her "You're not going to catch *me* out that easily, so you're not" and she tells the headmistress – oh, yes, she doesn't deign to address me directly, might make me think I was a human being or something – that Ben had claimed in class the other day to have read John Steinbeck's *Of Mice and Men*. She had gone to some trouble to make sure he didn't mean it was read aloud to him, but no, he was claiming to have read it all, start to finish. *Steinbeck*. I went and got Ben, I told him I was going to ask him some questions and he was to give the answers to the headmistress. (In other words, you brainless cow, I haven't missed your dumbass won't-talk-to-the-lowly-parent crap, I can do the same.) I asked him where the book was kept in our library. He described where it was. I asked him what books were near it. He gave all the titles.'

Cassie, the cordless phone to her ear, walked into the library and sat down on the floor. She must not lose, she thought, the habit of physically mimicking Ben's height in order to see the world from his point of view. It would not have occurred to her that he would remember the titles of the books surrounding *Of Mice and Men*.

'I'd love to have heard his pronunciation of *The Gulag Archipelago*,' she said.

'I asked him why he picked *Of Mice and Men* to read, rather than the others, and he said because he thought it was going to be about mice, and also the book was smaller than most of the ones on the bottom shelf.'

Less intimidating, she thought, smiling. True enough, at less than an inch across, the spine of the book was narrower than any of its neighbours. Polo completed his account of the various proofs he had elicited from Ben in the headmistress's office with a description of the conditional climb-down of Ben's teacher. She did not quite apologise to the boy, but accepted he might, genuinely, have read the book by himself.

'Big of her,' Cassie spat.

By way of shifting the goalposts, Polo added, the teacher went on to request that he and Cassie get Ben assessed by a psychologist.

'Why? If the problem's been cleared up, where does the psychologist come in to it?'

'She thinks these problems emerge because Ben may be a gifted child and we should get this confirmed. It would help his teachers bring out the best in him. We can think about it,' Polo said, losing interest. 'You haven't forgotten Saturday?'

No, she hadn't forgotten Saturday. Gobnait would be over later in the day and the two of them would get started on getting the house ready for the 'casual party' Polo was planning for some friends. She was also going to invite Marsha and Erik, she told him, because, just as Polo wanted to celebrate recent company successes (she did not add 'and secret political manipulations'), she felt they should celebrate the fact that Disney had optioned the children's books with a view to a TV series. Other than those two, she wasn't going to invite anybody else. Polo loved to preside over the mass of his friends, interacting. Cassie preferred more cellular relationships, meeting pals singly, on the phone or over a meal.

On Saturday, doing final checks with Ben early in the evening of the party, Cassie found herself trying to work out why she was so casually comfortable about that night's gathering. It must be, she decided, the lifting of the pressure of Liam's silently pissed presence, common to most of their previous parties. Out of habit, whenever they invited Marsha to anything, they had tended to invite Liam, too, which meant each of them was forced to spend time listening to his slurred monotone on some aspect of his life in which they had no interest. In addition, there were all the myriad little adjustments, warnings, explanations to be given to Ben, to other guests, and whenever a few freelance waiters were called in, to staff as well: Liam's no harm, he'll just get quietly plastered, water his drinks as the night goes on, he won't notice but it'll slow him down, try to get him to eat something, don't mention it to Marsha.

'Auntie Marsha's not bringing Uncle Liam tonight,' Cassie said. Casually. Of course, the little voice in her head commented, if you were really casual, you'd have talked about her coming without him, not 'bringing' him as if he was a spare blanket for the guest bed.

'Why not?'

'She's stopped being married to him.'

'How?'

'There's a thing called divorce that rubs out marriage.'

Ben considered this for some time before checking was Marsha happy with this new arrangement. Yes, Cassie assured him. Not only was Marsha happy, she was delighted to get into a new apartment on the beach and far away from her son, who had grown up to be unpleasant and unkind to her. Overhead, they could hear the shower being turned off. Ben took off up the stairs. She could hear him telling Polo about Marsha's impending divorce. Say one negative thing about my best friend, ran Cassie's mental threat, and I'll come up there and make you very sorry, Polo. As far as she could tell, Polo's only comment was that Marsha was a great bit of stuff, and until he was sent off to bed, Ben should make sure she was never on her own tonight. Marsha'll take care of that all by herself, Cassie thought. In point of fact, Marsha was *less* likely to be on her own tonight than at previous gatherings, where she would break away from a laughing, drinking group to go check on Liam, pretend to have a quiet conversation with him when in fact he was incapable of words.

It was Ben who greeted the first arriving guest. Erik the Red always left himself a superfluity of time, in order to get out of his car, into his wheelchair and – in this case – up the ramp now installed beside the front steps before helpful guests could offer him their assistance. Ben, coming downstairs, found Erik in the big stone hall and flung himself on him with glad cries. If Ben persuaded his mother to give Erik the biggest double gin in captivity, Erik said, he would drink it sitting on the couch and Ben could do wheelies in the electric wheelchair.

'Remind me to plug that in when he finishes with it,' Erik said, a few minutes later, nodding towards the hall, where the surging revs of the wheelchair could be heard as Ben greeted half the incoming guests by terrorising them with it.

'Why do you never want people to help you?' Cassie asked him.

'People in this country know shag all about disability because we never had a war. They go at it without knowing how to go at it. Terrify me. I once met a guy in a car park who got me out of the wheelchair and into the car and the wheelchair into its slot on the back – except that I'd only just managed to get myself *out* of the bloody car and into the goddamn wheelchair. He just wouldn't listen to me. I was a cripple, he wasn't, therefore he knew how to take care of me.'

One of Polo's lawyer friends joined them, as did the girl who had taken over Orna's job. Introducing her, Cassie mentioned that since Orna left the company, she'd never heard a word about her. Karen looked surprised. 'Ask Polo,' she recommended. 'He knows every move the two of them have made since they left. Has their phone numbers and everything.'

'You don't escape Polo.' The lawyer smiled. It was praise.

'But how would he know things like their telephone numbers?'

'Cassie, you'd never make a journalist,' Erik said. 'You're never, in Ireland, more than one person away from the person you want to find out about. You just work out who'd know them. No man is an island. Everybody's surrounded by – no offence,' he said, patting the lawyer's forearm, 'lawyers, doctors, priests, teachers, co-workers.'

'But people like that don't talk, don—'

'Lawyers gossip more than any other profession,' Erik said. 'Ask any good hack, and he'll tell you that. Next in line, as leakers, are the cops. Politicians come in there, too. And if you want to reach someone, find someone, revive a cold trail, then nothing's as good as the old clerical network.'

As he talked, Cassie watched Peter Thornton arriving, was surprised to see Ben rated him highly enough to get out of the wheelchair to hug him. She could see Thornton being introduced to others, asking brief questions, then disengaging to wander on his own into the room where they sat. This man seemed committed to avoidance of any network, clerical or otherwise. He drifted into the group around the fireplace to hear Erik's descriptions of his media interviews across the United States promoting the children's books.

'The interviewers with the strongest opinions on the books were the ones who hadn't looked at them at all. That's the thing that takes getting used to: the interviewers talking more than you do. Then there are things you can't get used to. One blonde on an afternoon show, just as we were about to go back on the air after a commercial break, suddenly went like this at me.' Erik peeled his lips back from his clenched upper and lower teeth so he looked like an illustration of how murdered people can be identified by their dental work. 'I'm looking at her, thinking, Lady, I'm phoning for the guys in the white jackets, and then I discover she expects me to tell her has she got lipstick on her teeth. I told her no. She had oodles of it on her teeth,' he finished, with an evil snigger.

On one programme, a fellow-guest was Maeve Binchy. Weird, Erik agreed, that two people working on national newspapers in Ireland would never meet before they found themselves sitting side by side on an American TV show to promote their respective books. 'Just before that particular programme went on the air, the compère turned to her and said, "By the way, Maeve, when precisely was it that you became interested in restoring antique furniture?" She told me afterwards that, for one crazy moment, she was going to go along with it. She was even trying to work out how much she knew about antique furniture. Which, as it turned out, was nothing. So she said to the compère, "I think you may have mixed me up with someone else – I'm Maeve Binchy the writer," just as the red light comes on, and he starts asking her about her books as if he never would have believed she'd know an antique chair from a fried sausage.'

One of the group asked Cassie if she'd found the media tours as peculiar as Erik did. 'It took me a while to realise they wanted no surprises. If they had you on for three minutes, that meant four questions, predictable answers and the obligation to laugh hysterically at anything mildly humorous said by the presenter. Full stop.'

'So Polo would be a disaster on that kind of show?' Peter Thornton asked.

She nodded. The presenters who coped well with Polo Cadogan when he guested on their shows were the ones who managed televisual time the way an angler manages a hooked fish – feeding out the line to exhaust the fish, then reeling it in at just the right moment. Presenters who tried to chop him into little sections or to top his jokes tended to come worst out of the encounters.

Ben appeared beside them. 'My dad says not to forget to pick out the records you wanted to copy,' he told Thornton.

'I'll report you to the music-royalty people,' Erik threatened.

'These are old vinyls I've tried to buy and simply can't find,' Thornton said, allowing Ben to lead him towards the library, where one corner was devoted to Dr Cadogan's extensive record collection, some of them old, breakable seventy-eights. Cassie pointed a finger at her watch and Ben nodded. It would soon be long enough past normal bed-time for him to go without a fuss. Cassie left the group to make sure Erik's wheelchair was plugged into a socket somewhere and discovered an unexpectedly large group of people draped over the backs of couches, an assortment of chairs and a few rugs in the small sitting room with the big TV on. 'What on earth are you looking at?' she asked, standing in the doorway. 'It isn't even news time yet. You expecting some major disaster?'

'We're watching the Ard Fheis,' one of the group said.

'The annual festival of the worst that television can offer,' another said.

A close-up shot of the Taoiseach doing his keynote address gave way to a long shot of the hall.

'Any minute now they'll give us the big close-up of an oul' fella with a cap and one tooth, from the wilds of Clare.'

'Careful about the Clare references,' someone from the other side of the room said.

'OK, Leitrim, then.'

'To say there's wilds in Leitrim is to flatter Leitrim,' someone else began. 'Leitrim is—'

He was shushed into silence, gestured at by almost everybody in the room, hands flapping downward – shut up, shut up, would you watch – as the camera work suddenly went MTV-wobbly. Something happening in the body of the hall attracted the attention both of the Taoiseach and of the camera operators covering his speech. He halted, started to speak again, halted again as a figure sprang from the body of the hall on to the stage. The director cut to another part of the hall, where a disruption that the sound system failed to pick up was creating concentric circles of people standing up to get involved or move away. The next shot showed the Taoiseach getting back to his autocued speech in spite of the intruder from the body of the hall being subdued a few feet away from him.

'*YES!*' several people in the room shouted, fists in the air. Those nearest Polo began to thump him on the back. Laughing at the vigour of the congratulations, he half turned and his eyes met Cassie's.

'Shhh,' somebody said. 'They're running into the bulletin. Please – keep it down.'

Polo half smiled at Cassie, turning back to the screen, where the newsreader was solemnly telling the nation that, in the last few moments, a group of pro-life protestors had disrupted the most important part of the annual conference of the country's governing party, the Fianna Fáil party. He handed over to a named political correspondent who, pink in the face with excitement at finding one of the ritual TV corpses of the year spring to life, said that credit must be given to the protestors for the timing and skill of their intervention. (A muted roar of approval rose around Cassie.) They had concealed themselves throughout the two-day conference, passing up opportunities to speak at committees in order to get themselves centre stage at the precise moment they knew the TV coverage would be watched by most viewers.

This, the correspondent went on, was a sophisticated and well-planned intervention. (A girl behind Polo hugged him around the chest and he patted her as if she was a pet dog.) The political correspondent, perhaps to help herself through a long piece to camera for which she could not have had the time to prepare a script, began to count her points off on her fingers. Holding on to her index finger, she pointed out that the Taoiseach was visibly disturbed as he reached a key point in his speech, although he had recovered with remarkable speed. Moving on to her second finger, she stated that there had been drama on stage as a minister tackled a protestor who

273

might, for all any of them knew, have been carrying a weapon. Isolating the third finger, she told the camera that this was arguably the most significant aspect of the protest, 'this' being the simultaneous eruption of protestors in several different parts of the hall at the same time. Maximum commotion, disorder and distraction, she said, but minimum illegality.

'Finally,' the correspondent said, reaching her little finger and for one visible second unsure what, in her story, it stood for, 'finally, the protestors who are currently being questioned by the police may spend Saturday night in custody. But they know that they have swept every other aspect of the Ard Fheis off the front pages of the Sunday newspapers and taken over the prime space in those newspapers to high-profile the abortion issue in a way it has not been high-profiled in recent times, and in a way that will send shivers up the spines of every politician watching tonight's events unfold.'

The TV turned down, the group in the room gloated about timing, about choreography, about courage, about understanding of TV. Cassie was tempted to point out that the Taoiseach, not knowing either the person who leaped on to the stage or his purpose, had shown a fair amount of courage in continuing his speech when, for all he knew, he was about to be gunned down. Not the time, she thought. Not the place. She slid quietly from the room and went to the kitchen, where Ben was drinking orange juice in semi-darkness and indicating he was on his way to bed.

When the door closed behind his weary small form, she stood amid mid-party chaos, trying to guess the level of Polo's direct or indirect involvement in the pro-life protest. The door-shape filled with brightness and closed again, Polo inside the kitchen with her.

'You didn't tell me.'

'No.'

'Why not?'

'Keep it cellular.'

'Polo, there are plenty of places where pro-life points can be made on media.'

'Put someone on any of the usual current-affairs programmes, all it does is confirm everybody's pre-existing prejudices,' Polo said. 'Do what those guys did tonight, and they're gladiators, they're cool, they're rule-breakers. And, by Jesus, do they know how to work the system. The most important system of all: media. Why would you want them to use media in an orthodox way, which can only result in the defeat of what they stand for, when using it in an unorthodox way is so visibly successful?'

He began to load the dishwasher. She left him to it, wandering through the ground floor of the house, checking that each cluster of people had food and that the bores were kept moving. The library door was half open but, because inside was dark, she was about to pass it by when she heard music. Without turning on the light, she stepped inside the heavy oaken door. Some light came from a dying fire in the big old grate.

Peter Thornton was seated, head against the side piece of one of the old leather armchairs, listening to a record spinning on the turntable. Watching her with the cool observation characteristic of the person whose eyes are used to semi-darkness. Holding a glass, he pointed, with no movement other than the unwrapping of his index finger from around it, at the chair opposite the one where he sat. When she sat down, he set his glass on a side table while he threw three logs on the fire, a starburst of sparks as each hit the reddening embers. He poked the ash beneath so that fresh flame began to seek and soar around the dry logs.

She sat, elbows rigid, hands tense, trying to force her

limbs to relax. Thornton padded around the room, then put a glass beside her. Red wine. It would give her a headache, but what the hell?

'Another triumph for the forces of good.'

It was clear, the way he said it, but not crisp. The clarity was the effortful concentration of someone fighting the slurring effects of alcohol. She thought about playing dumb, about making him tell her he was talking about the pro-life demonstration.

'Polo explained it all to me,' she said.

'And?'

'What he says makes perfect sense. It is persuasive. I am convinced.'

He raised the glass, before drinking from it, in half salute.

'And I am ashamed.'

The fire was blazing now, filling the room with warmth, casting great shifting shadows across the books, up to the high ceilings.

'I am persuaded that these are good people who believe they must fight to prevent what they know to be murder. Yet I have a great need to think the worst of them, to find them out in something evil.'

He drank and said nothing. The American voice singing on the LP behind him seemed to be doing a French song. Or maybe a song about a French song. The phrase *'chanson pour les petits enfants'* kept coming up. Ironic timing, she thought.

'If Polo had anything to do with what happened tonight, he made no money out of it, will take no credit for it. It is pure altruism. Yet I know I would be afraid to describe it that way to any of my friends. I hate being a coward, but I am one. I am a confused coward. Most confused of all because I admire most people who give their time for free for something they believe in, even if

I don't believe in it, but I don't admire Polo for this and I can't pin down why.'

There was a short pause between tracks before the American began to sing again. Something about moth-balling battleships and sending soldiers home. No. Sending one particular soldier home. A general or some-thing. She tried to concentrate on the story in the song, to distract herself.

> *All he'll have is memories*
> *And great books by James Jones –*
> *They're sending the old man home.*

It was sentimentally moving.

'Country-and-western,' she said, satirically, at the end of it, when the disc, too, finished.

'Country,' Thornton said, sleeving it and selecting another big black LP.

Corrections must be easier, when you're drunk, if you can do them in one word, she thought. Might check that with Marsha. Although Liam operated one-word sentences drunk or sober.

'Boot scootin' cupsa cold coffee,' she said.

'Best lyrics in popular music in recent times have come from country music,' he said, not bothering to turn round as he said it. The next LP dropped, the needle locked into the groove, and a pianist began a highly theatrical introduction. What followed was the oddest song. A song about sado-masochism, complete with whips, missing limbs and worse. Thornton sat back, smiling to himself, eyebrows raised in query: you know this guy?

She shook her head as the pianist/comedian began another, equally weird ditty, this time about the pleasures of poisoning pigeons in a park. Totally distracted from her earlier thoughts, she found herself giggling unwillingly at the outrageous bad taste and cruelty of it.

'Tom Lehrer,' Thornton said.

'Who was he?'

'Was?'

She shrugged. Even as a parody, the performance reeked of twenty or thirty years earlier.

'He's a persssif –' Thornton narrowed his eyes and started again. 'He is a professor of mathematics at Harvard. Or Yale. Used to do this as a s-sideline. Stopped.'

'Why?'

'Why'd he do it or why'd he stop?'

'Stop. He was very funny.'

Thornton pushed back in the chair, the long limp hair flopping sideways as he tilted his head to look at the flames through the whiskey in his glass.

'Very rarely, very, *very* rarely,' Thornton said, so slowly and after such an interval that Cassie had forgotten she had asked a question. 'People know when they've done their best work. Muz-most people never know when they've done their best work. But a few do. A very few. And an even smaller purz-percentage, having come to that knowledge, stop. Salinger. Lehrer.'

'Hemingway?'

This time, the pause was so long, she thought he might have fallen asleep, then realised he was slowly shaking his head.

'Why not Hemingway?'

'Not the same. That was – that was – a man with no energy left to keep confecting himself. Lehrer never confected himself. Never needed the heat of 'proval to keep his blood moving, know who he was. Mss-most performers not truly alive without one last fan to sing to.'

She leaned forward towards the fire, remembering times when she had sat in this kind of companionable darkness, toasting bread, with her father. Her father, she thought, would point out to her that Polo was more than the kind of performer who simply needed to warm himself at the responses of audiences. Her father sought the fulcrum, the point of balance, in anything. Tonight, he would point out to her that in an Ireland over-supplied with politicians claiming beliefs because focus groups made those beliefs safe and inescapable, Polo was note-worthy as the exception: a man cleverly serving genuinely held beliefs – beliefs that could do him nothing but damage. He would not often be surrounded by the kind of collective enthusiasm coming from the well-groomed group in the small TV room. The zealots in the room, she thought, wondering at the reflex nature of the pejorative gloss.

'It's so much easier to like the likeable,' she said to the fire.

'*Quis non amantum amat,*' Thornton said, finishing his drink. 'Do not even the heathens do this?'

'I don't know what the fuck you're talking about,' she said, in a sudden spurt of temper, putting down her drink and standing up. 'Being drunk is no excuse for being a pompous pain in the tits.'

'You're quite right,' he said, just as she reached the door. 'I'm sorry.'

'Don't give it a thought,' she said. 'Frankly, you're the least of my worries.'

CHAPTER SEVENTEEN

Street Theatre and the Angel of Death

Getting Ben out of school early on just one Friday proved to be no problem. Ben's teacher was now treating him with a defensive formality. She seemed to believe Polo had the classroom bugged and the smallest step out of line would cause her trouble. That was Cassie's theory. When she mentioned it to Polo, his face soured at the recollection of the *Of Mice and Men* episode. 'Bloody great idea, to bug that classroom,' he said. 'Dead easy, too.'

'Oh, *Polo*.'

Eyebrows raised, he took a pen from the breast pocket of his jacket and handed it to her. For a moment, she wondered what he wanted her to write, then realised the pen was heavier than most. She turned it, taking in the details, pushed a button on the side. '. . . the fact that a member of the Arts Council is an expert in street theatre would certainly help . . .' a voice said.

Polo took back the pen. 'Whenever I don't quite trust the people I'm negotiating with, I record the meeting,' he said.

'That's illegal. To record someone without their knowledge.'

'Nonsense. Doesn't matter, I'm not going to bug Ben's classroom.'

'She was perfectly nice about letting him go early,'

Cassie said, wondering why she felt the need to do PR for Ben's teacher, why she wanted Polo's focus to be somewhere else, on some other hate figure.

'That's partly because she'll have an easier time when he's gone. Ben spends so much time with talkative adults like you and me and Marsha and your mother and Peter and Gobnait he thinks he's an adult. No respect for authority, is how that's interpreted at the PTA meetings I've attended. He interrupts all the time, has opinions on everything, asks questions about everything.'

Polo loaded the last of his goods into the successor to the Pajero, Cassie sitting on the stone steps watching. 'This is going to be a great summer,' he predicted.

'Because *Bards* is the new *Riverdance*?' she asked, quoting a recent review of the street-theatre show Polo planned to bring to the summer festivals.

'Partly that. It's good to know you have a great show. But it'll mean you and Ben spending time in places around the country you've never even seen. Once school closes down, you can both spend a week here, a week there, and we'll all three of us be able to explore wherever it is the show's in that week. Be tourists. See castles.'

'Do Bunratty.'

'Do Bunratty,' he agreed. 'Believe it or not, Bunratty's very good. I checked all of those yokes out before we put together the *Bards* show.'

'Secretly recorded them,' Cassie said. 'Left a bug in each castle to steal any new jokes they came up with after you'd gone.'

'Now, *there*'s an idea,' he said, laughing.

He climbed into the driver's seat. It would take him, he estimated, the guts of three hours to get to Galway. Might take her a little longer, starting at eleven. They'd want to break for lunch. A good place would be the Hideout in Kinnegad. Or Harry's if Ben wanted to see truck-drivers laying into chips and beans. Go on, she thought, you don't have to decide which restaurant we eat a hamburger in. He checked again did she remember about the unexpected turn-off in Kinnegad. She nodded, silently. It would be more logical to go straight, he said, poking his hand out ahead of him in case she missed his meaning, but that would take her to Mullingar. She assured him she would turn left in Kinnegad.

'Don't forget to bring your mobile phone.'

Another nod. 'See you this evening in the City of the Tribes,' she told him, and watched the car disappear down the driveway. Galway, she thought. Of all Irish cities, she liked Galway best. There was always a bit of excitement in Galway, a sense of something going on.

The first time it happened, it happened this way.

The chair beside the bed had been moved. Its normal place was in parallel with her, so she had to turn sideways to see whoever sat in it. The man sitting in it now was facing her. He must have moved it, she thought. He nodded to her.

'You did,' she said.

'Probably,' he said.

'What do you mean, probably? Either you did or you didn't.'

'Didn't what?'

'Move the chair.'

'I definitely moved the chair.'

'I know you,' she said, to see how it sounded.

'My name is Peter Thornton.'

'The drunk at our party.'

He nodded again. Seriously, as if the description was as valid an identification as a magnetic strip on a credit card.

'I'm sorry, that was rude.'

'Doesn't matter.'

'Why are you here?'

'Just.'

The word fell like a softly flattened hand on to water.

'Just,' she mimicked, and laughed.

'Just,' he said again, and smiled.

'Just *because*,' she said, thinking of times she had played this game with Ben. Reacting to the thought.

'Don't try to get up,' the man said. 'You're attached to a million tubes.'

'I have to get Ben.'

'No, you don't. The tubes are keeping you alive. You've been hurt.'

'Where is Ben?'

The man pushed the coverlet back into place where she had dislodged it.

'You don't know, is that it?'

He looked at her, silently. The door into the room opened and in a movement of his head he dismissed whoever was trying to come in. He was in charge, she decided. He must be a doctor. This must be a hospital. Ben – the question and the horror of the possibility came out of her in a gibberish scream. Ben must be in the hospital too, was he alive, he must be, where was he, how badly hurt was he, was he alive, of course he was, what happened, was he alive, was he alive was he *alive*? Some woman held her in place and the man sat while the screams croaked away down into a whispering hiss of a question. Is Ben dead? He nodded.

'Ben died,' he said softly.

Ah, no, she said, hushed-calm in voice while her hands clawed at air, as if staying calm would persuade him to change the truth of it, not Ben, not my beautiful boy, my son, my son. Please, she begged him, trying to turn, held, pinned to the bed by plastered legs, tied and tethered by fluid-filled flexing tubes. No, no, no, she soothed him, head rocking frantic, yet confined. No, no, no. Please, no.

He sat through the longing litany of hope and desperation until the grief reached the last barrier and came out of her in a growling, choking howl and boiling tears blurred out the sight of him. The tears burned into the abrasions in her face and she tried to believe that this prickling pain was real, the other not, trying to croon the cramping horror of it away into sleep. Someone put a hand on her arm. Through half-open eyes, she could see a shiny-faced nurse, leaning close to be heard over the raucous grief.

'Cassie, hang on, hang on, I'm putting this into the IV, it'll give you a rest, you—'

The second time it happened, it happened this way.

She lay with her eyes closed, knowing from the feel, the smell of the room that it was strange. A hotel room. Holidays? No. There were office noises in the room with her. Computers. An office, then.

'You're in a hospital,' the voice said. 'It's OK. Don't be frightened.'

She knew the voice, but when she opened her eyes, could not put a name to its owner.

'Peter Thornton,' he supplied.

The computer noises were coming from things at her shoulder level or above. She tried to get a look at them. Pain and the man said no together. The pain was more forceful.

'Up behind you are machines to measure how much oxygen is getting into your blood, how your heart is doing,' he said. 'You had a car crash. A bad car crash.'

A bad car crash, she repeated obediently. A bad car crash.

'Was it my fault?'

'No. According to the Guards, no.'

'Is the driver of the other car alive?'

'Yes. In hospital. Down the corridor here. But alive, yes.'

The ease of the exchange brought it home to her that she was somehow asking the wrong questions. The man was looking at her very fixedly, as if he knew the right questions, but she had to come up with them herself.

'I was on my own in the car?'

He shook his head. She was not alone when the accident happened, then. Who could have been with her in the car?

'Ben?'

He said nothing.

'Was Ben hurt too?'

'Yes.'

She came up out of the bed so suddenly, so violently, that he put his hand against her, against the hard bone below her neck, as if she was attacking. The big hand preventing her coming up further, forcing her slowly back.

'Why are you not letting me – I have to – where is he?'

He tidied the coverlet where her movement had disarranged it.

'Where?'

His eyes searched her face as if she knew something he only half knew, and she knew to ask the right question.

'Is Ben killed?'

Ben was killed, he said. Yes, Ben was killed. He was. Yes. She closed her eyes and his voice died away. After a moment, she opened them again, but he was still there and what he had said was still coming out of him, not now in words, but in something like a sheen of sorrow. The door opened and this time he tweaked his fingers at it – come on, come in – fingers together, moving as one. A nurse with a silver tray, twittering words about just going to put something into the IV and just going to do something else and just not taking a minute. The man ignored her, still watching.

The woman in the bed closed her eyes, squeezing them tight to make him go away with what he had said. Because if he was not there it would not be true and she could make him go away if she refused to open her eyes again.

A cooler feeling ran into the arm held rigid on a small wooden block for the IV. If she opened her eyes, she thought, he would still be there, insisting on telling her something awful, but she was not sure now what the awful thing was or what his name was, and he was probably not there anyway, if she opened her eyes, but she could not remember how to open her eyes and it was all gone.

The third time it happened, it happened this way.

She would surface into the pain, tell someone and then the someone would be gone and she was surfacing again. Once, when she surfaced, a man, sitting at the end of her bed, gestured a nurse away. She waited for the coolness in the vein of her arm that would announce the softening of the pain, loosen her grip on consciousness, but it did not come.

'Singing the same fucking chorus six million times,' she said.

The man laughed.

'What's funny?' she asked.

'What chorus are you singing?' he asked back.

'The chorus that my arse is hurting.'

'Just your arse?'

She thought about this. Most of her seemed to hurt, but the pain centred at her lower spine. She tried to move and could not. If she concentrated properly, she decided, she would be able to move. She concentrated and there was a jolting, but it did not amount to moving to where she wanted to go.

'You can't sit up,' the man said.

'Who says?'

He laughed again, softly. 'It's not a question of who says. Your two legs are broken and surrounded with plaster.'

'Why?'

'You had a car crash.'

'You've said that before,' she said. There was something familiar about the way he said it.

'Yes, I have,' he said, and seemed glad to be caught out.

She opened her eyes and looked at him. He stayed still, like he was having his picture taken. 'Your name is Peter Thornton,' she said.

'Right,' he said, as if she had passed an exam.

'You're not a doctor,' she told him. 'Why are you always here?'

'What do you mean by "always"?'

'Always,' she said, impatiently. Everybody knows what always means. But how could he be here always when this was the first time she had seen him in the hospital?

'You remember me being here before,' he said, very quietly, like a parent prompting a child to the next line of a prayer. She scrabbled in memories that shifted and slid away from her like song-titles, and the sound of him saying it, rather than the reality of it, came to her first. She repeated the sound of him saying it and as she did, the reality of it came to her in a splitting, stabbing scream.

'Ben is dead. Ben was killed. Ben is dead, he's dead, he's *dead*.'

Someone else in the room moved and the man turned towards the movement. They battled, distantly, without words, bent blearily as if through the thick-bottomed glass of an old bottle. Then the nurse spoke to her again. Softly, but with a stiff reproach to the man in her voice. 'I'll come back very soon, very soon, Cassie. D'you think you'll be all right?'

Cassie's face-bone pain was surging hotly under her swollen skin but she nodded, not knowing why she nodded. The life seemed to be bleeding out of her with every misery-clotted breath, the effort of pulling in air past the crying turning into its own hoarse keening. Damp coolness touched the coarse-crisped abrasions again, mopping the salty tears. It stayed, the coolness, on her closed eyelids for a few seconds. A softly heavy coldness, infinitely comforting, gently pressured by some hand. Her breathing quietened somewhat. She half opened heavy-lidded eyes. The man was still there. Expressionless. Empty as a cave. Holding the wadded wet white thing.

'He is dead, then.' She said it carefully, searching for a response. The man sat still. Neutral as a pool of dark cold water, she thought.

'He is dead?'

This time it was not an exploration, but a prayerful mistake, awaiting correction.

'Ben is dead,' the man said, robbing her for ever of the fleet comfort of the indefinite 'he'. 'Ben is dead, yes.'

Terror spasmed through her and, one-handed, she clutched at him, fingers encountering shifting metal, nearly tearing the watch off his wrist.

'No.' He said it loudly. 'There was nothing like that. It was over before he even registered. No pain. No fear. Do you hear me?'

I hear you, she thought at him, as he bent to free her

fingers, trapped in the expanding bracelet of his watch, his hair falling forward over his forehead. I hear you and I hate you and I believe you. He put her hand carefully across her chest. As if, she thought, he was arranging a Victorian picture of the quiet consumptive dying. I wish, she thought and said.

'You wish?' the man prompted, and wordless surging tears came again. I wish I could die, could have died, had died before I knew my beloved boy had died, died, not in the linen layers of a snowy bed, but bucketing like a demolition dummy, the round downed firmness of his head crushing, giving way, giving blood and bone and the lovely sun-filled face of him warped, bloated, the shining soft gold of his hair soaking up the dark blood, each curl a circle of browning congealed brick red, brick hard blood – Oh, Jesus, how can this be, how can this be?

The cold dampness was fitted into her hand and she automatically brought it to her face, pounding it clumsily against the already wet skin. She could hear and feel the sobs revisiting through the all-pervasive pain: aftershocks of an earthquake warning the wounded.

'Why you?' she asked, without opening her eyes.

'It's my job,' the answer came. Tonelessly.

You are the angel of death, she thought, the force of a furious God, the bearer of terrible tidings. And I know you. But the pain prevents me remembering how I know you.

'How I know you,' she said, and the very clarity of the nonsensical non-question made her ashamed.

'You need the morphine, don't you?'

Yes, she thought, that's what I need. She could hear him moving around the room and then busy footsteps.

'Won't be a minute, now, Cassie.' The nurse's voice was full of reassurance.

'He Polo friend.'

There was a clinking of little bottles and a tearing of Cellophane.

'Know him.'

'Just count to ten and you'll begin to feel it. Just count to ten.'

'*Know* him.'

'Peter Thornton,' the man's voice said. 'The drunk at the party.'

Fingers were tapping at tubes, checking the flow.

'It's going in, Cassie, you can probably feel it—'

The chill of the medication hit. She could see him sitting. See him through the swimming swirls of the pain going. Sorry, she thought. Called you the angel of death. Doesn't matter, my sorry. Can't affect. Can't change. One truth. Ben dead. Just that. For ever. Ben dead. She spiralled into unawareness, still aware of the dying, a voice saying it softly, repeatedly, somewhere far distant like a choir hymn.

O Absalom, my son, my son.

CHAPTER EIGHTEEN

Tests and Lists

There came a time when she knew it without being told it. Knew it the moment she came out of drugged sleep. After that point, the man seemed to disappear.

There came a time when she knew it without being told it and did not fight it because there was no fighting it. After that point, other people seemed to appear.

Polo was there a lot. It was best, she found, not to let him know when she woke. That way, he would sit with his elbows on his knees, face in hands. Or he would wander the room, standing for long periods looking out of the window. Gravity had pulled his face down. His nose looked longer, the lines from nose to mouth deeper. She was so used to him smiling. Yet now those score-lines gave the impression that he had never smiled and never would smile again. His face was like a thunderstorm day when everything is so cold, so grey and black, dark shining with water, the sky hanging low, that it is unimaginable that there would ever be another sunny day. It was not even possible to call up the memory of past sunny days.

Sometimes, when she was pretending to be asleep, he would take her hand, the hand not fastened to the rigid board, and hold it. He would talk to her, telling her he understood how awful it must be, promising that the future would be tolerable, that time was a great healer. She learned to pump noises into her head to distance his words.

When he knew she was awake, he would fountain words, telling her where these flowers came from, reading aloud letters from people wishing her well. Sometimes, the letters would include some incident, some detail about Ben, and when he read that bit, he would cry. She would reach out with her free hand and touch him. He would bend his head down to her hand, the tears wetting it, and she would pat him. It seemed the least she could do.

Her mother was there, too, but her mother did not require minding. Her mother, terrified that Cassie, in the bed, would need anything from her, worked the room on every visit, culling dead flowers, dropping soluble aspirins into the water so the vases talked sibilantly to each other. Her mother read the letters, too, muttering them to herself, reading those from famous people twice. She never asked Cassie anything, but sometimes Cassie would hear her ticking off nurses and maids about a stain on the floor she said was there three days. Those circular dusting machines were not a patch on someone getting down on hands and knees and scrubbing properly, she said. Say what you like, the nuns had standards. You wouldn't see a stain left for three days on the floor in a hospital run by nuns.

Marsha was there a lot. Cassie had the impression Marsha was in a towering rage all the time she was there, but the rage seemed directed somewhere else. Everywhere else, maybe, other than at Cassie. Her aunt would come into the room, put a load of items on to the tall tray thing at the end of the bed, lift the chair (everybody else seemed to drag it) so it was right beside the bed. Cassie could see her sitting there without moving her neck. Marsha would pat her on the hand and, unless Cassie held on to the patting hand, take it back. Cassie liked that. Having her hand trapped in moist warmth was so discomfiting that she would end up asking Polo to get her a drink, simply to free her hand from his.

'Well?' Marsha would ask.

Cassie would never answer, and that seemed OK, too. Marsha would examine her, up and down, and after a while might tell her something she could not know herself. That the scabs on her face had fallen off. That the swelling around her eyes was down. That they had taken away one of the monitors. If Cassie said nothing, Marsha would sit awhile and then unpack whatever she brought with her. Mostly, it was a variety of drinks because Cassie could eat nothing that required chewing.

'I'm putting these in the fridge down the corridor,' Marsha would say, before shifting the chair back to its original position and disappearing for a while.

Cassie would forget she had been there, but gradually learned that if she came in at the door and did not move the chair, she was on the second phase of her visit. It seemed important to remember that, although Cassie was not clear why it was important, and once Marsha was gone, she ceased to think about what was or was not important. It was like watching an endless rerun of episodes from a TV series. Polo visited, read letters, told her things, cried, held her hand. Her mother visited, tidied things, read letters and complained in the corridor. Marsha visited, said little, brought things and came back after going somewhere else.

The first time Marsha's rage seemed to include her was the day Marsha discovered three days' worth of drinks untouched in the fridge. 'You haven't had a single one of them,' she told Cassie, coming back into the room. 'You're drinking bloody goddamn tapwater.'

Cassie stared at her fearfully through a blurring of tears. 'I'm sorry,' she said.

Marsha looked at her. 'I'm not mad at *you*, for Chrissake,' she said.

This frightened Cassie more. Marsha went down on her knees beside the bed and took hold of Cassie's hand in a strong, warm, one-handed grasp, the other hand wiping away Cassie's tears with a gentleness unexpected because of the rage. Cassie felt things going back into place. She and Marsha were at the hub, and Marsha's rage went out like the spokes aimed at a wide circle of targets. All out there. None in here where the two of them were together.

'Honey,' Marsha said firmly. 'Honey, they took you off the drip because you can swallow. But you can't chew. You need to drink nutritious stuff all the time. You're losing too much weight. All you have to do is ask them for the drinks. They're yours, it's not like you're asking them for a favour. OK?'

'OK.'

'You will ask them?'

'For the drinks?'

'Yes.'

'I will ask them.'

'Promise?'

'Promise.'

'Fine, then,' Marsha said, corking the rage.

When Marsha asked Cassie a few days later if she was asking for the drinks, Cassie did not feel guilty.

'What drinks?' she asked.

'The drinks I leave in the fridge down the corridor for you.'

'Thank you. You're very good.'

'Frig very good. Have you been asking for them?'

Cassie looked at her, mystified.

'You didn't know they were there, right?'

'I know they are, now,' Cassie said, willing to take on the responsibility now she knew about the drinks.

'Don't you worry about them,' Marsha said decisively. 'Forget about them.'

'All right,' Cassie said.

Marsha suddenly laughed out loud, as if Cassie had made a riotously funny joke. 'I don't need to tell you to forget anything, do I, honey?'

Cassie watched her prowling, pacing the room, and thought about what she was saying. Maybe the reason everything seemed like TV reruns was that she was forgetting a lot. 'I always remember Ben is dead,' she said.

'Do you, sweetheart?' Marsha sat down. 'You never think—'

'Except in my dreams. But I always know they're dreams.'

'And as soon as you're awake—'

'I remember.'

'Oh, Jesus, love.'

'I remember first thing.'

Marsha made a noise without words, agonised at not being able to say something useful.

'It's all right,' Cassie said. 'I don't get surprised any more. That's the good thing. I always know.'

Marsha was writing a note on a lined yellow pad. She tore it off and stuck it to the bedside locker on the side where Cassie could see it. 'Ask for drinks in frig,' it said.

After Marsha was gone, Cassie read it several times. It confused her each time because it did not say 'fridge'. By the time she worked out the meaning of that word, her thoughts would go somewhere else, so she never asked anybody for the drinks.

The next time Marsha visited, Polo was there. Maybe Polo was one of Marsha's targets. Cassie thought. Because Marsha was not as kind to Polo as Cassie expected her to be. Ben was his son, too, she thought. But then it came to her that Marsha expected Polo to be in the middle, at the hub of the wheel, seeing to Cassie, and was unsatisfied with him on that score. She did not criticise him, just attacked him by telling him actions she was going to take. 'I'm hiring an agency nurse from tonight,' she told him. 'I need someone who's looking out for Cassie and only Cassie.'

Polo did not object to this, although he did say it was strange to have an agency nurse now, six weeks after the accident, when Cassie was no longer on the danger list. Six weeks ago, Cassie thought. That's when it happened. 'When is it now?' she asked.

'July the twenty-fourth,' Polo said. 'I did tell her that already today,' he added, to Marsha.

'Better get used to replays,' Marsha said. 'Teflon memory.'

Cassie tried to work out what this meant, but after a while got tired of it.

'Be sure to keep records,' Polo said. 'All of this will be taken care of in the court case.'

'Oh, Jesus, tell it to the Compo Queen,' Marsha snapped. 'I'm trying to make sure your wife doesn't starve and you're thinking of the fucking damages.'

'You know that's not true,' Polo said.

'Yeah, well, you don't have to talk to me about keeping bloody records. She should be here soon.'

'Who?' Polo asked. Cassie was glad he asked it. She was noticing nurses getting impatient with her when she asked questions, so she was trying not to.

'For fuck's sake, Polo, *you* didn't get hit on the head,' Marsha said.

'No, but I can arrange it if you want me to badly enough,' Polo said, and Cassie burst out laughing.

'Oh, Cassie, it is so good to hear that sound again,' Polo said, taking her hand. She thought for a minute she might hit him with the other hand, because it was still attached to a lump of wood and would be very satisfying when it connected with him. The laughing had hurt her face and she needed her free hand to palm away the pain, but it was too complicated to say that, so she left her hand where it was.

'The agency nurse will be—' Marsha began. 'Is here,' she finished, as the door opened and a little round woman carrying a basket came in.

'Little Red Hooding Ride,' Cassie said.

'Little Red Riding Hood,' Polo gently corrected.

'Shut up, you,' Cassie said.

Shut up, shut up shut up, she thought. My dad used to say Little Red Hooding Ride to make me laugh. He had a whole lot of words he would bend like that.

'Derbis,' she said aloud.

Polo opened his mouth then shut it again. Good, Cassie thought. I would smile but I know that hurts, so I won't. Derbis is debris, and I know that. But I'm not telling you. She could hear him telling the Little Red Riding Hood woman that Cassie got confused when she was tired.

'Shut up,' Cassie said, much louder this time.

The three of them turned to her, Marsha looking as if she, too, wanted to laugh but had a sore face.

'Shut up and go home,' Cassie said, suddenly not caring.

Polo smiled at her and half shrugged at the basket woman. See, God love her, what I have to put up with?

'Go home *now*,' Cassie shrieked. 'To Meath. To your big old house. Go home, just. Shut up and go home. Go home. Now. Just go home, would you?'

'I'm going,' Polo said, looking so sad she wanted to hit him more than before.

I'd like to hit you with both my hands, she thought. Smack smack real fast with my free hand. Bang to hurt you with the other hand and the plank. If you come over here and kiss me, I'll do it, too.

But he took up his coat, seemingly too defeated even to put it on, and went away. The Little Red Riding Hood woman put her basket in the corner and took off her coat, hanging it on the back of the door. Then she came over to the bed and sat in the chair. 'Hello,' she said.

'Hello,' Cassie said.

'My name is Joan,' the woman said.

'All right,' Cassie said.

Marsha lifted the other chair so she was close to the woman, and the three of them were silent for a while. Cassie liked that. It was like one of those things you shook with snow in them. The snow was settling down to the bottom again.

'What's your name?' Cassie asked the woman.

'Joan,' she said.

'Joan,' Cassie said. 'All right.'

She looked at Marsha to see was it all right, and Marsha's eyes were full of tears.

'Why are you sad?' Cassie asked.

'Christ alone knows,' Marsha said, rubbing her sleeve over her eyes.

'Is it OK to call you Cassie?' the woman asked.

'Yes,' Cassie said.

'Thank you,' the woman said.

'Don't mention it,' Cassie said.

'Joan's going to be here all night,' Marsha told her.

'I'm sorry,' Cassie told the woman. 'I'll probably be asleep a lot of the time.'

'That's fine,' the woman said. Cassie thought she would say more, but she didn't. Instead, she looked at Marsha, and that was good, because Cassie had no idea what came next.

'There's a room, three doors down on the left,' Marsha

said to the woman, angling her hand so the woman would know which side of the corridor she was talking about. 'It has a fridge in it. The fridge is full to over-flowing—'

'With drinks!' Cassie said, delighted to know that she knew this.

'Right,' Marsha said.

'Drinks Marsha bought,' Cassie told the woman. 'Marsha is my aunt, but she's my best friend, too.'

The woman nodded as if it was important to understand this.

'She manages my career,' Cassie said. 'I'm a cartoonist.'

'*Pinheads*,' the woman said.

'That's right,' Cassie said.

Just as she was beginning to wonder if there was something else she was supposed to say, the woman turned to Marsha. 'Why don't I go and get one of the drinks now?' she said, touching the glass on the bedside table with the back of her hand. 'That's a bit warm.' She didn't wait for Marsha to give her permission, but just got up and left the room.

'She's nice,' Cassie told Marsha. 'What's her name?'

'Joan,' Marsha said.

'Did you tell me that before?' Cassie asked.

Marsha nodded.

'I'm sorry. I should concentrate,' Cassie said.

Marsha seemed to get upset again, but the woman arrived back and held out a glass to her. It had a tissue around it. Cassie reached out and took it. 'Thank you, Joan,' she said, trying it out.

She would like to tell the Little Red Riding Hood woman she preferred that way of being handed something, instead of the way the hospital nurses did it, putting it right into her hand. But she must concentrate. One of the nurses even closed her fingers around glasses when she gave them to her, and she really hated that. Cassie tried to remember the thing she was concentrating on, but it had gone away.

'The staff nurse will fill me in,' the woman said to Marsha.

'I suspect the disapproval will be obvious,' Marsha said.

'Nothing new,' the woman said.

'I should probably go and let you two get on with it,' Marsha said suddenly, as if she was interrupting something important. 'I'll be back before you go in the morning, we can talk then.'

The woman didn't say anything to Marsha, who began to gather her things, came to kiss Cassie, and went. The woman sat for a while and then asked Cassie if she'd had enough of the drink. It reminded Cassie she was holding the glass. She drank some more. While she was doing it, the woman pushed the bedside locker into a different position, where it became the obvious place to put the glass when Cassie was finished drinking from it. Then the woman got up and went to her basket, taking a folded garment out of it and a cap, putting them on.

'Now you look like a real nurse,' Cassie said. 'Joan.'

In the morning, when she woke up, the woman was moving around the room. Cassie pretended to be asleep in order to retrieve her name.

'Good morning, Cassie,' the woman said. 'I don't know if you'll remember. I'm the agency nurse. My name is Joan. Does Marsha drink coffee or tea in the morning? I thought I'd make us a pot in the room down the corridor.'

'Tea,' Marsha said, coming in the door behind her, to Cassie's relief, because she couldn't remember.

After the agency nurse had left the room, Marsha asked Cassie how she'd got on with her. 'I think maybe we talked in the middle of the night,' Cassie said. 'She doesn't make a production out of anything. Joan is her name, did you know that? I felt – it was the best night. I really hate it here, do you know that?'

The statement surprised her more than it seemed to surprise Marsha. She thought it through again. This place was awful, with its systems and nurses who behaved as if they owned you. But then, so what? No place would be any better, with the agony of knowing Ben was dead ready to well up and over her at any moment. Home. The word put a chill in her. She lifted the arm that was free and could see, against the whiteness of the sheets, the hairs standing up at the thought of the big old house. Each room filled with the sounds of him, the laughter of him, the shining glad face, the rushing hug of him.

Marsha's hand was on her forehead, warm and strong as Cassie remembered her father, holding her when, as a child, she was being sick. After a few minutes, the strangling sensation came under her control. Marsha sat down, silently. The agency nurse came in with a cheap plastic tray. The three of them watched the dawn rising over the trees in the hospital grounds.

'Does she still need to be here?' Marsha asked.

'If someone competent is around all the time probably not,' Joan said.

I should mind that they're talking about me and not to me, Cassie thought. But it's all right because it's the two of them. She drifted in her thoughts. Joan touched the back of her hand to remind her she was holding a mug. She drank from it and put it down on the bed table. I must remember it's there and drink from it, she thought. Joan was asking Marsha something about neurological tests. Marsha took out a pad and started to write down things Joan said. At one point, when Marsha was embarked on writing a long piece, Joan smiled at Cassie and said, 'You're not forgetting your tea.'

'No, I'm not,' Cassie said, and took a drink of it.

After a few nights of Joan arriving at about seven, carrying her little oval basket, Cassie summoned up her name without effort. It was a relief to know that she would not wake up in half-darkness alone.

Most of the time, she felt strung between lamp-posts. One lamp-post was the stupor brought on by painkillers, the other lamp-post the high-grade grinding grief threaded through with physical pain. One lamp-post was the odd moment when she would not think about Ben, the other was the blind terror as she tried to summon up his face in her mind and failed.

When there was someone in the room, it was easier to be alone. Joan never initiated conversation and Cassie had no conversation to initiate, nothing to talk about. She was without curiosity, even about herself, even when the specialist explained why her right hand was not working. Nerve damage, he said. Some function would come back, probably. In due course. The hand that once earned her living for her was now completely autonomous. Even freed from the taped-on wood, it moved without her instruction, even counter to it. They put a half-glove on it with a rigid plastic piece running up the inside of her wrist to stop it flopping flaccidly. She learned the habit of putting that hand in a pocket. It might not obey, but there, it was at least inert.

'I'm sorry, Marsha, I'm not able to draw,' she said.

'You probably won't ever be able to draw the way you used to,' Marsha said, the way you'd say, 'Cork is a hundred and sixty miles away.' 'But why're you apologising to me?'

'There will be no money coming in.'

Marsha came over to the bed and ruffled Cassie's hair as if Cassie was a small child. 'You poor bloody eejit,' she said affectionately. 'You're worried I'm gonna be out begging in the street, aren't you?'

'Well . . .'

'Well, kid, being crippled in a car crash is probably the best career move you ever made. First of all, the insurance ship is coming in. Better than winning the lottery. I don't mean the general car-crash stuff – Polo is working hard on that,' Marsha said, her tone indicating a difficult determination to be fair-minded about Polo. 'I mean the insurance we took out on your hands. It probably won't be finalised for about a year, when it's clear how much damage has been done and how much you can recover, but the payoff will be worth the premiums, and that's putting it mildly.'

The *Irish Examiner*, which had started Cassie off, was going to do a framed limited edition of some of the classic cartoons and was linked up with a major American catalogue to sell them by mail order in the US. 'The fact that your output has stopped is advantageous in that context,' Marsha said apologetically. 'You have no financial worries. None. You clear on that?'

Once that was sorted out, Cassie slipped without choice into the grey Polar steppes where she searched for bright memories of her son. Like the moment in Dublin Zoo when he tugged at her, afraid to take his eyes off the hugeness of the elephant, nodding frantically towards it. 'Look at him *creeping*,' he said, making her, for the first time, understand the way an elephant moved. She must remember that, she would think, trying to freeze the sunny moment, the conspiratorial gleefulness of Ben, knowing for that split second he was stumbling on a great secret only she should be told. She must remember because, other than the shining facets of a short remembered life, there was nothing. An absence. A void.

'Was it you who told me it was worse because the funeral was over long before I knew?' she asked Marsha, who started in surprise at her speaking, then shook her head.

'Might have been Thornton,' she suggested. 'Peter Thornton? The bereavement counsellor?'

So that's what he was. Not the angel of death. A bereavement counsellor. It was probably Thornton who had said that the ritual, the litany, the shared celebration of a life and grieving for a loss of a funeral was important. Without it, she felt spun loose, unconnected for all eternity. Ben had not died. He never died. Never died so her hands could register the chilling of his childish limbs, hold the motionless contradiction of everything he was for her and learn to relinquish him into a shimmering satin-cushioned nest. Ben never died. He ceased to be. There had never been a death that she would learn in the core of her, no matter how often it was said, the words tap-tapping without purchase.

Sometimes, when the chemicals interacted in her, the shining satin-cushioned nest would become a stained parody of puddling corruption, of seeping decay, soap-hardness forming in the rounded baby shape of him and she would come off the pillows screaming, staring, flailing at the smell and sight.

Mostly, there was not even that ghastliness to reach what feelings she had left. Mostly, there was a despair dispirited into apathy, way past grief, a despair so profound, so solitary in its genesis and completion that it mocked the trivia of tears, sneered at the possibility of common ground or sympathy or sharing. It was a despair that made her a stranger in a strange land, listening to people speaking in effortful, pointless tongues.

'You have nothing to blame yourself for,' somebody said to her.

She tried to find the consolation in this. They must mean, she imagined, that if she were responsible for the accident, she would feel worse about Ben's absence, the void where he once was. The thought was well intended but could connect only with who she had once been. That Cassie used to read newspaper accounts of parents being 'beaten back by flames', knowing that if she was one of those parents, she would spend the rest of her life with the copper-tasting certainty of covert condemnation half hidden behind the ready acceptance by others of the 'beaten back by flames'. Now in a version of the same situation, lack of blame was a coin kept pointlessly, a token for a ferry on a waterway she would never traverse.

At some point, Marsha lifted the ban on visitors and was livid when so few came. For Cassie, visitors were hard work. Hard, purposeless work, with their awkward apologies for not coming sooner or oftener, when she could scarcely remember who they were, with their generic remembrances of Ben, their stories of him that jostled her own real memories of him over some edge, so they floated: feathers distanced further by her every grabbing effort to catch them.

A few were OK. Erik the Red came and fiddled his wheelchair back and forth saying nothing, other than once when he muttered, 'Oh, fuck this.' But mostly, when people came, they made her conscious of how she would never be comfortable meeting them again, because they would always be asking her how she was doing and there would never be an answer that would not provoke them into sweet, shallow, tacky, optimistic lies about the future, illustrated by some unmatched personal experience of theirs that left her stranded, unreached, unreachable. The worst thing was the need to reassure others, to prevent herself tainting Ben's life by seeming to need the tragedy of his death – when she had not even the completion of a sense of his death.

When Polo came, he would try to cheer her up, tell her stories of the people working in his company. She got good at following the intent of each anecdote and could laugh in the right places. He kept telling her how much she was coming on, until one day when Marsha was there too.

'Cassie is not coming on,' she said. 'The psychiatrist here wants to put her on anti-depressants. He says she has flat affect. Meaning no ups and downs. Emotionally, she's flat-lining. Sorry, honey,' she said to Cassie, 'but that's the way it is.'

Polo looked at Cassie with a kind of anxious hope, hazarding a guess that maybe anti-depressants would help. Cassie looked at Marsha. Marsha looked at Polo, then closed her eyes and sighed such a long, controlled sigh it was patently a substitute for hitting him.

'Cassie is depressed as all hell for a very good reason. I appreciate you share some of the reason, Polo, but, bluntly, you're not Cassie.' The comparison and implied criticism were brutal. 'Furthermore, I'm not satisfied with the tests they've given her for brain damage. Fitting bloody shapes in holes and matching up words. I went back to that bloody psychologist and you know what he said to me? He said she had a good visual sense and vocabulary and IQ and without tests of what she was like before the accident all they could say was that there was maybe some subtle damage. Subtle my arse. There's a dame in London who's a world expert and I'm taking Cassie to her.'

'That would be a very good idea. The sooner the better.'

Cassie was surprised and relieved to hear Polo so vehemently approving what Marsha was proposing.

'Firstly – day after tomorrow – I'm taking her home.'

'How'd you mean, home?'

'Home as in my apartment.'

'But that's not her home.'

'No, and her home – your home – has neither got a lift nor is it located where the agency nurse she likes can be every night. I'll be there in the daytime, Joan'll be there at night, and it's quite close to the airport for journeys to London.'

The logic of this defeated Polo, who said, patting Cassie on the hand, that this sounded like a plan, but of course they would understand his preference for having her at home in Meath. The way Marsha listened to him gave the impression that she had already written his script and allocated time for its delivery. When he finished, she nodded and assigned him tasks relative to Cassie's going to the apartment.

The next few weeks passed for Cassie in journeys to the psychological testing place in London followed by slow walking, using crutches, around the grounds of the apartments. The crutches could not be used in sand, acting, she found, the only time she tried it, like punt sticks in old cartoons, rooting her in one spot as they sank into the softness.

The London clinic woman was unsentimental and to the point. What the Irish psychologist had called subtle brain damage she had more precise terms for. She briefed Cassie and Marsha together, with a tape-recorder running. 'You'll take away the cassette of this session,' she told Cassie. 'You can listen to it whenever you want to, because you won't remember what I'm going to tell you.'

'I'll concentrate,' Cassie said, not wanting to waste her time.

'That's a good place to start,' the woman said. 'People will tell you all you need to do is concentrate. Now, let's say you concentrate very hard on what I tell you for the next hour. Let's say you and your aunt concentrate. At the end of the hour, if I ask your aunt to repeat the key points, she will remember somewhere between sixty and seventy per cent. If, after this hour, I ask you, Cassie, to tell me the key points, you will remember less than ten per cent.'

Cassie shook her head, frantically.

'It doesn't matter how hard you try, your short-term memory has been reduced. But your confidence in your short-term memory never reduces. So you are convinced you'll remember, and when you don't remember, you'll feel guilty. That's the first point I need to stress. No matter how vivid or memorable something appears to be when you are witnessing it, within an hour most of it will have evaporated. But you will never get used to that. You will be determined, you will be hopeful, you will try very hard every time. Every time you fail, you will feel guilty. The problem is that being determined and hopeful is a waste of time. You cannot fit this amount of water' – she gestured at the fat blue plastic spring-water container in the corner of the room – 'into this glass. That's going to be your situation for the foreseeable future. Feeling upset and guilty about it is a bloody waste of time. You need to ring-fence yourself with assists.'

'What's assists?'

'Lists. Notes. Reminders. Give you an example. You drive, right?'

Cassie nodded. She was already driving again. Total amnesia surrounding the accident meant she had learned no fear of traffic from it.

'Driven on your own, yet?'

Cassie shook her head.

'You'll set out on your journey knowing where you're going and why. Ten minutes on the road, you will not remember the purpose or place. Because of this unjusti-fied confidence, you may guess at where you're going. You'll guess wrong and irritate a lot of people in the process. Instead,' the woman half-turned to Marsha, 'you'll need a mobile phone with a speed-dial number for someone who is always accessible to you and who always knows where you should be. Plus you'll need a notice in the middle of your steering-wheel to remind you to ring that person.'

Cassie began to drift as the woman went on. There would be classes in London every few weeks, she heard, where she would work along with other brain-damaged people to come to terms, to build what the woman called 'mental capillaries'; tricks and methods to get around the deficits. In time, some of these would become reflex, and in time some of the damage would repair itself, if things went well. It would not be easy. There would be suffering involved.

'The person who will suffer most in the next few months will not be you but your aunt,' the expert told her, but Cassie knew she was really talking to Marsha, really checking did Marsha know what she was letting herself in for. 'Short-term memory loss is the best analgesic ever created,' she went on. 'What you cannot remember, you cannot grieve over. Or worry about. Or take responsibility for. Good resolutions are pointless if you can't remember them. Past failures are doubly infuriating for the innocent bystanders if you can't learn from them. Be aware,' the woman said to Marsha, 'that, in the short term, Cassandra is a numb psychopath. She is dangerous, not in any big dramatic way, but in a million maddening small ways.'

Cassie listened to the cassette several times on the journey back from London, beginning to write down reminders as she listened. Even the reminders, in the beginning, were of limited value. She would come across a Post-it note stuck on the front of a notebook with three reminders on it:

Marsha – be sure and tell
Tuesday 3.30 sharp
Gear change.

Only the last had any resonance for her. Polo had bought her an automatic Volvo, red in colour, probably because it was least like the car in which the accident happened. But what Marsha took to calling 'Cassie's reptile brain', some primitive long-term brain cells, remembered only stick-shift driving, so she would be doing forty miles an hour when the reptile brain would cue her to change gear. The result, in the automatic Volvo, was the car sticking to the ground totally, without any brake-light warning so other cars screamed swerving to the outside and on to the hard shoulder to avoid hitting her. After a while, she learned the automatic again, but whenever her mind would drift, the learning evaporated. This meant she should not have the radio or CD-player on. Pleasant music seemed to put her into a kind of fugue in which she would decide to change gear.

When people asked her about the trips to London, in the beginning she explained, but quickly learned that, either because they thought she was imagining problems or out of misplaced sympathy, it just provoked them into telling her about *their* forgetfulness. How they would often find themselves upstairs in their homes thinking, what did I come for? They could not understand the difference between that normal forgetfulness and finding yourself in a room without any idea why you were there, but unworried, readily distracted by anything on offer in that room, regardless of a saucepan of oil setting fire to the kitchen or an iron burning clean through the padding of the ironing-board or a phone-caller left hanging for two hours because they could not disconnect themselves from a phone call they had initiated when you forgot either to go back to them with the number they asked you for or to hang up.

The good thing was discovering that old motor skills were still there. She was frightened, the first time Marsha suggested she try her laptop, but once it was opened and turned on, she knew how to use it. The fingers of her right hand did not respond properly, but she could still remember the password, still input ideas and employ it to work out what she thought about her life.

The weekend she began to use the computer, Polo kidnapped her. He said he wanted to take her for a drive, have a meal. But once they were in the car, he drove for what seemed a long time, arriving at the end of the journey at the house in Meath.

'Welcome home, sweetheart,' he said, with tears in his eyes.

She got out of the car and, using one crutch, walked up the wheelchair ramp into the big hall. Against the wall, at the bottom of the great curving stairs, was a chair. A new, different chair. Obedient to Polo's invitational stance, she went across to it, the crutch crossways on her lap as she sat. He showed her where the control panel was and which button to press. The chair moved slowly up the wall, taking her to the floor above, Polo walking up the stairs beside her.

'I can walk upstairs,' she told him. 'They teach you how to manage the crutch before they let you out.'

'That's fine,' he said. 'But with the amount of metal pins you have in your legs, it's going to be painful for a while. I know you. You'd want something from up here, but you'd postpone getting it because of the difficulty of climbing the stairs. With the chair lift, you don't have to worry.'

Like a tour guide, he led her to the right at the top of the stairs, into Ben's room. Except it was no longer Ben's room. It had not gone back to what it had been before Ben, but was a bright buttercup-painted room with white wicker furniture. A room from a tropical resort, transported into an old stone house in Meath. She wandered around it, touching chair backs and shelf units until she became aware of Polo crying. He was standing in the doorway with his head hanging down loose, shaken by the sobs. 'No point in keeping it the way it was,' he said hoarsely, begging her to approve. 'It would remind us every day.'

Remind us but never deliver the reality of the shining, smiling boy coming plunging out of it, trainer-laces flying. She nodded. He held on to her for dear life, sick with relief. She waited until he was done. Then walked across to their bedroom. Repainted in new colours, unfamiliar bed linens. On the bedside table on her side of the bed, in a silver frame twelve inches tall, her favourite picture of Ben. It showed him at about eighteen months, hair still blonded with babyhood, looking upward. You could almost hear the happy giggle as he discovered the source of the drops of water falling on his head: a leak in the gutter overhead.

In the photograph, he was dressed in his Humpty-Dumpty rompers: Humpty beaming away above a wall represented by a big pocket on the chest of the rompers. When dressing Ben, Cassie would tweak the rompers so Humpty disappeared into the pocket, pretend to search for him, then be astonished and gladdened when Ben would pull up the romper front to reveal Humpty.

'Only hiding,' he would reassure her.

Her fingers longed for the softly knitted fabric of the rompers. She was about to ask Polo where all of Ben's clothes and toys had been put, when some instinct she could not quite understand intervened. She put the curlicued silver frame back on the table and walked out to sit down in the chair lift. At the bottom of the stairs, she stayed sitting, the crutch across her lap, looking at him.

'Welcome home,' he said again.

'I have to stay here?'

'It's time, Cassie. You don't have the agency nurse any more. You don't need her. I've arranged my time so I can be here a lot, really from mid-afternoon, and Gobnait will be here every morning.'

She could walk out of the big front door and get into the driver's seat of his car, but then she would have to ask him for the keys and he would give her a big long argument.

'Marsha has been wonderful,' Polo said.

'But,' she thought. 'Go on, you have a "but" . . .'

'But she moved into that apartment to be away from dependants.'

The word was like a smack, sparking tears into her eyes.

'It's better for all of us that you come home. Your car is being delivered in an hour or so. You'll be able to go and see Marsha whenever you want.'

Technically this is not a kidnapping, then. You rely on me to be reasonable. You have worked so hard to remove the triggers of grief. You want your wife back home. It may even be good for Marsha, not having the endless repetition, the constant reminders, the timers going off all day to remind me to check have I left something plugged in or something on the cooker. She is funny about it, but it is like an Elastoplast on too long, beginning to curl and fray at the edges, functional but dirtied.

She got up and walked into the library. A fire was set. As soon as she sat down in one of the big ruby red leather chairs, he lit the fire in several places, put a spark guard in front of it. 'I would like a cup of tea,' she said quietly.

He nodded, eagerly, as if she had given him a permission, and went off to be noisy in the kitchen. He would

313

have fresh doughnuts, she knew, and would warm them for just twenty seconds in the microwave because he knew she liked that. He is a clever man, she thought. He knows it is not the big ties that bind. It is the multiplicity of tiny ones. Gulliver held by Lilliputians using strings of trivial intimate knowledge. Doughnuts. Tea in a favourite mug.

The phone rang. It was somewhere in the room but it took her three rings to work out that it was beside her. When she lifted the receiver, she was confused into silence by hearing Polo's voice giving the number. Marsha was the caller. Marsha in a towering, spitting rage. Marsha calling Polo a lying, contemptible bastard. A self-absorbed shit. A duplicitous control freak. Polo saying very little, letting the fury break over him. Saying quiet words, keeping his voice down, forcing Marsha to stop shouting in order to hear what he was saying, thanking her for all she had done for Cassie. She told him it wasn't his place to thank her. She hadn't done anything for him. Or done anything for Cassie because of him. And if he was being Cassie's *owner*, Cassie's *keeper*, in thanking her, he was bloody lucky he was in the middle of Meath, because if he was any nearer to her she'd take the two eyes out of him.

'You know I will take good care of my wife,' Polo said firmly.

'Amazing, what good care of her you took when it came to telling her Ben was dead,' Marsha shrieked, incensed all over again.

'I was advised—'

'You ran behind ex-Father Thornton's skirts. In behind old cassock. "You do the hard bit, didn't you used to be a priest?"'

'Peter Thornton is a trained bereavement counsellor.'

'Yeah. Get a professional in. Never let an amateur at an important job.'

314

A confusion, this, for Cassie, because she could not imagine wanting Polo, her husband, to be the one to tell her about Ben. She would, she thought sadly, have had to mind him when sadness swept over the ageing boy face of him. The uninvolved repetitions of the counsellor had been the better option. Just like confession, she would never have to see the professional again unless she asked to.

'Being kind to my wife gives you no entitlement to be gratuitously vicious to me,' Polo said.

Marsha back-tracked, trying to get him to agree that Cassie should not have her routines disrupted when she was trying to come to terms with deficits left by the crash. He agreed very civilly, pointing out that it would probably be wrong for Cassie to become dependent on essentially false routines.

She was, after all, his wife, she did, after all, have a home, and now the home was properly adapted for her, it was appropriate that she move back into it and allow Marsha go back to being a manager rather than a full-time carer, which must have been extremely hard on her. He sprinkled the occasional legal term into his sentences, the way he did whenever he talked with his senior counsel friends. Cassie was hoping Marsha would not agree, but eventually she did. The moment she did, Polo got very pacy again, all jokes and tasks, told her he was late with Cassie's tea, that he would get a hard time from her, so goodbye, Marsha. He put down the phone and Marsha did too, leaving Cassie alone on the singing line. She put down the receiver carefully and pulled the spark guard away from the fire, so she could watch the shapes and chimeras flickering in the warm glow of the logs.

The following morning, Polo waited until Gobnait arrived before he left the house. There was no embarrassment with Gobnait, mainly because she arrived in the kitchen and burst into tears at the first sight of Cassie. Hugging her hard and apologising for crying, announcing that she had promised her mother she would not cry. Cassie was suddenly fixed in position, remembering Ben hadn't liked Gobnait's mother. Why was that? Oh, yes, because she was always wishing siblings on him.

'No matter what I say, it's going to be wrong,' Gobnait said, after Polo had gone. 'So I'm sorry in advance, all right?'

'The thing about brain damage is that no matter how many things you say wrong, I won't remember them for very long,' Cassie said. 'So don't worry about it.'

Polo left detailed instructions for Gobnait. Appointments to be made for Cassie, contact with Marsha, tablets to be taken, exercises gone through. She kept taking up his list of directions, holding them out in front of her as a town crier would to read aloud whatever was the next item on the list. Mid-morning, she announced that Polo wanted Cassie given a pot of tea ('Not a cup, mark you, a pot,' Gobnait sniffed) in the library, where he had set a fire ('Brownie points for Polo,' Gobnait said, on a louder sniff) and Cassie would find documentation on the table beside her she might like to go through.

'This is all very mysterious,' Cassie said, trying for a light tone.

'I wonder do I bring you into the library and give you the documentation first or give you the pot of tea and then the documentation?' Gobnait asked.

'It's because of my brain damage,' Cassie said.

'The way he's leaving these instructions, he obviously thinks I'm going to catch the brain damage off you,' Gobnait said, banging kettles and teapots around in somewhat rebellious good humour.

The documentation left by Polo was contained within

316

a leatherbound scrap book, heavy on Cassie's lap when she transferred it from the table.

FUNERAL OF BEN CADOGAN

it said in elaborate lettering.

Maybe, she thought, Polo was concerned about her not having been around and conscious when Ben died, so he wanted her to have some portion of the formal mourning of him. Slowly, unwillingly, she began to turn the pages. Most of it was from media. First came cuttings from the evening paper, with big headlines: 'Cartoonist, Son In Horror Crash.' She read the accounts, but could get no understandable story out of them because they were so careful to avoid saying either driver was responsible. Then came a series of news reports saying Ben was dead, Cassie on the critical list. These came four – no, five days after the story of the crash. The timing was so unexpected that she assumed her brain damage was causing her to misread or misunderstand. But on every reading, it came up the same. Five days elapsed before Ben died. Five days, he was in hospital. She must know this, she thought, but a shuddering dread ran through her. Someone had told her Ben did not suffer. But if he lived five days . . . She clutched the outer edge of the scrap book as if it was a wall she must hang on to, wild horror chilling her.

'Hey, what's up?'

Gobnait was there, holding a tray. Cassie shifted so Gobnait could get the tray down on the table beside her.

'What's up? What's wrong? Tell me?'

Mute, Cassie pointed to the date on the first story and the date on the second swatch of reports.

'Ben was in hospital,' Gobnait said. 'D'you not know about Polo suing the hospital, too?'

Cassie shook her head. Too? Who else was he suing?

'Pour out your tea,' Gobnait said gently, so she did.

'Ben was in the neur-neur – oh, feckit, the brain bit of the hospital and – this is according to Polo, now – they didn't read the X-ray right and they didn't realise Ben's—' Gobnait lost confidence and looked abject. Please let me off this duty, her expression said. But you can't leave me without the rest of the story, Cassie's face replied.

'Ben's spine was cracked?' Gobnait said.

Cassie could not understand why Gobnait seemed to be asking her to confirm things Cassie could never have known. 'Up here?' Gobnait said, on another rising inflection, putting her hand behind her head, just above its junction with her neck. 'But the X-ray was from the front and the hospital didn't see the broken bit. This is all according to Polo, mind. So Ben was moved in some way he shouldn't have been or wouldn't have been if they'd known and he might have survived if they hadn't moved him.'

For the first time in weeks, something broke through the soft-focus numbness that surrounded Cassie. Like an animal bucking intolerable pain, she howled, her head beating off the scrap book on her knee. My son, my boy, my baby, my Ben. They killed him twice, my hands were not there to gentle him, he need not have died and he died. While I slept, he died. Gobnait got the scrap book away from her so Cassie ended up rocking, racketing back and forth, until Gobnait, like a little tackler, got her shoulder in front of Cassie's forehead and tightened her arms around her, vice-like. He wasn't awake, she kept telling Cassie, never woke up, not for a moment during the whole four days, never opened his eyes, they said his brainwaves showed he couldn't feel anything, he would probably never have survived properly anyway, but the main thing is he didn't know, he never knew, one minute he was driving to Galway with his mum and the next minute he was in heaven. One minute going to Galway, the next minute in heaven.

Eventually, still locked in Gobnait's restraining clutches, Cassie's bellowing misery died away to snuffling apologies. Very slowly Gobnait let go of her, watching to see if the seizure of grief would return, then tested the teapot with her hand, announced it was lukewarm and went off to make another one. With difficulty, Cassie retrieved the scrap book from the floor to read on. The next pages were about the funeral. There were pictures of people carrying a coffin. Not a tiny white box like you might bury a newborn in, but a little heartbreak of a coffin, all grown-up bronze fitments contradicting the small size of it. Pictures showed famous people from politics and showbusiness commiserating with Polo and with her mother. Marsha was caught in one of the pictures, her face shrivelled into a concentration of misery that aged her past sixty.

The papers quoted sections of Polo's oration from the altar. They particularly liked the anecdotes showing Ben to be old beyond his years (choosing Stilton in a restaurant when he was only four, reading Steinbeck at six) and the ones where Ben and Cassie figured together, such as the story of Cassie, terrified on a carnival big wheel, being minded and reassured by her own five-year-old: 'Be all right, Mamma, be all right. Big hug and the pain's all gone.'

Also quoted was a bishop who officiated at both the taking to the church and the funeral service. He talked about the modern tendency to regard children as consumers and passive recipients of adult largesse and wisdom. How it took an unusual child, a child like Ben, to remind us of the Christ-child, enlightening the scholars in the temple at seven years of age, knowing, even that young, what insights he could offer and how the imperative of his life lay in offering them, no matter what pain they brought with them. Ben had been such a child, the bishop said. Cassie was torn between wanting to accept everything said as definitely Ben's due, and wondering how the bishop knew anything about Ben except at second-hand. Probably Polo wrote stuff down for the bishop, she thought. Gave His Grace or His Eminence, or whatever you called a bishop, the more serious illustrations, kept the light, touching personal stories for his own oration. Now for the funny incident, she thought, a rising lump in her throat at the promiscuous sharing of her boy, her son, the uniqueness of him scatter-shot in a church to strangers who would applaud, wipe their eyes, and by the very illusion of briefly comprehending how special he was, taint that specialness, turning it into a commodity for consumption and retelling.

She drank the hot tea, conscious of Gobnait coming to the door now and again to check how she was doing, how she was coping.

'You were there, Gobnait?'

'Course I was there. We were all there, the whole lot of us.'

'What . . . ?'

'Polo and the bishop did a good job. Maybe better the first night. The following morning, they said some of the same things: it was kind of second-hand, they could've come up with newer stuff. Although in fairness, a lot of people were only there for the taking to the church or the funeral mass, not for both. It'd burn holes in you, it was so sad. There was so many important people. I kept thinking it would be nice if it was just you and Polo and family and us. Maybe Father Thornton – not Father, you know who I mean. And your friend Erik, maybe.'

Gobnait leaned back, looking incongruously easeful, in the big leather chair on the other side of the fireplace, the two women silently imagining the perfect funeral.

'I didn't want that number of people thinking they knew Ben just 'cause of listening about him,' Gobnait said, wiping her eyes on her apron. 'He was much more interesting than anybody was going to tell at a funeral, even though Polo is probably the best if something like that has to get done. He reminded me of things I'd totally forgot. Listen, I'm going to go and do some work. Am I safe to leave you on your own or will you set fire to yourself?'

Cassie promised to be safe. When Gobnait became a busy noise three rooms away, she went back to the scrap book. The final pages contained the leaflet given to worshippers. Front and centre, her picture of Ben glancing upward in expectant delight, the shot cropped so Humpty-Dumpty was just a bald-headed hint. She read through it. The readings. The hymns. Then, a small line about a final few words and prayers at the crematorium in Glasnevin. The crematorium. One-handed, she held her temples as if without this strong grip her head would come apart. The crematorium. There was never a grave, never a slow dissolution. There was a blinding, searing, scorching wind of fire, fire turning the wood casket, the satiny cushions into fuel, into flame consuming what they cradled. 'Oh, Jesus,' she cried into her knuckles, slow, grinding gulps of air sucked into her lungs at every inbreath. 'Oh, my Ben. My beautiful boy.'

After a long time, she wiped the tears off the page, closed the heavy scrap book, put it carefully where it had been. She sat alone in the silent room, her hurting hands lonely for her son. Her hands, so used to the casual caressing of him, they went rounded and soft at the thought. Polo once commented that in pictures he took of the two of them, Cassie's hands were always touching Ben, whether as a baby, a toddler or a sturdy little boy. Sitting here, in this chair, she remembered once letting the weight of her hands drag her arms down the outside of the same chair in exhaustion, and him coming up from behind, a warm, needy little animal, butting into her palm, demanding she stroke him, knowing it pleasured her as it pleasured him.

If she could just believe that death wasn't an end, a writing-off. That somewhere, at some different level, her hands might hold the warm, bundling, tawny, satiny strength of him again. But there was, she knew, nothing after what was here.

Weak tears slid warmly from the corners of her eyes. She struggled to her feet, trying to remember where the computer was. Bedroom? Bedroom. Definitely. In the hall she encountered Gobnait. 'Don't tell Polo I'm not using his chair lift,' she requested.

Gobnait put her finger to her lips – child keeping a secret – and frothy, fizzy laughter blurted out around the finger. Concealing Cassie's improving strength appealed to her, probably as a payback for Polo's over-detailed instruction list.

At the computer, Cassie opened the password-protected document she regarded as her thinking place. The words came through her inept fingers in a furious outpouring, a blind reckless catharsis so hurried and uncaring that it took her ten minutes to correct it into coherence afterwards.

You buried him and you kept me the cuttings, you preserved the evidence of your tears and of your capacity to draw tears from others. The street theatre of your sadness. Reported and photographed. You did a Bible reading, so you did, but first you talked about your son, our son, my son. You tarnished for ever the shining moments of his remembered life, turning them into vignettes to make a church full of VIPs laugh softly, laughter echoing into the arches of the dark wood-boned roof. You made them laugh at his archaic sentence structures, so you did, to wring a round of applause from them, tinkling transient tribute in that context of eternity.

You stood, your back to the tall thin stained-glass windows with tall thin angels, great feathered wings curving to their ankles, talking to breast-touching pale-faced virgins, each picture Gothic-pointed at the top. They knelt, the congregation, the middle ones in the pews, reading shiny brass plates set into the seat backs adjuring them to remember in their prayers a stranger of whom they knew nothing other than this engraved affirmation that he had generously contributed. When the short dark coffin passed them they cried as if they cared, though but a minute earlier they had been side-glancing to see who famous was there, who famous trying to look anonymous but be noticed, who famous whose name would be listed in the next day's papers as a validation of one little life they hardly knew. The ones near the top thought you looked boyish yourself, never think you old enough to have a little boy, really. Everybody would have noticed how, in the churchyard afterwards, as you clasped the clasping hands, you constantly spoke of me: how grateful Cassie would have been, how appreciative, how touched.

There would have been a smaller group in Glasnevin, a fall-off in numbers making it from the church to the graveyard. 'Forgive me, but I have a job to go to, limited time off, you know how it is . . .' 'I'm really sorry, but . . .'

In Glasnevin, without a full audience to whom you held a responsibility, you would have looked inward,

323

not outward, been inundated with the real pain. You would have knelt in front of that ominous curtain and been overcome at the horror that the rollers would forward move his little body into the furnace.

You burned him. You burned Ben, incinerated him and kept the ash of him for me to make decisions about. Because that, too, you would have surrounded with a nimbus of care. I know you will not have scattered that ash, those ashes, those infinitely plural dust-motes unrelated to my solid boy, my flesh-firm son. Yet each one of those dust-motes, those grains of ashy grey carries the scientific essence of him into an environmental eternity, wherever they are scattered, wherever they blow, wherever they damp down into solid soil.

You would want me to decide. And if I let you, you would ask me questions, millions of questions about his places, his preferences, where would he like. You would put gritty, grainy ashes in one part of your mind and ask me what an alive boy would want done with them when they are all that is left of him?

Now I know I must leave you.

Now I know I must leave you.

CHAPTER NINETEEN

Partners and Parasites

Once she had made the decision, she knew it was not enough of a decision. It was not enough to leave Polo. She must leave the totality of her life.

On Amazon.com she bought an instruction book about suicide, holding the book in one hand as she checked supplies with the other: this number of this kind of sleeping pill, this amount of that kind of painkiller. The book described how they must be carefully, slowly swallowed so as not to sicken and trigger regurgitation. How the plastic bag over the head, secured around the neck, gave extra surety, letting you breathe and rebreathe the same air as the pills relaxed every tendon, speeding oblivion, making it doubly certain.

She studied those who had done it. The notes left behind: subtle stabbings of survivors rendered sordid by the mere fact of survival. Some suicides left neither explanation nor cry for understanding nor general absolution. Some chose instant agony over slow, seeping unconsciousness. There were those who walked into the sea, pockets full of stones. The threat in Ancient Rome, to curtail an epidemic of female suicide: the bodies of the next perpetrators would be dragged naked through the city on open carts.

There was the primal selfishness of a poet's head cradled in an unlit oven with two children asleep upstairs, deadly fumes curling, seeking to make that

325

childish sleep pinkly permanent. The poignant puzzles: the writer – his book about his own handicapped son treasured by her for years – who did away with himself in a motel bedroom, black plastic garbage sack rubber-banded around his neck. Such a watchful observant man to die blocked in, blacked out, closed down, unseeing in a room not worth seeing . . .

It became more practicable to do it, as time went on. The prescriptions for the painkillers had a few more repeats in them, so she filled them in spite of rarely using them any more, hoarding them where neither Polo nor Gobnait would come across them. As she became more competent, less likely to set fire to something or fail to locate the hidden keys when she locked herself out, she was less supervised. Sometimes Gobnait was not there for a whole day, with Polo arriving late in the evening. Cassie could, if she chose, disconnect the phones, drive the big car into the garage, lower the garage door and in semi-darkness thread a hose from exhaust to window, sit in the car, engine purring lethally, music playing.

There was no fear involved in her decision not to do it. It came all of a piece, integrated, inarguable, one day. The day Polo's feature appeared in the newspaper.

A week before, when he asked her to read something written by him, she refused, more ruthless, as time went on, about preserving her necessary numbness, shuttering out the chatter of the normal day. But he was thinking of giving it to a newspaper, he said. It was about her.

'Is it true?' she asked.

'Yes.'

'Then I don't need to check it.'

She shrugged off his talk about the truth sometimes hurting. Shrugged him and the feature off. On the day of publication, he telephoned her the moment he got to his office, half excited, half fearful. They used it, he confirmed, with a picture of the two of them to illustrate. She tried to get a fix on what a normal wife would say at this point.

'Why don't you fax it to me so I can read it?'

That was what a normal wife would say, she thought, pleased, when his reaction confirmed it. He would photocopy it and put it on the fax straight away. Minutes later, the faxphone rang three times before stuttering its way into delivering a dirtied version of the newspaper page, divided in two, since one A4 page could not cope with what took up the top half of a broadsheet newspaper page, with explanatory paragraphs, boxed, about *Cassandra's Pinheads*, about the accident and the resultant brain damage.

We thought she was recovering when she asked for her diary [the feature began]. She has always carried a big desk diary, using it as a cross between a scrap book, a telephone book, a journal and a Filofax. Once the date has passed, the page it occupies in the diary can be used to stick a press cutting into or write down a quotation from a book she's reading. It is not the kind of diary an adolescent keeps, with a gilt lock to indicate how secret it is. Cassie's diary could be read by anybody, because it is so impersonal. It just shows what interests her at any given time, and what she is planning to do on a particular day.

Or, rather, that's what it used to show. What is heartbreaking, when I look at the pages for the months since she came home after her accident, is how impoverished a life it portrays. She still makes lists of the ten tasks she plans to tackle, still crosses them out at the end of the day. The difference is that none of the tasks get done, nowadays. Cassie knows, at the end of every day, that she has not finished off one single element in her ten-item list, but it does not bother her. Every day now begins systematically. When that day unravels to its fruitless conclusion, she cancels out the tasks and writes the same list for the next day.

Her circle of friends has contracted to a tenth its normal size, because nobody's face is familiar to her any more. She could meet someone she knew quite well, and if they don't tell her who they are, how she knows them, and give her examples of shared experiences, they stay strangers and she is merely polite to them.

Cassie's attention was drifting from Polo's ruminations when the doorbell rang. Expecting his phone call, she was confused, conflating the sound of doorbell and the sound of the phone. She went out to the hall to see Marsha, sectioned vertically in the panel of glass at one side, a tight-rolled newspaper smacking against her leg like a riding crop. Her aunt came through the door like a whirlwind, scattering bags, coats, scarves while brandishing the newspaper.

'Did you read this?'

'Most of it.'

'Did you know he was going to do it?'

'Yes.'

'Why didn't you stop him?'

'I didn't care enough.'

'You didn't care enough?'

'I'd prefer he did it to me than to Ben.'

'Why would you let him do it to anyone?'

'What harm does it do?'

For the first time since the accident, Marsha's always-ready temper flared directly at her, blowtorched her. Even when she constantly made mistakes in the very early days, even when she asked Marsha the same question ten times, Marsha was never furious directly with her.

'What *harm* does it do? Cassie, you're a fucking world-class artist trying to cope with the greatest challenge possible and your husband is peddling his pathos like that creepy shit married to whatshername the novelist vomiting out all the stuff about her Alzheimer's.'

The phone startled the two of them, and because she was nearer, Marsha picked it up and barked a greeting into it, then became very still, coiled as a countdown, when she knew who the caller was.

'Our hero,' she said silkily. 'Tell me, Polo, should I be afraid you'll take notes of this conversation or do you only use wives to fuel your ambitions? Does one have to be brain-damaged in order to serve Polo Cadogan, minister-in-waiting, future Taoiseach?'

Cassie could hear Polo doing a theatrical laugh, as if Marsha was making an elaborate and outrageous joke.

'You want to know what I think of it, Polo? Lemme tell you what I think of it. I think necrophiles usually wait till you're dead before they rape you.'

Polo's voice got louder, half-way between tut-tutting at Marsha's over-the-topness and a more threatening, more righteous, more personally offended tone. Marsha stood, chewing something non-existent between her front teeth, eyes narrowed, listening to him. Cassie sat down, because her legs had begun to tremble.

'You know something, Polo?' Marsha asked, cutting through whatever he was saying. 'Fuck the response. Sideways. Fuck the radio programmes that want interviews with you. Fuck the stupid readers who'll send in letters praising you for being so nakedly vulnerable, for sharing your own flawed responses, blah, blah, buggering blah. Iris Murdoch has a husband like you, generously sharing his wonderfulness and, well, OK, his occasional understandable little failures in the face of her complete intellectual deterioration. The way anybody will ever think of that lovely model – Something de Cachard – again is ragged and destroyed and ghastly because she had a husband like you prepared to ghoul over her while she died, prepared to record every falling away from perfection, sketching her every day of the fucking four months it took for cancer to eat her. But, of course, the portraits were the hardest thing he'd ever done. God, yes. I mean, it must have taken such a lot out of him. Shit, he had to sketch her dying, all she had to do was die. Even when he exhibited them later, *that* took a lot out of him. But he knew she would have wanted him to do it. He knew. Oh, shit, as if any woman, any beautiful, bright, brilliant woman in her right mind would ever want a partner parasite to suck her blood and puke it up for the public.'

When she finished, there was no response, and then Cassie, hearing Polo asking formally to speak to his wife, half stepped forward, met Marsha's rapid headshake and halted.

'Fortunately, your wife is not standing right beside me, listening to all this,' Marsha said, icily. (Truthfully, too, Cassie had to acknowledge, since she was sitting down listening to it all.) 'When I have the time, I'll tell her you rang to celebrate your triumphant exploitation of her. When she has the time, she may even be fool enough to ring you. In the meantime, maybe, as a card-carrying religious freak, you might reflect on why confession was always a secret. Private. One-to-one. And why it always dealt with the confessor's own inadequacies, not those of his wife.'

She banged down the phone with such force that the handset split neatly in two, tried to pick it up again and found herself looking at the fat speaker section and the fat ear section connected only by coloured wires.

'If that wasn't about me, I'd've nearly enjoyed it,' Cassie said. 'Jesus, Marsha.'

'Jesus, what?' asked Marsha, fiddling with the phone.

'Who're you ringing?'

'The goddamn speaking clock.'

'Why?'

'To see if I can hear it.' She nodded to herself, fitted the broken bits together and abandoned the phone.

'Marsha.'

The other woman looked at Cassie silently, willing her to be wounded.

'How soon will the insurance cases happen?'

'Yours or Ben's?' Marsha asked, visibly, tetchily unwilling to be distracted from Polo's offence.

'They separate?'

'Very. There are two for Ben. The case against the other driver's insurance, and that'll be settled out of court because Ben died. The other one for Ben is against the hospital, because your husband has decided he – sorry – you both have a huge case against them for negligence, punitive damages, dah de dah de dah.'

'And mine?'

'The insurance on your hands they'll make an offer soon, we'll refuse it, they'll make another, and we'd better hope they don't decide to use your stupid husband's feature in today's paper to argue that your hands would be basically OK, that the real problem is someone scrambled your brain, so it's insurance on brains that has to pay up, not insurance on hands. So help me God, if that happens, I'll swing for him.'

'And the other insurance?'

'That's you against the other driver again. They're talking about that coming up in the next three months.'

'What's the least I could get?'

'From which? From any of them? From all of them? God, I don't know. Maybe if God was having a really bad-hair day, two hundred thousand. I'd be amazed if you don't come out of it with eight hundred thousand or more.'

'Do I own that?'

'As opposed to sharing it with Polo the Parasite? Yeah. Free and clear. Clear of tax, too.'

Cassie thought about this for a long time. Marsha waited.

'I can put it in a bank and not tell anybody what I'm doing with it? Good. Marsha, some time – no hurry, just some time – would you talk to a lawyer for me? I don't know if it's a will I want or a contract with you or what. I just want that if I died or anything, you would have complete control over everything. Not just who got to use *Pinheads*, but you'd have control over the money.'

'You pay me very well,' Marsha said, puzzled. 'I've control with you over the money now. You saying you'd want me to have control *without* you?'

'Done so nobody could ever say I was nuts when I did it.'

'Why?'

'I don't know why. I just know I need to do it.'

'Cassie, anything that will keep that—'

'Polo has never wanted my money,' Cassie said. 'That's not the issue.'

'Well, what *is* the frigging issue?'

'I'm tired.'

'I'm sorry, kid, you've had a hell of a day and you don't need me picking at you too. Consider it done.'

As she walked into the hall, she tripped over the rolled-up discarded newspaper, picked it up and pitched it accurately into the middle of the fire, where it blazed up amid a shower of sparks from the low-burning embers. Cassie waved until the car disappeared, then as the light died round her, began to input to her computer.

Now, I must concentrate on escaping.

Whence the need to be dramatic about it?

Because if I'm not, the urge will fade. Anything I decide to do without becoming obsessed with just slides to the side of my mind.

Define 'escaping'.

I want out of my life.

Meaning?

Meaning, I want to go somewhere where nobody knows me. Where day after day, month after month, year after year, I never meet anybody who is family, friend, acquaintance, anything.

You're not that famous.

I'm not famous at all. I had an identity, and in a small country like Ireland, that can masquerade, briefly, as fame. Fame – irrelevant. Identity – central. Once I was someone and I am not that someone any more. I was Cassandra, the woman who drew the *Pinheads* cartoons. Cassandra, the woman who illustrated Erik the Red's books. That me is finished. I don't see people that way any more, and my right hand doesn't draw with anything like the ease I used to have. The other thing I was . . . I was Ben's mother.

You were Polo's wife, first.

Chronologically, yes. But that was just giving in to pressure and making the best of a not-bad result. Like agreeing to go on holidays with a bunch of people who keep nagging you and you quite like. It didn't define me to me.

Giving birth to Ben did?

Falling in love with my own baby did.

The anti-children activist?

Ben's presence in my life made sense of my life. I saw everything differently, I had different priorities . . . I'm not getting to what I want to say. He was like the glue that held a bunch of disparate friends, activities, contacts together. Without him, I wonder why they were ever in my life. I wonder what they saw in me. I wonder what *I* saw in me. Without Ben and without my capacity to draw the way I used to draw, it's just drift. Maybe that's why I wasn't mad the way Marsha is over Polo writing about my brain damage: it's something to be useful as raw material. If I were even in a drug trial where someone gained at the end of it . . . But nobody really gains from me being here. People work on me, now. Or they work around me. Or they work me to their own purposes.

Polo is trying to help other people through you.

Marsha is right about Polo. He respects no boundaries. He thinks he owns me – not in the old-fashioned way men did thirty years ago, goods and chattels and stuff. He just thinks I am part of his act. Permanently. He will decide how I can serve him best.

Serve him?

Serve whatever he believes are the objectives he should have.

They're good objectives.

Questionable.

Well, let's put it another way. He is trying to do good.

Why doesn't he just do good all on his own? Why does he need Ben to do good out of? Why does he need to do the equivalent of letting the world see me sitting on the loo?

You're the most touching example.

Fuck being a touching example.

You'd like other people to think it was the feature he

published about you that made up your mind. But your mind was made up the day you came home, wasn't it?

How?

You never bothered your arse with any of the exercises the rehab people wanted you to do, but the day after he brought you home, you practised going up the stairs without using the chair lift.

That's true. I'm not clear on much since the accident, but one thing I'm incredibly clear on is knowing when he's trying to persuade me to get comfortable in crippledom. As a mental cripple, I'm interesting. But as a physical and mental cripple. I'd be more visually interesting. Leaning on him as we walk. Tragic but brave, and every half-wit we meet saying, 'It's him I'm really sorry for.' Whole, he could never own me. Damaged, he thinks he can. Don't tell me that's kindness. That's control. Grow your own victim. Keep it in a pot beside your bed. Water it daily. Well, watch me pull up my little roots and get out of here.

To where?

Anywhere. Doesn't matter. Just freedom is all I want. Not to be checked on and owned and used. I'm not looking for happiness. I have no capacity to be happy again. I could go to Hong Kong, Paris, Nairobi, anywhere.

But where *will* you go?

(Hey, I remember how to do italics. Whee! Of such tiny competences are triumphs made, for the brain-damaged.)

America.

Why?

Because I no longer have good French, and one of the things about having your short-term memory shot to shreds is you can't learn new languages with any facility. So I'm stuck with somewhere that speaks English.

But Britain isn't big enough to hide in. So it has to be America.

Could be Australia.

I'm too old for Australia.

You're thirty-one.

Going on sixty.

They'll look for you.

Who do I mean by 'they'?

Polo will pay a fortune to private investigators to find you. Not to mention his connections with what he calls the most effective network in the world, the Catholic Church. First time you're seen, the message gets to him within hours.

And I'm back to square one.

How bad is square one?

Infantillist.

No such word. See, the computer's put a little red line under it.

I don't care. Infantillist, even if the word doesn't officially exist, is what square one is. I'm like a permanent infant. Minded, well cared-for and controlled. Back when I did the cartoons, I defined myself. Now, I'm just the wife at home. The damaged wife.

He doesn't stop you doing anything you want to do.

He stopped me staying in Marsha's.

Not physically.

That's to imply coercion is only physical. But I am convinced that if it came down to physical, he would use force. If he knew I was trying to escape, he would go into overdrive. He's suspicious that something has changed, so he's keeping watch on me. Makes me carry the mobile phone everywhere—

Without it, how would you reach Marsha when you can't remember why you're in Heathrow?

I know. But there's never more than a ninety-minute gap between calls. The first thing he asks me is where I am. As if he was plotting my progress on a grid.

Habit, on his part. Looking out for you, not controlling you.

You know something? With Polo, there's no difference between the two.

Tell him you want out.

No.

You're just a coward.

Because you're a coward doesn't mean you have nothing to fear.

He's going to beat you up?

No, he'd wear me down. Same end result.

Wear you down how?

Never stop at me. Talk, talk, talk. He would take every point and dissect it until there was neither logic nor life in it. Until I didn't know what I believed or felt any more. He would paint pictures that would frighten me into staying. He would keep reassuring me that he would never let me go, that no matter what it took to keep me, he would do it.

Not exactly third degree.

When you read reports of a man beating up a pregnant woman, that's third degree, right?

Right.

Same third degree when a man with a fast, healthy brain intellectually beats up someone with brain damage. I begin to breathe in short gasps at the very thought of him coming at me with words, words, jokes, sitting-down-intense bits where he holds my hand, mentions of Ben – no. I can't let that happen. I'm definitely not going to tell him I'm leaving him. But I wouldn't just be leaving him. I'd be leaving everything.

Everything?

Everything.

For ever?

For ever.

Nobody does that.

Sometimes, they do. There's all sorts of problems. But I'm going to do it.

Never see Ireland again?

Never.

Never walk across the Ha'penny Bridge, or drive under the arch at Christchurch?

Or walk the Cliffs of Moher.

You never *have* walked the Cliffs of Moher.

No, and if I miss something about Ireland, it's not going to be Tourist Highlights, either.

You going to tell Marsha?

No.

Your best friend?

No.

Who gave nearly a year of her life to getting you able to cope with your brain damage?

No.

Shitty.

Yes.

Leave a letter for her?

No. I'm not going to involve or implicate her in any way. Because she's the first person Polo would go to or have someone go to on his behalf, and he'd question and barrack her until she gave something away.

This is all pie in the sky.

You'll have pie in the sky when you die.

You're going to fake your own suicide?

We'll get to that. Later.

Around that time, Polo got into the habit, when he came home in the late afternoon or early evening, of turning on a radio or the television. Along with the rest of the nation, he was obsessed with the unravelling of a thirty-year pattern of corruption involving major political figures. This was happening in tribunals set up to investigate this possible link, that possible bribe, and in a parliamentary committee called the Public Accounts Committee, whose members, inevitably, were dubbed PACmen.

At first, Cassie was merely glad because the interaction required of her was less, sitting quietly while he seethed at the immorality revealed. One night, the earnest red-haired reporter who had so disapproved of Cassie's presence on the plinth eight years earlier held up a list of 'well-known figures in the world of business' owning offshore accounts.

'What's wrong with holding an offshore account?' Cassie asked Polo.

He looked at her with so much surprise she realised that it must reflect how rarely she asked him any question, how rarely, since the accident, she initiated contact of any kind between them.

'Nothing,' he said, looking tentative.

He was, she saw in a flash of sympathy, afraid to

over-answer the question, lest she glaze over and put him at an even further distance from her.

'D'you want to know why Copperhead there is getting her moral knickers in a twist? In Ireland, we have this thing called a Deposit Interest Retention Tax. Meaning if you put money in the bank and earn interest on it, you pay tax on the interest. There's a lot of business people think it's an iniquitous tax.'

'Iniquitous,' she repeated with pleasure, not quite sure what it meant, but positive it meant they didn't like it.

'So they take a hundred thousand quid or fifty thousand and put it into an account in the Cayman Islands, where I don't think they've come to terms with the concept of tax at all. Their money earns interest, the Irish tax authorities don't know about it.'

'But you said there was nothing wrong with having an offshore account?'

'You could have twenty offshore accounts and it isn't a problem. If you pay tax on the interest earned, the Revenue Commissioners don't honestly care if you keep your money in Outer Mongolia. It's highly unlikely those guys paid tax. They had legal offshore accounts, but they illegally failed to pay tax on the interest earned. None of them are jumping up and down waving tax-clearance certificates, that's for sure.'

'But if they *did* pay the tax, there wouldn't be any point in having . . .'

'Yeah, there might.'

'How?'

'Let's say you and I were married fifteen years and I decide I'm going to divorce you and marry my mistress.'

She nodded obligingly at this scenario.

'We have three kids, and I know that because, in the early days of my business, you painted walls and did book-keeping, you think you should get half of every-

340

thing I own. Not to mention child support, pension scheme and the Ming vase. Assuming a Ming vase. I decide, hell with that, she's not getting all my stuff. So, over a year or so, I sell off a few properties, get rid of a few stocks and put a million quid into a bank in the Cayman Islands. If I do it cleverly—'

'If you have your book-keeper in your pocket,' she said.

'– which, as you know, I have, then there's going to be no paper trail. You'll suspect I sold off things, but I could have bought other things or just lost the money. I divvy up half of what's left, but I'm divvying half of half.'

She thought about this in silence. The red-haired girl on the news bulletin was now explaining to the news-reader the significance of the list she was revealing exclusively (she kept repeating) on that station on that night.

'For many of these men, this is the worst possible night-mare,' the reporter said. 'They would have opened offshore accounts in the absolute confidence that there was no way it could ever be revealed. If the tribunal did not have extraordinary powers, powers nobody could have anticipated, it never *would* have been revealed.'

Of course, thought Cassie, one of the beauties of an offshore account would be that you could use a credit card in another country based on that account, and it would not link back to Ireland: nobody could locate you as they could by a normal credit card or travellers' cheques.

Polo asked was there anything else she wanted to know. No, she said, trying to look as if her mind was on other matters already. No, she probably shouldn't waste his time; after all, what he just told her she wouldn't remember tomorrow. He tousled her hair affectionately as he passed. 'Poor oul' Scramblebrain,' he said, and she smiled, hating him.

She smiled, thinking, I must ask Marsha, then deciding against it. She must ask nobody who would ever remember being asked.

As it turned out, she didn't need to ask Marsha, because Polo, arriving home from a trip to Cork the following week, planked his briefcase on a surface in the kitchen and got launched on a saga about his flight back. 'The Celtic tiger roars, the economy booms, so Aer Lingus, ever responsive to customer need, has extended its Cork service,' he told her, in mock-admiration. 'There's an extra flight every evening. Subcontracted to Aer Arann.' She looked blankly at him. Aer Arann?

It was the little airline, he explained, the little local airline that carried locals and tourists on the short hop between the Galway mainland and the Aran Islands. 'The Aran Islands,' he said, expansively. 'Home of the great playwright J. M. Synge. Locale for his play *Riders to the Sea*. Where the wonderful Irish language is spoken as a first language.' This last was ironic. Polo regarded the Irish language as having been created solely to torture school-goers who never wanted to speak it. 'So we walk across the tarmac, the wind cutting us in two, because this is not one of those real planes you reach by an airbridge, right? This is one of those telephone-kiosks-on-their-sides jobs. Where the air hostess flings out something like a rope-ladder and everybody pretends it's serious steps. So we get on. The air hostess hauls in the ladder, which in this case doubles as the door, just to give you extra confidence in the airworthiness of this tiny joke plane, and over the intercom comes the voice of the pilot. I'm waiting for a full Irish greeting. Instead, I get this flat Brummie accent.' He imitated the announcements made by the pilot, then imitated the announcements made by the single cabin staff, a woman, who seemed to hail from Yorkshire. 'I have nothing to read, so I think, I'll read some nice magazine about the Aran Islands and learn something about them, because you never know the day or the hour we might include them in a tour. So what do I find in the pocket of the seat in front of me?' He threw his findings across the surface. She picked them up. Three separate brochures. Two from the Channel Islands, one from the Isle of Man. Financial services. 'I assume they do a run to Guernsey or the Isle of Man and someone just forgot to switch the literature in the seat pockets.'

Frowning to indicate she was trying to make a connection, she looked at him.

'Offshore accounts? Remember the other night you asked me about them?'

She shook her head, untruthfully, and let him repeat himself until he reached the point that although the important businesspeople mentioned in the news report tended to have their offshore accounts in the Cayman Islands, the places the brochures came from also offered the same facility. She nodded dutifully and gathered them up as if she was, in deference to his bringing them home, determined to read them even though they bored her rigid. As she passed him, he put a hand gently on her shoulder. 'Three weeks from now is the anniversary.'

She froze, his hand cupping her shoulder, making a weird circular movement, half containment, half caress, as he talked of notices in the paper, in memoriam services, visiting the river where he had scattered Ben's ashes when she finally got it through to him she would have no part in it.

A year, she thought. Twelve months without Ben. It was like the ocean, she thought, this unceasing beat of misery, this background noise ready to move into the foreground if you let it. Sometimes, the tide of loss went far out, leaving nothing behind but great mud-flats, sand-flats, hard-ridged, dark, holding lozenges of water to remind you of the sea that had been there and would return. Would always return. Sometimes, the feeling of loss, the yearning for Ben would be a quietly growing thing, like the sea moving back in, coated and calmed under a plastic film. But often – mercifully when she was on her own – the tide would come roaring, thundering in, cold as eternity, untouched by prayer or pathos, impersonally, biblically destructive, and she would be like gravel grinding in its backwash. They would panic her, these tides of grief, because they reminded her of how little she had left of him. At the beginning, the world seemed awash in memories of Ben, memories belonging to her eyes, her ears, her hands to every part of her.

One day she would be lying on her side and a warm, welcome hallucination of a memory would re-create for her the time he came home, when they were on holiday, at the end of a tarpon fishing trip begged for. The men who'd taken him with them nearly rocked him off his feet as they returned with him, thumping him between his shoulders to congratulate him for actually catching a good-sized fish. Then he came up to the hotel room with her, responding to her questions, the heart dying out of his answers until he stood there, so small and sturdy and frightened, trying to bite his lower lip into courage. 'He was beautiful,' he said to her. 'It was sad.' The eyes filling with tears of guilt, filling with puzzlement and shame at feeling guilty. She lay down on the bed and gestured him into her embrace. He reversed into her like a little spoon, and she put her head against his back while he cried, open-eyed, looking at the wall of the hotel room and seeing the magnificent fish, downed and tortured and dead. 'I'll never go fishing again,' he said, quietly, when the crying was over.

She never thought she would want to remember his suffering, the suffering too big for a little boy, the sensitivity requiring more courage than the kill. But when it happened, it was welcome, this hallucination, in bringing in all its agonising reality. It became a commodity, an item: the day Ben caught the tarpon. She dreaded hearing Polo talk of any incident involving Ben where she had been present. It was OK if he talked of things she'd never known about, but when he talked about something she'd been there for, his talking was so vivid, his mimicry so perfect as to give a brief blazing illusion of reliving it, and then it was gone for ever, the life sucked out of it by his use.

He always wanted to examine pictures of Ben. Until the day she screamed at him, the screams turning into a long-haul keening that frightened him so badly he called the doctor to tranquillise her. Even after the injected diazepam, the keening went on, telling him that every picture he showed her wiped out the Ben in her head, so that instead of a warm, laughing, three-dimensional figure barrelling at her out of a glowing past, making her stagger as he plunge-hugged her around the legs, her hand dropping to its cosy, curved, comfortable place on his forehead, the place her hand was made for, she would end up with nothing but a Kodak-bright flat primary colour, single shot of one instant in a reality-chain. She could understand primitive peoples who objected to anybody taking their photograph because it stole the life out of them. They were right, those people, except it was not the taking of the photograph that stole the life, it was the showing of the photograph that sucked, vacu-umed the remembered life out of the soul, leaving the dream-time barren, empty, level as a wind-scoured grey beach.

His hand tightened on her shoulder, to remind her of where she was and of what they talked. Ben's anniversary.

'I'll be in London,' she said.

He didn't often look horrified, but he looked horrified then.

'You would be absent from your own son's memorial service?'

Don't push me, Polo. Don't push me. You are persistent and controlling. Over the long haul, you'll beat me, every time. But in the short term, the blowtorch short term, I can terrify you and I know it. Because if you madden me enough, there is nothing I won't do or say. Since the accident. Only since the accident. It fills me with appalled panic and firestorm exhilaration, this possessed rage you can provoke in me, because I could kill without compunction in it. Imply that I need a special day to remember Ben, infer I do not remember him with dull agony every minute of every day, and I will score you, scorch you. Mouth tight, narrowed eyes unblinking, she thought it at him and he put his two hands up, palms to her. 'I wasn't there for the reality, why should I be there for the replay?' she asked him, and he winced at the bitterness of it. 'You can tell people my coping skills are not up to it. They'll understand.'

They won't, ran the subtext as she sat in the chair lift and let it do the climbing she was now capable of doing. They won't understand. The oul' wans will cluck their beaky mouths in reproach and the younger brigade will ask if I'm getting enough counselling, Counselling, the solution to everything. Lose a son: get counselling. Get a killer fungus in your ancestral oak: get counselling.

Marsha scheduled a number of meetings in London to coincide with the services, suggesting a flight on Thursday, back on Saturday.

'Leave me over there for a week, would you?'

'Sure. You be all right?'

'Let's see how I'm doing after nearly a year of these brain-damage exercises.'

346

'Seven and a half months, not a year.'

'See?'

'Kid, if you can't remember the difference between a year and seven months, it worries me, you being in London without a purpose for five days, six days.'

I won't be in London, Marsha, and I won't be without purpose, she thought.

'But it's your life and you run it.'

'Compromise?'

'Yeah?'

'I take my mobile phone and you ring me every day, but you give me a signal. It rings twice, then stops, then rings again, I know it's you. I don't have to answer anybody but you.' Marsha, she thought, this is a test. No multiple-choice options. Only option is silence. You know and I know that I don't want to talk to Polo when I'm on my four days away, I only want to talk to you.

Marsha said nothing. You win the prize, Cassie thought. I'll work out what the prize is later, but you definitely win it. 'If Polo checks anything with you, just agree with whatever he says I said, right?'

'Cassie, the chances that Polo would ring to check anything with me are slimmish. I find calling a man a necrophile rapist chills one's relationship with him just a tad.'

Cassie told Polo that she would be spending time in the London neuro-rehab place. (True.) That the next test for her was to survive five days there without making contact with home. (True, although she had set the test herself and planned to accomplish rather more than survival.) That she would ring him if she got desperate, or pick up the phone if he rang her and she was desperate, but that the best option was no contact. He argued with her. Said he could not believe this was a good test. Took her through every negative possibility he could think of. Indicated he would ring her 'coach' at the London clinic to talk it through with her. This last threat paralysed her. She stood in the bedroom (having raised the issue just as they were going to bed) mute and motionless, panic roaring in her ears like static, staring at him. Fortunately, what was the outward manifestation of abject, impotent fear was read by Polo as the white heat of rage, and he backed off his threat to ring London.

'I don't trust you,' she said, her mouth dry. 'You're saying you won't ring, but you will.'

'I don't know her direct line or anything. Marsha has always dealt with her.'

'I'll warn Marsha,' she told him. 'She'll find out if you ever contact them, and you know I'll leave you if you ever do something like that.'

He came over to her side of the bed and put his arms around her, pinning hers down when she tried to fight him, corralling her into a mad, funny, limping dance across the room where she could see the two of them in the mirror, where he stopped and put his head on her shoulder so he looked winning. She closed her eyes.

'You'll never leave me, Cassie,' he said, soft voice huge in her ear. 'I'd never let you leave me. What would I do without you?'

In one movement, he got an arm beneath her legs and carried her to the bed, roused, she was convinced, by binding her in his embrace, controlling her movement by lifting her off the floor. She went along with it, her thinking taking on his rhythm.

Oh, yes, I'll leave you, be in no doubt about it.

I'll leave you in my own time, at my own pace.

I'll leave you without a backward glance.

I'll leave you and you'll not know how.

I'll leave you and you'll do without me.

Or maybe you won't do without me.

But one way or the other.

I'll leave you.

I'll leave you.

Leave you.

Leave, leave, leave, LEAVE you

Soon . . .

CHAPTER TWENTY

Credit Cards and Sea-Walking

Long before she set off for London, she was terrified. Terrified Polo would find out or Marsha would. Terrified, most of all, that her brain damage would leave her beached, gasping, all property gone, a crime committed, identification lost. There were advance visits to banks to withdraw money. There was constant list-making, using her computer. There was the urge to write things down, but the fear she would not remember where she left them so Polo would find out her intentions.

The first thing to go seriously wrong happened before the flight to London even took off. Today, she decided, she could not afford the distraction that duty-free packaging offers to a skittering mind. She must concentrate, keep going through the plans in her head. Walk down the much duller corridor on the outside of the duty free. But because the duller corridor ended at the Bank of Ireland's final *bureau de change*, which she scarcely noticed normally, coming out of the duty free, and because there was little else to look at, she spotted a notice for the first time. It told her that anyone taking more than ten thousand pounds out of the country was breaking the law.

A guilty blush started in her bra and washed up over her face, bathing her in perspiration. She blundered into the CD shop and bought three or four CDs totally at random, then went to the café and bought a sports bottle of chilled mineral water to cool her down. At the point where the ground staff checked tickets, tearing off the relevant section, she dreaded apprehension so much that when the ground hostess clutched her by the forearms and pushed her back, preventing her making progress, a deadly resignation came down on her and she asked no questions.

'I'm sorry,' the ground hostess said, in a tone that made it abundantly clear she was anything but sorry. 'Your drink.' She pointed at the sports bottle, half empty, tucked under Cassie's arm. Gestured at her own feet.

Slowly, Cassie understood that the woman's intemperate reaction had been to Cassie inadvertently pouring ice-cold water over her feet. 'I do apologise,' Cassie said, with as much fervour as if she had cut the woman's throat. A girl of about fourteen standing behind her giggled, then roared with laughter. Cassie ran downstairs quickly so that the ground hostess wouldn't think she was being first drenched then derided.

On the plane, the teenager, seated beside Cassie, kept chortling. 'You were like a man peeing,' she said at one point. 'This curved hose of water came out of you, and none of us could see where it was coming from.'

In London airport, Cassie picked up her case from the conveyor belt, stuck her carry-on on top of it, and walked through the various concourses, convinced, every time someone bumped into her, that she was being arrested.

When her phone rang, only the fact that it took her some time to find it stopped her answering it instinctively. No coded rings. Therefore it was Polo. Finger on the green receive button, she halted, knowing the story of her water-pouring would come spewing out of her the minute she heard the familiar voice, and would lead, as night follows day, to a recounting of why she was so excessively apprehensive in the first place. She put the phone, still ringing, back into the carry-on and zipped it so it sounded as if it was in the middle distance. It seemed to ring for hours.

Even there, Polo, you are a stalker, a reader of minds, she thought. You ring to check on me when I have asked you not to ring, confident you can joke and charm me out of resentment. You ring past the point where I might have mislaid the phone and be having difficulty finding it, because you are a good me-watcher and you know the pattern. You ring past the point where I would have found the phone and be deciding against answering it, because you know my damaged mind presents me – mostly – with either/or options, so you figure it may be easier for me to answer it than explain to those around me why I'm not answering it, yet not turning it off. You ring long past that point in the belief that I don't have the resolution to keep my finger off that green button – you are trying to terrorise me with your persistence. Walking past the Sock Shop and the Body Shop and Tie Rack, she saw other travellers automatically patting pockets and reaching into handbags to check if it was their phone making that peculiarly distant racket. The effect of this ringing, ringing, ringing torment, Polo, she thought, is to efface any doubts I might have about leaving you and underline for me how very carefully I must do it.

She found the terminal for flights to the Channel Islands. Paid for the next available flight in cash. It was a small plane, although not as small as the one Polo talked about as the source of his leaflets about offshore accounts. Sitting in the narrow seat, another wash of retrospective panic doused her in hot sweat: if Aer Arann did this run, she could just as easily have found herself on an Aer Arann plane on this trip. The wave receded. So what? So double what, since the pilot and cabin staff on Polo's flight were English, anyway?

The plane landed in a miniaturised sun-catching island

decorated with picture-perfect tiny coves and castles. At the first bank pictured on Polo's leaflets she asked to see someone about opening an account. Of course, madam. Step this way. An ambassadorial forty-year-old asked her a minimum of questions, then did a hypothetical outline for her. Let's say she was Irish, and wanted to open an account. They could certainly do that, without it being externally verifiable she was the beneficial owner of the money.

Frightened at his willingness to conspire where she merely needed him to co-operate, she suggested she might offer an alternative hypothesis. He assumed – it was written all over his nodding face – that she wanted something even more crooked than his first proposal. 'I want this to be legal in Ireland,' she said. 'I want to pay tax on it. I want you to calculate how much Irish DIRT tax would be due at the end of any year on whatever money is in the account, to withdraw that money from the account and send it to the Irish Revenue Commissioners.'

He called in a lawyer and they went through the legal logistics of deducting and despatching the tax on interest accruing. Which, the manager pointed out, would be less with every passing year, because she'd be using some of the capital sum via the credit card the account would carry. They were to pay the interest for as many years as the money was there? Even if she died? Very unusual. They huddled. How much money was she of lodging? Two hundred thousand Irish pounds? And how would that be transferred? She opened her carry-on bag and took bricks of money out of it. They goggled. She opened her mouth to tell them that she hadn't known it was illegal to take that amount of money out of Ireland, then closed it again. They counted the money, double-verified the totals and gave her receipts. She asked that the credit card

353

be in her maiden name, as she was parting from her husband. Sandra Browne. Short for Cassandra, hence the Cassie. By evening, she was on the flight back to London, her carry-on considerably lighter, a new credit card in a pocket inside it.

It took her two days in the hotel in London to recover. Then she did it again. Another island. Another bank. A credit card with a different logo on the front of it. The last step was a flight to Glasgow, where she never left the airport, simply located a coin-operated locker into which she put the new credit cards and a hundred and twenty thousand dollars, having changed money in dribs and drabs at every *bureau de change* she came to. She caught a flight back to London and from there to Dublin, where she was so visibly shaken and exhausted that Polo, meeting her, felt free to point out that he had warned her she wouldn't find being away for so long easy.

'I wouldn't do it again,' she told him truthfully.

'That eases my mind,' he said.

'Good,' she said quietly. Meaning it.

He laughed when the three new pairs of shoes came out of the cases, the matching handbag set down beside the snakeskin pair. 'You can still find Harrods, then?'

She worked hard at looking guilty, at evoking the furtive funniness that used to come naturally whenever he would spot the evidence of a spending spree. A curious task, this, to prove an impersonation of self by exaggerated conformity to expectations. The guilt was real the day she wore the shoes, carried the handbag, to distract Marsha. The following day, she confessed culpability to her computer.

Marsha is the problem. The only problem. I feel so guilty, doing this to her.

You're not doing it *to* her.

354

It's an unkind return for how good she has been to me.

But you're going to do it, anyway.

I can't see a way around it.

Around what?

Around not telling her.

Actively deceiving her, you mean.

That's what I mean.

You could write an ambiguous letter to her that would leave her with some hope.

Marsha hates hope.

So: frig her.

No, not frig her. I'm sorry.

If you're sorry in advance of doing wrong to someone, you don't do it.

That's not always true.

What about Polo? Changed his entire life around to be of service to you. Ben was Polo's son, too, case you had forgotten. Polo will be left in limbo without either his son or his wife. Undivorced, unseparated. The wife undead.

Yep.

Why are we being glib?

I don't know.

Child's response.

I don't care.

Truer.

He's a survivor. Everything that happens to him, good or bad, provides him with more energy, more options for the future. Three years ago he didn't write. Now he regularly writes features for newspapers. Three years ago he was a success but not an authority. Now the BBC includes his opinions when they're making documentaries about how tragedy deepens comedy. Alive and present, I am being fed into a woodchipper called Polo, mulched and bagged for incorporation into his soil to grow his harvests. Let him feed my disappearance into the woodchipper. It'll suit him just as well. Serve him just the same.

You portray him viciously.

No. I portray him as I have no choice but to portray him, standing where I stand. 'What you see depends on where you stand.' If I stood in love, I would see him differently. Because I love Marsha so much, I gild and gloss what if I didn't love her I would interpret as stridency or harshness or manipulative humour. Because I do not love Polo, I have neither gilt nor gloss for him.

So no matter how much your actions may hurt Polo, or your mother, you're taking those actions anyway. If you don't love people, they are not entitled to expect from you even the kindness of strangers.

I wish I could contradict that, but I can't.

You come first.

What's left of me comes first.

Oh, let's get out the violins.

I come first.

No compunction.

Compunction is a myth. Most people put themselves first. They just drum up justifications for what they're going to do anyway. If they put themselves ahead of a dead person or a comatose person, they project on to that person what they want to do: 'Joe would want me to marry again.' If they put themselves ahead of a child, they fabricate benefits for the child: 'It's better for a child for their parents to separate honestly, not be fighting all the time.' If they put themselves ahead of a spouse, they make the choice seem cosmic in its inevitability. Or they use the ultimate twenty-first century rationale: 'Something that feels so right couldn't be wrong.'

You're more virtuous than any of them, then, because you know how selfish you are being and can't be bothered even to muster a defence for your shitty self?

I suppose the truth of it is that I no longer believe in virtue. I was never much for God or religion, but I always thought someone was counting.

Counting what?

Counting when someone was good, brought sunshine into other lives, had no evil in their actions. But nobody was counting if Ben could be killed. I'm a louse leaving its shell behind, but crawling away.

A louse?

Yes. There is no romance, nothing heroic in what I am doing. It is an acknowledgement: I am hollow, in a hollow place. I would rather be hollow anywhere other than where I am reproached every day by the shadows of what I was.

You want to outline the Louse Escape Plan, then?

OK. The date is the fifth. Monday night. Around three in the morning, I get out of bed, get dressed in a black sweater, leggings and trainers, get into the car.

Polo sleeps through this?

Polo would sleep through the Last Trump.

Her mind would want to skip, at that point, from Polo in bed in Meath to herself, the escape complete, in bed somewhere in the United States. The question-and-answer format of the computer, the brick-by-brick boredom of it was, she knew, essential to its success. Sometimes, when she reread her plans, she would see a big gap where her damaged mind saw no problem, and would have to insert a new question. She postponed her plans by three months when she realised that, to get rid of her distinctively thick glasses, she would need laser surgery. If Polo was not to know, it would have to be done in England, ordinary glass inserted in her spectacle frames so she could continue to look short-sighted. Fortunate, she thought, that she had put enough coins into the Glasgow airport locker to cover six months.

The surgery was successful. So successful that if she *hadn't* been brain-damaged, she would have been in trouble, forgetting to put her glasses on. In this instance, however, the old reptile brain was a friend, prompting her hand to reach for her glasses before she got out of bed any morning.

The postponement did not bother her. It just gave her more time to get the details right, hammering away at the computer, although never when Polo was in the house, lest he come up behind her unnoticed. She selected a long cardigan coat with big patch pockets and a pair of trousers as the outfit most suited to carrying shifting weights of stones. Days later, it struck her that she could not afford to actually wear those clothes, since someone seeing her in them might remember the combination.

While planning to wear something he'd never seen before, she needed to make the clothes she was *supposed* to be wearing very memorable to Polo. Mend one of the pockets on the trousers. Strengthen the threads holding the trouser button on. Apparently normal repairs that would have a later resonance for him. But, having done those repairs, she would then need to destroy the entire outfit so it could never be found. She knew how she would do that, too. Polo often had a meeting on a Sunday night with some religious group. She would burn the clothes then, mix and mince the ashes, check that there were no buttons, no unburned bits. Then, when she got up in the middle of the night, she would put on an outfit he had never seen on her.

Gradually, the gaps between some of the bricks of her plan filled themselves in. About a fortnight before she was due to do it, she mentioned to Polo that she had left her laptop somewhere, fending him off when he began to reconstruct the day in which it had been lost, even getting huffy about it. She did not take her laptop that many places and she didn't need his intervention to find it. Nor – she said, planning for his next predictable action – did she want to be reminded every day it was missing. She would locate it, she didn't currently need it for anything, there was nothing on it that a thief or a crook could use, so would he kindly forget she ever mentioned it? Watching him under her lashes, she could spot him quietly lifting piles of books and magazines, eager to get the credit for finding it, but he said nothing.

She didn't hide the computer until everything was straight. Until she had worked out that she could not escape on a Friday, Saturday or Sunday night because of beach-revellers staying out late without the imperative to rise early for work or (on Sunday night) too far gone in the weekend's festivities to care about an early start. Monday was the day when everybody felt like hell so would identify with someone deciding to abandon their life.

She tried out walking the distances, timing them. Rehearsed what to say if a Garda accosted her on that early morning. Bought the train ticket. Burned the cardigan coat, cargo pants, even a matched set of underwear, poking the ashes again and again to detect metal, a clump of unburned fabric.

On the Monday night, she slept not at all, lying beside Polo going through the details, ready to abort the mission

359

if she discovered some lethal complication her brain damage had allowed her to miss. At half three, filled with dread and determination, she slid out of bed, went to the spare bathroom at the other end of the house, showered, dressed in running pants and sweater, the new pair of underpants, the new sports bra, socks and running shoes. Put on her watch. Checked through the bag: computer, wallet, passport, ticket. Took the car keys. Went out of the front door. Closed it quietly behind her.

The car started immediately, and she moved it slowly, quietly, down the serpentine driveway, putting on the lights only at the point where it moved out on to the road. She kept within the speed limit, concentrated on her driving. There must be none of the veering and over-correction characteristic of her brain damage, but typical, too, of drunks at the wheel. Nothing must attract attention.

When she reached the causeway, she passed a couple of cars. Late-night lovers, drowsily sated. There was no moon. That was one of the first things she thought about, the way a teenager would think of something so eerie, so much a part of every Gothic novel, every paperback with blood dripping from embossed title-lettering. No moon. No cars anywhere near the spot she had selected, but she parked, doused the lights and sat for a long, long time, to be sure that no lonely walkers, no dune-dwellers were around. The darkness became a friend, the white edge of the sea faintly visible a hundred yards beyond the rim of shells and seaweed where the Volvo was parked. When the tide came back in after dawn, it would nudge and dribble to within a few feet of it, not reaching it as it might during a winter storm.

She pulled the hidden shoes out from under the car seat, tugged engagement and wedding rings off and stowed them, together with her watch, glasses and car keys, in the toe of one of the shoes. Tucked them where they would not immediately be seen. Took off the shoes and socks she was wearing, stuffing the sock into the toe of each, then tying them securely by their laces to each other. Pulled the bag towards her, looped it over her body. Hung the shoes, milkmaid fashion, so the laces were round her neck, the shoes hanging just below shoulder level. Got out of the car, pushed the door to, so that it half latched, but did not bang. Walked barefoot towards the white edge of the retreating tide.

A straight line, she walked, her feet sinking first into the firmer, impression-holding sand, then creating foot-shaped marks on the wet, cleated lines of wave-created sand. This she had done many times in daylight. Each footprint would fill with water, so dawn coming up over the bay would cast a pewter sheen on each, old metal footprints leading to the water's edge. When she looked back, she stopped but kept her feet pointing to the sea. The car was an occasional glint of metal, now, no more. No shadows, no other cars.

She walked and walked, the white edge coming closer until she was into it. She pulled the legs of the trousers up above her knees and walked out in the calm cold of it until it was almost at her knees. At that point, she turned right, walking parallel to the shore, counting the steps. One hundred. Two hundred. Three hundred. Four hundred. Five hundred.

Another right turn brought her into the shallows, on to the hard-ridged wet sand, then gravelly drier sand, scraps of seaweed. She took the shoes from around her neck, and, looping the laces over her wrist, dragged the shoes back and forth behind her as she walked, to obscure her footprints. Fifty steps and it loomed at her: a great circular lump of cement, three feet tall, with a warning sign sticking up out of the middle of it. She sat on the edge of it, bounced the shoes off it to free them of sand, retrieved socks to put on her cold, now drying feet, then undid the knots in the laces and slid them on, lacing them firmly. Settled the bag and began to move up on to the road, sure of every rock, every hill because she had rehearsed this so often, at so many different times of the day and night, in brightness, dusk and dark.

A curious freedom attached to not having a watch, she thought, as she walked, her feet warming to the pace. Every section of the walk was timed, leeway allowed where necessary. Places where a few minutes' rest could be taken. At one of those places, she pulled the coppery hair into a rubber band. In the pocket of the bag was a beat-up baseball cap, its logo faded into illegibility. She pulled it on before resuming the walk.

Thanks to the local authority, a cycle path ran parallel to the road all the way, sometimes hidden from the road by trees and granite walls. More places to rest, shielded from the view of any of the cars on the road. The dawn streaks were beginning to sicken the sky. She walked, able to see and distinguish taxis, early buses or the turquoise minibuses collecting Aer Lingus staff while they were in the distance, each time breaking into a casual jog, the bag on her offside where it would not distract onlookers from the judgement: fitness freak, out for the early run.

By the North Strand, she was running easily but with fewer stops. Whenever a stop was necessary, she would do the ritual stretchings of the runner: hand on the instep of her running shoe, pulling her leg up against the back of her thigh. Clocks began to appear, confirming to her that she was on time, hitting the marks. The great grey railway station loomed.

Once up the cement steps, she went to one of the toilets, wetting toilet paper to wipe away perspiration, drying herself with the morning's fresh roller towel, sitting in one of the booths until the back of her hand to her cheeks told her the wind-scoured cold-flush was dying down. She bought a paper, found the platform, presented her ticket. On the train, she threw her bag on to the single seat opposite to deter anyone who wanted to sit there.

Passengers got on, clutching their own newspapers, their bags and briefcases. No familiar voices among the ones who settled in her coach. No familiar topics, either. Men discussing the glitch in a piece of software. Another group going over the possibilities for Wednesday's match. Five minutes to go, the guards walking up and down, last-minute arrivers running resentfully to get aboard. Three minutes. An announcement. Doors banging. That strangely secretive beginning, the train sneak-sliding away before its heartbeat thudded into action, gaining pace, breaking into brightness, speed building and nobody sitting opposite Cassie.

The man who checked the tickets told each set of seats they could go to the dining car for breakfast. Or there would be a trolley with coffee coming through. Some of the groups of men trailed him to the dining car, glancing at the capped girl reading the paper, but registering little about her. Baseball caps, she thought, the ultimate anonymity-givers. Wear one and, be you film star or waiter, you become generic.

When the trolley came through, she bought two paper cups of instant coffee and a Cellophane-wrapped limp Danish from a young man who would definitely be awake in an hour or so, tilting her paper to read and eat in an artificial cell. A panicky coldness came over her when she realised she should be turning the pages more than she was: nothing of what she was reading was staying with her. She began every story, and within five lines was thinking of something else. Maybe this was a bad brain-damage day? No, she told herself, shaking the paper to teach it manners. Of course, on a day like this she would be thinking of what she would do next. The incongruity of the phrase 'a day like this' struck her. My mother *never* told me there'd be days like this . . .

Cold sweat coated her forehead and chest. Crossed legs, feet cocked carelessly into the walk-space between the seats. Sand on her shoes. If any of these people noticed the sand on her shoes, the incongruity would stick in their mind. She shifted her feet so they were up against the wall of the carriage, glancing down behind the shield of the newspaper to see if there was sand on the floor. None. Her pulse gradually slowed, her breathing started again. Of course, she had run and walked for miles on grass, on tarmac, on concrete after leaving the beach. It would be something of a miracle if even one grain of sand was still lodged in her shoes. The relief was so great, it brought her to the verge of tears.

Just where the train crossed the border, she was never sure. She did become aware, after a certain point (the point at which she was failing to take in any of the details of the personal ads at the back of the newspaper) that the telephone boxes in the towns scudding past were bright red. Her mother would not like to think of her going Up There as she called it, lumping recalcitrant Orange and Republicans together in one blob characterised only by their desire to come Down Here and be on Our Radio with their northern accents.

When the train pulled into Belfast station, Cassie abandoned the newspaper and moved out ahead of the burdened businessmen, getting a taxi with ease to take her to the airport, where she was put on standby for the next flight to Glasgow. More coffee, another newspaper, a visit to the loo. All the time listening for announcements, never anticipating the blow when it came.

'Stand-by passengers McKenzie by two, passenger Browne, please report to the check-in desk in Area Two.'

The tide of red rose into Cassie's face. If she moved immediately, any observer would know she was passenger Browne, but if she didn't move, they would repeat the announcement. She moved. They did have a seat for her. Luggage to check? None. Boarding straight away. The woman at the desk circled the number of the boarding gate with her ballpoint. Cassie found herself sitting on the window side of two Indian businessmen who talked to each other all the time. Once landed in Glasgow, she found a business hotel, checking in for two nights, cash in advance, claiming her case had gone missing on the flight. They tut-tutted, telling her she would find toothpaste and shampoo in the room, and that they were five minutes' walk from an M&S. She took the walk, bought a duffel bag, three pairs of underpants, three pairs of socks, three plain white T-shirts, retreated to the hotel, more weary than she could ever remember, and slept until seven in the morning.

She had breakfast in a coffee shop, then found a hairdresser with a sign saying, 'Walk-ins Welcome.' Cut it radically shorter, she told the man. He pulled a strand of her hair aloft, suggesting an overall length of perhaps two inches. No, shorter. *This* short? Yes. Whatever Madam wants, he agreed, grateful for any business on this slow Tuesday morning. Her uniformly shoulder-length hair fell away in coppery shards occasionally commented on by other staff in the place. He began to get dangerously enthusiastic about the look he decided he was going to create for her, spinning her in the chair when he finished, poncing around behind her with a double-handled mirror so she could admire back and sides.

It was a lovely job, she told him, tipping as generously as she could without memorable munificence, walking out catching faceted glimpses of the gamine cut in the mirrored windows of the salon. Around the corner, she jammed the baseball cap back on, checking in another window. Nobody at the hotel would perceive any change in her appearance, she was sure.

A cab took her to the airport, where she went directly to the airline desks, finding a tourist-class ticket at a reasonable price that would take her into Chicago, returning in four days. She had no intention of using the second half of the ticket, but knew how single-way flights made immigration officials uneasy. The flight would leave the following morning at around ten. She went back to the hotel where, in the room, she washed her underwear and sweatsuit, hanging them over radiators to dry, ordered room service, listened to no radio, turned on no television and slept dreamlessly.

The airline check-in saw no difficulty in her taking the small duffel on board. Almost all the accents around her were Scottish, with the exception of a pocket of people three seats away to the left, who were either German or Dutch. She watched the movie, checked her progress through the plan on her laptop, read magazines, enjoyed the food. Immigration in Chicago was slow but uncomplicated. The official asked to see her return ticket, asked the purpose of her visit ('holiday') wished her an enjoyable time and waved her on.

It was lunchtime, she was in America. Nowhere to go, nobody to meet, no timetable. Thursday. The first day of freedom. Nothing left to lose.

CHAPTER TWENTY-ONE

Innocent Bystanders and
Guardians of the Peace

It was an eye-in-the-sky traffic reporter who first spotted the car. The helicopter was setting out on its early sweep, following the coast road when the reporter yelled for the pilot to have a look to see if there was a driver in the red car, because if there wasn't, in an hour the tide was going to be lapping at its front wheels. The pilot banked his machine, flying low along the sea's edge. Neither of them could see a driver. Both of them simultaneously spotted the single line of footprints leading directly into the sea.

'Am I seeing what I think I'm seeing?'

'You are.'

'I'm going live.'

The pilot muttered something about notifying the police first, but the reporter was already on to his producer, who agreed to take a live from overhead as part of their six thirty a.m. news. Two Gárdaí swinging on to the James Larkin Road in an unmarked car happened to have the station on. One of them turned up the volume in response to the excitement in the reporter's voice.

'There may, of course, be a very ordinary explanation for what we're seeing, but I can't imagine what it is,' he told the newscaster. 'We're directly above a big red car

– looks like a Volvo or a Saab – that's been parked at the point the tide comes to. Leading from the passenger door is a set of footprints – they go directly into the sea. We can't see any footprints coming out of the sea. Nor does there seem to be anybody in this mysterious red car.'

The newscaster, who was either slow on the uptake or playing for time, asked the reporter for his 'read' on what he was seeing. 'Looks like we may have a suicide here,' the reporter said.

The newscaster thanked him in an awed way (it beat the hell out of the normal stuff about Drumcondra building up and the Naas Road being slow) and expressed a pious hope that he was wrong. The police driver changed the direction of his signal and gathered speed. His companion reached out of the window and jammed a blue light on the roof, activating a siren at the same time. 'Thanks a lot, Brighteyes,' he said, leaning forward and trying to see if the helicopter was overhead. 'You've made sure every gawker in the county gets there to crap all over the scene. If it is a scene.'

'We must hope and pray,' the other officer said, mimicking the newscaster, 'that it is *not* a scene.'

'Fifteen minutes before we're off duty, what's the odds on it *not* being a scene?' the other asked rhetorically. Their buzz box squawked. An officer in the Clontarf station also listened to the same radio programme.

'We're on our way,' they told the buzz box.

Seven minutes after the broadcast, they were parked four feet behind the Volvo, involving two middle-aged men who had been out for a run on the beach in keeping others away, calling for help. The eye-in-the-sky man might have been dramatic about it, but they couldn't fault him on his logic. They noted the unlocked door, checked that neither of the two men with the towelling headbands had touched it. A careful probe within the car revealed the shoes, rings and keys.

Fifteen minutes after the broadcast, a squad car from the station in Kells was making considerable speed on the road to Stackallen, computer checks having revealed that the car belonged to Cassandra Cadogan. The man and woman heading from Kells both knew of Polo Cadogan and the tragic car crash that had killed his son. 'Didn't I hear him on a radio programme saying his wife was depressed or something afterwards?' the female officer asked aloud.

'Yeah, well, what else?' Dawn visits to comedians to tell them their wife might have drowned in the middle of the night were not Timmy Bourke's idea of a great start to the day.

The female officer pushed the doorbell when they arrived. They waited. Then Timmy leaned on the doorbell as if it required greater strength than she had employed, even though both of them had heard it squealing inside the house. There was another noise, and the shadows in the hall changed. The front door was opened by a dazed, dressing-gowned Polo Cadogan. They asked to come in. He stepped aside. They asked him if he knew the whereabouts of his wife.

'The whereabouts?' he said, disbelievingly. 'The whereabouts?' The official phrase resonated with dire implications. So much so that, sleepy as he was, surprised as he was, he nonetheless reached the conclusion before they needed to say anything. 'Cassie's dead, isn't she?'

They explained. He told them she was asleep beside him from eleven or half eleven the previous night, but when the bell woke him, she wasn't in the bed. Her car? They described it. Gave the reg number. The phone rang, and if he was fast moving to pick it up, Garda Doreen

Linder was faster, getting to it before he did and holding down the receiver.

'You need to know it's been on the radio already,' she told him. 'This is not likely to be Cassie. This is either a reporter or someone who's put two and two together. D'you still want to take it?'

He nodded, managed a strangled 'Yes?' into the phone, then cupped his hand over the mouthpiece to tell them it was Cassie's aunt. 'I'm sorry, Marsha, the cops are already here. It's her car, all right. That's all I know. That's all I know. I'll ring you back, all right?'

He disengaged, then took the phone off the hook. Somewhere in the house a mobile phone began playing a silly tune. After a second, another started with a different tune. The unmistakable outward and visible signs that media chaos was unleashed.

As if the gift of his concentration on the task of helping them, answering their questions, would in some magical way prevent her being dead, he got clean and dressed within minutes, speedily able to tell them that there was one set of clothes – casual clothes – missing. He described them. Cassie had mended the trousers recently.

They asked him if she was depressed. She had been continuously depressed since the death of their son, Ben. Not on medication, though. But she had not been extra-depressed recently. She'd lost her laptop, but she seemed confident she'd find it, wasn't worried about it.

He must ring her mother, he told them. Would one of them talk to her on the phone if she wanted more information than he had? He got Mrs Browne, who told him that although RTE was saying, at each of its news bulletins, that the Gárdaí weren't releasing the name of the car owner until relatives were told, in fact a local radio station had said it was Cassie. Mrs Browne was not hysterical. She asked would the Gárdaí put planes out to see if there was a body in the bay and how long it would take a body to surface. Timmy, whose first putative drowning this was, said that that hadn't been confirmed to him yet.

'What'd you want me to say?' he demanded, later, in the car, when his companion folded in remembered laughter at his euphemisms.

'You might have tried something truthful like "I know nothing."'

He said the reason he was so inept with Mrs Browne was that, every now and again, she would say aloud, 'My only daughter,' as if there was a national daughter allocation in which she'd been gypped, making the suicide of that one daughter doubly unacceptable.

By mid-afternoon, the car was off the beach, being examined by forensics experts who found in it nothing inconsistent with the possibility of Cassie walking out into the sea. The following morning, because it was a slow news day, Cassie was the lead story. There were pictures of her as Little Miss Muffet, pictures of her marrying Polo, pictures with Ben. On inside pages, critics placed her within the pantheon of cartoonists, an exception in that most political cartoonists gave their drawings huge heads and faces, whereas she drew attention to the individual characteristics often overlooked in people's physiques.

She sank through the news bulletins and the newspapers as time went on, sinking towards the bottom, the newsreaders opening their stories with phrases like 'The search for cartoonist Cassie Browne is to be wound down today, according to . . .'

That was the first Thursday.

*

One corridor of the airport had a gigantic replica of a dinosaur on loan from some museum. Clutching a cup of Starbucks coffee, she sat down in the shadow of the dinosaur and opened her computer. It was not a good place to be, she knew. Irish passengers inevitably went through such a big hub, but she could not remember what she was to do next. Scrolling back, she found the relevant section.

Don't decide where you're going until you're in the US.

Why not?

You might leave a clue here.

I'd love to go somewhere on one of those trains where you go to bed at night in the carriage.

Can't. Nobody travels on them any more except tourists. Anywhere there's tourists, there's Irish tourists, anywhere there's Irish tourists, someone's going to recognise you. If they do, you're toast.

Play that one out.

Someone recognises you in Boise, Idaho, or Poughkeepsie, New York, they do one of two things. Tell the cops that this woman is wanted in Ireland for faking her own suicide. Or let everybody at home know, so Polo's on the next flight.

Reading this, she realised that sitting under the dinosaur was incredibly stupid, and, computer still open in her hands, walked until she found a coffee shop with a dark interior seat. A bookshop on her way to the coffee shop had displays of European papers. No, she reminded herself. No checking. No backward glances. If you know planes and divers are searching for you, and you do nothing about it, you're undoubtedly wasting police time, whether that's a crime or a misdemeanour. The more you know about what's happening in Ireland, the more you'll try to second-guess it. Just leave no traces.

Give no identification. Don't use credit cards as long as you have cash. Do nothing noticeably *unAmerican*. It was, however, very American to sit in a coffee shop with your computer open in front of you. She went back to the screen.

So, no trains?

No trains going to touristy places.

I could take an ordinary train going to an untouristy place.

On ordinary trains going to untouristy places you'd stick out a mile because you won't know the little rules.

What little rules?

I don't *know* what little rules. But here's an example. D'you remember the time you were in an Arby's – wonder if they still exist . . . ?

Yeah. Sliced-beef sandwiches.

Had your meal, then gathered everything on to your tray and went looking for a garbage disposer bin. Until a man at a table nearby laughed and said, 'You were trained by McDonald's: here, they come take away your trash!' Didn't matter, in that context, you didn't know the rules. Going to matter this time, if you want to fade into the woodwork. No trains.

Shit.

You escaping your life or just having a holiday?

Where else can I not go?

Any of the eastern cities traditionally a Mecca for Irish emigrants.

Boston.

Almost anywhere moving south of Newfoundland. Including Newfoundland.

Oh, my America.

That's another thing you're going to have to learn to curb.

Gratuitous comments like that provide references back to your education, background, reading, everything.

I wouldn't have thought I did much in the way of gratuitous comments any more. I'm always trying to close down conversations.

You can't go to the places Irish tourists go to. Orlando. Miami Beach.

San Francisco.

You can't go to university cities.

That cuts out an awful lot of places.

You can't go to places like Indianapolis, the HQ of multinationals with big plants in Ireland with half their Irish people doing their American tour of duty. You can't go to Chicago because an Irishman runs the big cultural place there.

Jesus, for a small country, Ireland sends out a lot of people.

Breed like rabbits, leave like lemmings.

You can't go to places so completely Hispanic you'd be at a loss to know what was going on. Or places so black you'd look weird. Or places like Silicon Valley.

America is shrinking fast.

You can't go to interesting places. That's the key thing. Nowhere interesting.

She closed the computer and wandered the airport in search of ticket-selling desks, standing back from them to read the list of places to which she might go. Some she had never heard of. But that didn't mean they were uninteresting. What decided that Greensboro was less interesting than Greenville? Down through the alphabet ran the names. At P, she stopped.

Peoria. She knew something about that place. What was it? Oh, yes. In the film industry, when they were discussing a major new movie, someone would always say, 'But will it play in Peoria?' Meaning, will it please Middle America as defined by its dullest, most average little city?

When she stepped up to the desk to ask about a flight there, the woman seemed to have difficulty understanding her.

'Oh, Peoria,' she said. 'Gotcha.'

Cassie realised she had been emphasising the wrong bit of the word: Peor*ia*. Like that gum disease. Pyorrhoea? Pe*o*ria.

The flight, she was told, would cost five hundred and seventy dollars. That surprised her, but she could not say to the woman, 'It's not that far away, is it?' The desk clerk would surely remember someone who couldn't pronounce the name of the place she wanted to go to and didn't know where it was.

'Unless . . .' the woman said to herself. 'Why don't we?'

She started to punch buttons on her computer. Beaming, she told Cassie that if she was prepared to fly an hour from now and come back Sunday, she could do it for a hundred and eighty dollars. There was a special. Cassie nodded, smiled and produced the cash. Gate 11A? Gate 11A turned out to be an underground annex of Gate 11, with a few dispirited duffel-carrying, baseball-cap-wearing, sweatsuit-garbed travellers sitting around, reading each other's leftover sections from *USA Today*. She fitted right in, she thought.

The flight was perhaps forty-five minutes, the airport in Peoria roughly the size of the one in Cork. Its little gift shop had children's T-shirts in the window, with the slogan *I played in Peoria* on the chest. There's positive thinking, Cassie thought. She had never been one to buy T-shirts with smartass captions on them for Ben. Once or twice, he asked for a particular message to be printed on a blank T-shirt, and Marsha always made sure he had spanking new neat-fitting versions of the ones with famous *Pinhead* cartoons on them. His favourite of all was one printed with the *National Geographic* photograph of an apparently furious bird. The mad bluebird. No matter how many times he wore it, he still wanted to look at it in the mirror to laugh at the raging little bird. It stopped her, statued her in the middle of a corridor in Peoria airport, the memory of him looking at her in the mirror, inviting her to giggle at the picture on his chest. People semi-circled around her, slightly defensively. Air rage might be found on the ground, too.

She moved to the side, pretending absorption in the glassed-in, brightly lit displays. All for great earth-moving equipment, photographed in virgin condition, so its yellow paint was unblemished. Caterpillar. Peoria, the signs claimed excitedly, was the world headquarters of Caterpillar.

A little finger, poking the tiny green articulated worm with the yellow head to move faster. It's a she. All caterpillars are she, don't they turn into butterflies?

She waited for it to fade, trying to focus on the boasts in the displays. This number of employees at this modern plant turning out this number of units sold to this number of overseas countries. Caterpillar appeared to be not just Peoria's big boast, but rather, its *only* boast. A two-winged plaque on a wall offered, on its first wing, the highlights of the place. In question-and-answer form, imputing to the arriving traveller a pig-ignorant and curiosity:

Average home price? $84,870.
Newspapers? 2
TV stations? 4

Radio stations? 17
Economy? Agriculture, manufacturing, information technology

On the other wing of the plaque were Peoria's claims to fame. It owned a medal winner in a nineteenth-century Olympics. Abraham Lincoln launched his political career there with the first denunciation of slavery. It had produced such famous people as Betty Friedan.

That was it. There was a wooden display case with free leaflets in it. She took five or six different bits of folded paper. One had a map. She picked a location in central Peoria and asked a taximan to take her there. How long was she staying? Couple days. It was the first time she'd tried that one: couple days. It worked a treat. Couple days meant she was no tourist, therefore could not be persuaded to hire him to take her to the local beauty spots. He dropped her at the municipal buildings.

She walked central Peoria until she came to an upmarket hairdresser, where she asked to have her hair bleached white blonde. The hairdresser became extremely nervous. Did she ever do this previously? No? Did she know it would sting? Take a while? That it would weaken the hair quite some? That she wouldn't be able to have a perm afterwards? She nodded casually to each query, and eventually the hairdresser got into the task. The end result was so pretty, he wanted to take a picture of it, but Cassie shook her head, considering various explanations before deciding that, since she was never likely to meet this man again as long as she lived, a shake of the head would do.

I have all the instincts of relationship-building, Cassie thought, and in any other situation, they would be profoundly useful, whereas if I want to escape my life, achieve anonymity, learn to be someone else, they are probably what most endangers me. Every time I meet someone's eyes longer than absolutely necessary, every time I explain something so as not to offend, every time I show interest in someone or ask a question inviting the other person to explain some aspect of their own life in more detail than the situation demands, I am on the way to building a relationship, which is likely to be counter-productive to me.

The problem she was already finding was that other people seemed to have a greater need to connect than – up to now – she had ever noticed. No matter where she was, whether in a drug store or a fast-food outlet, someone wanted to talk to her. Not really to her. Mostly they wanted to talk, but if she was in the line of fire . . . At first, she used words and props. Right, she would say. Mmm, she would say. Or she would take out one of the leaflets to study. Even on that first day, she was teaching herself the new habits of anonymity. Don't say anything. Don't nod. Don't meet their eyes. Keep your eyes on some sign you might be reading. Then they'll talk, unoffended by your silence because you haven't made them look ridiculous.

Silence was amazingly applicable, she found. Push the goods on to the cashier's desk, wag a few dollars at her if she asks is this going to be paid with a JC Penney card or a Sears card, because that's the ritual question, nod when she asks would you like the receipt in the bag, smile thank you. The entire transaction done without a word from you.

She flagged down a taxi and asked for the address where her map showed a cluster of motels. She checked into a Days Inn, handwashed her clothes, hung them all up and went to bed. It was the beginning of the weekend.

*

On Sunday, without warning, he arrived at Marsha's apartment. Two friends who had dropped in on her to sympathise quickly said they were leaving anyway. He made no effort to apologise to them. Simply waited until they were gone, shucked his windcheater, walked the apartment looking at the views of the sea.

'She loved it here, didn't she?'

'In so far as she could love anything, in the grief she was going through and with the brain damage.'

They were big mugs of tea, thick, heat coming through the crockery in a comfortably muffled way that welcomed a hand.

'You look like hell,' he told her, 'but I'd expect that. You're probably the person most torn.'

She put down the mug and began to cry, swearing at herself that she had got through five days without crying, what the hell was wrong with her now? He sat beside her on the couch, put his arm around her shoulders so her head was tipped against his chest. She cried for a long time.

'I keep imagining how desperate she must have been, if they're right about her putting stones in all those pockets. I mean, even to go picking up stones. Wondering if the awful strangling made her want to fight it, but the weight on her legs stopped her standing up, getting above the water. Drowning is the death that has always given me the screaming meemies. Anything is better than drowning.'

She straightened up, and he let his arm fall on to the back of the couch.

'Except maybe burning,' she said after a minute.

She took her mug and moved away from him, leaving him there, one arm along the cushions.

'She loved the sea,' Marsha said, looking out over the bay. 'Even when she panicked that she would end up in some kind of "assisted independent-living" place because of the brain damage, sitting watching the sea was the great calmer. The great solution.'

'Solution.'

It was not a question. It was a statement. An argument. A point. She turned to look at him. Then looked away again, playing for time. Not him, not now. Not when she hadn't fully accommodated it herself, as a possibility. She waited a long time before speaking.

'You don't think she did it?'

'More to the point, *you* don't think she did it.'

Hearing it said aloud was like having a tight band around her breathing loosened. 'I hope she didn't.'

'No, you more than hope.'

Marsha was suddenly frightened.

'You working with the police?'

'How d'you mean?'

'You know bloody well what I mean. Are you working with them to prove she didn't do it?'

'No.'

'Well, why are you asking me?'

'Because I don't think anybody else knows her the way you know her. I don't believe she did it, but I wanted confirmation.'

'Why don't you believe she did it?'

'First, because of what I know of her. She's like that battalion at Waterloo: "The Guard dies, but does not surrender." Suicide, for her, would be surrender. Take her a long time to lose the fight that's in her. But then, more concretely, there are the incongruities. Seems she walked out into the sea some time between two and four in the morning, right?'

Marsha nodded, hugging herself to control the febrile trembling deep inside her chest.

'Tide was going out. Full out at five thirty.'

Marsha turned to look out of the window to visualise what he was saying.

'Take it that she walked out at four. Take her five minutes to reach the water's edge at that time. Straight walking into the sea, within five minutes more she's up to her neck. Ten minutes, *in toto*, after she walks into the sea, if she keeps walking, she's out of her depth.'

In an agony of imagining and hoping, Marsha leaned her forehead against the glass, closed her eyes.

'Interesting, though,' he said, very quietly. 'By five o'clock, the drowning place would be under only a few feet of water.'

'But she'd have been swept away—'

'Swept by what?'

'Currents. The sea.'

'The tide's on the turn. Coming back in.'

'The sea's funny. Unpredictable. There are counter-currents.'

'When the tide's on the turn and it's only maybe three feet deep and her body is weighed down by thirty or forty pounds of stones?'

Eyes closed, Marsha tried to think her way around this. Six o'clock, she thought. Bright morning. Helicopter in the sky. Close enough to spot footprints and it didn't spot a body in shallow water in line with the footprints, in line with the red car? She turned and stared at him. 'Is this what the police think?'

'The police think all possibilities. What does it matter what they think? Nobody suspects murder.'

'But you suspect something?'

'No. I hope logic adds up to a conclusion other than the obvious.'

'What the fuck does that mean?'

'It means she may be alive.'

'Oh, please,' Marsha said, crying again, frantically

trying not to. 'Oh, please. Please let that be the way.'

She came to sit opposite him. He sat up off the back of the couch, his hands reaching out to hold hers, briefly.

'Tell me how you think she did it,' she said.

'The only way she could do it was to have walked out to a depth of a couple of feet, then walked along – parallel to the shoreline – for a mile or so, carrying her shoes.'

'But there's no clothes missing.'

He raised his eyebrows at her, and she gusted a laugh, waving away her own objection. Of course Cassie, the champion shopper, could have bought and concealed another outfit. Go on, her nod prodded him. Go on.

'Once she got out of the water and got the shoes on, she's the same as any of the early-morning walkers. So she just walks to wherever she's going.'

Marsha sat imagining this, fearful of finding in her visualising of it something that made it impossible. He rooted in a breast pocket, removed a hard-shelled spectacles case and clicked it open.

'How short-sighted was she?'

'Blind as a bat.'

'Did she have spare glasses?'

'Oh, yes, lots of different frames to go with different outfits. Plus contact lenses, although most of the time she couldn't be bothered putting them in. Especially since her hands got hurt – she was less dexterous.'

He handed the case across to her.

'These were the ones in the car?'

'Yeah. Cops have finished with them.'

She held them, bothered that she could not work out why they were being introduced.

'Put them on.'

'What?'

'Put them on.'

382

'Hey! They've ordinary glass in them. No prescription. What the hell?'

'Your guess is as good as mine.'

'Cassie could've gone off wearing another pair. In which case, why would she have left these in the car? Or gone off wearing contacts, although that's unlikely, but it still wouldn't . . . She couldn't have gone off without glasses. She'd literally walk into lamp-posts. She lived with these glasses. These ones in particular. In the last few months I never saw her without them.'

'But you wouldn't have known whether or not they were prescription by looking at them.'

'No.'

'So she could have been wearing these all the time with ordinary glass in them.'

'How'd she not walk into walls? Laser surgery. Shit, that's what you're getting at, isn't it? Her eyes were brought up to normal, but she didn't want anybody to know, so she kept wearing these, but it ne – Did the Gárdaí notice?'

'Yes. But it didn't strike them as very significant, because she also wore contacts. Some people apparently wear non-prescription glasses over contacts for appearance.'

'But it is significant, isn't it? It means she planned it. Where do you think she is? Jesus, I mustn't get too hopeful. If this happened, where do you think she would be?'

'I can probably best tell you where she *won't* be. She won't be in Ireland. I can't see her in mainland Europe. Possibly Britain. More likely the States.'

'She's in the States.'

'Why?'

'She's got a green card, she's got a visa, she knows America, how to live there cheaply. Most of all, America is one of the memories not affected by the brain damage.

383

She could sort of regress there. But how would she get there?'

'She hasn't taken a flight out of Dublin.'

'How do you . . . ?'

'Never mind,' he said, coolly. 'She hasn't. Nor out of Shannon. She may, yet, but if she does, she either does it on a false passport –'

Marsha shook her head in absolute certainty. Whatever were the possibilities, a false passport for Cassie was not among them.

'– or it'll be caught at the check-in desks. Ditto with Irish Ferries.'

Marsha looked defeated.

'It's not our problem,' he pointed out gently. 'It was her problem, and she may have found a way. Our problem is playing the odds. If you had to stake everything you own, would you take evens that she's alive?'

'I need her to be alive so much, I'd have no choice.'

'Even though she didn't tell you?'

Marsha batted it out of consideration.

'So there's a fifty-fifty chance she's alive? Is there a fifty-fifty chance she's in America?'

'Yes. Oh, Jesus, I hope so. Yes.'

He stood up as if this clarified everything for him and gathered the jacket he had thrown over a chair-back.

'You're going to find her,' Marsha said, wondering why this did not fill her with dread, why she was not ready to fight it. 'Does anybody know what you've told me?'

'What did I tell you?'

'Does anybody know you're going to try to find her?'

'I'll tell the very few people who need to know that I'm going to America for a while. They won't be surprised. What's to hold me here?'

'That's not what I asked you.'

'You asked me the wrong question, Marsha. First of all,

you know you're the only person I'm ever going to talk to on this.' He started for the door as if the second error was too obvious to discuss.

'And second?' she persisted.

'You asked me did anyone know I was going to try to find Cassie. I'm not going to try to find her. I'm *going* to find her. I'm going to trace her, I'm going to track her down, if it takes me a lifetime. But I'll find her. You can be sure of that, Marsha.'

The words were dramatic, the delivery casual, understated, certain.

'Why?'

He looked at her, impatient.

'I'm sorry,' she said. 'You obviously think I know why you would abandon your life here to find Cassie, when there's only a chance she's alive or there, but I don't know. I'm not going to do it, after all.'

He shoved his arms into the jacket, shrugged it up on his shoulders so the collar stood up behind his head, started to search in pockets for car keys, selected the black-capped one that let him into his car, more comfortable with the details of any routine departure than with talking about something far from routine.

'I'm good at doing things,' he said, after a long moment. 'But I'm not good at bullshitting about them. Join the dots, Marsha.'

'If you find her, will you tell me?'

'When I find her, I'll ask her if she'll let me tell you.'

'Well, fuck that for an option.'

'Thought you'd like it.'

'If you find her, tell her I'd love to give her a smack in the face with a four-day-old kipper, but I hope she's – Oh, fuck, you know what I want you to tell her.'

*

It was so easy to move from one impersonal motel to another in the early days in Peoria, she couldn't believe her luck.

The motel where she spent the first six nights was in a declivity forty feet from the main highway. In the same unlandscaped set of car parks set at angles to each other were five other motels, a Perkins restaurant, an IHOP and a McDonald's. A transients' paradise, she thought, sitting on the bed, watching the overnighters in the Red Roof Inn opposite leaving. The first to leave were the business lovers. The man with the suit-bag out first into his locally registered car. The woman ten minutes later, into hers. Dressed for the office, but arriving at crucially different times. Next came the older couples, carrying small bags to great old saloon cars already filled with luggage, looking tired yet unable to sleep past eight o'clock. Snapping at each other from familiarity and deafness. From the upper floors then came the guys in the oversized strappy dingy vests, the knee-length baggy shorts, the baseball caps, shoeless or in untied sneakers, tossing their belongings into their pick-up trucks or beat-up low-riders. Last came the holiday-making families, shouting at each other to check is Jason's Palm Pilot packed and did someone take Jessica's rompers out of the bathroom.

Working around them, the massively impassive black cleaning crews with their trolleys, surrounded in white-pocketed waterproof cloth, moving relentlessly, skipping the still-occupied rooms, looping back, calling to each other from the balconies, moving from sullenness to mutually abusive good humour as – by midday – they had the blocks of rooms almost to themselves. Only the occasional long-stayers like herself who indicated they would take care of their own rooms interrupted the pattern. A long-stayer, she thought. Six days.

I wish I could stay longer than six days [she typed into the computer on day five].

Don't even think about it. No spoor. No traces. No pattern. Remember?

I'm having difficulty remembering anything. It's frightening me, how bad the brain damage is. It takes me ten minutes each morning to work out where I am.

What would you rather spend those ten minutes doing?

Anything. For the first time I sympathise with alcoholics who have blackouts. I don't know what I did last night.

Let's cut through this self-pity. You prefer to be in Stackallen with Polo ringing you every hour on the hour asking you what you're doing at that particular moment?

Sometimes, yes. Oh, God, this is so shame-making. Once or twice this week, I'd have preferred to go back and live with my mother. The comfort of her certainties.

Why would you need other people's certainties, for Chrissake?

Because maybe I was born without certainties. If someone argues a point very forcefully to me, I agree with it, but then if someone else argues the direct opposite, I agree with that, too.

If that's the case, staying long enough with Polo would have turned you into a photocopy of him.

Probably. That's maybe why Erik was so important to the cartoons. I observed and drew, but it was Erik who saw what it meant. I think I'm shapeless.

You're actually in better shape than you've ever been. You were always a stone and a half overweight. Now, your jeans are loose on you.

That's a problem.

It *is*?

Sometimes I get dizzy and it's from forgetting to eat.

You should be so lucky.

When I was at home, if I started to eat something but got distracted, Polo or Gobnait would make sure I finished it. Here, I discover meals with two bites out of them the following day. It looks as if when the hunger is even slightly assuaged, I get distracted on to something else. I've decided to eat breakfast – a big American breakfast – every morning in some restaurant. After that, it doesn't matter. I'm going to put notices around the room to make me go out first thing to eat.

Fed but not healthily.

Like I give a shit. Fuelled to survive is all I need right now. Concentrate. Jesus, I can't afford to skate on to a different level when I'm trying to understand me. Shapeless, was the point.

Morally shapeless.

That sounds like I am amoral. To be amoral requires that you are self-defined.

You're talking crap.

I was nearly someone when my father was alive. I nearly added up to his faith in me, because his faith was so specific. He had faith that I was humorous, talented, that I was resilient, could get by on very little. Without that faith, I was between things, just buying stuff.

Defined by designer labels?

That remark defines the problem I face every day. On one side is a great shapeless life obscured by brain damage, and on the other is a series of facile glibberies giving the illusion that I don't need to try any more to get a grip on the shapeless thing. I need to be very careful of those glibberies.

It's like being left with all the Christmas decorations, but no tree.

'Get a grip on the shapeless thing'???

I have to.

You've been through courses to make you get a grip. Your constant efforts – constant self-righteous, leave-me-alone-I-can-do-it efforts, bored the shit out of Polo.

I'm not in the business of entertaining Polo.

No. You were solely, dedicatedly in the business of boring Polo. Most other husbands would have dropped you.

Fuck Polo.

That sort of sums it up, doesn't it? Life is Poor You. Poor you with the brain damage. Poor you who lost your son. Fuck Polo, who also lost his son – and his wife, too. Of course, you'd never admit it, but you think Ben was more your son than Polo's. The reality is that you were the needier parent. Ben was more your son than Polo's only because you needed so such more out of him. You were using Ben to rediscover life, because you preferred his child's version. Using him. Using him.

What you are saying may be true. But the awful thing is that typing it in starts a process of sullying how I remember Ben. From now on, when I get a welcome flashback, I'll be asking was this another example of me trying to live life vicariously through him.

Not much point leaving everybody you know, everything you're familiar with, coming to another country – and then spending your time pissing around in the past.

The next day, having moved into the Marriot Motel, Cassie breakfasted in an IHOP. So many businesses moving to acronyms, she thought, looking at the logo repeated throughout the bright laminated menu.

Wonder why IHOP is better than International House of Pancakes? Wonder why KFC is better than Kentucky Fried Chicken? That was one of the disadvantages of losing Internet access. The Internet meant easy research. It also meant a credit card, and so far, Cassie's triumph was that she had never been forced to produce identification anywhere that would leave a trail. The Internet could wait. Her thoughts intersected oddly with an overheard conversation.

'How'd'you get the guys on it so fast?' a man in the next booth asked.

'E-mailed 'em.'

'E-mailed 'em how?'

'You can do e-mail, most flights.'

'The airlines can give us the Internet in the sky,' the other man in the booth said, 'but they can't give us food that doesn't suck.'

Every day, she bought a newspaper, meaning to learn about this city she might come to call 'home', but revelling, instead, in the style of the *Peoria Times-Observer*. Breakfasting on eggs ('over easy', she reminded herself) bacon, hash browns and coffee, she would one morning learn about the decision of the Friends of the Library to 'do pigs' in deference to the area's strength as a pork-producing area.

The fun begins with the program's name: PIG, which stands for Peoria is Great! [the report began]. Life-sized fiberglass pigs are available to organizations and individuals through Nelson at the downtown library (497–2141). Half of the $525 cost is dedicated to help buy and equip a new book mobile to take library books to people who can't get to one or another of our libraries . . . participants buy a pig to be decorated and displayed at or in their place. Some 80-plus pigs have been bought

so far and you are seeing more and more round town.
Here are some.

The Harley Owners Group of Peoria designed the outfit
of a wonderful Harley Hog at Walters Brothers Harley-
Davidson at 615 S. Maxwell Road . . .

The story carried a photograph of a fibreglass statue in
a nineteenth-century suit, named Pigmund Freud, and
took up half a page. Cassie read it and reread it in
search of irony, of some indication that this could not
be true, trying to imagine any Irish newspaper, even one
of the local free-sheets, carrying such a story. Perhaps as
a result of the brain damage, she found that if she
was now almost obsessively reading the paper, nearly
mouthing the words, if she glanced away from it, sat
back to consider it, conversations from around her
flowed into her consciousness. Strangely one-sided conversations.

'If the kid doesn't go home and do his homework, it's
not my fault, am I correct?'

'I mean, nine kids, livin' in a two-room trailer. No
utilities.'

There were sounds of a straw squeaking in and out of
the plastic lid on a baby cup. The couple owning the
conversation also owned a baby in a high chair.

'I tellya, one more and I'm callin' 'em on it. Wouldn't
you?'

(A lower voice, male.) 'I do whatever they tell me.'

'*Whatever* they tellya?'

'If it's female tellin' me, you're damn right.'

'Gimme the diaper bag, wouldja?'

If no conversations were audible, Muzak would fill the
vacuum in her head. The family-type restaurants all
played songs she remembered from her childhood.
Thirty-year-old oldies.

California girls are really the most . . .

. . . sounds crazy, but it's true –
As long as we're together, honey, I'm OK.

Where the restaurants provided insulated jugs to keep
the coffee hot, she would linger for more than an hour,
doing a private quiz. That was Dusty Springfield. Alive
or dead? Dead. Couple years dead. Left her money to
cats.

Same – old song, with a different meaning since you been
gone.

Singer? No name offered.

When the coffee ran out, she would pick a location
mentioned in the newspaper, find it on her map, and
walk to it, each day filled with fallacious confidence that
she was now familiar with the shape and layout of Peoria,
next day relearning what she thought she knew from the
day before. Merciful amnesia preventing her realising
how slow was her progress. After three months as a motel-
drifting walker, she knew that if she came out of the
motel cluster, got on to the main road and turned left,
after three miles she would find a vast Barnes & Noble
book store. That if she crossed to the other side, there was
a cheap strip mall with a dollar shop. That between the
motels and the Barnes & Noble was a marginally more
upmarket mall.

She rarely turned right coming out of the motel cluster,
learning early that a few intersections down was a big
avenue leading to a third-level college. While it was not
likely that Irish students in large numbers would make
their way to Peoria to study, it was enough of a consideration to make her avoid the area.

By late afternoon, wherever she had walked earlier in the day, she was at her laptop.

What's the point of reading the local paper if all you do is compare it to papers at home?

Anything I see reminds me of home. Or triggers a comparison with home.

That's pathetic. You can't meet any new experience without scrubbing around for reference in your past?

I don't know if it's pathetic or not. Yesterday, for example, I walked for hours because I got lost in some of the most run-down areas, places with the grass coming up through cracks in the pavement, great swatches of jungled wasteland with builder's rubble abandoned and grassed over. Everything defeated. Even the realty signs read 'Offered by company X' as if they couldn't drum up the courage to actually sell, just offer. I'm walking along, and thinking, this is how huge sections of Dublin used to look when I was going to school. Before the millennium boom.

Your point?

Wouldn't most Irish people think that way, in the same situation?

Not twenty-year-olds.

Maybe up to twenty or twenty-two, you're laying down basic experiences, views and visuals which will be base-line definitive: these will be the mother lode of memory, of identity, against which later incoming materials are measured.

Or maybe you're just so limited, you got frozen at twenty with a grab-bag of circumstantial evidence you apply to everything rather than encounter new things in a new way.

That's a real possibility. One of the places I passed yesterday was this house and surrounding wall covered – by some obsessive – with hundreds, perhaps even thousands, of hub caps. Old hub caps, dented, warped, but cleaned up, polished and fixed to the walls, so there's a sign saying 'The Hub Cap House'. The moment I saw it, what came to mind is some cottage attached to some old big house in Ireland, where the cottage is covered in shells and called the Shell House. Marianne Faithfull lived in it for a while.

The comparison didn't tell you anything useful about the Hub Cap House.

No, and I didn't – don't – want to be reminded of things Irish. The opposite. I wonder if there's an automatic search in the brain when you meet something new: quick, look up, have we encountered anything like this before? It could be part of a learn-and-file system.

Shell House and Hub Cap House remembered and filed together?

Yes.

Or it could be part of a search-and-destroy system whereby someone middle-aged refuses to learn and file new experiences under 'new', insisting that she's been there, done that, nothing new under the sun, it all fits into existing categories.

But if unbidden thoughts come into my mind, what do I do?

Get a thick rubber band, put it on your wrist, and when you feel a comparison with Ireland coming on, snap it, hard, against your skin. Cognitive therapy. Interrupts negative thoughts.

The thoughts about Ireland aren't necessarily negative.

Any thoughts about Ireland are negative if you're trying to become a new person. But you're not, are you?

Trying to become a new person? To be honest, no. These

first few months, I've just been trying *not* to be the old person.

Honest?

OK. I've been trying not to get caught, trying to survive. Those two things. That's all. Trying to survive, because the brain damage 'assists' are difficult to get right without someone like Marsha helping. Trying not to get caught: keeping the hair short and dyed. Trying to think of myself as Sandra, not Cassie. (No good at that.) Trying not to be noticeable or out of the ordinary.

That must be like 'don't think of a pink elephant'?

Exactly. No – worse than that. There's this mental loop, all the time: *Be ordinary, don't say anything, don't be noticed because if you're noticed they'll tell on you who'll they tell? There's people around. Keep looking out for them.* Because I'm on the watch, I constantly see people watching me. I never realised before how many men automatically do a visual assessment of any woman under fifty. When it happens, I immediately think they're private detectives spying on me, I get jumpy, get red in the face, begin breathing shallowly, clench my hands—

This, while you're trying not to be noticed?

Yes. In shops, if the same person is near me in one area who was near me in a previous area, I get shaky. I don't go to supermarkets any more, because people follow other people in supermarkets by virtue of the aisle system, but to me it feels like surveillance. I constantly, *constantly*, see a movement, a back-view, a profile that for a split second convinces me the person is Marsha or Polo or someone else from home.

Tell the whole truth.

Ben. Sometimes it's Ben. But always in the distance, and only for a dreadful second. I see the back of a boy his age away ahead of me in a crowd. My hand goes out – Ben, is he with me or is that him up ahead? Then the reality comes back. For that fraction of time, the cruelty is that Ben seems there, but I've lost him: he's wandered away from me or been stolen by that couple he's between.

Now you've typed that, it won't happen again.

I hope so. But I have to go on 'seeing' Polo and private eyes everywhere. I have to be vigilant. Until at least a year goes by, he won't give up and believe I'm really dead.

CHAPTER TWENTY-TWO

Private Eyes and Pursuit

The first thing he did in the private investigator's office was hand over the computer disk. The PI shoved it into its slot in the server, moving and clicking the mouse rapidly. 'OK, compatible, that's the first hurdle.' (He pronounced it 'hoidle'.) 'Passport number. Check. Visa number. Check. Green card details. Driver's licence – what's this?'

'She held a licence in New York when she was there as a student, ten, eleven years ago. Out of date, but I thought it might be relevant.'

'Might be. Irish driver's licence. International driver's licence. OK. Credit-card numbers. These accounts still open?'

'Yeah.'

'Why? S'pose to be dead?'

'If she's not, it's her money.'

'And she might use it, and get found that way?'

'Right.'

'E-mail address. Password. This crowd – Indigo – they still paid up?'

A nod.

'Computer was a Toshiba Tecra 8000. Additional software loaded – hey, fella, you're thorough.'

'I did tell you, though, that she said she'd lost it about two weeks before she – disappeared. Mislaid it. Wouldn't let its loss be reported to the police, was convinced she'd find it herself, that it was just mislaid.'

'Physicals. Cute little redhead, right? Maybe bit on the chunky side. Short-sighted, but maybe not. Hey, you got her eyeglass prescription in here and all – cool. A detail man. Distinguishing marks – none. Scars – whoo . . .'

The investigator took his time, making sure to input the technical detail of each of the scars accurately. Keloid, he thought. This lady ain't gonna moonlight as a stripper. It was not a thought to share with the client.

The client sat, impassive, waiting for the PI to scroll up the next series of data points about Cassie.

'Oh, fuckin' hell. Dental chart. You think we gonna be pickin' the redhead out of a creek?'

'No, but you said to put together every bit of verifiable data I could.'

'You done good. OK, shoe sizes, clothing sizes. Need to ask you a couple questions, OK? Leisure. When she's not working, where is she?'

'Home. In the gym.'

'She into fitness?'

'Used to be. Not too much, recently.'

'Go on.'

'I can't. She had a career, she had a child, they socialised – what can I tell you?'

'Clubs? Pubs? Preferred drink? Recreational drug?'

'Did ten years ago, not much recently. She always said she was a cheap drunk: one glass of wine and she was flying. White wine. Red wine gave her migraines. Didn't do drugs, didn't smoke since her student days.'

'She go shopping?'

'Oh, God, yes.'

'For what?'

'Shoes. Matching bags.'

'Type of shoe?'

'High heels, bright colours. Expensive.'

'Matching purses?'

'Pur – yes.'

'What else? Shopping?'

'Clothes.'

'Designer labels?'

'Always.'

'Colours?'

'Every colour.'

'Jewellery?'

'She wasn't much into jewellery. Had a gold chain she wore most of the time, a watch, a bangle, wedding ring. I don't think she'd browse jewellery shops.'

'She browse housewares stores?'

'Maybe.'

'Computer stores?'

'No.'

'Video stores?'

'No.'

'Book stores?'

'I – I don't know.'

'Her car was a Volvo? She like it?'

'I suppose so.'

'She choose it?'

'No.'

'She choose the car before the Volvo?'

'No.'

'Music.'

'What do you mean, music?'

'What kind of music she like?'

There was a long silence, the PI's fingers poised over his keyboard, his expression puzzled. How could he not know what music she liked?

'I could tell you types of music she didn't like and—'

'What types?'

'Didn't like country music, didn't like . . . I can't remember.'

'Her missing laptop ever turn up?'

'No.'

'Smart girl.'

'Very.'

'Catholic, right?'

'I don't follow – you mean, was that her religion? Yes, in so far as she had one. She wasn't a church-goer.'

'How ethical is she? Would she steal someone else's credit cards or driver's licence if they gave her an identity?'

'I doubt it. No. Not necessarily because of ethics. She'd be scared. It wouldn't fit into her normal pattern, so she wouldn't feel she was in control of something like that, some action like that. I did some reading up about methods of getting false identity – taking names of kids whose birthdates were close to her own, but who died not long after birth, applying for their social-security numbers and so forth. I don't believe she'd go that route.'

The questioning went on for two more hours, the investigator verifying details as he inputted them into his computer, saving it all before handing the floppy disk back to the client, who was now stretching, looking out of the twenty-sixth-floor window over Manhattan. The retainer cheque for twelve months was on the desk, pinned by a paperweight.

The investigator spun his chair round so he faced into the room. 'Here's the health warning,' he said to the big man opposite him. 'I'm not gonna pull on a trench-coat and go out searching the streets for Cassandra. That's not how people are found who don't want to be found. Nine times out of ten, they're found because they want to be found. They make mistakes. Huge mistakes nobody could miss.'

'Like?'

The investigator thought for a while, rejecting several of his personal cases because they would unnerve the client, settling on one without personal connection. 'You heard of Abbie Hoffman?'

The man came away from the window, snapping his fingers to force the memory to come to him. 'Political – revolutionary? Back in the sixties?'

'Yeah, well, on a cocaine charge, early seventies, he jumped bail. Had it planned. Got the kinky dark hair straightened, bleached. Got off a trail of letters to people from different cities, mailed by a pal. Wrote out his life story – his *new* life story – to get the details down pat. Had plastic surgery on his face, went off, laid low in small towns, taught school. Has it all squared away. What does he do then?'

The other man shrugged.

'Gives an interview to *Playboy* that reveals his location. Dumb and dumber. It's a helluva strain, though. Hiding out under a new identity. The Witness Protection Program proves that. Loss of identity, loss of community support, social connections, depression, ambivalence. Sooner or later, they need to make a reference to what they were, because they don't know how to be a completely new person. The reference can be choosing their old phone number when they buy a lottery ticket. Trivial. Or deciding they can let up on the secrecy because nobody would be lookin' for them so long. But unless they do a story on *America's Most Wanted*, you're not gonna have neighbours smackin' their heads sayin', "Hey, that guy next door is really Jimmy Hoffa."'

'That sounds as if you're saying nothing can be done. But you're not saying that, are you?'

'I'm saying a licensed private investigator has access to a whole lot of data a guy like yourself doesn't have access to. I'm gonna put a buncha little electronic ferrets out there today, and they'll keep ferreting around until she appears in some state or Federal record-keeping system. Minute she does, they'll let me know, I'll let you know. Additionally, I have a network across the nation I tap into. I do that, too. But don't call me every Monday lookin' for news. There won't be any. Make sure, no matter where you go, that I can reach you, and I will.'

Whenever a waitress arrived suddenly at her table, hollering, 'And how are *you*?' as if she knew her well, Cassie would jump in shock. They would apologise for startling her, she would tell them no problem, they would ask if she was OK, and at the end of forty-five seconds, she was sure, half the people in the restaurant knew she had something to hide. At first, when the waitresses then went into their 'I'm Alyssha, and I'm your server today' routine, Cassie would wonder if she was supposed to respond with her name and function.

Often, the same waitress would scare her all over again about half-way through the meal, by appearing beside her, demanding to know 'How we doin' here? Doin' OK so far?' As if, Cassie would think, a meal was a challenge, survival of which was praiseworthy. The fact that she was on her own frequently provoked waiters and *maître d*'s to mitigate her presumed loneliness by coming over to her and making small-talk. She would be trying to follow a story in that day's paper, to the effect that 'the Civic Center isn't as pretty, popular or wealthy as the Mark of the Quad Cities', when she would become aware of a lurking figure. She would glance up, cautiously, over the paper. How was she doing? Fine. How was her meal? Fine. What was she reading? (A flap of the paper.) Interesting story? Yes.

Sometimes, waiters would recognise her and gently parade their proof of paying attention the last time she was there, unaware that the moment anybody indicated to her that she was remembered from an earlier visit, it guaranteed she would never go to their establishment again.

The exception to that rule of run-if-you're-recognised happened when she went the third time to the Cottage Inn Motel, to find it swathed in great dusty sheets of thick polythene, carpets torn up, plaster torn down. The squat woman with the ruby-coloured hair at Reception twinkled at her as she hesitated her way into the reception area. 'Well, hi, there,' the woman said, cheerily. 'Nice to see you again.'

As the 'again' triggered in Cassie the desire to run, a man's voice from somewhere overhead asked a hoarse question, then issued some kind of negative.

''S OK,' the woman said, winking collusively at Cassie. 'It's Sandy. She's been here a buncha times. I can give her 3A.'

Jesus, I've gone from Sandra to Sandy in three visits – is this a good thing?

'Honey, you're real welcome to head over to the Marriot, they got rooms over there,' the little woman said. 'As you can see, we're smack dab in the middle of reconstruction here, but I do have a room we haven't got to yet. You been in it before. Course you may not want the racket and the dust we're creatin'.'

No, Cassie said, racket and dust were no problem. Why were they reconstructing, anyway?

'Kenny's idea,' the woman said, rolling her eyes towards the floor whence the hoarse comment had come. 'Convert into efficiencies. One efficiency per two rooms.'

Cassie didn't know what an 'efficiency' was. 'So you break out the walls between the rooms?' she prompted.

'Install cooker, refrigerator, extra sink, couple cupboards.'

'Right,' Cassie said, trying to sound enthusiastic.

'New software plant startin' up, two blocks up from Eagle. Gon' hire six hundred software engineers, six months down the line. They gon' be comin' in here from all over. Barry, he's been readin' in *Time* magazine 'bout the pressure on accommodations in Silicon Valley, he got the idea to build us the beginning of a franchise. Gon' call it the Dorms. Couples, Groups, whoever, move in, pay six months' rent in advance. Cheaper'n a hotel. Cheaper'n a rental. Everything they need, nuthin' they don't need. Those guys work seven to seven or eight or nine, come home, fall into bed with a Chinese or a pizza, watch TV, sleep, go to work again.'

'The Dorms,' Cassie said, recognising the link to dorm rooms for college-goers. 'It could work. The ultimate starter-homes.'

MaryLu (as her chest label announced her to be) nodded with determined cheerfulness as she produced a key and suggested they leave off the payment until she worked out what discount Sandy would have to get because of the noise and the dust.

CHAPTER TWENTY-THREE

Ace and Moon

'I brought a buncha books,' the younger man said, dropping a backpack on the banquette bench beside him, looking around to find a waiter.

'Ace! Howya doin'?'

The waiter looked curiously at the older man, who ordered root beer. 'I'll be back to take your orders.'

'Ace?'

The younger man looked embarrassed and mumbled an explanation involving a sporting achievement in his college days. Most of his friends used the nickname rather than his real name.

'Before we get to the books, tell me something,' the older man said.

The waiter arrived with the drinks. Both men ordered steak.

'What are my chances?'

'Of getting hired at the end of it?'

'Yes.'

'You got to cross a couple speed ramps.'

'Like being old.'

'What are you? Thirty-three? Thirty-four?'

'Thirty-six.'

'You're in good shape, man.'

'This last year, yeah. But old.'

'Can't discriminate on the basis of age. You get the

exam, do the physicals, doesn't matter if you're eighty-three next birthday.'

'So what are the speed ramps?'

'They got to hire minorities to bring the balance up. I've known guys who aced the tests but got bumped in the selection by Hispanics or women who didn't do so good. They hung on for a while, then went to some other state where it's easier to get hired. Sometimes you get lucky.'

The waiter arrived with the food. Ace asked him if the restaurant, which incorporated its own brewery, was hiring at the moment.

'Flurry letting you off the leash?' the waiter asked, looking surprised.

'I'm off Flurry's leash permanently.'

'You're kidding?'

'She's in Boise, Idaho, right now, with her mom and pop.'

The waiter gestured at their food and walked off. The older man looked quizzical.

'My ex-wife,' Ace said, trying out the phrase. 'Fleur.'

'Good steak,' the older man said, after a minute.

It was, Ace agreed. He sometimes moonlighted here, and if there was one thing moonlighting taught you, it was where to eat and where not to eat. He had done less moonlighting during his marriage. Four and a half years. Fleur got anxious about him when he wasn't home, nights. Got to calling where he was working maybe three, four times a night. Places don't like that, you know? They could have done with the money, but it was easier to stay home. Except at home, he liked to watch sport, right? Specially hockey, in season. Beer, big-screen TV, you know? But Fleur wanted to talk. Mostly wanted *him* to talk. About his feelings. Jeez, after a forty-eight hour shift, he wasn't thinking feelings.

There were long pauses in the narrative while both men ate, steadily, checking the sports scorelines on the television screens hanging every twenty feet throughout the restaurant.

They'd'a drifted on, Ace muttered, except for her hitting him with the frying-pan. That broke it.

'The frying-pan?'

'The marriage. No damage to the frying-pan. It was a wedding present. I got to keep it.'

Fork on way to mouth, the other man looked a question.

'Fleur eats low-fat,' Ace explained. 'Additionally, she's too petite for it. That was the problem, night she hit me with it.'

Fleur, a tiny woman ('ninety pounds soaking wet') had employed the frying-pan the way a tennis player would use a racquet when serving. Out of habit – she had been a good tennis player. The weight of the cast-iron dislocated her shoulder.

'I'm a trained paramedic, I coulda clicked it back in for her, but she insisted we had to go to the emergency room.'

In the emergency room, they had attracted some interest: one six-footer weighing two hundred weight-lifter pounds with a massive swelling on one side of his head, bleeding profusely, but directing all attention to an accompanying tiny woman with no visible injuries. When Fleur's shoulder was fixed and Ace's forehead stitched, his mind was made up. So Fleur was now in Boise. 'I'm in the market for someone to share the rent,' he said.

The other man laughed. 'How do I qualify?'

'You qualify. According to Uncle Jimmy, you qualify.'

'And you can tutor me through all the things I need to learn to get the exam.'

Ace nodded.

'So I get marks so high, I can moon every minority I'm up against.'

The younger man roared with laughter as the waiter arrived with their check, explaining the background to him.

'Good luck with moonin' the minorities,' he said to the older man.

'Ace and Moon,' Ace said. 'Good name if we were a band.'

'That's next year,' Moon said.

'Right. You gotta have a career plan.'

'Built on your assets.'

'What assets?'

'A frying-pan.'

'Heavy-duty.'

'Proven in battle.'

'Battle is two-sided.'

'Proven in unilateral assault.'

'Uni-*what*?'

'One-sided.'

'Hey, I'd known that when we were drawing up the papers, I'd'a put it in. Fleur, you did me in a unilateral assault.'

'With a gravid culinary implement.'

Since Barry was doing most of the physical work to transform the motel into the Dorms, Cassie/Sandy was affected hardly at all. One man can generate relatively little noise, no matter how hard he works, and Barry was working at the other end of the long, straight building. Cassie was afraid that dust might get into her laptop, so she took it with her when she went on her long walk to Barnes & Noble. Between their displays of books, they had clusters of soft armchairs alternating with small work-tables and hard chairs, so customers could read, refer or study on the premises.

Setting up her computer on one of the work tables, Cassie began to input.

This is a new-year resolution time.

It's not the new year.

True. but I want to make a number of decisions that'll stick, so let's pretend it's new year.

You're going to be a better person?

New, different and better.

New?

Sandra.

Different?

Not constantly referring back to Ireland. (I'm doing my best with the rubber band. The inside of my wrist is black and blue. I get very strange looks from people who think I have my own portable masochist's kit with me, but I'm trying.)

Better?

I'm going to improve my mind.

That's an example. I'm going to, every day, learn something new to do on this computer.

Brain damage means you'll learn it and it'll be all gone by tomorrow.

No, I'll learn it and repeat it.

Point taken.

But I'm also going to read.

What?

Books. I've picked out this vast tome about Thurber to start with.

This could get tedious.

I need to learn.

Learn in your own time.

D'you know why I like this place? Because book-buyers are naturally secretive. They don't talk the way people in a supermarket will talk to each other. They move around each other in exaggeratedly big quiet arcs. They register, out of the corner of their eyes, when the person four feet away has scanned all the titles in front of them and needs to move this way, so they move behind. Tiny murmured acknowledgements, no more than that. Sometimes 'Excuse me,' I notice that if I slide in front of someone for a moment and say what I would say back home, 'Sorry!' they take it as much more of an apology than Irish people would, and make quite an effort to assuage the regret they assume I'm suffering.

Rubber band.

You're right. Rubber band. Oooh. (That stopped a man who was about to sit at the opposite side of this table. Nobody wants to share a table with a rubber-band snapper.)

Except a fellow-reader of *The Joys of Perverted Sex*.

Wonder where they keep sex books? Under Self-help, probably.

Self-help?

They're hardly going to classify them under Health.

How're you doing without it?

Nobody ever died of sex deprivation.

She closed the laptop, paid for the Thurber biography, and began the long walk back, switching book and computer from hand to hand as the combined weight tired the carrying arm. Passing a bus shelter, she noticed an ad for a cereal with the bright, smiling yellow

Pokémon figure front and centre. Pokémon didn't exist when Ben was alive. But Ben was not interested in electronic games. He knew how to find sites on the Internet, but took only occasional, spurting interest in it.

Strange, she thought, marching to the beat of an unheard drum, how Ben, appearing in her thoughts these days, never caused the screaming searing outbursts of agonised raging grief of the early days. Instead, there was a heavying of the day left by the recollection. Which, in itself, was sad. Perhaps there would come a day when to remember him would be to lighten and brighten a day. Or perhaps there would come a day when she would not think of him at all. For one whole day. Would that, she wondered, be a good thing or a bad thing? She no longer drew comfort from the notion that Ben was in some way still alive if she thought about him every day.

But, she thought, transferring laptop and book yet again as she waited for traffic to pass on the intersection she needed to cross before entering the area where all the motels were, Ben would never be subject to the rubber-band rule. Almost everything caused her mind to loop back to Ben. A penumbrous pleasure, if even that. But essential. Without it, she would cease to exist. Cease to have existed.

'Moon?'

'Mmm?'

'What's the major disadvantage of open web bar joists made of unprotected steel?'

'Tend to lose strength in high temperatures. Steel is non-combustible but has little heat resistance.'

'Keep moving. You're slowing.'

'How many more storeys?'

'Three.'

'Shit.'

'What are the essential steps for a successful foam operation?'

'Whooo.'

'You can think and move at the same time. Two to go.'

'Apply foam to burning surface.'

'Come on, Moon, you're losing time.'

'Whooo.'

'One to go.'

'Have suff – whooo.'

'Half-way there.'

'Suffish – whooo.'

'Come on, not gonna stop now. Four. Three. Two. One.'

The sound, as the big man collapsed, was like a multiple-vehicle collision. Air tanks and heavy metal tools went in all directions on the metal floor of the top landing. He crouched, his face pressed to the patterned floor, then rolled into a sitting position, his high forehead indented neatly with the metal diamonds embossed on the floor.

'Sufficient foam on hand to kill the fire. Observe pressure gauges on foam appliance. Supply foam at proper application rate for the specific hazard.'

'Your recovery time is getting shorter.'

'Write it on my tombstone.'

'Not many guys could carry thirty-two pounds of equipment up that many storeys at a run.'

'True. I'll say that to myself in bed tonight.'

'Moon?'

'Yeah.'

'Why you doing this?'

'To join the fire service.'

'Why do you want to join the fire service?'

'Why did *you* want to join the fire service?'

'You come from where I come from, you become a cop or a fire-fighter or a bum.'

'That's not the real reason.'

'Good benefits.'

'That, neither.'

'Best fire service in the country. Once you've been with the Boston fire service, you can get a job anyplace else you want.'

The two of them sat on the fire escape in silence for a while.

'All my life, I wanted to be a fire-fighter,' Ace said eventually, and Moon laughed.

'So why do I have to have a different reason – a better reason?'

'You're starting fifteen years later than I did. You were a success in a completely different area. You're not from here. And I'm not dumb. The dedication is unreal. Fire-fighting's part of something bigger. None of my business, buddy.'

His feet clanging on the metal, he started to rise. The other man's gloved hand held him back. 'It's quite a long story,' he said. 'But I owe you.'

'Bullshit. You owe me plenty, but if it's a long story, the only reason you want to tell it to me is to stop me asking you fire-fighter quiz questions and making you run.'

'You're right.'

'Tell me anyway.'

'OK.'

Cassie was too preoccupied with her new friends to move on to another motel. Her new friends emerged from the big biography of Thurber.

'One of the writers he was pals with, a guy named Peter de Vries, said Thurber was good at hitting the male on the head,' she told the computer. 'Any guy who says something like that I'd like to get to know. So I made a list of people mentioned in the book, including someone called John O'Hara, who was described as "the master of the fancied slight", and now I'm back in Barnes & Noble, I'm going to pick up copies of their work. Then they'll introduce me to other people and I'll have a little network.'

This system worked well. Whether in acknowledgements, dedications, biographical notes or the text of their book, authors pointed fingers at other writers they loved or hated, so Cassie began to form allegiances, to join clusters of authors, long dead most of them. Her absorption in their worlds became so total that when she would put the book down, it took her a moment or two to work out where she was. Sometimes, there was a sickly second or two during which she believed she was back in Ireland.

To balance the expenditure on big hardbacks, she would go to second-hand book shops, picking up, almost at random, yellow-edged old paperbacks. One, from the fifties, opened at random, made reference to Brendan Behan. She did a double-take, looking again at the book cover, which was all about how to make it in a man's world. When she brought the book home at a cost of five cents, she found the author was – when it was written – a book publicist who, finding a drunken Behan in amorous assault, got him to behave himself only when she told him she was 'a nice Jewish girl', which seemed to make perfect sense to him and provoked him to talk lovingly of Jews in Dublin. The book was dated but sparky and funny. Another friend, Cassie thought, making lists of Letty Cottin Pogrebin's later works.

Sometimes her new friends developed faces, appearing in the blocks of photographs in other people's biographies. Letty Cottin Pogrebin, a tiny, pretty blonde turned up in histories of feminism alongside the aviator-spectacled Gloria Steinem. And in an autobiographical offering from Helen Gurley Brown, first editor of *Cosmopolitan*.

They were more real to Cassie, these new friends, than were the people around her. MaryLu she chatted with each day. Barry she saw but mostly heard on the third floor. Particularly the day he came off the ladder. She and MaryLu made it to the third floor from different approach stairs at almost the same time in response to the agonised yell. He had fallen at a bad angle. Both women made the judgement simultaneously.

'I'll call 911,' MaryLu said, running down the stairs.

Cassie pulled out of the socket the plug to the paint-sprayer, which was continuing to spray a creamy colour called, according to the can, Mary's Lamb impartially over everything and everybody within range. Barry was so thickly covered by then that Cassie wondered if the *Goldfinger* rule would apply: that he would suffocate because his pores were all clogged up with paint. Then she realised the only portions of Barry actually exposed to the sprayer were his face and hands. The rest of him was probably breathing just fine under his overalls. She wiped his face gently. He was sweating profusely. MaryLu came running back up the stairs. 'On their way,' she said, kneeling beside him.

Within minutes, the fire brigade, ambulance and squad car were wheeling into position directly below. MaryLu was obviously a dab hand at describing where they should go. The paramedics examined Barry, put inflated supports around his legs, secured him to a stretcher and got him into the ambulance.

'I'll go with him,' MaryLu said, readying to throw her keys to Cassie. 'Sandra, you take my car and follow us?'

'Don't have a driver's licence.'

Everybody turned to look at Cassie. Hey, we got a live

one here. Imagine, must be thirty and no driver's licence.'

'Not a current one. I'm really sorry.'

'Follow the ambulance,' Barry growled at his wife. 'I'm gonna be fine, it's seven, eight minutes to the hospital.'

Promising to take care of things in their absence, Cassie waved at MaryLu as she pulled out of the car park in her beat-up Pontiac. She came back a few hours later. Barry had, she said, a comminuted fracture of the femur. Real bad. Eggshells in a Baggie, was the surgeon's phrase for it. He'd have to have a couple of surgeries.

The two women sat over coffee in the now-defunct reception area of the old motel.

'We got insurance,' MaryLu said, 'but it's going to slow us down here.'

'MaryLu? Barry wasn't able to make much progress anyway. His breathing's not great.'

'Emphysema. But there's no telling him.'

'Make a suggestion?'

'Yeah.'

'Two suggestions, really. Let me continue what he was doing. I don't know much, but I probably won't be any slower than he was. And let's think about getting other guys in to do some of the stuff.'

'He won't like it.'

'MaryLu?'

'I know, I know. So he lives with it, right?'

'Right. I also need to get a driver's licence and a car. Tell me how to go about it.'

'When I go to the hospital tomorrow, I could take you to the driver test place, pick you up after I visit?'

By the time she was picked up, Sandra Browne had managed to pass a driver's test and get a licence, mainly because of a series of no-shows. The two women laughed at the picture on the laminated card.

'Makes you look like the cover of one of those supermarket tabloids. You know, "Woman's Hair Goes White Overnight – UFO Aliens Raped Me, She Says." What's your real hair colour?'

'Black,' Cassie lied, feeling guilty and pleased with herself at one and the same time.

The following day she bought a car. A seven-year-old Chevrolet Lumina, wine-coloured. One aged owner. When she took MaryLu for a spin in it, MaryLu fiddled with the controls of the radio until she found a country-music station.

> *I guess you had to be there*
> *You really had to be there . . .'*

'I don't know country music, but I know that one,' Cassie said aloud.

'Lorrie Morgan,' MaryLu said. 'You know the one? Same colour hair as you.'

Cassie shook her head. 'It's not the singer,' she said, 'it's the song.'

With a chill, it came back to her. It had been one of the songs at her wedding. Rubber band, quick . . .

MaryLu wanted to pay her for the painting she was doing. Cassie wanted to know when she was going to get a bill for the room she was sleeping in. MaryLu asked what room. Cassie asked what painting. The Lumina cruised to a halt and she turned off the engine.

'We're gittin' there,' MaryLu said, only half believing it.

'We're *gittin'* there!' the private investigator yelled.

Ace, reading in a corner, was startled by the volume of the screech coming out of the phone. Moon shrugged, holding the phone out slightly. 'We are?'

'Oh, we are, my friend, we are.'

'As in?'

'As in, your girl's alive and well and living in Peoria.'

The big man sat, eyes closed, in absolute silence. When he spoke, it was a croak. 'Where?'

'Peoria. Peoria, Illinois.'

'How sure are you?'

'Unless ghosts drive cars . . . She got herself a driver's licence. You want the number?'

Without knowing what use he might ever make of someone else's driver's licence number, Moon obediently wrote it down.

'But that's not all.'

'No?'

'Within couple of days of getting the licence, she got herself wheels, too, didn't she?'

The details of the second-hand car Cassie purchased went down on the sheet of paper. The big man looked at them, a surge of triumph rising through him. *You are alive. I have you. I can reach you, locate you, find you, see you. Touch you.*

'Got an address, you'd care to take it down.'

The private eye's voice was silky with delight.

'This is a motel, right?'

'Has been.'

'Sorry?'

'Has been a motel. That chain went belly-up a few months ago, and most of the operators bought out the premises. My information is that the couple who bought the Peoria building are planning to turn it into efficiency homes to service new industries they're expecting to move in there. It stopped operating as a motel several weeks ago, but my information is that Ms Browne's on the premises. Your guess is as good as mine.'

The man put down the phone, unseeing in the ecstasy

418

of his relief. Ace watched him walk out of the door. He would run, Ace knew, and run until the rhythm of the running evened his breathing and his emotions. He would come back, walking as if on rough ground, every bit of fabric on him damp to sodden, the sweat running off his face, ready to step into a pounding shower. In his place, Ace thought, he'd be celebrating with a few drinks, but Moon never drank alcohol.

He must call Fleur, Ace thought. She was still his best friend, and was fascinated by the Moon story. This latest news would move her reaction from wistfulness to a more sloppy anticipation. Could he handle that, he wondered, hand on telephone. He decided he could, and started to dial.

CHAPTER TWENTY-FOUR

Fire Ants and Fire-Fighters

The good thing about Barry coming back, as Cassie saw it, was that there was no hope of him, in a wheelchair, getting to the third floor, where she was working from room to room. Once, the first week he was home, mainly to annoy MaryLu, he managed to bump himself all the way up the stairs on his bottom, roaring for her to bring up the wheelchair to him at the top, but the effort took so much out of him that he didn't do it a second time, opting instead to drill Cassie from below as to what precisely she was doing.

'You put the tape round the frames before you started that painting?'

'Course I did.'

'You remember to plug in the pest gizmo?'

'Absolutely.'

'Didn't forget to thin the paint like I told you for the walls?'

'Not for a minute.'

Half the time, she was lying to him, scurrying around to fix the deficit once reminded. MaryLu kept apologising to her for his nagging, but Cassie liked it. If God ever designed a man to be the remote-control boss of a woman with brain damage, Barry was that man. Without his constant interference, Cassie knew, she was quite likely to paint areas cream that should have been left without paint, or to paint over the glass in windows, whereas his sporadic interruptions reminded her of the specificity of each task.

Whenever she felt particularly good-humoured, she would go downstairs and consult him on something. Three weeks into the job, she brought down the pole from which the shower curtain was hung, to show him how much it was sagging in the middle and to draw his attention to rust so that in ordering replacements he got better supplies next time. He rolled the wheelchair back as if, getting so far out in the car park, he might be able to see into the bathrooms on the third floor. She stood on one of the small green patches outside the ground floor (first floor, she corrected herself, reaching for the rubber band) rooms. Like a pilgrim, she looked, she thought, catching sight of herself reflected in a window, holding the long pole, its further end stuck into the ground. Which, as it turned out, was the problem.

Barry was in the middle of a long story about the suppliers of the original shower curtain rods when stinging little prickles in her skin pulled Cassie out of the brain-damage daydream she was in. I shouldn't stand in hot sun to listen to him, she thought, then almost heard the contradictory thought: But it isn't hot sun. Her left leg, particularly her foot, was stinging all over. She glanced down. Her thong-sandalled foot was alive with tiny busy ants. She pointed the toe and hammered it off the ground, leaning more heavily on the pole to achieve balance. Which ensured that thousands of ants climbing up the pole got to climb on to her hands and, because she leaned her forehead against the pole in order to get better purchase in her increasingly frantic efforts to get the ants off her leg, on to her face.

The insistent multiplicity of stings demanded attention everywhere. She flapped in a demented way at herself. Barry watched, mystified.

'Ants,' she said, apologetically. 'Only tiny ones, but they're stinging.'

'Fire ants,' he said, and yelled over his shoulder, 'MaryLu!'

MaryLu came at the run, took one look at Cassie, grabbed the hose, spun the tap feeding it, and assaulted her with a precisely directed stream of ice-cold water. Stunned by stinging, by the breath-stopping cold of the water and by confusion, Cassie stood like a statue.

'Get on to the paving,' Barry ordered her.

She obeyed.

'Throw away the pole,' MaryLu shouted at her. She did that too.

'Step away from it,' Barry shouted. She did that as well.

The sound of the hose died down. Cassie stood where she was, afraid to move without instructions, unable to open her eyes because of the water flowing down her face from her hair. She could hear a car engine coming closer, drawing up, going silent, and doors opening, just as MaryLu said, beside her, 'OK, Sandy, towel,' jamming cloth into her hand. Cassie put her face into the cloth.

'Fire ants,' she could hear Barry saying.

'We're paramedics, you want we should take a look at her?'

Cassie, sure that her hair and face were reasonably dry, straightened up and opened her eyes. Or tried to. 'My eyes won't open,' she said to MaryLu.

'You're OK,' the voice said beside her. It belonged to a man.

'I'm not OK, I can't open my eyes,' she said, and someone snuffled a laugh.

'I know, you're all swelled up, but I need you to answer some questions.'

'Fuck questions,' Cassie said, 'my eyes won't open.'

'They will in due course.'

'Due *arseholes*,' said Cassie. 'Whattya mean, in due course?'

'Do you suffer from anaphylactic shock?'

'Look, this is not the time for market research.'

'Ma'am, do you swell up when a bee stings you?'

'How the frig do I know? I've never been stung by a bee. Jesus, my fingers hurt. My whole hand hurts.'

'Your hand is swollen up, ma'am.'

Cassie began to feel her legs, a procedure greatly hampered by the gross swelling in both hands. Someone took one of her hands, then the other. 'What are you doing?'

'Checking for rings,' a different, husky voice said.

'You were the one who laughed,' she said.

'That's true, ma'am. I apologise.'

Several people then spoke at once to Cassie, and before she had absorbed what any of them were saying to her, she was lifted and carried. Under her, she could feel the cool fabric of bedclothes. Within seconds, she found that the heat emanating from her arms and legs was heating up the fabric, creating, she imagined, a burning hot body-shaped zone in the bed, like a heated-up version of the drawings police did at the scene of the crime. She kept shifting to new spots, but heating them up faster and faster. Something was poking at her mouth. She opened it to protest and discovered a drinking straw. Cold liquid. Wonderfully cold liquid. Liquid so sweetly cold it rivered a stream of chill down into her so absorbingly pleasurable she drifted away from the noise for a few minutes. It got taken away. She croaked a protest.

'Sandy?'

There was a silence. MaryLu began to make worried noises about calling 911 and telling them Sandy was not responding. Who's Sandy? Cassie wondered. Oh, Sandy is Sandra, she thought, and Sandra is the end of

Cassandra, and that's how MaryLu and Barry know me.

'Yes?' she answered, and the snuffly laugher did another snuffly laugh.

'Sandra,' the other voice said. 'You can hear us?'

'Obcorsh I cnheary—' The sounds she produced startled her.

'Your mouth is swollen,' the voice said.

'Oh.' That's a relief. I thought brain damage had taken a turn for the worse, Cassie thought, and was then grateful she could not, on impulse, articulate the thought. Or, if she did, would not be understood by any of them. She made a huge effort and could see a narrow slit of light.

'We don't think you're going to swell up any more,' the voice said.

'Thank God,' Cassie said. What she wanted to say was 'Thanks be to Jasus', but that might be a little complex to get out between the two pneumatic tyres her mouth had turned into. It sounded ludicrously pious, and she laughed.

'Don't cry, honey,' MaryLu said. 'We gonna get you to the hospital.'

Cassie came up from under the stroking hand on her forehead like a greyhound out of a trap.

'No hospital,' she shrieked.

'What she say?' several voices asked.

'No hospital,' the husky-snuffle-laugh voice said, laughing again.

'What's so fucking funny?' Cassie asked. It came out like water from a hose someone tries to control by pressing a finger into the hole where the water is coming out.

'What she say?' voices asked again.

'She wanted to know why I laughed,' the husky voice said. It had a funny accent.

'Never mind that. Honey, you really need to go to the hospital,' MaryLu's voice said. 'If you swell up any more, your breathing – you might not be able to breathe.'

424

'No hospital.'

'It's not painful, what they—'

'I'm not going to hospital, is that clear?'

'What she say?' the voices asked each other.

'Oh, for fuck's sake,' Cassie said.

The straw was introduced between her great lumped immobile lips and, in desperation, she drank deeply.

'She can ingest, anyway,' someone said.

'Of course I can effing ingest,' Cassie said, spitting the straw out with the first words. 'I can talk, I can swell, I can spray-paint efficiency rooms. Jesus, if you force me to I can do sit-ups, but I am not going to any hospital at any time.'

There was a long, baffled silence after this offering, and then she could hear MaryLu whispering to someone, obviously hoping Cassie wouldn't hear her asking if the someone thought she was delirious. The someone snuffled with laughter again and said he thought Miss Browne was quite coherent and very clear in her own mind that she was not going to a hospital. If they were worried, he said, they could get her to sign something to the effect that they had tried to get her to go to a hospital and she had refused. Cassie nodded, frantically. They huddled while she considered the number of systems into which her name and address would be fed if she went into a hospital. Hospitals here probably had pastoral systems that involved visiting priests and rabbis, she panicked, seeing messages flashing to Polo Cadogan within minutes of her arrival in any ward. 'What time is it?' she asked, sitting up, fighting off restraining hands.

Five of eleven, she was told.

With great difficulty, she outlined a plan. Until lunchtime, she would stay in bed and, if it wasn't too much trouble, MaryLu would watch over her to make sure her breathing stayed the way it was. At lunchtime, they could decide the next step. 'In the meantime,' she muttered, 'I learn to plan sentences with no Ps, no Ss and no Fs.'

Her mutter was greeted by complete silence and then another snuffling laugh.

'Who he?' she asked, pointing in the direction of the voice.

'Moon,' a man's voice said.

'And stars,' she said. 'What's his name, for Chrissake?'

'Moon.'

'Oh. What's your name?'

'Ace.'

'What are ye? Comedians? Moon. Ace.'

'Want you to drink something.'

The straw was back. She poked it away with her tongue, wanting to know what this drink was. Something to control the pain, the swelling and the feverishness, she was told. She drank it, still trying to shift to a cooler space in the bed. After a while, she became aware that the room was empty. Or emptier.

'Hello?'

'Hi, Sandy. How'ya doing?'

'MaryLu?'

'That's me.'

'The guys with the funny names gone?'

'They're talking terms with Barry. They moonlight on building sites. Friend of ours gave us references.'

'MaryLu?'

'Sssh.'

'OK,' said Cassie, and fell asleep.

At first, when she woke up and could not open her eyes, she thought she was back in the hospital and that she had just learned from the counsellor that Ben was dead. She lay there, tears squeezing out of the side of her eyes, until the thirst became oppressive. Her hand was heavy, sodden with swelling, but she moved it up to where the drink was on the night table in her memory, tipped something and came down heavily on it to keep it from tipping over.

She lay there for some time, trying to work out what it was. Her hand was so swollen and misshapen that it could send only skewed messages of what it was cupped over. It was not a glass, she worked out, because it was warm to the touch. It was round, too. Like the roundy knob on a banister, she thought. It began to shake and she snatched her hand away. The knob on the end of banisters didn't shake or snort with laughter. Jesus. It was a head. A perfectly smooth shaved head. A man's head.

'Don't get frightened,' the husky voice said. 'I'm here for five minutes. MaryLu needed restroom break.'

'I put my hand on your head,' Cassie said. (It came out as 'I buh' but the rest of the sentence worked.)

'You did.'

'I'm sorry.'

'Why?'

Cassie thought about possible answers to this. One doesn't put one's hand, swollen or normal-size, familiarly on the powdered pate of perfect strangers. 'I don't like shaved heads,' she said. 'I'm sorry.'

'OK,' the voice said, equably. 'I'll grow it back'

I'm not going to forbid you to grow your hair back, Cassie thought, because that would imply I have some ongoing interest in putting my hand on your head, whereas what I was looking for was a drink, and could I have it, please?

As if in response to the thought, the straw tickled her mouth again. She tongued it to one side. 'I don't want any more of that drug,' she said. (Good sentence, she thought. Very few of the consonants that demand lip involvement.)

'It's iced tea,' the voice said.

She drank ferociously, chilled by the cold of the drink, then relinquished the straw and tried to sit up. The man helped her, expertly. 'Thank you,' she said.

'Any time,' he responded.

'What do I look like?'

There was a small pause.

'Compared to . . . ?'

'Compared to normal.'

'Do I know normal?' The question was put like a polite reminder.

She laughed. 'Never mind normal me. What do I look like compared to normal anyone?'

'You look,' he said thoughtfully, 'like someone used an air hose under your skin to inflate you to maybe twice normal size. Your face has no wrinkles at all.'

'I'm not that wrinkly normally,' she pointed out.

'But no wrinkles even here.'

She shrank back from the touch.

'Ma'am?'

'What?'

'I'm touching you with a pen.'

'Oh? OK.'

She relaxed.

'Your mouth looks ready to burst. Your hands . . .'

The tiny cold touch of the pen took a second to register through the puffed tissues.

'Your hands have no wrinkles, no veins and no knuckles. You have dimples where the knuckles should be. The swelling is hard, hot and red.'

'Thank you.'

'Any time,' he said, as MaryLu arrived back, quite disappointed that Sandy had woken when she wasn't there. The husky voice murmured something and the door closed.

'What's he called?'

'Moon.'

'Moon. You told me that before, didn't you, Marsha?'

'I'm MaryLu.'

Cassie fell asleep again.

The following day, the only man about the place was Barry, now using crutches to get up and down stairs, mainly, MaryLu maintained, for the kick of seeing her resultant terror. Cassie now had a narrow strip of vision, reminiscent of some videos of movies where the processing leaves a couple of inches of black above and below the colour picture stream. Watching Barry climb the stairs through this slit, she could see he had no clue how to manage crutches. But am I going to teach you and have you ask how I know? No. She stood, trembling with more guilt than MaryLu when shudderingly he made a mess of the top step and almost arrived on the pavement between them on his back.

'Did you look at yourself?' MaryLu asked.

'Difficult not to, when I was brushing my teeth,' Cassie said. 'Impressive, aren't I?'

'Impressive is one word for it. You must be *so* allergic.'

'I could walk right into court and get a restraining order on those ants just based on how I look.'

MaryLu suggested coffee. Cassie stumped after her, her shoes fastened loosely around feet tubed by swelling.

'Where's Amos 'n'Andy?' Cassie asked, pleased to come up with some duo reference, although not desperately sure who Amos 'n'Andy were. Or had been.

'They work today and tomorrow. Be here Friday again.'

'Won't recognise me,' Cassie said, dribbling her coffee slightly.

Overly fat desensitised lips made her misjudge the suction needed, so she either slurped like a soup-scooping derelict or dribbled. She held a napkin under her chin all

429

the time, like, she thought, an altar-boy. Rubber-band smack, she then thought, but did not do in front of MaryLu. Not that she could, anyway, she realised, fingering her wrist. Someone had removed it. Back in her room, operating through her postbox-opening slit of vision, it took her a long time to find the thick rubber band. She tried it on. Whoever removed it was wise, she thought, looking at the swelling. It would have cut off circulation to her hand.

Her toes, she found, taking off the shoes and socks, were not simply swollen, but distended and hard with oedema. It was uncomfortable enough to consider sticking a needle in the swelling to reduce it, but this probably would not be a good idea. Her fingers, on the other hand, were not swollen at all, poking thin and fragile out of puffed circular hands. Thin fingers encouraged her to try out the computer:

Why was I not evasive and you-don't-see-me with Amos 'n'Andy?

Because you were more disguised than if you were in the Witness Protection Program. If one of them was Polo, he wouldn't have recognised you.

There's a great freedom in total anonymity. Black like me.

No, there's a great self-flattery in being your wonderful unique self inside apparent anonymity. Anonymity – the real stuff – isn't that much fun at all, at all.

I'm in very good humour.

For someone who looks somewhere between ghastly and ridiculous and itches all over, yes. You feel so triumphant about not getting sent to hospital.

That's true. Being fed into that record-keeping system would have been fatal.

At this point, tired because her rate of hitting the right keys was so poor, she gave up, opting instead to read. She had a growing list of people whose books she wanted to get. Or in certain cases, like the man named Max who edited Hemingway, Scott Fitzgerald and some other famous writer, the book she wanted was his biography. Out of print, no doubt, some of them. It was the one great disadvantage of being off the Internet: that she could not use any of the book-searching services to find out-of-print books. She thought about opening an Internet account, but could feel herself shrinking away from the gratuitously higher level of risk. Leave it another three months. Another six.

She took the risk, on Thursday, of going out for break-fast to a waffle shop. Since the last time she was there, they had installed CNN on a big screen in a corner, presumably in deference to its location on the edge of the business district. The waitress took Cassie's order without looking at her peculiarly. Good, thought Cassie. I look like hell, but as far as this woman is concerned, I look more or less like the hell normal customers of hers look like.

The waitress took the menu, moved out of her line of vision, and Bertie Ahern spoke to Cassie. Her breathing suffocated her backwards, like a cotton-wool wad, and she saw stars. After a moment, she came to understand that he was on the TV, talking directly to the camera in that curiously confidential, just-between-you-and-me, wouldn't-want-this-to-go-further-than-the-two-of-us tone he used, the three or four times she had met him in reality. The stars stopped sparking against the roof of her skull, and she remembered to breathe. He was saying that whatever the IRA had announced an hour before was radically different from anything they'd said up to then: it meant peace, it was the hoped-for outcome of the peace process, it was a breakthrough. The newscaster took up the story, inviting his weatherman to be as orgasmic as everybody else was about this news from Ireland, and the waitress presented Cassie with her eggs and bacon.

She must remember to do a retrospective rubber-band snap when her wrist was deflated enough to tolerate the band, she thought, eating with considerable pleasure after a couple of days on liquids. She should not have been taking such interest in a report about Ireland. Ireland? What's Ireland? Little country out in front of England. Peaceful, these days. Good luck to it.

Despite her best resolutions, she was tempted, the following day, to go back to the waffle place, just in case CNN carried more reports incorporating people she knew filmed against backgrounds with which she was familiar. It was not that she wanted to go back to those places, she thought. It was a fairly pure nostalgia. But, then, wasn't that typical of Irish emigrants? Always sentimental about the old country, but never actually returning to it, when they had the money to go back, in anything like the numbers of Italians, say, returning to Italy. Exile was a curiously comfortable discomfort, like pushing gently against a bad tooth.

She turned, taking a quite different direction, and walked in the gathering daylight towards a Perkins restaurant. Coming near to it, a chattering bird protest halted her. Someone walking behind her collided with her. She apologised. He no-problemed.

'They're in the sign,' he said.

'Excuse me?'

'The birds?'

She nodded at the implicit question: that stopped you with their noise. He pointed at the elaborately crafted illuminated sign giving the restaurant's name, high over its front door. Birds had built their nests in the round section of the P, on top of the other letters. They were, she thought, giving out yards, those birds. Move on there, move on there, don't be standing looking at us, none of your business, staring is rude. *Don't stare at Gobnait's mother, Ben, staring is rude . . .*

'You OK, ma'am?'

The man was still standing, half behind her, she realised. She moved sideways to let him past, but he stayed where he was, a big hulk in a navy vest with narrow shoulder straps. A weight-lifter, by the look of him, the bulked-out shoulders. Bullet-headed.

'I'm fine.' She laughed, pulling herself together. 'Just got confused for a minute.'

He pulled open the door of the restaurant and nodded her through. The host at the little podium looked up, gathering menus, and smiled.

'Two? Smoking or N—'

'The lady's on her own,' Bullet-head said, and the host adjusted seamlessly.

At a banquette table, Cassie stayed for nearly an hour and a half, fascinated by a book bought on impulse as a result of a short review in the *New York Sunday Times*, which she'd taken to buying every week, throwing away the news, arts and travel sections, each of which was likely to contain material about Ireland she didn't need to know. The book was by a doctor who had experienced brain damage more severe than Cassie's. It was her account of the rehabilitation process and of her gradual compromising with her earlier ambitions. Cassie looked at her right hand, going back to its normal size after the fire-ant attack, but still slightly off-shape because of the car crash breaks. Would she be able to draw again? Take out the 'again', she thought, smacking her wrist with the rubber band. Take out the question and make it a statement. I will be able to draw again. I'm starting with the wall-painting I'm doing for Barry and MaryLu. I'll refine the lines I draw and eventually I'll draw cartoons. Or maybe something completely different. Something fresh and new.

The thought of MaryLu and Barry propelled her out of the banquette and back to where she lived. A pick-up truck was parked beside her Lumina. Amos 'n'Andy, she thought. Better get work clothes on before I go painting. Selecting the dingiest of the plain white men's vests she constantly wore, she matched it with the oldest pair of jeans, now faded and flittered at hem and knee.

All of the top storey of the old motel was now transformed into large, single-room efficiencies, except that the units still had two doors apiece. Amos 'n'Andy, according to MaryLu, were going to brick over alternate doors and stucco the outside so nobody unfamiliar with the building would ever suspect there had been a second door in the wall. Which meant, in logic, Cassie thought, setting up her paint-roller dish and her ladder, they would start at the other end of the corridor from where she was finishing off the interior painting job in the last room two floors above her own room.

She tied a bandanna around her head and slid on clear goggles. No paint drops were ever going to fall into lasered eyes if she could help it. Beginning to paint, she could hear, faintly, from the other end of the long landing, over the noises of destruction as the redundant doors were torn out, the contradictory noise of the two men singing. In harmony, at that. She climbed carefully back down the ladder and leaned against the wall just inside the exterior door of the room she was painting. A country-and-western song, one of them taking the melody line, the other the harmony. Something about elusive dreams, one partner following the other wherever the first partner's dreams led the two of them. Sweet sickly semi-truths, like all of those songs, she thought, climbing back up the ladder when the song was interrupted by the two of them co-operating on some physical task that generated groans and swearing.

Her father always sang when he worked, she remembered, trying to recall what his songs were. Paul Robeson songs. Gilbert and Sullivan, although, now she thought of it, that couldn't have been when he was painting or plumbing: the rhythms of their songs did not lend themselves to the long, even strokes of a painting job. What was that song he used to sing with her. She could remember the tune of it, but not the words, she thought, humming the melody as she painted.

'. . . to the beautiful Indian country that I love,' a voice sang clearly behind her, and she fell off the ladder, bringing the roller and paint tray with her. She half landed on the person, which finished the song, and in a wild attempt to deflect the falling paint tray, kicked out, bringing the ladder down on them. Her goggles were covered in cream paint. She reached out to get a grip on anything and found her paint-covered hand sliding on something round and firm.

'We can't go on meeting like this,' it said. The voice was familiar from the fire-ant encounter. And, she realised, the Perkins' birds nest conversation.

She snatched away her hand, trying frantically to get up, away from the mêlée of paint and people on the floor, getting her feet caught in rungs of the ladder, then stepping on the paint-roller, which went like a wheel and brought her down again.

'What is this? The Peoria Paint-store Massacre?'

The young man named Ace was standing in the open doorway, as Cassie discovered when she wrenched off the paint-covered goggles. It didn't seem possible, she thought, following his admiring gaze, that one painter with one can of paint and a shallow metal dish could do such damage. The other man was sitting on the floor, shielding his eyes from the still liquid paint flowing off his shaven head. It reminded Cassie of the 'instant shell' liquids sold in bottles for pouring over ice-creams, guaranteed instantly to form a hard shiny carapace on the outside of the ice-cream. 'Your head would be great for pouring ice-cream syrup on to,' she told him, before she could stop herself.

He tilted his head and his hand so he could see her from underneath its shelter, but said nothing.

'You gonna sit there all day?' Ace asked.

'No,' he said. 'I'm gonna sit here until I work out what's safe to do next.'

'You know what I think?' Ace asked from the doorway. 'I think the two of you should step outside.'

'Duke it out, slug paint at each other until one of us weakens?' Cassie suggested.

'No. If I hose the two of you down, that'd do it.'

Cassie tried to find something to argue with in that, but failed.

'I'll lay down some plastic for you to walk on.' Ace went off, all business.

Moon tested removing his hand from his forehead and decided the paint was no longer runny enough to need protection from. Although his hand had prevented it getting to his face, it covered the rest of his head and neck, joining below his chin.

'You look like a knight in chain-mail,' Cassie said, and roared laughing. 'I'm sorry,' she said, and laughed more.

He stood up and began testing bits of his clothing. The straps of his vest were stuck to his shoulders with rapidly drying paint. T-shirt, she thought, reaching for the rubber band. Vest means waistcoat here. The rubber band was stuck to her wrist by drying paint.

'Oh, *shit*,' Moon said suddenly, discovering that his watch was coated in it, the sectioned bracelet neatly outlined in cream paint. 'Oh, shit.'

'I'll replace it,' she said, getting serious.

'Sentimental value only,' he said, shortly, taking it off.

Ace, in the car park below, called them to make their way down to him. Moon made an elaborate after-you gesture, which made her laugh again because of how funny he looked.

'I suppose I don't look so good, either?' she said, as they ploughed along a path of plastic laid by Ace.

'I plead the fifth,' he said.

Ace was planted in the car park, near a sanitation ditch, which he was indicating they should stand close to, holding a hose, patently delighted with the prospect of sluicing the two of them down.

'Brace yourself, Brigid,' Cassie said, closing her eyes.

'Excuse me?' Moon asked.

The hose hit full blast. Cassie opened her mouth to protest and found herself swallowing cold water and paint. The taste was horrific, and – eyes still closed – she ducked sideways to spit the mouthful into the sewer. The sudden vigorous movement was stopped by her head banging hard into some part of somebody. From the sound of a wet body falling and the accompanying yell, even standing there with a mouthful of paint and her eyes jammed shut, she knew she had head-butted the shaven-headed man in the crotch. The hose died.

'Jesus, lady, you should play ice-hockey,' Ace said reverently.

From the ground came a strangled instruction to get the water going again. Now afraid to spit, because she was no longer sure where the sewer was, Cassie stood, eyes tight shut, letting the icy hard water beat up her hair, her clothes, her face. After a while, it was directed elsewhere, and she cautiously opened her eyes. Ace had come closer and was hosing down the figure of Moon, crouched in foetal curve on the ground, pale diluted paint issuing from him in a cloudy stream headed for the shore. When the water ran clear, Ace turned off the hose. 'You OK?' he asked her, and she realised that her face was now balloon-shaped from holding the mouthful of paint. Carefully, she went over to the sewer and spat it out. Ace hoisted Moon to his feet.

'Time out,' he said.

CHAPTER TWENTY-FIVE

Wounds and Wound Care

I think 'Time out' is when they put kids in kindergarten into solitary confinement after they've done something mischievous.

Cassie surveyed the sentence, wondering if it was she or the bald man who had been sentenced.

You're trying to fade into the wallpaper, remember? To be unmemorable. Headbutting a total stranger is a great way not to be noticed.

Having painted him all over, first.

Don't take pride in it.

Shit, it was enjoyable, though.

For who?

Me.

Oh. Right.

I cleaned up the room perfectly afterwards.

That'll greatly help his aching privates.

How long do they ache?

Dunno. I don't have that much experience. You could ask him, though.

I don't want to remind him.

You think he's not going to remember, every time he sees you?

On the third day that she met Ace working on his own, she asked him if Moon had sworn off further work on the Dorms. He laughed. No, Moon was on a special training course.

'To learn what?'

'Advanced skills to cope with toxic terrorist attacks or accidents.'

'In *Peoria*?'

Ace looked at her solemnly. 'You think Peoria is safe? Moon doesn't. Moon thought fire-fighting was dangerous until he met you. Shit, I thought *marriage* was dangerous until I met you.'

'We got that top floor habitable, though.'

The two of them stood in the car park, looking up at the top floor, where three separate efficiencies were now occupied.

'We're gonna move into the end one,' Ace said.

'I'm going to move into the one at the other end,' Cassie said.

'As long as it's that far away,' Ace said, and ducked as she swiped at him with the paper.

A week later, she was reading about the course Moon was attending ('Course Simulates Toxic Terrorist Attack On "Big City, USA"') when MaryLu came to the door. 'They're going to hang the sign today,' she said.

Sign, Cassie thought. Oh, yes. The Dorms. What's so serious about hanging a sign? She invited MaryLu to sit down.

'You know the problem Barry's been having with his back?'

Cassie nodded. Barry's recovery from his comminuted fracture was slow, painful and puzzling.

'They found what's wrong.'

Don't tell me, Cassie thought. Because in telling me,

440

you will get closer to me, and I don't want that, I can't afford that. 'Tell me,' she said.

'Bone cancer.'

'Oh, shit.'

'Everywhere.'

A truck pulled up outside and MaryLu instantly responded to the engine noise. It would be the sign-hangers, she said. Cassie followed her out and stood while she and the foreman worked out precisely where it was to go. Holding on to her own upper arms (for warmth? comfort?) MaryLu talked of the doctor who wanted to let Barry go on believing his pain was caused by infections following the fracture.

'Coward,' Cassie said.

He knew now, MaryLu said. Somehow, knowing stopped him pretending to himself that he was getting better. He was very much worse. They were talking about moving him to the hospice.

'Tell me what has to be done and I'll fill in for you,' Cassie said.

There was no overcome-my-objections protest. Just a defeated nod. Could Cassie come up to the office right now? 'D'you have a Dictaphone?'

MaryLu looked surprised. She thought so, yes.

'I'll need to record what you tell me. I have brain damage as a result of a car crash, so my short-term memory is shot.'

It was more personally revealing than anything Cassie had told anyone in Peoria in the previous year and a half. MaryLu nodded, absently, as if confessions of brain damage were a standard part of bad Tuesdays. An hour later, she was gone to the hospital and Cassie was seated in the office, playing the tape to herself again and again. She paid the sign-hangers, who left, THE DORMS beaming pinkly into the dusk. She dealt with the Vietnamese family who wanted to know if there were rules about pets. E-mailed responses to two queries about the prices of the efficiencies, using MaryLu's web address.

'This promotion or a way to prevent you killing the workforce?' Moon, a hard fuzz of crew-cut taking the shine off his head, big shoulders bulked by a leather jacket.

'I read about the course you were on.'

'Dull, compared to the excitement around here.' He threw the leather jacket on the back of a chair and helped himself to coffee.

'Do have some coffee,' she said sarcastically.

He smiled, pouring packet after packet of sugar into it.

She told him about Barry. The easy smile faded. 'I'm sorry,' he said softly. 'Just when it's comin' together for him.'

Without asking him, she knew he would have listened to MaryLu and Barry talking about their plans, their past, their dream. He was the kind of man people talked to. Why was that, she wondered. He wasn't a great talker. Rationed words, so it was difficult for a hearer to catch and locate the oddity of his accent. Didn't ask questions. Even working beside him for several days, he never asked her about herself, evinced no curiosity, shared nothing about himself. A man deeply, almost physically content within himself, relishing the physical power brought to each task, the precision of measurement and marking, cutting and fitting. So unlike Polo, she thought: no need of an audience. She snapped the rubber band, remembering too late that he was in the room. He raised his eyebrows, looked amused, but said nothing. Drank the coffee. Looked into the middle distance.

After he left, Cassie opened her own computer.

It's time I put it down and looked at it: the worst part of the brain damage. Which is that I now remember almost nothing of Ben's life. I have *knowledge*. I know the events of his little life. I know when they happened, how they happened. I know I was there. But what I have is not memory. It is closer to the numbed sensibility of a mouth anaesthetised for dental work: it is aware of a touch, but it does not feel it in a real way. A great numbness has spread, seeped through my memories so they are now no longer memories, but braincell *accounts* of what happened. They are like chewing-gum after hours of chewing. No colour. No flavour. Dead relics.

I do not know why this happens. Has happened. I have bought every book on memory I can find, learned all the mnemonics, the tricks to help me fake it as if my short-term memory were not so stunted. Now, it's difficult to tell whether it's the tricks that work or if I have grown – regrown? – some of the dead cells. It doesn't matter, and as of today, I'm not going to read any more or reflect any more on it.

None of the books mention this seeping erasure of what was important in my life. About five years have been damaged or disappeared. Deadened into facts I could have learned from a book. How strange to think that Polo's memories of Ben are more real than are mine – that he will get flashing colour remembrances of our son's face turned this way or that way, hear the voice say something as if it was real, whereas I am left with nothing but the shapes of memory, hollow. Like the contours left in Pompeii, preserved by the ash that killed them and vacuumed the reality out of them.

There is nobody to tell about this. Nobody would understand. For some reason, every fool in the world believes, when you talk about memory loss, that you are (a) attention-seeking, (b) confabulating. If I talked to anybody who knew Ben, they would start reminding me of incidents we shared with him, never grasping that these reminders helpfully, paradoxically point me to the ashy death outline of him.

I said this was the worst thing about the brain damage, but my father would say, God never gave a burden without broadening the shoulders to carry that burden, so I must honestly register a matching sad truth. I discovered a love for Ben that wasn't in me until he was born, and even after his death, the need to love – him? the memory of him? – continued, like a raging fire.

But the dampening of the memories has been matched by a dampening of the agony of loss. It is like feeling something through thick gloves.

None of this does Ben any harm. He lived. My greying memory does not wipe that out, and if there is a God, if there is a hereafter, sense will be made of it. If there isn't, it doesn't matter anyway. This must be like having a limb amputated: it is more merciful to have the nerve endings die than have the illusory sense-memory of a phantom limb, making you believe you can still dance. The dancing's done.

I've spent a long time working hard at not being me. Now, it seems to matter less. I suppose I was half waiting to be discovered, exposed. Or for some great event to happen to tie up the loose wires of my life. The way people used to ask me after the accident, did skies look more blue when I had been so near death . . .

Instead of becoming rapt with suddenly appreciated significances, I am pleased, every day, with conscious little pleasures. Routine – how I used to despise routine. Now it's like a tight belt holding up loose trousers. Doing competently the same set of tasks I did yesterday, even as a replacement for MaryLu, is satisfying. I enjoy being

444

a spectator at other lives. Watching the difference in the way the Vietnamese family treat their children to the way American parents treat theirs. Listening to Moon and Ace singing together when they're working. Getting them to talk about fire-fighting, then reading a book about a famous fire and asking them questions about it. Sitting with Barry, laughing with him in the twenty-minute high after the morphine injection, then quieting as he drifts to sleep.

It is strange to say, 'I am my own woman,' when I am less than whole. Sometimes, a terror and shame sweeps over me when I find I have reread a book with the same enjoyment I must have had the first time I read it, but with no recollection of ever coming upon it before. But increasingly, a logic clicks in that says, 'So you enjoyed it this time – what's the problem? That's the way it is. Never mind the way it was. Is the way it is liveable-with?' The answer is yes.

The answer is more than yes. I am next door to happy. Every day is harder than it was before the crash, because of the need for reminders and a dozen failures. But there is a startling pleasure, a newness to everything. Maybe, like an Alzheimer's patient, I have gone past the vexatious, maddened fighting phase and am content with the limitations.

Now and again, something I read, something I see, some slithering slanted sex memory revives the need, the groaning hunger for the building, tautened, tumid, crested excitement and the rhythmed release of it and, lone animal, I mimic and imagine to a small satisfaction and a short-lived sense of shame.

I do not, though, look at men, eyes sliding sideways in assessment, speculation. I sometimes look again at a man because he reminds me of someone back home. But less often, these days, and never with a need.

Barry died a week later. MaryLu took his ashes to New Hampshire, where they had met, leaving Cassie in charge of The Dorms. She was now installed in her efficiency, with its view out over a wooded area and the sweeping highway. It had a three-tier bookshelf, half filled: the first concession made to possessions. For the best part of two years, if the need arose, Cassie would have been able to pack all her belongings into the bag used for her journey out of Glasgow. Books bought were wrapped in plastic bags and left outside the local Goodwill store at night. When socks or T-shirts wore out, they were thrown away. Belongings and purchasing patterns, according to one of the books she bought that purported to tell the reader how to disappear without trace, were as personally revealing and distinctively individual as a fingerprint.

On the top shelf, lying flat, was a hardback dropped in for a loan by Ace. *Young Men and Fire.* She took it down to the reception area and was so immersed in its account of a mountain fire and the deaths of a group of young 'smoke jumpers' air-dropped on to the hillside to fight it, that when the phone rang it took her several seconds before she worked out that it was MaryLu at the other end of the line.

Yes, everything was fine. No, of course MaryLu didn't need to come back quickly. A couple weeks? No problem. Had MaryLu got a fax number where she was? Then she could send her at the end of each week an accounting of money banked, leases taken out. That help? No, there was no need to change their informal arrangement: use of an efficiency, rather than wages, in exchange for her time. (Looking through the ledgers, Cassie found that the two moonlighting workmen had much the same arrangement with MaryLu.)

The fortnight stretched to a month. Then to five weeks.

Idly, Cassie inputted an analysis of the business into her computer, then faxed it to MaryLu.

> In summary [she finished], the 'dorms' idea is not working as well as Barry hoped. The top floor is filled, but I would recommend that, instead of converting the other two floors, we simply upgrade them and put them back on the market as motel rooms three months from now (first floor) and six months from now (middle floor). People who want efficiencies will be served by the top floor, and people who want motel rooms by the other two. Calling it The Dorms doesn't prevent this dual approach and it would both reduce your outgoings and improve your income.

She was unsurprised to receive a fax almost by return agreeing to the new business plan. The Dorms was Barry's elusive dream, she thought, wandering outside in the watery sunshine, not MaryLu's.

It was ten o'clock in the morning. Quiet time. No cleaners along the floors – cleaners came to the efficiencies once a week. The families and couples living on the top floor were all out at work. Ace and Moon, she figured, should have come to the end of their forty-eight hour stint at the fire station the previous evening, so any time now she would hear them setting up their ladders and toolboxes on the balcony-corridor above. Indeed, it was unusual that they weren't already set up. They mustn't have got in last night, she realised. The pick-up truck wasn't in its parking space. She took a newspaper from the vending-machine and turned to go back in, when a beeping horn halted her.

The pick-up caromed into the grounds, coming to a precipitate halt beside her. 'Coffee for the hero!' Ace demanded, jumping down out of the cab.

'Who's the hero?'

Running around to the passenger door, Ace missed the query. Moon seemed to be fending off his assistance, but then fell out of the cab so limpidly that Ace, catching him, staggered back into the flowerbed and lost his footing. Moon seemed contented enough to lie on top of him, but Ace was making jumping movements with his hips. It looked like they were having sex.

'Get him up,' roared Ace at Cassie. 'My ass is in a thorn-bush.'

'Rosebush,' she corrected, reaching out for Moon.

'Don't touch him!' Ace yelled.

'Make up your fucking mind,' she snapped.

This had the effect of collapsing Moon in laughter. He was beginning to get on to his hands and knees and his collapse drove Ace more forcefully into the thorns.

'Touch him anywhere but on the shoulders,' Ace clarified, through gritted teeth.

'I second that,' Moon said. 'Anywhere at all. Take your pick.'

Cassie went round to the front, then got behind Moon, her arms around his chest, and tugged. Ace pushed him at the same time. With much staggering, he was brought upright. Ace, clutching his own backside one-handed, tilted his friend against the front end of the truck, holding him by his plaid workshirt so he couldn't fall down again. Cassie came around from behind Moon. 'Is he drunk?'

Moon gave her a smile so vast, it mesmerised her.

'Is he?'

'No,' Ace said impatiently, trying to examine his bottom without much success. 'Drugged.'

'Oh, that's OK, then, isn't it?' Cassie said. 'For what it's worth, that was a new rosebush I bought to give this place some class. And your arse is bleeding.'

'My *what*?'

'Ar– ass,' Cassie corrected.

'Rubber band.' Moon giggled, and she looked sharply at him.

'Arrrse,' he said, with infinite pleasure. 'Ace's arrrse is bleeding.'

'Look,' said Cassie, trying to get a handle on the situation, 'could we go inside? I've a first-aid kit we can use. You get under his left arm and I'll support him this side. Put him into the little room beyond Reception.'

They decanted Moon on to the soft couch in the inner room. His jacket had fallen off his shoulders *en route*. He was now naked to the waist, with a vast bandage running across the back of his neck. The nakedness was normal: the two men normally worked in shorts, sneakers and baseball caps. The bandage was new and impressive. She started coffee. Ace came back into the room, clutching the jacket and a box of donuts from Dunkin' Donuts.

'Hey, don't *do* that,' he said, flipping up the newspaper from where she had dropped it. 'Betcha haven't read it. The Story of a Bad Hose Day.'

'Shut up,' Moon invited.

'Do you want me to put peroxide on your ass?' Cassie asked Ace.

'On his arrrse,' Moon corrected.

'Neither,' Ace said, flapping the paper at Cassie. 'I'll serve.'

The story was bannered across the top of the front page, with an aerial photograph of several blocks of War Memorial Drive. Unusually, there was no traffic on the big main highway, although scattered at the margins were dozens of cars, evidently pulled over for some reason. Running right down the middle of War Memorial Drive was a pale buff stripe. Looking close at the picture, she could see people, tiny, ant-like, investigating the stripe. It was absolutely straight, the stripe, except where the people seemed to be lifting it off the surface of the road.

'The hose,' she said, looking up at the two of them. 'The hose off the fire truck.'

Ace, handing her a mug of coffee, nodded, delightedly.

'My friend here is driving the truck yesterday morning when we respond to a call from University Plaza,' he told her. Moon hung his head and regarded his mug of coffee glumly. 'Now, my friend here is Mr Perfect Fire-Fighter. Spit and polish. Also the only fire-truck driver in history to drive defensively. If it's a three-unit fire, you can bet your last cent the other two units are gonna get there before us. Which is what happened yesterday. We arrive and the Captain's jumpin' up and down, get your hose on to it, move, move, and we move. My friend Moon comes out of the truck, round to the back and you know what?'

'No. What?'

'No hose. We got jaws of death, we got halligans, we even got a space for a hose, but no hose. Captain's shitting ballbearings, yelling at us to get over there, rubberneckers are telling us to get on to it, and he – you know what he's doin'?'

Moon, head down, was beginning to laugh, shaking his head at the memory.

'He's sayin', "Ace, go tell the Captain we ain't got no hose." I'm a fire-fighter six years longer than he is, but what do I do? Right. I go over, say, "Moon says we ain't got no hose. Sir." And the Captain says bullshit. So I say, "Yessir." And he says, "Whattya mean, you got no hose?" I say, we got a hose deficit, sir. Absence of. And he says "Why?" and I say I'll go ask Moon, but the captain says if we got no hose, we're no value to him so get the hell back to the station and he'll deal with it later. His investiga-

450

tions will reveal that the hose began to pay off the back of the truck along the straight of War Memorial Drive, us drivin' down the middle, because the siren has cleared all the cars to the sides.'

'Paid off in a perfectly straight line,' Moon said, as if straight-line driving counted for something, even as you lost the tools of your trade down the main street of a city.

'Tellya what was no fun at all,' Ace said, sitting down and immediately standing back up again, his bottom evidently sensitive after the rosebush attack. 'It's no fun at all to rewind a hose the length of War Memorial Drive and car drivers makin' comments all the way. At that time, we did not know the helicopter had taken shots of my friend's unique achievement.'

'Helicopters play a major role in my life,' Moon said, chuckling to himself.

They ignored him.

'Did the Captain then flog him?' Cassie asked, in reference to the bandage.

'No, that was this morning. Six o'clock, call to an apartment fire. Taken hold. Nobody indoors, everybody accounted for. Put a lot of water on it, then the two of us go to the ground-floor window, next thing he's pullin' up the neck of his jacket pointing to me – put the hose on him. I can't hear him, but that's what he's sayin', I can tell. He wants me to put water down the back of his neck from a two-inch hose? I do, and the rubberneckers shout that he can have a shower any time, we're s'posed to be savin' property and securin' premises. Turns out molten soffits fell off the frame of the window, straight down on him, and they're burnin' him up. Burnin' PVC – whoo. The paramedics say he has to go to the hospital, they take care of it, give him shots and here we are. I got to work two days from now – he gets a week off. More, maybe.'

'I'm a good healer,' Moon said.

'What?'

'I heal real well,' he said.

'They shaved the back of his head, too, see?'

Cassie went around to look. Moon had a half-inch crew-cut everywhere except down the back, where he looked recently peeled. The contrast looked ridiculous.

'You'll have to go back to shiny all over and then start growing again,' she told Moon.

'OK,' he said.

'And you better not try shaving when you're full of painkiller, because you won't be able to see straight.'

'OK,' he said.

'A man of few words, getting fewer by the minute,' Cassie observed to Ace, who allowed as how it might be a good idea to shift Moon up to where the two men lived. It took some time, not least because Moon had developed a deep contentment with his present position.

On Thursday, Ace, going to work, told Cassie how to dress Moon's wounds. 'I've done it for today, but tomorrow morning, I'm not gonna be here, OK?'

Writing down the instructions, Cassie nodded, and Ace spun the pick-up truck in the car park. He's thirty or thirty-one, she thought, and he drives with the show-offery of a sixteen-year-old. Later, Moon put his head – shiny again – around the door. He was going on a long walk. Bring her anything back?

She smiled at him. 'You're really bothered by not working out, aren't you? You an exercise addict?'

'God, no,' he said. 'Hate goddamn training, always did, even when I was playing matches . . .' His voice trailed off.

'So why d'you do it?'

'I'm ten years older than most of the guys in the fire

house, twenty years older than a couple. Not going to be the weak link, the guy who doesn't quite carry his weight.'

He hauled himself up off the doorframe and headed off. She opened her laptop.

I'd like to join a gym, myself.

Why don't you just revert to all the behaviours that'll infallibly identify you?

I don't honestly think that there's some forensic genius pissing around the backwoods of Peoria adding up things, like 'Ooh, the bleached blonde does push-ups, she must be a former cartoonist.' But even if there was, and even if they told Polo, and even if Polo arrived here tomorrow, I could cope. I could lift the phone and Ace and Moon'd be up here so fast.

Say if it's the police?

Who arrive here?

Yeah.

Which police? If the local cops arrive, it'll be because I'm here too long on my visa. So I get turned out and I get the next flight back. I don't honestly think the Garda Commissioner is going to send a battalion of officers over here to deport me or extradite me or whatever they do to people who waste police time.

Now that you're on the Internet through MaryLu's account, you could check on yourself.

I shouldn't.

If you've got careless and gay, why not?

Cassie logged off and turned on the Reception computer and modem. Ireland.Com she typed in. Up came the *Irish Times*. She typed her own name into its archive and was astonished by the number of references coming up. She took them in chronological order, from the day she had walked into the sea. A helicopter doing traffic reports gave the alarm. Helicopters play a major role in my life, too, Moon, she thought, recalling his comment about the aerial photograph of his lost hose.

As the months of coverage went on, she found her name appearing less frequently as central character, more frequently in lists of actual or suspected suicides in features about people taking their own lives. She figured frequently, too, in bracketed supplementaries to descriptions of Polo. Polo Cadogan (whose wife, cartoonist Cassie Browne, is believed to have committed suicide in Dublin Bay six months ago) today said . . . On the anniversary of the day she had gone missing, Polo published a letter to her. I should find this nauseating, Cassie thought, reading it, but all it does is give the bad taste in the mouth you get if you touch your finger to your tongue after holding old pennies for a while: coppery curling of the upper lip.

Then came the indications that one of the major political parties was inviting Polo Cadogan (whose late wife, etc., etc.) to run in the next general election. He would be virtually guaranteed a seat, the writer said, because of the makeup of the constituency, but that was not to downplay the considerable personal charisma of a man who could surmount two personal tragedies, nor to underestimate his ability to represent, with charm and wit, a right-leaning wing of that party and of developing Irish thought.

Cassie disengaged from the web, eyes narrowed. Narrowed with the thought: You're not following me, Polo. You decided I was of more currency to you dead than alive. Good. None of the coverage suggests anybody had major doubts. Couple of dissenting comments in the beginning about currents, raising a slight question-mark over the fact that a body had not been washed up, but – as far as her searches could be relied on – no Lord Lucan-like sightings.

That's what Andy Warhol really meant, she thought contentedly. It isn't just that everybody gets their fifteen minutes of fame. It's that fifteen minutes is all anybody gets. You disappear and are spotted in Indonesia a week later, it's exciting. But disappear and leave no trace for a couple of years, and it becomes Cassandra who? Which cartoons were they, now? Visiting the bathroom, she looked at herself for a long time in the mirror. White-blonde hair, cut short and choppy. Face looking older than thirty-something, no makeup, ever. White T-shirt, jeans. Thin but not gaunt. Funny, she thought. People talk of fame as a drug. Never mind talking it, they live the addiction on every TV screen in this building, willing dupes and accomplices of chat-show hosts seeking increasingly bizarre sources of controversy. To be famous, even briefly, seems the ultimate high of our times. Yet for me, to be anonymous, to be the nobody in the mirror there, spun loose, rolling along like a bead unstrung from a necklace: that's the drug. Inattention must be paid.

The following morning, she slid a note under Moon's door at six a.m., to tell him she was on call for shoulder-dressing whenever he needed it.

'How about now?' he asked, opening the door as she straightened up, her hand against it for balance, so that when the door disappeared inwards, she went in after it, crouched as if to head-butt him as before. He bent himself back from her like a banana, catching her with an arm before she went head-first into the TV. She pulled herself upright. 'Could we get a health warning printed on those carefully anonymous T-shirts of yours?' he asked.

'Did I hurt you? Your arm must be pulled.'

'No,' he said, giving her a wide berth.

He sat down on the edge of the bed. The ointments and bandages were neatly laid out on a surface. She took off the previous day's bandage and shuddered at what it revealed.

'Get the loose tissue off, even if it bleeds,' he instructed.

She went to work. I am good at this, she thought, in surprise, good at not making the pain worse for him by being tentative. He knows what has to be done, he's familiar with the pain involved, he doesn't need me wilting and looking for referred sympathy. She worked in teeth-gritted silence until the wounds were clean and clear. Stood back. He let out a long-held breath and blew some of the gauzes across the surface. She took the ointment, rereading her own handwritten instructions dictated by Ace before she applied it. Strong palm-stroked cover, glossing the brown skin, the red lesions: and like a kick in the heart came the physical memory of Ben's much smaller, softly rounded shoulders, bones fragile within, the time he got sunburned on a holiday in Florida and she had wept as she worked, convinced he was set up for later skin cancer.

The memory was so fiercely present, so assaultive in its painful pleasure, she stood, eyes closed to it, hands holding his shoulders, stock-still, breathless. For how long, she didn't know, opening her eyes to see the man's reflected image in the mirror opposite, distorted by her tears. He looked at her without urgency or judgement or question or sympathy. There is no hurry, the look said. Cope with it. It's yours to cope with. Whatever it is.

She smiled at the reflection, gave his shoulders a squeeze – thanks. Held up her greasy hands. 'Let me wash this gunk off before I put the bandages on,' she said, going to the sink.

'Don't rush,' he said. 'Air is good for them.' Absently, he retrieved the gauzes from where his breath had skied them.

'It's a hell of an injury,' she said, scrubbing her hands like a nurse. 'I had no idea.'

'Stuff continues to burn when it falls,' he said. 'Like bad ceiling tiles.'

She began to dry her hands, smiling at the roughness of the towel. Fabric softener must be a girl thing. Two guys living together were not going to waste dollars on it.

'There was a fire in a disco, at home, a long time ago,' he said. 'The tiles dripped flame from the ceiling.'

There was a fire in Ireland like that, too, she thought. The Starlight disco. No, not Starlight. Star something. Stardust. That hospital she was in after the accident had a small garden of remembrance commemorating that fire. With that Armistice Day poem incised into stone: 'They shall not grow old, as we who are left grow old. Age shall not wither them, nor the . . .'

'Oh, shit,' she whispered. Ben will not grow old. She stood over the rucked towel, head down, trying to make no noise, to recover before he noticed. Big hands took her by the upper arms, bracing her against her own misery, holding her from behind, firm. Not an embrace. A support only. When it faded, the hurt of it, she rubbed her face in the towel and he let her go.

'Those towels are *rough*,' she said, half admiringly, coming back to where he was again seated. She bandaged and taped efficiently, then stoppered the containers. 'Will you have scars?'

His expression conveyed surprise – never thought about it – and lack of interest: what's it matter? She set the medications beside a pile of books, many of them about fire, but several about history, perhaps a dozen about recent murders and serial killing, and a couple of biographies. There were cuttings, she noticed, from recent newspapers about the fires raging through thirteen or more western and mid-western states. 'When you're in the middle of a fire, how frightened are you?'

'Not frightened at all,' he said, shrugging into a T-shirt. 'You've no time to be frightened. Too much to do, too many things to factor in.'

'Oh, you *must* be frightened.'

He looked puzzled. 'No. It's like the black-box recordings on planes that come down. You don't ever hear evidence of fear in those recordings. The guys are too busy going through checklist after checklist. Could it be this, maybe it's that, did you try the other? They'd be plenty scared if they had the time. But even at the very end, the last seconds, when they realise they're going to impact, what they say is always the same: 'Oh, shit,' or 'Oh, *fuck*,' and it's the noise you make when you've done everything right and you're still getting screwed. Not fear. Never fear.'

She thought about this in silence before turning to go.

'Thank you,' he said, kissing her lightly on the forehead as if she was a child.

It was a gentle intimacy without invasion and she was surprised by how much she enjoyed it. When Ace came back, he made a big production of checking to see if her work was up to scratch.

'You two are gonna have to do double time,' she told them, cutting through his grudging compliments. 'I want the ground floor ready to rent as motel rooms by Easter.'

'You buying it from MaryLu?'

She looked sharply at Moon. What a strange question, she thought, assuming, as it did, that she would have the money to buy a motel. 'No,' she said, and made no further comment.

For which added wisdom, I owe you, Mr Perfect Fireman, she thought. (Oops, rubber band: fire-fighter.) Because the books you lend me about murderers and forensics and serial killers ram home the fact that killers constantly nail themselves by talking. The cleverest of them, the quickest-witted, talk convolutions and complications around themselves and suddenly, they're trying to explain the explanation of the previous explanation and cope with the minor discrepancy between the third and the second. Never talk, was the lesson. Even if silence doesn't seem to solve the problem, don't talk. Minimal communication. No verbal hostages to fortune.

The two men were marvellously matched as workers, good at shared tasks, just as good at undertaking long solo runs such as spray-painting a series of ceilings. In the weeks after his burning, the older man wore a transparent flexible covering on the new scars, designed, Ace told her, to keep them flexible. Don't talk to me about scars, she thought. I've got more of them than any woman of my age you're likely to meet. Greatest living expert on scars, I am.

MaryLu came back, that week, and failed to recognise Moon. 'Jeez, you have hair,' she said, looking at the abundant dark covering where she was used to shaven shining skin. 'I thought you were like Bruce Willis – shaving it all because you had so little of it.'

'Greying, though,' Ace said, flicking at his friend's temples. 'Git out the Grecian 2000, guys, we got an oldie but goodie here for concealment.'

'You're both goodies,' MaryLu told them. 'This place looks great. I thought about selling it off, you know, when I was out east. But my brother said I should make no major decisions the first year after Barry's death, and I'm glad I didn't. It looks great. It's gonna work.'

'Brothers are great,' Cassie said, and then giggled, realising that in the absence of real brothers, she was promoting Ace and Moon to the position.

'She doesn't have any,' Moon said flatly.

'Any what?' asked Ace, whose attention span was short.

'You happy with the mix of motel and efficiencies?' Moon asked MaryLu.

'Very. I don't think this town's ready for a complete efficiency block. Sandy says you guys can complete it by June, so we might get some summer trade. When do you two plan vacations?'

Ace said, self-consciously, that he planned to visit his ex-wife for a long weekend. Expecting derision, he met with a careful silence as he stood up to go.

'I'll walk with you,' Cassie said. 'Want to give back a couple of books I borrowed.'

They climbed the stairs together, Cassie remembering when every step hurt the pinned bones in her legs. Wondering what, in her behaviour, made Moon sure she had no brothers.

Ace looked out over the big highway, semi-artics taking the hill through the woods like distant toys. 'Fleur was my high-school sweetheart,' he said, as if this explained something. 'I've never found anyone like her.'

She searched for a plastic bag to put the books into. 'If you marry her again, Moon'll be kind of lost, though,' she said, handing them over.

'Oh, no,' he said, with absolute certainty. 'Moon's not gonna be lost. Moon's found what he was lookin' for. Moon's all set up. He's squared away.'

She could hear his footsteps walking away on the hard concrete of the outside corridor. Squared away, she thought. Wonder where that phrase comes from?

*

Easter was busy and happy, with new hires coming onstream, MaryLu and Cassie joining a gym and Cassie, when the Easter rush died away, retreating from office work, going back to painting the motel rooms before the two men moved in with carpeting, followed by MaryLu with curtains.

She had never given up the habit of breakfasting in a restaurant every day, on Sunday working her way pleasurably through the *New York Sunday Times*, particularly its book-review section, before walking the few miles to Barnes & Noble to pick up or order books spotted in the *Times* book supplement.

On one Sunday, coming into summer, the paper carried several heavily illustrated features on the fires continuing to burn in some of the major national parks. Some of them suggesting that the no-fires-at-any-cost policies of the previous twenty-five years were turning out to be inimical to the environment, preventing the natural burn-off of trees, leaving a dense dry tinderbox where the eventual damage would be a quantum leap away from what nature, uninterrupted, did every year. Another background piece dealt with what it called the Wildland-Urban Interface: a homebuilding boom on the undeveloped doorstep of nature, which it described as literally playing with fire in some western states.

How pleasant, Cassie thought, pouring herself more coffee. How pleasant to be curious about, partly informed about, something I never registered in my previous life. For a moment, she considered a rubber-band smack, but left the band alone, as she was tending to do more frequently, beginning to believe that it was impossible to accommodate new experience without an automatic sorting of its applicability to past experiences. Her life story was written, she thought, up to a point, and after that point her function was to fit the new details into the existing structure. Not to continually try to kick away and disavow the structure.

She was half in love with fire. The science of it. The horrors of it. The management of it. The behaviours it evoked. As a result of her interest, The Dorms' fire notice, on the back of each bedroom door, was not standard. The fire authorities were still considering whether or not to insist on the usual notices, but were interested in a submission Cassie had made, based on research of some famous hotel and motel fires, which indicated that people in fires do not panic quickly enough, and when they do panic, ignore instructions about where the nearest exit is, going instead to the entrance where they came in.

She put the fire features to one side, to add to her growing collection.

'Still a Sly Wit, Now Mostly for Himself,' ran the head-line over a feature in the Arts and Leisure supplement, illustrated by a colour photograph of a haggard man seated at an upright piano. 'Tom Lehrer at his house in Santa Cruz. Calif,' said the caption. 'He says political satire has become "obsolete."'

Tom Lehrer. She knew the name from somewhere, but was unable to remember where. Or what exactly this man did. He was before her time, anyway. The feature placed his last paid appearance thirty-three years earlier. Yet, it went on, his work continued to sell, without a public persona or continuing promotion. To such an extent that his record company was now issuing 'a lavish, three-disc boxed set of his career oeuvre'.

The name stuck with her so that when she arrived at the big bookstore she wandered to the music section at the back. Sure enough, they had a display of the new boxed set. She put the set in her basket, distracted, as always, by a visual half-seen out of the corner of her gaze path. A girl with hair like her own: white-dyed blonde. Idly, she picked up the disc. Country music was the category. The girl's name was Lorrie Morgan.

No familiar titles here, the little voice in her head predicted as she turned it over to see the list of tracks. Half-way down, one halted her. 'I Guess You Had To Be There'. Something familiar about that, she thought, turning over the box to have another look at the artist's face. No. Strange to her. New to her. On impulse, she took the disc to the listening station, put on headphones and requested the track.

Like all country songs, it had a story. A clichéd story. The archetypal story of the wife seeing her husband sharing a meal with another woman. Except that the understated intensity of the singing impaled the listener on the exquisite pain of the unseen witness coming to terms with the happiness between the two.

Cassie listened to it twice, then paid for it and the Tom Lehrer collection, walking slowly back to The Dorms, its melody playing in her head moving her by memory until she was again seated in tight-bodiced white, a pointed cuff making her hand even smaller than it was, drawing attention to a new gold band. That was when she had heard it before. At her wedding. Who sang it? Not one of Polo's company. No. That ex-priest. The angel of death. Thornton. It was him. What an extraordinary song to sing at a wedding. A song of loss, of relinquishing a love to someone better able to meet the needs of the lover.

Playing the discs over the next few days made her want to walk out on to the concrete corridor outside her home and invite perfect strangers to listen to Tom Lehrer with her. And maddened her by the ready tears at the back of her throat in response to another of the tracks on the Lorrie Morgan disc, where a girl successively bought a dress to attract a man, a dress in which to marry the same man, and then an outfit for the resultant baby.

This is so puke-making, she thought, cutting it off and saying it again, out loud. 'This is pure tawdry. Pure "Drop-kick Me, Lord Jesus, Through The Goal-posts Of Life".'

CHAPTER TWENTY-SIX

Elections and Quiz Shows

She was sorely tempted, the day Polo Cadogan was elected, to telephone and congratulate him. The Irish newspapers gave him arguably more column inches than any other successful candidate.

MaryLu, busy with holidaymakers, was in the outer reception area, happy to let Cassie work on the computer in the inner room, once looking over her shoulder at a story that happened to include a picture of Cassie Browne, cartoonist. Untroubled, Cassie left the picture onscreen, knowing how different she looked. That was another country and, besides, the wench is dead. Long hair, Cassie Browne had, dark in the black and white picture. She was round-faced and untouched, was the pictured Cassie Browne. Doll-faced, bright-eyed. Heading for the wall.

She found the RTE site. Got the video feed. There he was. Large as life and twice as natural – literally. Polo. Doing his self-derogation performance. Making his supporters laugh. Becoming grave in response to an interviewer's question about his interest, his very personal interest, in the epidemic of suicide in the country at the moment.

The door to Reception opened and Moon came in, a protective mask hanging on his chest. Hearing the sound of the newscast, he left her alone, going to the coffee machine. 'Sorry, I forgot to refill it,' she said.

He flipped a hand at her, fishing clean filter paper out of the package. Polo was talking about her. Gently and kindly. Historically. Speaking with dignity of her achievements. You have let me go, she thought, smiling at his tiny image. Believing me dead, you no longer control me. Or try to. You give me independent status in my absence and, watching you, I recall the best of you. Across a distance of time and change, washed clean by an ocean of tears, you stand, admirable in your passions, likeable in your new modesty. You are a good man and I wish you well. You are not my man, and perhaps I did us both a disservice to collude in your belief that you ever were my man and that I was your woman. I never was. I was Little Miss Muffet and you were the funny spider. Be happy, Polo, she said softly to the screen. Be all you can be. And thank you for all you gave to me.

The newscast moved on to the party leader, promising that Cadogan's enormous financial sacrifice in severing his connections with his business would be recognised, as would his talents, although the leader smilingly refused to be drawn on how precisely that recognition would be delivered. She closed down the program and turned, smiling, to Moon, who was standing with two mugs of coffee at the ready. Surprised, as she always was, by the great warmth of his returning smile.

'You always happy, Moon?' she asked, taking the coffee from him.

He thought about this for a moment, as if there was measuring to be done. 'I am now, yeah,' he said.

She knew he would say no more unless asked, and she knew she would never ask him. His past was his business. But, for the first time, she was tempted. Tempted to ask him what event in his life had got him 'squared away', had given him this visible sense of completion without complacency.

'Invitation,' he said.

'Mmm?'

'Ace got a video we've been hunting for a while. Going to watch it tonight when we finish. Get pizza delivered. You on?'

'Sure,' she said. 'What is it? *A River Runs Through It?*' Ace had talked of a Robert Redford movie based on a book by the same man who wrote the book about the young men fire-fighting, and dying, on the side of the mountain.

'No. Robert Redford did direct this one, though. *Quiz Show.*'

For a moment, she hesitated. It didn't sound like much. Hell, let's not be ungracious, she thought, and asked what time she should arrive. Seven thirty? Ace would be heading for the fire station at ten and would drop it into the video shop after they'd seen it. Moon finished his heavily sugared coffee and left her to it. She wandered over to the bathroom, looking at herself in the mirror, liking the ash-blonde hair. It wouldn't matter, now, if she let her natural coppery colour grow out. But the bright whiteness suited who she was now, she thought, noting that her long walks – continued, in spite of owning the Lumina – had given her a golden tan, so that even without makeup, she looked good.

'Didn't dress up for us, though,' Ace commented, when she arrived at the other end of the concrete corridor as evening fell.

'Well, shorts,' Moon said.

'Good to know she has something other than the jeans,' Ace said, going to deal with the Domino's Pizza man.

They had created a pyramid of pillows on one of the beds for her. They took the two chairs. Triangles of pizza in napkins, cans of drink within reach, they sat through the inevitable trailers at the top of the videotape, several of them dealing with movies they had seen, a few doing a hard-sell on movies none of the three would ever be seen dead at. That's me, today, Cassie thought. Being seen dead at Polo's victory. Of course, now he'd been elected as a saddened widower, there would never be an incentive for him to discover and reclaim her. On the contrary, he would want to avoid any possibility of finding her.

The movie enthralled her, telling the story of Charles Van Doren, an academic who, in the early days of American television, became a household name through a heartstoppingly successful run on a quiz programme involving hundreds of thousands of dollars in prize money. Van Doren, brilliant scholar, played by Ralph Fiennes, was naturally good at coming up with the answers to the most obscure questions. But not good enough to ensure he stayed at the top, and so, as the film went on, it showed him being corrupted by the producers, who badly wanted an attractive ratings-friendly figure like himself, as opposed to his predecessor, a polymath whose speed of mind was not matched by looks or charm.

'It's so easy to like the likeable,' Moon muttered.

Even the somebodies do that, Cassie thought, Heathens? The quotation evaded her, and the thought drifted away on the tide of tension as the quiz programme was investigated, then exposed, bringing down Van Doren with it.

At the end, Ace wound the tape back to a couple of particularly revealing scenes for them to watch again. 'Told you it'd be good,' he growled at her, as if she had resisted the invitation.

Warming up some of the pizza in the microwave, she laughed at him. He boxed the tape, grabbed a loaded plastic plate out of her hand, and ran for the pick-up. Moon turned off the television and went around the room switching on lights. She made to get off the bed, but he sat down on the end of it, looking, thoughtfully, at the black screen.

'The horror of being defined for ever by the worst thing in your life,' she said.

He got up and put on an electric kettle, then searched among the unsorted pile of books beside the television.

'This guy mentions him,' he said, tossing the book to her. It was an autobiographical account by an academic of the thirty-year mental illness of his brother. 'Van Doren was his tutor, at some point,' Moon said, handing her a cup of black tea, 'and was good to him. But even when the author's praising Van Doren, he still feels called on to identify Van Doren as the man who knew the questions in advance on the quiz programme . . .'

She sipped the tea, carefully. He did likewise, making a face.

'Ace bought this packet of herbal teas in your honour,' he said, pouring his down the sink. She drank some more of hers, finding it more palatable as she got used to it. He watched her as if she might explode. 'Chamomile,' he said.

Laughter shook her and she had to put down the mug. 'You make it sound like a swear-word,' she said, coming up off the nest of pillows to examine the scars on the back of his neck, touching the raised skin gently. 'You were right about being a good healer.'

He reached up and held the hand. 'I had help,' he said to their reflection in the mirror.

'You did,' she said, to the same reflection, turning, smiling, to him, knowing he would kiss her. Not knowing that she would lean back from him to pull the white T-shirt over her head and sit there, waiting for him to make love to her. There was no talking, then. No endearments. No names. No jerking anxiety, either, but an infinity of easeful pleasure in the textures and the strengths of each other, a swimming satisfaction, a trusting sweetness of harmony and pulse-pace, warmth, sureness and quiet certainty in the way they moved, were moved, joined and pleasured each other, so, at the end, there was no closed-eyed sweating isolation, but a full-sighted submersion in each other. He held her, finger-tracing her face, learning her to touch, she watching the gloss of soft sweat at his throat, stroking the tendrils of silver in his hair.

How strange it is, she thought, as he clasped her bra at the back and turned her T-shirt right side out, how strange it is to feel more at home with a stranger than with my husband. To be unthreatened by our silence, at ease with an unplanned encounter that carries no future with it. To have no questions to ask, no reassurances to seek.

He walked her back to her room, not holding her hip-to-hip with him in awkward embrace, but with one arm a casual weight over her shoulder. At her door, pinked by the nearness of The Dorms sign, he kissed her forehead.

CHAPTER TWENTY-SEVEN

The Remains of the Day

'I love it when a plan comes together,' MaryLu said, straightening with difficulty in the last room on the corridor. In the absence of Ace and Moon, who had pulled two back-to-back duties, which immured them in the fire station for the following five days, the two women had finished the decoration, equipping and commissioning of the final rooms.

'Now, you can make money,' Cassie said.

'I never thought we would, you know,' MaryLu said, shamefacedly. 'I was used to Barry's dreams never quite working out. But this is going to work.'

'You going to throw me and the guys out on the street, now you've got paying customers knocking on your doors?'

MaryLu laughed. 'Two fire-fighters on the premises? Available for any maintenance work I need? I'm not crazy enough to lose that.'

'And me?'

'You'll move,' MaryLu stated flatly. 'Don't know when, and it won't be at my behest, but you'll move. You got places to go to.'

'I do?'

'You do. Trust me.'

The two women walked the three corridors of MaryLu's business, checking for the smallest snag, exulting in the dearth of problems emerging. On the top storey, they leaned, side by side, on the strong balcony fence. Looking at the building sites where activity was happening, indicating that the booming national economy was reaching Peoria. 'They better build things right, this time,' MaryLu muttered. Peoria, in its early days, had been damned by collapsing bridges and other structures.

On the highway, they both simultaneously spotted the pick-up truck, heading for the exit ramp.

'You want to put money against Ace remarrying that girl?'

Cassie laughed at the question, freighted as it was with resentful resignation at the foolishness of other couples. The pick-up came to the edge of the declivity, and Moon jumped down out of the cab, closing the door and thumping the side to send Ace on to wherever he was going.

'You do what seems right at the time, I suppose,' Cassie answered, then found MaryLu had already moved away. She could hear her footfalls in the stairwell.

Perhaps half a mile away, Moon came into sight from behind a cluster of trees, stuffing a book into his back pocket, prowling forward. Walking as if the smooth Tarmac under his feet were broken, untrustworthy, requiring soft-footed effort. Serious, even dour face shadowed by the hair, never cut since he abandoned the swimmer's shaven pate, now looking across at The Dorms, attention caught by something, flicking the hair sideways out of his eyes to see who was on the balcony.

In that instant, she was not leaning over a rail on the third floor of a motel in Peoria, Illinois, but standing beside a young Polo in the long, subdivided oblong of a deep window in a big old house in Meath, watching a man walking up from the river's edge, the grasses long and lovely and lush around him, head tilting to get the too-long hair out of his eyes. 'Walks like he's walking on cinders,' she could hear Polo saying.

The certainty grew with every step the big man took through the remains of the day. Back then, he had seemed defeated, melted by a solitary sadness, no eagerness in him to reach the end of the walk. Today, there was an undefeated purpose to his prowl. And she was the purpose. She leaned into the comfort of it, watching him, knowing him.

He stopped. Ten, perhaps fifteen feet away from the building, looking up at her as if that was all there was to be done about it.

'You going to let me starve?' she asked.

'Where would you like to eat?' he responded.

'Oh, somewhere classy like Red Lobster,' she said, and relished the flickering acknowledgement of the irony in his expression. 'My car in fifteen minutes?'

He went automatically to the tower of stairs at his end of the building, and she could hear him skip-climbing, three stairs at a time. You have learned joyfulness, she thought. There was a time when you climbed stairs slowly, dutifully.

When he came to her door, sports jacket over open-necked shirt, he pointed out that they could walk to the restaurant.

'Want you to hear a disc,' she said, handing the CD to him. 'Track nine.'

As she started the car she was aware of him looking at the picture of Lorrie Morgan on the play side of the CD. He read through the list of tracks carefully as she drove out on to the highway, watching out, almost immediately, for the exit ramp to bring them to the franchised seafood restaurant. Just long enough for the song to be sung in its entirety. 'I Guess You Had To Be There'.

Without comment, he followed her into the restaurant, wandered silently in the waiting area while she sat, watching the livid lobsters in the big tank crowded up on top of each other in one corner. Like people fire-trapped inside a door that opens the wrong way, she thought.

A girl, perked into squeaky-voiced delight by the task, led them to a table, fazed only momentarily when the man asked for a banquette. Of course. Would this do? Perfectly. Their server tonight would be Timothy and she hoped they would enjoy their meal. When he arrived, Timothy was – in personality terms – a diametric opposite, dragging himself through his syllables with such sadness as to convey the message that, if pressed, he would share the six most recent disappointments of his life with them. The big fire-fighter seemed almost punitively positive, by comparison.

'Tell me something,' Cassie said, as Timothy drained away, leaving them with ice-noisy drinks. 'Do you ever have a tentative moment?'

'Yeah. Before I make up my mind I'm right.' He grinned, confusing her by touching her face at the same time, the gentleness of the touch saying, 'This is real, the other just mischief.'

Timothy was back with a bevy of enormous plates, cluttered with little pottery sauce-holders. Folding up his plate-stand, he stood wistfully beside them for a moment, then retreated.

'What the hell is he yearning for?' Cassie asked. 'A round of applause?'

For a while, they ate in silence, Cassie watching him, watching the big hands, brute strength at the massive wrists tempered to a precise dexterity in the fingers, flooded with a series of memories recalled without effort, laid down, it seemed, without knowledge. She remembered seeing the right hand cupped, casually waiting for the fall of uptossed car keys. She remembered, too, the first gesture at first meeting: Sit down. Or don't. And the drink-lazed invitation to join him, that night in the library.

He asked no questions about the Lorrie Morgan song, and yet its melody and associations were more present than the restaurant's Muzak. The tacit postponement between them, she thought, was pleasant: close to the afterglow reminding reddening skin of a day spent in the sun. He sat back, drinking from the tall glass slowly.

'Why do you never drink alcohol?'

He looked at her over the glass, weighing the question. Unhurried. Laying down the answer like the terms of a contract.

'I was once told that alcohol made me a pompous pain in the ass.'

'Arrse,' she said, mimicking Ace. But quietly, because Timothy was heaving to. Reassuring him – in the end, somewhat forcefully – that their half-eaten meal was fine, delicious, no problems with it, they dislodged him by ordering coffee.

'That's not what you were told,' Cassie said. 'You were told alcohol was no excuse for being a pompous pain in the tits.'

The waiter came and went, without breaking the quiet rapture of the big man's smile. 'Oh, Cassandra,' he said, as if the saying of it was a reward, a confession, a caress, a conclusion.

'I know you,' she said, without fear.

'I found you,' he confirmed, without triumph, holding her hand.

I am home, she thought, illogically. Home. The homesickness is gone. That's what it was, the last remaining shadow. It was homesickness. Wherever I am, with this man, is home, now.

He began to talk, quietly answering the unasked questions. He had followed her, he said, not to bring her back, not even to identify himself to her. It was simply that he could not let her be lost, without someone looking out for her. That would be too bleak. Too bleak, not to have someone looking out for her . . .

'But you didn't like me. Every time we met, you argued with me, dismissed me.'

'The old priest's habit: defocus them. When the girl comes into sharp focus, when her name, mentioned in another setting, jangles your entrails, then you defocus her. Undo the flattery of the situation, pick at the weak places, fix your gaze on something else, somewhere else. Except that whenever I met you, the certainty grew heavier. The certainty that here was the only woman I would love, and that she was not only married, but married to a man who thought me his best friend. Putting distance between us, but watching. Listening. Even wondering, through the pleasure of listening to your son talk about you, wondering was I using him.'

'Polo used you.'

'How?'

'Getting you to tell me, after the accident.'

'You misunderstand. Polo knew he would hurt you worse – worse than a stranger would. If I'd told him he had to do it, he would have. And it . . . would not have served.'

She told him of learning ways to cope with the brain damage. Of how central Marsha had been. 'You must be in touch with Marsha,' she said. 'It never struck me. Does she know?'

'That you're alive? Not for sure. But when I told her I was coming after you, she had enough hope to give me a series of rude messages for you.'

'We'll ring her tomorrow.'

'Will we?'

The amusement was total, as if she had made a joke. Was it because she had said 'we' as if they moved and spoke as one? Or because of the easy abandonment of the secrecy that had framed her recent life? Did he think she was bossing him?

'You don't have to understand everything,' he said.

You smile at me, she thought, when I look at you at the end of a fugue, one of each day's brain-damaged cul-de-sacs. I come out of the confusion and you are there, easy, not able to follow or help, but calmly confident that it is I who will emerge. 'You'll be my minder,' she said.

'Oh, I'll be a lot more than your minder,' he told her.

'Why?'

The question seemed to floor him, as if the answer was obvious. The waiter took advantage of their silence to put a bill in front of him. He signed for it, absently adding a tip, retrieving his credit card and slip. 'Long before I met you, I was a priest. I was a very good priest. I believed in what I was doing. I was good at it, I was made for it. When I stopped doing it, there was nothing comparable to do, no better choice. Just a void. A void that was never going to be filled by a clever career move. Loving you is what I do. Now.'

They were walking as he talked, getting into the car, him driving the short distance, she watching his profile as he talked of following her, searching for her, convinced that if he did not, she would be truly dead, truly reduced to the scribbled signature on the edge of an old cartoon.

'I was happy, searching. Happy for the first time in years. I believed in what I was doing.'

'And you had a job like the fellows you used to envy, digging the roads. Just reacting, just action.'

'Then, when I find you, you're Sandra going on Sandy,

another goddamn diminutive,' he said, suddenly furious. 'Well, fuck that. You don't get given a great name in order to mess around with it. You're Cassandra.'

'I daren't call you Pete, then?'

'Ben never called me anything but Peter Thornton. The whole lot.'

He was not trying her out, she knew. Recognising that he had times with Ben locked in his memory that he would never tell her, because to tell her would be to share and disperse and destroy the integrity of them. You will keep them shining deep as warm sea water and Ben will be alive always in you, not ashed in me. We will have no circle of deadly reverence around my boy, but heft the memory of him, unspoken, between us, as if sweeping him off the ground, swing-style, walking three abreast.

He suddenly remembered something he had to fetch from his room, running lightly along the balcony, coming back within minutes to hand over the spectacles she had left in her car. Long ago. 'No prescription?'

It meant nothing, and he had to explain it to her, sitting up straighter to watch her, fascinated to realise that she had never known about that error and – even at this distance – was freshly terrified by the possibility of failure. She told him of walking in the black water of the sea at night, the sneakers tethered round her neck, knocking against her chest. He told her of finding a private eye, of being introduced to Ace by the young fire-fighter's uncle, a priest friend of his. Of weeks of training to destruction, his mind numbed by muscle-tearing repetitions, load-carrying runs. Of winning a place in the best fire service in the country. Of learning where she was and finding Ace, unexpectedly, willing to upstakes and come to Illinois with him. Of seeing her, the red stripped out of her hair, the fight in her tamped down. 'Did you get what you ran away to find?'

The room had darkened around them, unnoticed. He put away the glass and she stumbled to the bed. 'What did I run away to find?' she wondered aloud. 'Life, liberty and the pursuit of remembered happiness? I don't know. Breathing space. A place to be not me, or to make the not me into me. Oh, shit, that makes no sense. When I'm tired, words go from under me.'

'I know,' he said, as if it was a precious talent, wrapping her in bedclothes and his own warmth.

'I suppose I have rediscovered the capacity to be happy with very little,' she said sleepily. 'Because things won't ever be complete, unbroken, any more. It's damaged and drained and so am I.'

'Would we through our lives forgo, quit of scars and tears? Ah, but no, no, no . . .'

She watched him in the shadows, loath to relinquish him to the darkness of sleep. 'You could quote things to me,' she said, the words fumbling. 'I can't quote any more. It's all gone and it won't come back, now. It won't. I've tried to get it back. I'm not even as sad as I should be about what's gone.'

'All we have is what's left,' he told her. And she slept.